Praise for

HARRY SIDEBOTTOM

'Makes you feel as though you are there'

BETTANY HUGHES, *THE TIMES*

'Harry Sidebottom's epic tale starts with a chilling assassination and goes on, and up, from there'

MARY BEARD

'An amazing story of bloodlust, ruthless ambition and revenge'

KATE SAUNDERS, *THE TIMES*

'An extraordinarily vivid take on the ancient world. Think of *The Killing* crossed with Andy McNab crossed with Mary Beard, and you're there'

DAVID SEXTON, *EVENING STANDARD*

'Ancient Rome has long been a favourite destination for writers of historical military fiction. Much the best of them is Harry Sidebottom'

SUNDAY TIMES

'Swashbuckling as well as bloody, yet curiously plausible . . . a real gift for summoning up a sense of place'

TIMES LITERARY SUPPLEMENT

'The best sort of red-blooded historical fiction – solidly based on a profound understanding of what it meant to be alive in a particular time and place'

ANDREW TAYLOR

'Absorbing, rich in detail and brilliant'

THE TIMES

'Sidebottom's prose blazes with searing scholarship'

THE TIMES

'Superior fiction, with depth, authenticity and a sense of place'

TLS

'A storming triumph . . . wonderful fight scenes, deft literary touches and salty dialogue'

THE DAILY TELEGRAPH

'He has the touch of an exceptionally gifted storyteller, drawing on prodigious learning'

TIMOTHY SEVERIN

WARRIOR OF ROME

FALLING SKY

HARRY
SIDEBOTTOM

WARRIOR OF ROME
FALLING SKY

ZAFFRE

First published in the UK in 2022 by
ZAFFRE
An imprint of Bonnier Books UK
4th Floor, Victoria House, Bloomsbury Square, London WC1B 4DA
Owned by Bonnier Books
Sveavägen 56, Stockholm, Sweden

A CIP catalogue record for this book is
available from the British Library.

Hardback ISBN: 978–1–83877–801–9
Trade paperback ISBN: 978–1–83877–802–6

Also available as an ebook

1 3 5 7 9 10 8 6 4 2

Typeset by IDSUK (Data Connection) Ltd
Printed and bound in Great Britain by Clays Ltd, Elcograf S.p.A.

FSC www.fsc.org MIX Paper from responsible sources FSC® C018072

Zaffre is an imprint of Bonnier Books UK
www.bonnierbooks.co.uk

Harry Sidebottom was brought up in racing stables in Newmarket where his father was a trainer. He took his Doctorate in Ancient History at Oxford University and has taught at various universities including Oxford. His career as a novelist began with his *Warrior of Rome series.*

Fiction

(The Warrior of Rome series)

Fire in the East

King of Kings

Lion of the Sun

The Caspian Gates

The Wolves of the North

The Amber Road

The Last Hour

The Burning Road

(The Throne of the Caesars trilogy)

Iron & Rust

Blood & Steel

Fire & Sword

The Lost Ten

The Return

Non-fiction

Ancient Warfare: A Very Short Introduction

The Encyclopedia of Ancient Battles

(With Michael Witby)

In memory of Michael Dunne
16th December 1958 – 17th August 2017

Contents

GAUL AD 265

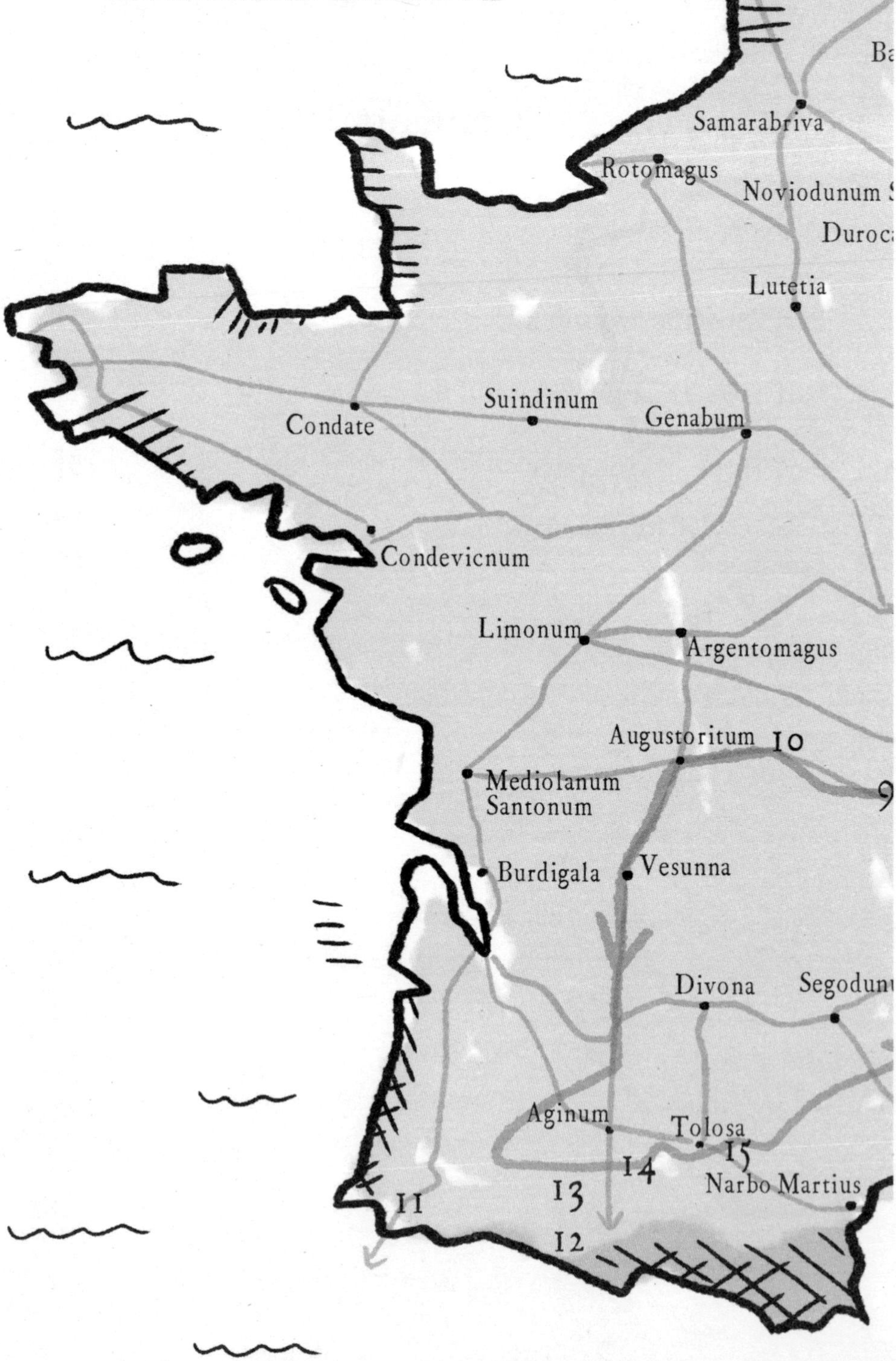

Samarabriva
Rotomagus
Lutetia
Suindinum
Condate
Genabum
Condevicnum
Limonum
Argentomagus
Augustoritum
10
9
Mediolanum
Santonum
Burdigala
Vesunna
Divona
Aginum
Tolosa
15
14
13
11
12
Narbo Martius

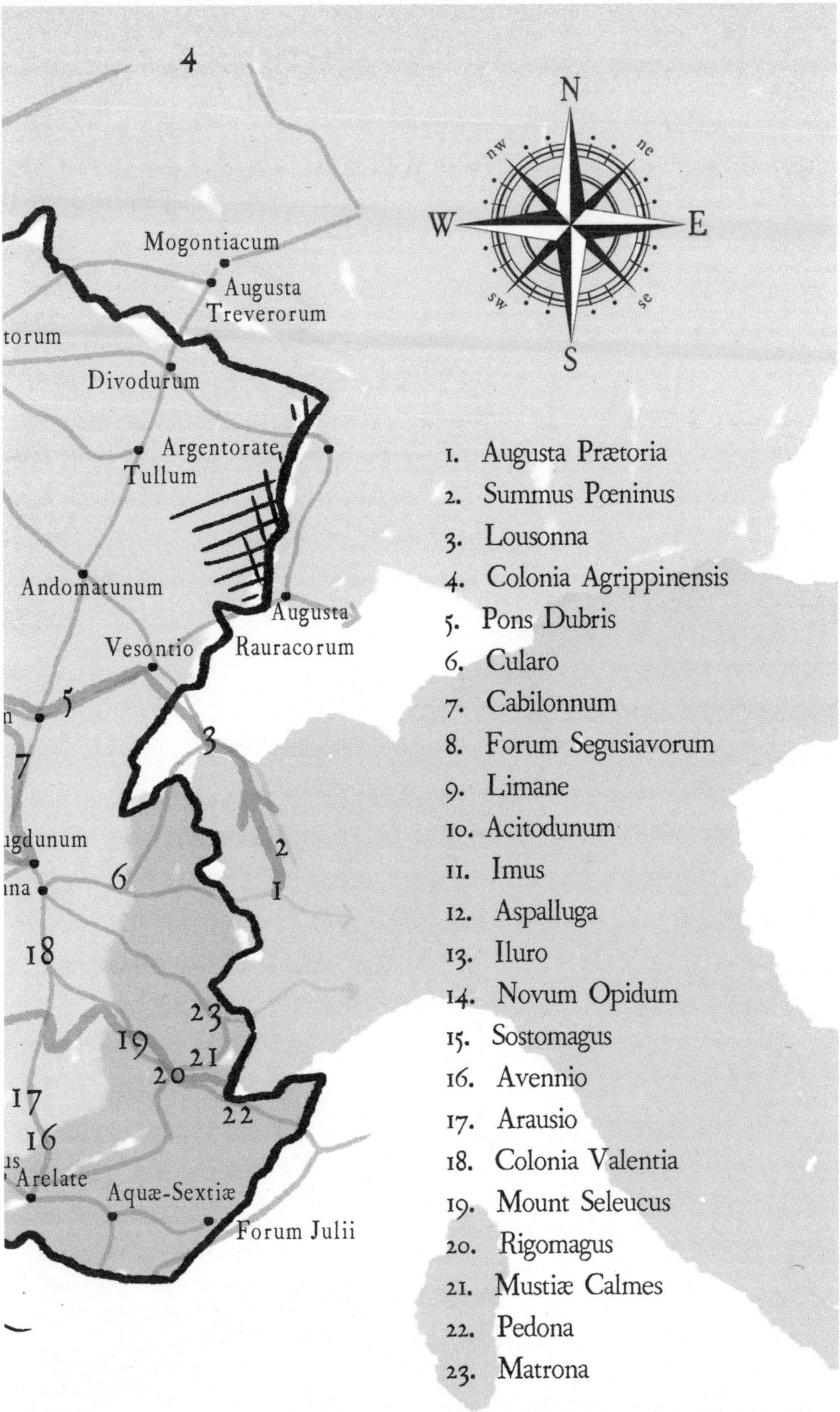

4
N
nw
ne
W
E
sw
se
S
Mogontiacum
Augusta Treverorum
torum
Divodurum
Argentorate
Tullum
Andomatunum
Augusta Rauracorum
Vesontio
ugdunum
Arelate
Aquæ-Sextiæ
Forum Julii
1. Augusta Prætoria
2. Summus Pœninus
3. Lousonna
4. Colonia Agrippinensis
5. Pons Dubris
6. Cularo
7. Cabilonnum
8. Forum Segusiavorum
9. Limane
10. Acitodunum
11. Imus
12. Aspalluga
13. Iluro
14. Novum Opidum
15. Sostomagus
16. Avennio
17. Arausio
18. Colonia Valentia
19. Mount Seleucus
20. Rigomagus
21. Mustiæ Calmes
22. Pedona
23. Matrona

‘A cavalry raid at its best is essentially a *game* of strategy and speed, with personal violence as an incidental complication. It is played according to more or less definite rules, not inconsistent, indeed, with the players killing each other.’

S. A. Forbes, Captain, Company B,
Seventh Illinois Cavalry

PART ONE
THE MOUNTAINS

CHAPTER ONE

The Pass of Summus Poeninus in the Alps

The Day before the Kalends of June

THIS WAS ALL WRONG.

Ballista looked at the enemy at the top of the pass. A cohort of Roman auxiliaries, about five hundred infantry, well armed and close packed, blocked the narrow road. To the left was a bare, unclimbable cliff, to the right a sheer precipice. No way around. This would be murder.

'We have our orders,' the Praetorian prefect said.

Ballista did not look at Volusianus. Instead, he gazed at where the pass notched the skyline, the rocky slope near at hand, the great mass of the mountain beyond. There had to be a way around.

'The Emperor Gallienus will be here with the main army tomorrow. We have to clear these heights.' There was resignation, perhaps sadness, in Volusianus' tone. The Praetorian prefect had risen from the ranks. He knew what this would cost.

'You can teach a monkey to ride a goat, but a northern barbarian can never learn Roman discipline.' Acilius Glabrio was with the staff assembled in the small area of flat ground to the side of the road some way behind Volusianus, but his patrician voice carried.

Ballista ignored the insult to his origins. He turned to Volusianus and saluted.

'We will do what is ordered, and at every command we will be ready.'

'May the gods hold their hands over you,' Volusianus said.

Ballista nudged his horse, and went up along the road towards the pass.

Maximus and his other two bodyguards were waiting upslope. Scarred and lined and ugly, that their faces were pinched with the cold did not improve their looks. Despite their appearance, Ballista regarded them with pleasure. These were men he could trust. Maximus had been with him for almost a quarter of a century. On his way to Hibernia, Ballista had needed a native to teach him the language of that remote island in the west. Sold into Roman slavery after a tribal war, Maximus had been fighting as a gladiator in Massilia. Passing through, Ballista had bought the Hibernian. Friendship and freedom had come later. The companionship of the other two was more recent. It was three years since Ballista had saved Tarchon from drowning in a river in Suania high in the Caucasus mountains. Apparently that made them inseparable, like blood brothers in some obscure but fierce Suanian way. It was only the summer before that Rikiar the Vandal had given his sword-oath to Ballista. In his previous hearth-troop, a drunken joke had led Rikiar to be held in contempt as a thief. The new allegiance had offered a chance of redemption, and the Vandal had proved his worth since along the shores of the distant Suebian Sea.

They were a map of his life since he'd entered the empire. Of his youth in the north there was nothing. There had been one, but he was dead, and still unavenged. Ballista pushed away the sadness and the guilt.

'Our britches are down, I am considering.' Tarchon the Suanian spoke in a heavily accented Latin acquired in army camps. 'Most fucked beyond redemption.' He had an inventive and foul-mouthed way of mangling any of the several languages he had almost mastered.

'An elegant summary of our position,' Ballista said. He swung his big frame down from his mount. 'Rikiar, would you take Pale Horse back to the camp, and bring up my war harness.'

As the Vandal led the gelding away, Ballista walked over to where the vanguard of the expedition, a detachment from the Thirtieth Legion, sat huddled against the rock face. The centurion got to his feet and saluted.

'It does not take a man skilled in physiognomy to read our future in your face, sir.'

Not all centurions were ex-soldiers. Some were commissioned directly from well-off equestrian families. Ferox liked to remind people of his educated origins.

Ballista smiled. 'Indeed, Centurion, we are to have the honour of leading the way into the pass. As we go in, the archers from Emesa will distract the enemy by shooting over our heads. When the men are ready, I will say a few words.'

'We will do what is ordered, and at every command we will be ready.'

Ferox bustled off, snapping out orders, gesturing his legionaries into place with the vine stick that marked his rank. Affluent background or not, the centurion had served with the legion for years. On the march up, Ballista had come to appreciate that Ferox knew what he was about.

Where the snow had melted, the road was wet and slick underfoot. Elsewhere, patches had been trodden down to sheet ice. A slip might be fatal. Ballista leaned against a boulder, drew his dagger, and began to clean the hobnails on his boots. He worked methodically, careful not to cut himself. His fingers were cold, and clumsy with the beginning of an all too familiar apprehension.

The strategy of the emperor had been good. The rebel Postumus held Gaul and commanded the routes through the Alps. Spring had come early. As soon as scouts had reported the first signs of the thaw, Gallienus had marched from Mediolanum to Augusta Praetoria in the Italian foothills. Two passes led from there through the mountains. A decoy force had gone west into the easier passage. Gallienus and the main body of the imperial army had taken this less frequented northern path. The Praetorian prefect Volusianus had been sent hurrying ahead with three thousand men to seize the heights.

The strategy had been well thought out, but it had not worked. They had caught an enemy picket that morning on the other side of the last ridge below the summit. The four frightened auxiliaries had told their story. Last autumn Postumus had posted their cohort in this desolate place called Summus Poeninus. All winter they had been cut off. The snow never stopped. It had threatened to crush the buildings in which they were barracked just beyond the pass. Supplies had run short. Raised in Aquitania, they had never known such cold in the gentle plains by the Atlantic. No, there was no other way through the peaks. Nothing but jagged rocks and awful chasms.

Volusianus and the other officers in his war council had accepted the statements of the prisoners. Ballista had been a lone voice, arguing that they should take the time to question the local shepherd they had also captured. Ballista had been overruled. There could be no delay. The auxiliaries had been stationed here for months, and would have known any alternative tracks. The pass had to be taken by the next day, or the whole army would be trapped, strung out along the bleak and treacherous road.

Ballista wiped the dagger clean on his britches, and sheathed it.

There was something very wrong about all this. At Thermopylae a traitor had revealed a goat path around the narrows. The emperor Septimius Severus had only forced the Cilician Gates when the defenders had feared they would be outflanked. No one stormed a mountain pass head-on in the face of determined troops. There was always a way around.

The crisp sunshine gave no warmth, but illuminated the mountains with a startling clarity. Snow lay thick on the crests and in the hollows, dazzling white against the black of the rocks. No trees or grass up here, nothing green. It was a harsh world devoid of other colours.

From where Ballista stood, the road up to the pass was steep, no more than ten paces wide, and carved out of the sheer cliff on the left. The rocks above looked loose, prone to avalanche. Climbing, one false move, one piece of ill fortune, and a man would be lost, sliding and scrabbling, tearing his fingernails on the sharp rocks in a hopeless attempt to stop himself crashing back to the unyielding road. Most likely he would be swept over the side, down into the ravine below in a hail of debris, taking his companions with him to their doom. The mountain on the other side of the pass was higher – if anything, more rugged and daunting. Yet on the march Ballista had noticed valleys opening off the route. Not every one could be a dead end. They should have been explored.

The stamp of boots and the jingle of equipment heralded the return of Rikiar, and ended further speculation. Ballista unbuckled his military belt and slipped his sword-belt over his head, and placed them on the boulder. He sank to his knees and held his arms aloft to make it easier for Maximus to help him into his mail coat.

How many times have we gone through this performance?

Getting back to his feet, Ballista felt the heaviness of the armour dragging down on his shoulders. His belt refastened tight, he pulled some of the mail through it, up above his waist, to take a little of the weight from his shoulders. He slung the baldric over his shoulder, and tied the thick scarf in the neck of his armour. Finally, he went to settle his war helm on his head. The laces under the chin tangled in his fingers. Like a mother fussing over a child, Maximus pushed Ballista's hands away, and tied the laces.

'Sure, we have been through worse places,' Maximus said.

Sometimes the Hibernian infuriated Ballista. He was like an animal, living in the present, to whom cause and effect were meaningless – an animal blissfully unaware of its own mortality. Certainly they had lived through dozens of fights: famous battles, the storm of great cities, minor border skirmishes, and nameless fights in squalid backstreets and bars. They had been lucky. Every survival had robbed Ballista of a little of his luck. Now it was threadbare and frayed. Perhaps here, on this cold track in these remote mountains, its material finally would rend and tear.

'What is it you always mutter? *Don't think, just act.* We are good at this.'

Maximus was right. It was not just luck. The Angles of the far north, Ballista's people, believed a man did not die until the Norns, the implacable goddesses who weaved a man's destiny, cut the thread of his life. And, tempered by a lifetime of violence, trained by renowned warriors in *barbaricum* and the most skilled sword-masters of Rome, Ballista knew he was good at this. Not a natural like the Hibernian, but hardened and shaped over the years into a killer of men. Empty the mind of fear, and let training and experience take control. A coward dies a thousand times, a brave man just once.

'Reminiscences of times past,' Tarchon said. 'Beautiful mountains, a sharp blade, much killing – it reminds me of home in the Caucasus. Such happy days!'

The three bodyguards were grinning like yokels in town on market day. Rikiar had a far-off look in his eyes. At any moment the Vandal might start reciting poetry.

'Today we will behave as good Romans.' Ballista spoke quickly to forestall whatever verse was composing itself in Rikiar's thoughts. 'A Roman officer of exalted rank, such as myself, manages the battle from the rear. He does not hurl himself into the fray, like some hairy-arsed Hibernian or other savage barbarian.'

'Things never work out like that,' Maximus said. 'And, unlike me, those two are not Roman citizens. They are the most benighted barbarians you could ever find – filthy, ferocious, and quite beyond reason.'

'Enough.' Ballista was laughing, despite himself. 'It is time to address the troops.'

Having clambered onto the boulder, Ballista could see all the way back down the track. Ferox was at the front of five centuries of his legionaries. The men were in ranks ten wide, with a few paces between each century. Each century was five or six deep. They should have been eight. The detachment was under-strength after years with the imperial field army. That they were veterans showed in their mismatched and patched equipment. Beyond the legionaries, the cohort of bowmen from the Syrian city of Emesa had come up, and now stood in a mass. The easterners must be feeling the cold. Further down, Volusianus and Acilius Glabrio still sat on their horses in the patch of level ground off the road. Their staff had gone, and the two men were leaning together, deep in conversation. Right down on the floor of the valley, troops were milling in the camp. Now and then the call of a trumpet sounding assembly floated up the mountain.

'Silence for the officer!' Ferox shouted.

The legionaries gazed up at Ballista. They had taken off their cloaks, and uncovered their shields and helmets. Equipped for battle, their upturned faces betrayed no emotion.

'Soldiers of the Thirtieth Legion Ulpia Victrix.' Ballista was accustomed to making himself heard on parade ground and battlefield. '*Ulpian* for the family of your founder, the divine Trajan, *Victorious* for your conquest of the proud Dacians and your many defeats of the savage Franks, today you will write a new chapter in the illustrious annals of your legion.'

The appeal to history had produced no sign of enthusiasm in the quiet ranks. There was something Ballista had to say – something that could not be omitted. It was a delicate subject. Ballista took a deep breath.

'You fight for the legitimate emperor. Our noble Gallienus Augustus was invested with authority by the Senate and People of Rome. He rules with justice, not for himself, but for the benefit of all his subjects. Those who stand against you here serve Postumus, a pretender with no claim to the purple, a tyrant who desires power for nothing but his own advantage and pleasure. On the one hand the majesty of Rome, on the other a mere Batavian upstart. On the one hand Gallienus, a loving father, on the other Postumus, the murderer of an innocent child. Have no doubt, the gods favour your cause.'

Some of the legionaries looked sidelong at one another, and a low, unfriendly muttering came from the rear ranks.

'It is true that the rest of your legion has been forced under the standards of the usurper. That is nothing but an accident of geography. How could they not pay lip service to his cruel regime, with their base on the Rhine cut off so deep inside the territory of the rebel? Have no doubt that when we descend from these mountains your tent-mates will cast off the shackles of the impious child-murderer. They will welcome you with open arms, join you in casting down Postumus.'

The legionaries looked unconvinced. Ballista needed to find words that might kindle their spirits – earthy things that appealed to old soldiers.

'The day draws on.' Ballista looked at the sky; perhaps three hours of daylight remained. 'Another cold night for the army camped on the mountain. But not for us. The prisoners say that on the other side of the pass is an inn and snug barracks, storerooms full of wine and food. Clear those bastards out of the way, and they are ours – shelter, a warm fire, a hot meal, a few girls to pass around, perhaps a pretty boy for your centurion. No one enjoys a pretty boy more than that bugger Ferox.'

The hostile murmuring had ceased. Many of the legionaries were grinning. That the prisoners had moaned of privations, and that Ballista had no idea if Ferox was a pederast, were immaterial.

'You are legionaries. The men up there are auxiliaries. You have enjoyed the winter warming your arses in the bars of Mediolanum, they have spent it freezing their balls off watching this desolate crag. You want to cross the mountain, they wish to leave. Would you fight to stay here?'

The soldiers were laughing.

'And there is one thing of the utmost importance. A thing which unites all the squabbling schools of philosophy, a single thing on which all the long-bearded lovers of wisdom agree, and that is . . . no one fucks with the Thirtieth Legion!'

A roar of approval greeted the profanity.

'And no one fucks with old Ballista!' someone shouted from the ranks.

Ball-is-ta! Ball-is-ta!

The chant echoed up the cliffs.

Ballista raised his arms. The noise died away.

'Time to earn our pay, boys. Ferox, sound the advance.'

The trumpets sounded, the standards inclined forward, and the legionaries began the ascent.

When the first century had passed, Ballista got down from his perch. Maximus handed him his shield, and Ballista and his bodyguards joined the column.

Immediately the world narrowed: the backs of the legionaries in front, the shields of the second century behind, the dark cliff on the left, the horrible drop to the right. Ballista was a tall man, and he could see over the helmets of the legionaries in front. He chose not to look. Head down, he trudged up the slope.

A thrumming in the air overhead, like the beating of innumerable wings, startled Ballista. The black shafts of hundreds of arrows arced overhead. Now Ballista looked ahead. The auxiliaries had formed a testudo, roofing themselves with their big oval shields. The arrows of the Emesenes streaked down, fast and wicked. Almost all thudded harmlessly into the leather-covered wooden boards. Ballista saw only a couple of places where the testudo shifted as an arrow got through, and a wounded or dead auxiliary was dragged away under the sheltering shields.

Ballista almost lost his balance, stumbled for a pace or two, as his right boot skidded on a patch of impacted snow. This was not going to be easy. Battling uphill, and there was little worse than fighting on an uncertain footing. Volusianus must know that Ferox's men would not break the auxiliaries. Unless – the unwelcome thought came fully formed to mind – the Praetorian prefect did not want this attack to succeed.

'Shields up!' Ferox's command boomed over the hiss of arrows and the stamp and rattle of the advancing legionaries.

Just in time, Ballista hefted his shield. The impact jarred up his arm as a stone caromed off its surface. The auxiliaries were hurling javelins, rocks – anything to hand – at the legionaries. The incoming arrows had ceased; the legionaries were too close to the enemy for the Emesenes to continue shooting over their heads. No longer threatened from above, the auxiliaries had moved out from their testudo. Their arms snapped forward, and a hail of missiles rained down from their commanding position. Ballista ducked down behind his out-thrust shield. Not long now.

A legionary in the rear rank spun around. Dropping his shield and weapon, he doubled up, his hands covering his bloodied face. Ballista stepped around him.

'Prepare to throw.' Ferox sounded as calm as if on a routine manoeuvre. 'Throw!'

Ballista peered around the rim of his shield.

Launched uphill, the heavy javelins of the legionaries were robbed of much of their force. Some of the pila fell short; many of the others failed to penetrate the enemy shields. Only a few of the auxiliaries found they had to cast away their encumbered shields. Ballista did not see a single one fall.

'Draw swords!' Ferox bellowed. 'Into them, boys!'

The auxiliaries did not wait to meet the charge of the legionaries. They broke their tight formation, and raced down the path to seize the initiative.

The noise of the collision was like something elemental: a cacophony of steel on steel, wood on wood, body thumping into body, men yelling and screaming. The auxiliaries had the momentum. The ranks of the legionaries were battered to a halt, then sent staggering, foot by foot, downhill.

'Stand firm, the Thirtieth!' No mistaking Ferox's voice. 'Push the bastards back!'

Ballista could see the distinctive red transverse crest of the centurion's helmet. It dipped and jerked, as Ferox cut and thrust in the front rank. Unlike a senior officer, a Roman centurion led by example. After every battle, when the butcher's bill was settled, the centurions always had paid far over the odds.

'Hold them!'

And little by little, despite everything – the slope and the uncertain footing – the legionaries stopped giving ground.

The combatants were wedged together. As if by tacit agreement, both sides had moved a step or so away from the awful precipice. Too close for textbook sword-work, they jabbed and heaved as opportunity offered, ferocious with desperation, grunting with effort.

The first casualties emerged from the throng. They filed past Ballista. Each clutched his right arm or left leg. Those with wounds to the head would be down under the dozens of stamping boots. If any of the latter survived, they would be in bad shape.

The clangour of battle echoed from the mountains. The melee was stationary. Legionaries were falling, but the leading century of the Thirtieth was holding. Perhaps, Ballista thought, discipline and the desire not to disgrace themselves in the eyes of their messmates might yet inspire them to achieve the impossible.

The thought was no sooner formed than it was undone. The bright transverse crest vanished. Ferox was down. Moments later, two legionaries dragged the centurion out of the crush. Ferox was unconscious, his face a bloodied mess.

The legionaries took a step back, glancing sidelong at one another. Their talisman gone, Ballista could sense the fight draining out of them.

Do not think, just act.

'With me!'

Ballista knew his bodyguards would follow. He ran into the slender opening at the edge of the drop. Agile on his feet for a big man, yet he knew any stray elbow or shield would send him headlong over the edge. Hundreds of feet of sharp rock face. The thread of his life would be cut. Once, he felt stones crumble under his boot. They skittered away into the void. He did not break stride, did not look down.

The front fighters had drawn three or four paces apart. Both sides stood panting, like hunting dogs after a long run.

'One more push, boys!' The blue crest of the auxiliary centurion was half hacked away; his armour was splashed with blood. 'Give me one more rush, and they will run!'

Ballista knew the centurion was right. He took his stand in front of the legionaries, Maximus and Tarchon on his left, Rikiar on his right. Giving one another room, they blocked the track.

'Not today, Centurion.' Ballista glanced over his shoulder at the legionaries. Many did not meet his gaze. In those that did, there was little encouragement. Their eyes betrayed private calculations of survival.

'These auxiliaries do not know the Thirtieth, boys!' Ballista had to put heart into them. 'Ferox will live. Imagine what the old bastard will do if you leave me here!'

No time for more words. Ballista dropped into the ox guard: left foot forward, half turned, shield thrust forward, sword up and horizontal, its tip near his right ear. Ballista and each of his hearth-troop would face two men.

'Kill that hulking barbarian and the legionaries will turn tail.' The centurion was whipping his men up. 'Drag them down! Finish this! On the count of three . . . one!'

When they came, it would be fast – every man eager for this just to be over.

'Three!'

The centurion set off; a heartbeat later his men followed.

As the centurion closed, Ballista thrust his sword, angling down, towards the officer's face. The centurion hunched under the blow, and rammed his shield into that of Ballista. The collision drove Ballista back. The wicked tip of his foe's blade darted at his left thigh. Ballista hauled his shield across and down, turning the strike inches from the flesh. Reversing his grip on the hilt, Ballista jabbed overhand at the centurion's head. As the officer stepped back, an auxiliary lunged from Ballista's right. Ballista pivoted, high on his toes, twisting away. The edge rasped across the mail covering his chest. Off balance, the soldier blundered against Ballista. They were locked together. Ballista smashed the pommel of his sword into the bridge of the soldier's nose. The auxiliary howled, and reeled off, entangling the centurion.

A briefest of lulls in the maelstrom. Breath rasping in his throat. The clatter of combat to Ballista's left. Ominous near silence to his right.

Rikiar was on the ground. He had lost his weapon, but he was still alive. Two assailants above him, both seeking to get past his raised shield, to land the killing blow.

Ballista sidestepped. With a backhanded cut, he chopped into the back of the nearest soldier's knee. The man collapsed as if the bone had been hit by a hammer. The other, eyes wide with surprise at the unexpected threat, lost his nerve and retreated.

Ballista stood over Rikiar, one foot either side of the prone Vandal, guarding them both with his shield. The precipice was at Ballista's back. His right boot was all too near the sheer drop.

'Can you walk?'

'Leg gone,' Rikiar said.

'Pity.'

The centurion was not finished. 'One down, three to go!' he called to his men.

After their first encounter, Ballista expected a cautious approach from the veteran. He was wrong. The centurion surged forward.

Allfather, he wants me over the cliff.

Ballista bent his knees, dug in his heels. The collision of shields forced him back, hobnails fighting for purchase on the smooth stone. Rikiar was under his left foot, getting stamped on. The dread of feeling nothingness under his rear boot was strong on Ballista. At any moment he expected to topple into the abyss.

Locked in a hideous embrace, Ballista could smell the sweat on the man's body, the garlic and wine on his breath, the iron reek of blood. He wrenched himself sideways, trying to use his opponent's own strength to force him past. Too wily to fall for that, the centurion eased his pressure. Summoning everything he had, Ballista shoved the man away, and scrabbled forward over his wounded friend.

They stood eyeing each other like gladiators in the arena. Flickers of movement in the periphery of Ballista's vision. The sounds of fighting. The temptation to look was almost overwhelming.

Watch the blade. Watch the blade.

The centurion feinted low, then slashed high. Somehow Ballista got the shield up in time. The steel bit through the leather rim. The centurion swung again, like a man chopping logs. This time, the binding of the shield gone, the blade bit down deep into the wood. With all his weight, Ballista yanked the shield sideways. Embedded in the boards, the sword was jerked from his opponent's grasp. Ballista dropped the ruined shield. Together with the sword, it clattered to the road.

Unarmed, the centurion backed away, his own shield up.

Ballista altered his stance – sword out, two-handed – but did not advance.

The other combatants were hanging back.

'Enough,' Ballista said.

The centurion said nothing. Only his eyes were visible between the top of his shield and the peak of his helmet.

'Enough for now,' Ballista said. 'We have both done our duty. You have held your ground. By the custom of war, the victory is yours.'

Still the centurion did not speak.

'If you will let us recover our fallen, my men will go down the hill.'

The centurion set his shield aside.

'Take your dead and wounded.'

Ballista looked across for Maximus and Tarchon. When he saw they were both standing, he felt a fierce exultation, before a terrible emptiness descended as he signed them to tend to Rikiar.

CHAPTER TWO

The Pass of Summus Poeninus in the Alps

The Night before the Kalends of June

THE NIGHT WAS BLACK. You could barely see your hand in front of your face. Each man in the column gripped the belt of the man in front. In the vanguard, Ballista kept a firm hold on the shepherd. It was slow going. The moon would rise in an hour or so. It would be up well before they had to start climbing, so the shepherd had said. If it was not, things would not go well for the old man. As they stumbled along the dark valley, from behind floated the oddly muted sounds of renewed fighting in the pass.

The centurion of the auxiliaries had been as good as his word. Not only had his men not hindered the retreat of the legionaries; at his command they had helped collect the injured and the dead. Ballista had been the last man down from the mountain. He had been unsurprised to see the detachment of the other legion, the Tenth, drawn up in battle order on the flat area off the track. Volusianus and Acilius Glabrio were with them.

Maximus had put a restraining hand on Ballista's arm. 'You have no proof. Nothing for any of it.'

Too angry to speak, Ballista had hardly heard the Hibernian. He had stood glaring up at the two mounted officers. Neither the broad peasant face of Volusianus nor the thin patrician visage of Acilius Glabrio had given anything away.

'You did not think they would fight.' Ballista's voice had been tight with fury. 'Because their tent-mates are with Postumus, you thought the Thirtieth would run.'

Volusianus and Acilius Glabrio had looked at each other. There was an unsettling complicity between these very different men.

'You sacrificed them, hoping their rout would bring the enemy in pursuit down from the pass.'

'It is called generalship,' Acilius Glabrio had said.

'You sent good men to a needless death.'

'A feigned retreat seldom convinces,' Volusianus had said. The Pretorian prefect had gazed up at the heights. 'Now we will have to send in attack after attack, wear them down. Many more men will die.'

'Let me talk to the shepherd,' Ballista had said. 'See if there is another way.'

In the darkness the old man stopped abruptly, and Ballista bumped into his back.

'This is the place,' the shepherd said.

On the slope to the right, Ballista could just make out the faint paler line of a path.

'We wait here.'

The word passed quietly down the line. The twenty volunteers hunkered down. Ballista sat, his back against a rock, and pulled his cloak about him. The cold was intense. Almost at once, a couple of the men were snoring. People considered the ability to sleep the night before a battle was a sign of steady nerves and courage. As he had got older – forty-three winters – Ballista had come to doubt that judgement. Several times he had had to kick men awake before a fight. Once, many years before, storming a settlement in Africa, he had discovered two of the defenders wrapped in blankets, oblivious to the uproar. Fear brought exhaustion. Sleep was a form of escape from the horror. Perhaps some men believed that no one would harm them while they slept, or, if they did, they would know nothing. Ballista was certain such hopes were unfounded. Both the men in Africa had been aware as he killed them.

Ballista shifted his back against the hard rock. Allfather, it was cold. Again his thoughts wandered back to earlier in the evening.

The shepherd had been forthcoming. This civil war meant nothing to him. Yes, he had told the others that there was no other way an *army* could get around the pass. But, of course, there were goat tracks. The others had not asked. There was one opening off the valley next to the camp. It was early in the season – there was still much snow – but a few men, experienced in climbing, may venture the ascent. Some might fall, but life was never easy.

Ballista had called for volunteers from the auxiliary cohort of Cantabrians. They had been recruited in the mountains of Spain. He had promised them rewards, as if they were assaulting a city wall. Four trumpeters had been offered twice as much. Without them the exercise was pointless.

Waiting for darkness, they had stripped off their armour and helmets, discarded their shields. Each man wore dark clothes, and had smeared his face with mud. Tarchon and four of the Spaniards had lengths of rope coiled over their shoulders. Ballista and Maximus had tinderboxes tied to their belts. The rest, apart from the trumpeters, carried nothing but their swords and the little pickaxes they used as entrenching tools.

As the light leached out of the sky, they had left the camp. With luck, their departure would have been unnoticed by the defenders. At the head of men from the Tenth Legion, Acilius Glabrio was leading his second assault uphill into the pass. There were many bad things that could be said about the patrician, but he did not lack physical courage. The intention of Volusianus was to make numbers count by sending in relays of attacks intermittently throughout the night. In between, the bowmen would rain arrows down. By dawn the auxiliaries holding the road should be exhausted, and their ranks diminished. More important to Ballista, their attention should be diverted from his hazardous attempt to get around their flank.

'Time to go,' the shepherd said.

The moon could not yet be seen above the peaks, but its light silvered the edges of the clouds. The air was still at the foot of the cliff, but high above, the wind drove the clouds across the heavens like tattered black banners.

At first the track was straight, the slope gentle. Soon the incline increased, and it began to switchback across the cliff. Never more than a pace wide, sometimes much less, in places the path was powdered with snow, which crunched and shifted underfoot. It would be worse for those in the rear, when it had been trodden down to hard, slippery ice. Following the lead of the old shepherd, Ballista leaned in with one hand on the face of the rock. In the gathering moonlight, it was possible to see all the way down. Ballista was good with heights. As a child, with his half-brothers, he had scaled the cliffs of his homeland by the Suebian Sea. They had gathered the eggs of seabirds from their remote nests, sometimes dived into the waters far below. They had taken insane risks. When you are young, you believe yourself immortal. Now Ballista only looked down the once.

'Best we crawl,' the shepherd said.

Arranging his sword-belt across his shoulder, over his cloak, so the scabbard and the entrenching tool were secure on his back, Ballista gazed up. The summit seemed as far as when they had begun.

How long had they been climbing? Half an hour? An hour?

The stars were obscured.

The climb was slow and painful. Ballista's hands were frozen, the rocks sharp under the sodden knees of his britches. Was the cliff in Hades up which Sisyphus pushed his boulder dark and ice-bound? At least Ballista would have to make only the one ascent. The shepherd claimed the descent on the far side was smooth, easily walked.

'Now it gets difficult,' the shepherd said.

For a moment Ballista thought it was irony.

The old man had stopped. Unnoticed by Ballista, the moon had shown itself above the peaks. Its light was bright. Peering around the shepherd, Ballista saw a break in the track. For perhaps twenty paces was a sheer, blank face of snow. It had settled where the path navigated a hollow. The snow was almost blue in the moonlight.

'I will cut handholds, places to put boots.' Without hesitation, the shepherd edged out, and began the slow process of hacking at the snow with a small pickaxe.

Waiting could be worse than the ordeal itself. Part of Ballista wanted the old man to hurry; part of him wished he would never finish. The wind had started to blow along the slopes. It lifted flakes of snow, threw them into Ballista's face. He was chilled to the bone, shivering.

'Better it was colder,' Tarchon said. 'The thaw make snow loose, untrustworthy like Roman whore. Let man down badly.'

Born and raised in the Caucasus, Tarchon knew all about mountains. Ballista wished the Suanian had kept his counsel to himself.

The wind moaned. Now and then it carried around the shoulder of the mountain snatches of the din of the fighting back in the pass.

All too soon, the shepherd was done. Two lines of small black holes punctuated the slope. From the far side, the old fool gestured for Ballista to cross.

Some men thought their gods listened when they prayed. Christians were convinced of it. The devotees of the traditional deities of Rome spent vast sums attempting to win their favour. The gods of the north were less amenable. Woden the Allfather was Ballista's ancestor. Somehow he doubted the one-eyed death-bringer would intercede for his descendant.

Tentatively, Ballista reached out and clasped a handhold. Driving his fingers into the compacted snow, he put some of his weight on his arm. The hold did not give.

Deep-hood, do not desert me.

He put a boot into the first foothold.

One limb at a time, with agonising slowness, Ballista inched out across the slope.

The wind was rising. It fretted and tugged at his clothes. The weight of the scabbard was heavy on his back, the sheath containing the entrenching tool digging into his shoulders. For all the cold, he was running with sweat.

'Nearly there.'

The aged shepherd squatted like some senile satyr where the track resumed.

No more than a couple of arm-lengths from safety, as his right boot groped for the next foothold, the one under his left gave way. Ballista's fingers were yanked from their fragile purchase. He was sliding. Desperately, he clawed at the snow. The slope was getting even steeper. He was moving faster, the loose wet snow coming away under his fingers.

'The pickaxe!' A voice was yelling.

Ballista felt the nails on his fingers tear as they scraped under the snow against the unyielding cliff. Any moment now and he would plunge into the abyss.

A stinging pain as his right knee jarred against a projecting rock. For a few seconds his fall was halted. Feverishly, using his hands like blades, he shovelled the snow from the cliff. Nothing but glassy black rock. His knee slipped on the tiny outcrop. It had been just a momentary reprieve. Then his left hand found a fissure. Blind to the way it lacerated his fingers, he jammed them into the minuscule crevice.

Gingerly, Ballista balanced his weight between the two points. As slowly and gently as a man could move, he reached back over his right shoulder. His cloak had risen up, tangled around his belt. Eventually he groped it out of the way, and his fingertips found the metal head of the pickaxe. The thing was stuck in its sheath. Flexing his numbed hand, he took a firmer grip. With infinite care he slid it free.

Something told him where to strike. Just above and to his right was a thin crack in the stone. The steel clinked against the rock. Splinters stung his face. At the third blow, the pick stuck firm – a third purchase binding him like Prometheus to his high place of torture.

He rested his cheek against the surface. Every muscle was trembling, and he knew they would not obey him. This could not last long. Unlike Prometheus, no hero would intervene to save him.

'Take the rope!'

It was dangling behind him, swaying in the chill wind.

All self-preservation urged him not to relinquish either grip.

'We can pull you up.'

Do not think, just act. But which hand?

Ballista let go of the pickaxe. With the release of the pressure, it fell. It clanged and clattered off the exposed rocks. The sounds went on all too long.

Getting hold of the rope was one thing; leaning slightly out from the cliff to pass it over his shoulder, then twice around his waist, took more willpower than Ballista had known he possessed.

The flow of time was not a constant. He held the rope – no power, human or divine, could have slackened his grasp; they hauled, and his boots scrabbled. In less time than he had seemed to fall, he was prostrate on the goat path.

'Sure, but you have got horribly heavy,' Maximus said. 'When we get down from this hill, I am going to cut down on your feed.'

'Fuck you, too,' Ballista said.

'And will that be all the thanks me and Tarchon get? After shinning across that snow, like an ibex or some such, risking our precious necks, and nearly giving ourselves a hernia.'

With a strangely paternal gesture, the Hibernian leaned down, and kissed Ballista on the forehead.

'By the way, it has taken quite a bit of the skin off your face. Your looks are gone, and you had better get used to children screaming, and running away from you.'

The others came across roped together. Ballista watched in horrified fascination. He was shaking violently; hugging himself under his cloak did nothing to help. They looked like black insects crawling on a sheet of papyrus. It seemed unjust that not one of them slipped or fell.

They rested for a time, strung out along the path.

'Nearly dawn,' the shepherd said. 'You should be going. Not far to the top.'

'And you do not know if they have lookouts up there?'

The old man shook his head at Ballista's obtuseness. 'I told you before, last autumn they sent a couple of soldiers up here. When the snows came they stopped. After the thaw, they sent no more, but when your army arrived they may have thought again.'

'But never more than two?'

'I have acted as your guide – I am not a diviner.' The old man stood. 'I will be going now, with my money.'

Ballista took the wallet from his belt. It was a miracle that it had not been torn loose when he fell. The wallet was small, and contained few coins, but they were gold. It was more wealth than a shepherd would see in several lifetimes.

'You are really going back down *that path*?'

'Safer than staying here with you.' The wallet was stowed out of sight. 'First Gallienus ruled these mountains, then

Postumus – tomorrow it may be Gallienus again. All I know is that the tax collectors will take the best of my flocks.'

Ballista listened to the shepherd leaving. The sounds quickly vanished. The wind was gusting from the pass, keening over and around the peak. If there were guards at the top, the shouts and the clatter of the falling pickaxe might have been snatched away from them.

'Best indubitably I go first,' Tarchon said. 'You not having good night on this hill.'

Ballista did not argue. Tarchon and Maximus slid past.

The final approach was easy, the path angling up almost parallel to the crest.

Tarchon held up his hand to stop the column. He crawled ahead, peered over.

Clouds raced across the moon. Disconnected bursts of sound could be heard from the invisible struggle in the pass. They came without warning, startlingly loud, then were gone, leaving only the whine of the wind.

Tarchon returned. Jerking his thumb over his shoulder, he raised up two fingers. He pointed to Maximus and himself, then repeated the motion of his thumb. His final silent instructions were to gesture Ballista and the soldier behind him to climb straight up, and cut off any retreat, while the rest remained where they were.

With no reason for delay, and no evident qualms concerning the murderous work he was about, Tarchon returned the way he had come, Maximus at his heels.

The slope above was not that steep, and not much higher than two tall men. There were many handholds. Even so, Ballista ascended carefully. Neither he nor the Spaniard made a sound.

The top was flat. A track, gleaming in the moonlight, ran up from the far side, and off to a rough shelter at the extreme end on the right. The hut was half collapsed, the roof sagging, and one whole wall was gone. The light of a brazier flooded out. It threw two hunched shadows of the sentinels huddled over its warmth.

Ballista did not look directly at the light, wanting to preserve his night vision. Apart from the tumbledown building, the summit was bare of cover. He put his hand on his companion's arm to indicate they should remain where they were. Ballista slid out his sword from where it lay in the scabbard still on his back.

What happened next had an air of unreality, as if some imagining of the infernal realm, conjured up in the theatre. Two dark shapes flitting towards the bright cave-like opening of the hut, steel flashing in the pale light. Yelps of surprise and fear. Elongated shadows intertwined, grappling. A crash and a shower of sparks when the brazier went over. A shaft of light as a door at the rear of the shelter banged open. A figure haring down the white path. Ballista clambering onto the even ground. The fleeing watchman unable to break his stride, slashing wildly. Ballista ducking under the arc of the blade, then chopping his own sword into the man's thigh. Balance gone, one leg failing, the sentinel running four, five increasingly ungainly strides, then pitching headlong to the ground. The Spaniard finishing him with a couple of neat blows to the back of the head. And it was over. No sound but the lamentation of the wind.

The corpses were tossed over the cliff up which their killers had climbed, and the brazier set upright again. There was not room for all the soldiers in the dilapidated shed. Ballista posted six of them as a picket down the track on the far side, below the skyline. They would not have to stay there long. By the height of the moon, it was about an hour until the false dawn. The rest of the men wedged together in the hut.

Ballista could not settle. His face and hands were smarting from his fall, his thoughts disjointed and troubled. He went out and stood in the cold, the wind buffeting him. Maximus joined him, and passed a flask.

'Old Rikiar will survive,' Maximus said. 'The doctor might not amputate. If he does, I have seen a lot of men with one leg. Rikiar is a tough bastard. And certain, he looked all right, talking no more bollocks than usual.'

Ballista took a drink. The wine was unwatered, rough and cold in his throat. Ballista had seen a lot of wounded men, tough men, who talked normally, and appeared all right, only for the fever to take hold, their jaws lock, and after several days for them to die in agony.

'I cleaned the wound with wine.' Sometimes Maximus seemed to know what Ballista was thinking. They had been together a long time. 'He would not want to die old and helpless, a straw-death.'

'We should go inside,' Ballista said.

The Spaniards squeezed up to make room. Ballista sat, wedged between Maximus and a trumpeter. He shut his eyes, dog-tired, but he doubted he would sleep.

Ugly as my head may be,
The cliff on which my helmet rests . . .

Only fragments of Rikiar's poems were in Ballista's memory.

Let us perform brave deeds,
Here before sunset . . .

Tomorrow, down in the camp, when they got off this peak, he would encourage the Vandal to recite, would write the lines down. It was not so much that he cared for Rikiar's verse, but he wanted to preserve something of his companion.

It seemed wrong that death would take everything. Rikiar had grown up in the same northern world as Ballista. As children, they had been told that if a warrior died in battle, he might be carried to the Hall of Woden the Allfather, to feast and fight until the end of days. Ballista had often doubted, but he still hoped it was true. Here in the empire, strange mystery cults promised their initiates an afterlife. The Christians appeared convinced of bodily resurrection, although their Heaven sounded a dull place compared with Valhalla. Still, it might be better than an eternity flitting, insubstantial, through the cold, black meadows of asphodel, which was all most Romans might expect in Hades.

If, at last, all returns to sleep and quiet, why worry?

Ballista's wife, Julia, had been raised as an Epicurean. Her belief was innate. The appeal of the philosophy was obvious and beguiling. Yet to Ballista the idea that the world would continue with him unaware was monstrous.

The thought of Julia brought an ache of longing. He was not getting any younger: forty-three winters – old for this endless campaigning. He wanted to go home. Not to the home of his childhood in the north; there was no going back there. All he desired was to retire to his wife's villa on Sicily. Julia was there with their younger son. Ballista would be content if he could collect their elder boy from Rome and join them. All he wanted was to spend time with his wife, and, after all these years away, get to know his sons.

The gentle touch of a thumb behind his ear, and Ballista was awake. It was one of the elements of the silent battle language the hearth-troop had created over the years.

'Almost dawn,' Maximus said.

Ballista could not have been asleep long, but every bit of him ached. Maximus helped him to his feet, and he followed the Hibernian from the shelter, with the stiff gait of a much older man.

Outside the air was so fine, the cold so exquisite, his breath caught in his chest, as if surfacing from clear, crisp water. The sun had not yet risen over the peak to the east, but the sky above was free of clouds, nacreous with light. The wind had dropped to a murmur. It would be a fine day.

Ballista stretched, and took in his surroundings. At the foot of the shadowed cliff face was a small, black lake. On its shores, the tiny outlines of inns and storehouses and a temple were emerging from the night. Thin lines of smoke rose from the buildings – a harbinger of worse things to come. Ballista was looking down at the settlement beyond the pass, behind enemy lines. The old shepherd had earned his reward.

To the south the view opened. Jagged range after range of mountains, receding one after another, the highest already splashed with gold. On the floor of the valley, the pale road, up which the Emperor's army would appear, snaked and coiled through the lingering gloom.

A trumpet call, thin and insubstantial far below. A sharp and broken knife-edge of rocks blocked any view of the position of the defenders. But the shoulder of the mountain dropped to the south-west, revealing the camp from which Ballista and his men had set out. A phalanx of infantry was forming – too far to make out which unit – ready to march up towards the unseen enemy.

'We might be making things easier for them,' Maximus said.

'Best get moving,' Ballista said. 'Rouse the men, quietly. Keep them off the skyline.'

Ballista remained, gazing down again at the isolated hamlet. What he intended struck him as wrong at some primordial level. Duty often did not run with what was right. He thought of Julia, his younger son, and his household, and hoped no man such as himself ever looked down at their home in distant Sicily.

'They are ready.'

Ballista had not heard Maximus return.

'What are we doing here?' Ballista said.

'A man has to be somewhere.'

Ballista did not reply.

'To your people you are Dernhelm, son of Isangrim, descendant of Woden the Death-bringer. The Romans know you as the tyrant-killer, the Persians as Nasu, the demon of death. Set your conscience aside – be the man others see.'

The Hibernian reading his thoughts was unnerving. It did not help that Maximus was right.

'Let's get this over with,' Ballista said.

The soldiers had taken off their cloaks, wrapped them around their left arms as makeshift shields. Ballista told the four trumpeters to remain. They knew the signal. The rest followed him down towards the settlement.

The old shepherd had not lied. The path this side was broad and easy, and mainly screened from the settlement down by the lake. When they reached the men on picket duty, Ballista sent them back up to the hut. They might as well rest. If this went wrong, six frozen and exhausted men would make little difference, and, with a head start, the path they had climbed last night offered just a faint chance of escape.

Not far above the hamlet, the track became fully exposed to view from below. Ballista raised his hand for them to stop. Instantly, the soldiers hunkered down. Some produced food and drink, others closed their eyes. These Spaniards had been in bad places before.

Keeping close to the ground, Ballista peered around the last outcrop. The temple was bigger than it had appeared from the heights. It was built of dressed stone, roofed with tiles. Only the foundations of the other buildings were stone or brick, their walls and shingle roofs constructed of wood. Inconsequentially, he thought of the labour of hauling timber up to this treeless place. There had to be a reason, but he did not know what it was.

At any moment the sun would crest the mountain. There was no time to delay. Just as he was about to move, the door of the largest inn was opened. Ballista felt his heart sink. A squad of auxiliaries trooped out. As they formed up by the lake, Ballista counted just over fifty men – probably an understrength century. His estimation of the commander of the defenders rose. Despite the pressure of the attacks sent in by Volusianus throughout the night, the officer in charge of the pass had rotated his men. At any point, at least one of his five centuries was out of the line, resting in the hamlet.

Ballista realised that he must alter his plan. Although they had surprise on their side, his men would be outnumbered by more than three to one. They could not storm the settlement. Stealth would have to replace force.

Having inched back into cover, Ballista issued new instructions. He and Maximus would go on alone. Tarchon would remain here with the men. If the Suanian saw his two companions apprehended, he was not to attempt a rescue. Instead, Tarchon should lead the others back up to the crest, and give the word to the trumpeters. That might prove enough on its own.

Tarchon was not happy. But for all his bluster, the Suanian was no fool, and he recognised the necessity.

Ballista and Maximus pulled the hoods of the cloaks over their heads, kept their weapons sheathed. If spotted, those in the settlement might mistake them for the two guards posted on the heights. Of course, that in itself might draw attention. Why would the guards be returning before they had been relieved? And, now the thought occurred, when would the next watch be coming up the path? Ballista tried to put such things out of his mind.

'Grand morning for a stroll,' Maximus said. 'Shall we be off?'

It was hard to walk normally, to feign unconcern. The track now was in full view. Any of the auxiliaries by the lake could look up at any moment. Anyone in the settlement could see them. The subterfuge did not have to be exposed. All it would take was for one person to ask the obvious question: Why are those lazy sods leaving their post?

Home we bring our bald whoremonger;

Romans, lock your wives away!

Maximus was humming an old marching song of the legions.

'I once read a treatise by a philosopher in praise of baldness,' Ballista said.

'Sure, philosophy is a wonderful thing.' Maximus shook his head in wonder. 'I cannot conceive why the ignorant think it does not prepare a man for life.'

'You should take it up, when we get back to Sicily,' Ballista said. 'Any of the schools would welcome a man of your perspicacity.'

'Now I have nothing against a bald man. But a short bald man, that is another case. Aggressive little bastards, probably because everyone calls them *short-arse* and *baldy*, keep rubbing their heads for good luck, like they were deformed or something.'

'I see you as a Cynic, a follower of Diogenes.'

'Not too sure about all that public masturbation, and the having no money.'

The track brought them down to the rear of the hamlet. They cut into an alleyway between an inn and some stables. There was a strong smell of horse muck and rotting food. Grooms could be heard, out of sight, working in the stables.

The kitchen door of the inn opened, and an elderly maid threw slops out. She looked at the two men.

'Good morning, darling.' Maximus pushed back his hood. 'Would you be into coming for a quick gallop in the stables?'

The ill-favoured woman regarded him with silent contempt, then went in, slamming the door.

'Thought she would have been grateful. Do you know how long it has been since I had a woman?'

'Here will do.'

A narrow gap opened between the inn and a storehouse. The wooden eaves were almost touching, low enough to reach. The enclosed space reeked of the urine of years of drinkers.

Without a word, each man kneeled on the foul, damp surface. Swiftly, but without undue haste, they took the tinderboxes from their belts. Ballista piled the wisps of hay on an oil-soaked rag, took the flint and steel.

An auxiliary walked into the passage, fumbling with his britches. He nodded to them, and began pissing against the wall of the inn, before the realisation that something was amiss made him look at them properly.

'What . . .?'

Maximus was on his feet.

The natural urge to put his penis back into his britches undid the auxiliary. Maximus tackled him to the ground. A glint of steel. Boots drumming in the mud. A final convulsion, and it was over.

'Time is not our friend.'

Maximus dragged the corpse deeper into the passageway.

Ballista angled the sparks down, blew on them until first the hay, then the rag, caught. Reaching up, the licks of flame already scorching the hairs on the back of his hand, he stuffed the incendiary under the eaves of the storehouse. It was bone-dry up there. Tendrils of smoke issued out, even as Ballista waited for Maximus to do the same to the inn.

'Time to go.'

They had reached the track, begun the ascent, when they heard the first shouts of alarm.

Not breaking stride, they looked back. Great roils of smoke puffed up from the roofs of both buildings. Men rushed towards them. No matter how great their efforts, they would not prevail. The buildings were well alight. Most likely, the conflagration would spread.

There went the cosy billets Ballista had promised the legionaries of the Thirtieth the day before.

'I hope they let the horses out.'

Before Maximus could venture an opinion, the brassy note of trumpets rang out on high, as from the heavens. The notes rolled down the slopes, carried across the lake, echoed from the further peaks.

Nothing punctured the morale of soldiers like an unexpected threat – above all, the fear that the enemy had outflanked them, were poised to strike at their defenceless backs. The trumpets put an end to all attempts to fight the fires. On the instant, all discipline collapsed. As the wounded hobbled from every building, the hale streamed away down the road away from the pass.

In no time, those who had been manning the front line raced into view. Straight through the hamlet they ran, not even pausing to gather their possessions. Men who had held together against overwhelming odds for a day and a night, were transformed into a stream of terrified individuals.

The horses, indeed, were led out of the stables. The more enterprising among the routers fought over them. Ballista saw a centurion, the damaged blue crest on his helmet eye-catching, haul a soldier from a horse, mount bareback in his place, and gallop off towards Gaul.

'If there had not been soldiers in the hamlet,' Maximus said, 'if everything had gone as we wished, we might have been able to cut them off, stop the news getting out.'

'If everything had gone as we wished,' Ballista said, 'we would be safe at home.'

PART TWO

THE EMPERORS AND THE ARMIES

CHAPTER THREE

The Town of Lugdunum, Gaul

Seven Days before the Ides of June

THE EMPEROR POSTUMUS SAT with his Senate in the portico of the temple. To his right was the great altar dedicated to Rome and the divine emperors. It had been founded centuries before by Augustus, the first emperor, as a meeting place for his newly instituted council of the Gauls, a symbol of loyalty to the eternal city and to the new regime, literally set in stone. It was an auspicious place, and, up here on the hill, with the curtains drawn back, it caught the breeze on a stifling day.

The Senate was discussing a proposal to adulterate the coinage. The prefect of the camp, Marius, had the floor. He was arguing at length that the proportion of base metal to gold and silver should be increased. With war coming, the bullion in the treasury would go further.

Postumus only half listened. Although divulged to no one, his decision had already been made. Yet it was important that there was a display of free speech. An emperor was not some oriental despot.

Without moving his head – an emperor must maintain a certain dignity, could not gawp around like a peasant – he studied the hundred or so senators sweating under the heavy drapes of their togas. To have any claims to legitimate rule, an emperor must have the support of the Senate. Only the

Senate could vote a man the necessary powers. Without them, he was nothing but a pretender. Holding just the western provinces, Postumus could not call on the Senate in Rome. So he had created his own here in Gaul. There had been quite a few senators serving in the provinces who had declared for him, more living on their estates scattered across Spain and Gaul, even one or two on properties in Britain and Germany. They had not been nearly enough. To augment their numbers, he had awarded the broad purple stripe of a Roman senator to those affluent local landowners serving on the council of Gaul. These provincial worthies had been grateful for the high honour, and their loyalty to Rome was assured. Their fidelity to Postumus himself was more debatable.

'Yes, we pay the soldiers anyway, but a war costs money. The units have to be brought up to strength, broken equipment replaced, food and forage purchased, transport wagons hired. Civilians do not understand.'

Marius had risen from the ranks. A centurion under Postumus, he had been one of the first supporters of his commander's bid for the throne. His faithfulness had brought rewards: command of the imperial camp, wealth, and elevation to the status of a senator. Yet Marius still wore the cropped hair and beard of a soldier, and displayed the customary contempt for all those not in the military. He was a man of no education, and his last words were less than tactful.

Postumus let his gaze slide up the two porphyry columns that flanked the altar. At the top of each was a statue of Victory holding a crown. Postumus did not want this war, had tried to prevent its onset. And he did not want to sit on the throne, had never desired to be emperor.

Born on the banks of the Rhine, in the tribe of the Batavians, Postumus' own origins had been humble. The army had rewarded his diligence and courage. At the end of a long career, he had been appointed governor of Lower Germany. It had been enough. Ironically, his own military skill had been his undoing – that, and the malevolence of a man called Silvanus. At Deuso on the Rhine, Postumus had intercepted a raiding war band of Franks returning from Spain. After their defeat, he had distributed to his soldiers the loot the barbarians had gathered. Silvanus, the governor of Upper Germany, at that time had overall command of the whole frontier, and had charge of Saloninus, the young son of Gallienus. In effect, when Gallienus had returned to Italy, Silvanus had been left as vice-regent of the West. Silvanus had sent Postumus a peremptory order to hand over the booty to the imperial treasury. Postumus had been caught between Scylla and Charybdis. If he had attempted to get the plunder back from the troops, they would have killed him. If he had not, Silvanus would have had him executed for treason. There had been nothing for it, but to bid for the throne.

'The silver coins of Gallienus contain hardly any precious metal, and his troops have not deserted the tyrant. Why should our noble Emperor Postumus pay his men more than that degenerate?'

Marius may have lacked the rhetorical training of a member of the traditional elite, but he did not lack words.

Postumus looked out past the amphitheatre at the main town on the other side of the river. The temples and the forum on the heights were hazed by the smoke from the innumerable fires of the potters and glassmakers and bronze-founders down by the water. His eyes tracked to the south and the docks on the island. Even from this distance, the activity was evident: ships coming up from the Mediterranean. They would be laden with wine and oil, and precious things from across the empire. Those casting off and heading downstream would be low in the water, freighted down with timber and wheat and sides of cured meat. In the sight of such peaceful endeavours, it was hard to imagine that war was coming.

Postumus had done his best to avoid war. He had written to Gallienus saying he was content to rule those provinces which the gods had granted, that he would not march on Rome: 'Do not come north across the Alps, do not put me in a position of fighting Roman citizens.'

The answer of Gallienus had been that of a madman: 'Let it be settled by single combat.'

Postumus had besieged Silvanus and Saloninus in the city of Colonia Agrippinensis. Perhaps there had still been a way back. But then the city had surrendered, and, in that awful capitulation, war had become inevitable.

'Wars cost money. We cannot afford to run short. The coinage must be adulterated.'

Finally, the rambling speech of Marius had run its course.

The Praetorian prefect, Victorinus, stood up. Postumus signalled permission to speak. Victorinus, like Marius, had been one of the earliest adherents to the cause of Postumus. The two men had nothing else in common. Victorinus was younger than Marius, much younger – perhaps not yet thirty. He was tall and good-looking. His blond hair and beard were artfully groomed and curled. Everything about him had the polish that came from a family that had owned vast estates in Aquitania for generations.

'Gallienus has assembled a huge army across the Alps. The latest reports suggest that it is advancing through the pass that leads to Cularo, and so down to the Rhône valley. That is why we are waiting in arms here at Lugdunum.'

Victorinus had a pleasant voice, cultured and well modulated, but with a hint of a lisp.

'Whatever you think of Gallienus, he ha*th* good officers, and many men. In this time of danger, loyalty is at a premium. To take any action which might undermine the fidelity of our troops is madness.'

'Nonsense!' Marius was back on his feet, unbidden. 'The soldiers will not notice the change in the coins.'

Victorinus smiled. 'Perhaps I should bow to your intimate knowledge of the common soldiery. But, as Homer said of base-born Thersites, "fluent orator though you be, your words are ill-considered, you shall not lift up your mouth to argue with princes".'

The coarse features of Marius were flushed with barely contained rage.

'Yes, I served in the legions. It is well known that I was a blacksmith. I did my duty then, as I do my duty now. Unlike you, I do not shirk my responsibilities, do not squander my time in drunkenness and shameful attempts to seduce the wives of others.'

Victorinus appeared unmoved. 'Yet you found time just the other day to court the admiration of the troops with a vain display of brute strength. Apparently you can bring a rolling wagon to a halt with just a single finger. At least, so one of the slaves said. He was most impressed.'

This had gone far enough. Postumus signalled to one of the *silentarii*. The official rapped his staff on a paving slab. Both speakers fell silent, Marius breathing hard, as if he had been engaged in some strenuous physical labour, Victorinus unruffled and still smiling.

'Silence for the emperor!'

Postumus gathered his thoughts, seeking words to smooth over this unseemly disunity.

'Free debate is the essence of liberty,' Postumus said. 'It is fitting to the spirit of our reign. Good arguments have been put forward on both sides. Wars indeed drain the treasury. Yet the loyalty of the troops is paramount. However, while we have the mines of Spain, we will always have enough specie. Orders will be sent to increase the shipments coming across the Pyrenees.'

Had that been an unfortunate phrase? *While we have the mines of Spain.* Might some interpret it as a lack of confidence, or, worse, an omen? All the statements of an emperor were scrutinised, every possible implication discussed. Something more uplifting was needed on which to end.

'The precious metal in the coinage can be reviewed after the war. Yet after our victory, the riches of the tyrant will fill our coffers. The baggage of Gallienus will go to the troops, his estates to the treasury. All who serve us will be rewarded.'

The assembled senators shook back the folds of their togas to applaud.

The coinage had been the last item of business. Some prayers, a few chanted acclamations, and the meeting would be at an end. The thoughts of Postumus turned to the baths.

Hercules, it would be good to get out of these suffocating robes.

The icy plunge pool in the *frigidarium* beckoned.

The emperor's pleasant anticipation was ended by the arrival of the Master of Admissions. The court official led an incongruous figure into the decorous, shaded confines of the Senate. The centurion was travel-stained, and walked with the stiff-legged gait of the exhausted. Half the blue transverse crest of his helmet had been hacked off.

Postumus felt his heart shrink. The centurion looked familiar, but Postumus could not place him.

The officer went to perform adoration.

'Get up off your knees,' Postumus said. 'While I reign, no one will prostrate themselves before me. I am emperor, not a tyrant like Gallienus.'

The centurion saluted, took off his helmet, and tucked it under his arm.

'Make your report.'

Squaring his shoulders, the centurion cleared his throat. Postumus was reminded of the famous words of Augustus to a nervous petitioner: *You look like a man offering a bun to an elephant*. Whatever was coming was no bun, no treat.

'My lord, the pass at Summus Poeninus has fallen. The army of Gallienus is across the mountains.'

A low murmur ran through the togate ranks, like the susurration of a gentle breeze through foliage.

Postumus knew the man now: Tuscus, acting commander of the First Cohort of Aquitanians.

A senator from the rear called out: why had the centurion not died with his men?

The click of the staff of a *silentarius* on the marble floor performed its intended function.

'The news had to be brought.' Postumus addressed the centurion. 'By your appearance you have ridden hard. You have done the right thing.'

'First horse died under me in the mountains, sir.'

'You are sure it is the main army?'

'Yes, sir. The advance guard was led by senior officers – Volusianus, the Praetorian prefect, Acilius Glabrio, and the Angle Ballista.'

'There is no chance that their presence was to add credibility to a diversion?'

'In the night, during the fighting, I heard Acilius Glabrio encouraging his men. He shouted that Gallienus would arrive the next day, they had to clear the pass.'

Postumus nodded. Too elaborate for subterfuge, the evidence was conclusive.

All eyes were on Postumus. He ignored them. The enemy would come down from the mountains to the plain of Vesontio, between the Jura and Vosges ranges. The town of Vesontio was the key to the gap.

'How long ago?'

The centurion paused, trying to remember through his fatigue. 'Six days. No . . . seven, including today.'

Seven days. How far would the enemy have got?

The pass was steep and narrow. The army of Gallienus was large, encumbered with baggage. Most likely they would have needed to break their march to rest and reorder at Lousonna by the shores of Lake Lemannus. There might still be time. Postumus had to act decisively.

'Marius, give the order to break camp. Have the army ready to move the day after tomorrow.'

An army was not like a single unit; it took time to get under way.

'Victorinus, take the cavalry in advance. No baggage – it can follow with the main force. Ride night and day. Get to Vesontio, and hold the town.'

A forced march, and they might get there before Gallienus. But it would be close.

Both officers waited, expecting further commands. Postumus gazed, unseeing, out of the portico. Birdsong was loud in the silence. The enemy advance towards Cularo had been the diversion. For all the talk of his indolence and effeminacy, Gallienus had done well. Of the passes through the Alps, Postumus had least expected the one through Summus Poeninus. As Victorinus had said, there were good commanders with Gallienus.

Gallienus clearly hoped that it would all be settled by one throw of the dice. Not single combat, but a pitched battle between the two field armies before the walls of Vesontio. And if Postumus' army lost . . .

Hope for the best, but prepare for the worst. Should he lose, Postumus needed a position to which he could fall back, somewhere he could prolong the war, frustrate Gallienus' plans for a quick victory. If the fighting dragged on, sooner or later some crisis elsewhere in the empire would call Gallienus away. A barbarian invasion on the Danube; a threat to Italy; a new pretender somewhere: diplomacy and Spanish silver might procure such events. A recent clandestine approach indicated the possibility of treachery within Gallienus' high command. But the question now was where to make another stand, and with what troops.

Postumus looked up at the ceiling, transformed its panels and beams into a map, into the lines of mountains, passes, rivers and roads, towns strung out along the roads. There were so few walled towns in Gaul.

'Trebellius.'

Postumus looked down at the senator, who got up from his seat.

'Call in the detachments guarding all the other passes. Tell them to march post haste to Augustodunum. Go ahead yourself with the Second Cohort of Britons. See to the walls, gather in provisions, put the town in a state of defence.'

'We will do what is ordered, and at every command we will be ready.'

'Augustodunum will be our base for this campaign.'

Postumus now was in his element. The planning of military operations was second nature. He widened his view to encompass the whole of his western empire. The garrisons in Britain and along the Rhine were depleted. Detachments from their legions and auxiliary units had already been drawn to augment his army. Some had been summoned many years before, and were serving on the other side with Gallienus. Yet Postumus had campaigned on both frontiers. His recent victories should keep the barbarians there quiet, at least for a few months.

'Victorinus, instruct the governors of the provinces in Britain and Germany to send another thousand men from each of their legions, and a matching number of auxiliaries, to Augustodunum.'

'My lord,' Victorinus said, 'should we also summon reinforcements from the forces in Spain? The Seventh Legion is nearly at full strength, and there are auxiliary units, as well as the barbarian mercenaries, both the Angles and the newly recruited Moorish horsemen.'

Postumus considered. There were four legions in Germany, three in Britain. With the attached auxiliaries, fourteen thousand troops would be added to the eight thousand or so troops being withdrawn from the mountains. Trebellius would have the making of a second sizeable field army – more than enough to keep Augustodunum safe.

Postumus made a decision. 'If our troops in Spain are weakened, the Frankish raiders will descend from where they are trapped in the northern mountains. They will lay waste the whole peninsula. My reign will not be secured with the blood of innocent civilians. I am emperor, not for my own sake, but for the citizens of Rome.'

The nobility of the sentiment brought a muted, though reverential, applause. Postumus was still thinking when silence returned.

'Trebellius, the mint and the imperial treasury will travel to Augustodunum with you.'

'My lord.'

Postumus took in all those assembled.

The military officers stood like greyhounds in the slips. The unlooked-for tidings had not overly disconcerted them. War was their trade. Unexpected things happened on campaign. War brought death, and for the survivors that meant promotion. War wrought destruction, and that translated into opportunity for the victors. If anything, the officers looked eager.

The same could not be said for the majority of the senators. They sat very quiet and still, eyes downcast, as if hoping not to be noticed. Most likely, they were thinking of their own safety. When the imperial court and the army had departed, they would slip away to their estates, sit out the conflict in peace, then return to lavish praise on the victor, ingratiate themselves with whichever of the two emperors remained on the throne.

'Conscript Fathers.' Postumus used the archaic term to flatter the senators, to soften the blow he was about to deliver. 'These are dangerous times. Brigands roam the countryside. With civil war, the depredations of these *bacaudae* will increase. For your safety, it is my command that you accompany Trebellius to Augustodunum.'

The unwelcome proclamation was received in silence.

'It will be a comfort to you to be with your sons who are being educated there.'

There was a pause, as the realisation dawned that they would be as much hostages as their children. Then they forced themselves to begin the ritual chants.

Postumus Augustus, most blessed, may the gods keep you!

You are father, friend, righteous senator, true emperor!

Deliver us from the tyrant, deliver us from the bandits!

As the sonorous cadences rolled out, Postumus thought of his own son. The youth was in the south, serving as tribune of the Vocontii tribe. A minor magistracy, it had been envisioned as the beginning of his training in governance. Now he could not stay there. Postumus wondered whether to summon him to the army. But the boy was young, bookish and unmilitary. Augustodunum – he would be safe behind its walls.

. . . may the gods keep you!

Gallienus would have thought his son Saloninus safe behind the walls of Colonia Agrippinensis. After the surrender, the boy had been led out in chains. Postumus had not wanted to harm him, but his advisors had been adamant – Victorinus and Marius among them; they had all insisted. Postumus remembered the terror on the child's face before the sword fell.

This was war to the death. Postumus knew that if Augustodunum should fall, no more mercy would be shown by Gallienus.

CHAPTER FOUR

The Town of Vesontio

The Ides of June

THEY RODE HARD DOWN from the mountains after they had left the main army. Forty hours in the saddle, just five dismounted. At first the road had been steep, its surface bad. Horses had gone lame, riders had fallen back from the column. Then it ran broad and smooth through upland pastures. The meadows were green from the recent rain, jewelled with flowers – narcissi, orchids and yellow gentians. One last show of spring before it surrendered to the withering heat of summer. Even in this gentle going, the number of stragglers had continued to rise. The Third *Ala* of Thracian cavalry was an experienced unit, but Ballista was unimpressed.

Now they were close. A couple of miles ahead, a final ridge of high ground screened the town of Vesontio. Ballista called a halt. It was the eternal rhythm of horse soldiers: walk, trot, walk – the gait varied to prevent repetition fatiguing the muscles – then dismount and see to their mounts, before starting again at a walk. Ballista was tempted to push on, but wanted the horses as fresh as possible after such a journey. If the enemy were already in the town in strength, the Thracians would have to beat a fast retreat.

Maximus and Tarchon followed as Ballista led his bay gelding off to one side. They poured water into their canteens, slipped the bits out of the horses' mouths to let them drink.

'You do not know for certain that the Praetorian prefect wants you dead.' Maximus spoke quietly, so as not to be overheard by the troopers.

'Volusianus ordered us to make the first assault on the pass. Now, despite the numbers of cavalry in the army, we are sent ahead with just one unit to ride alone into Vesontio. Men can only return from so many missions like these.' Ballista stroked the ears of the bay. 'If I had been part of a plot that had failed to kill the emperor, I would want anyone who might know dead.'

'Are you sure it was Volusianus you heard?'

In Rome, back in the spring, a dying man in the shadows of the Mausoleum of Hadrian had told Ballista of the conspiracy. The conversation had been cut short. Swordsmen had pounded up the stairs. They had finished off the informant, and tried to kill Ballista. From below, out of sight, a voice had urged them on. Much later, as the imperial entourage was leaving the city for this campaign, Ballista had thought he recognised the voice as that of the Praetorian prefect.

'After all, it was Volusianus that actually struck down the assassin in the Colosseum,' Maximus said.

'To cover his tracks. By then the attempt was doomed. Better that than let the senator be captured alive, and give him the chance to talk.' The horse had drunk enough. Ballista tipped out the rest of the water. 'Volusianus was thorough. He also killed the senator's son and secretary, and arranged the death of the only other known conspirator.'

'If you are right,' Maximus said, 'you should tell Gallienus.'

'Volusianus stands high in the emperor's regard.'

'You are Gallienus' friend.'

'I would need evidence.'

'Sure, these Romans are terrible, untrustworthy people. We had best be keeping a close eye on old Volusianus.'

Tarchon shook his head. 'Much better we are killing him. Creep into tent, slice off balls, stuff down throat. Bad end for him, keen pleasure for me.'

'Now,' Maximus said, 'I may not be as well versed as some in the ways of the Romans, but, I am thinking, they may take exception to a wild barbarian from the Caucasus castrating their Praetorian prefect.'

'Fuck them,' Tarchon said.

'Anyway,' Ballista was smiling, despite himself, 'even with Volusianus gone, it would not be enough. There must have been others in the plot.'

'Why?' Maximus said. 'If you had not stopped that bald senator getting his knife into Gallienus, your man with no hair would have been emperor before you could say kiss my arse. With the Praetorians of Volusianus, Rome would have been in their hands by nightfall.'

'It already was nightfall.'

'It is a figure of speech.'

'The imperial army was in Mediolanum,' Ballista said.

'Ah.' Maximus made a non-committal noise.

'Which would you back in a civil war – the field army or a bunch of ceremonial palace guards like the Praetorians?'

Neither tried to answer the rhetorical question.

'Volusianus would have had to have had someone he trusted already with the army in northern Italy. At least one man, an officer, someone who could make sure that, as soon as the news of the murder of Gallienus reached the camp, the troops declared for the new emperor in Rome.'

'Because left to their own devices, they might have chosen one of their generals in Mediolanum?' Maximus said. 'Select a commander they knew, or perhaps even offered the throne to the rebel over the hills?'

'Exactly,' Ballista said. 'Postumus is known as a good war leader.'

'That cavalry commander from Dalmatia, Cecropius – he is very close with Volusianus,' Maximus said.

'Cecropius was in Rome.'

'Then who?'

'I have no idea.'

'Well, that is grand,' Maximus said. 'There is at least one more man than our beloved Praetorian prefect that wants to kill you.'

'Not kill *me* – wants to kill *us*. They might be under the misapprehension that I share my innermost thoughts with the two of you. For example, things like my suspicion that Volusianus is a traitor.'

'Bugger.'

Ballista laughed. Sometimes, no matter the gravity of the situation, it was difficult to remain downhearted in the company of Maximus and Tarchon. It was time to be moving. He called over to the trumpeters with the column to sound the order to mount.

'What about Rikiar?' Maximus said.

'They will not go after him,' Ballista said.

'But he is part of your household.'

'He has not been with me as long. I doubt Volusianus knows he exists.'

Maximus grinned. 'Thank the gods, I am more notable than that Vandal, even if it is likely to be the cause of my death.'

They swung back into the saddle, walked their horses to where Ballista's personal standard – a white dragon – flew at the head of the troop.

'So, all good,' Tarchon said. 'Rikiar live, leg get better, no one cut throat.'

'Unless he starts reciting his poetry,' Maximus said. 'Then they might be cutting his throat.'

Ballista ordered the half a dozen outriders of the vanguard to their station a couple of hundred paces ahead, and then the main body to advance at a walk.

Standard-bearers and musicians to the front, the Third Thracians moved off in column of fours. Ballista pulled out of the line to watch them pass. Each man rode with his leg over his oval shield, which hung along the flank of his horse, suspended from the two left-hand horns of the saddle. The shield-covers were off, but it would take a few moments for them to ready themselves for combat. Still, weighed down with helmet and mail, and with their right hands gripping their javelins, the troopers were hot and tired enough without the extra encumbrance.

Rank after rank plodded past. The first squadron was mounted on blacks, the second chestnuts, the third greys. As far as possible, the troopers of each of the sixteen squadrons rode horses of the same distinctive colour. Was it a sign of vanity, or of pride in the unit, to take such trouble to distinguish its *turmae*? Now all the men and horses were caked in dust. The intervals between the squadrons were not well maintained. Ballista counted about three hundred horsemen. There had been almost five hundred when they had set out. It was an indictment of the troopers' horsemanship and training, and of the quality of their mounts, but most of all it was a condemnation of their commanding officer, a man of equestrian status called Solinus. Yet those soldiers who were still with the standards looked serviceable enough. The stragglers would be swept up by the main army, and rejoin the unit in a day or two. Given time, if Solinus were removed, a good officer could get the Third Thracians into shape.

Ballista turned his horse, and cantered up the line. The bay gelding had been a good choice. Although not fast, it was sure-footed, and had stamina. Ballista was glad that he had left his own charger to be brought up with the rest of the army. Pale Horse was no longer young. Shipped from retirement on the estate of Ballista's wife in Sicily, the grey was only to be ridden in battle. They had been together too long for Ballista to risk Pale Horse breaking down on this mad dash across the country.

Reaching the head of the column, Ballista gave the command to trot. The trumpeters put their instruments to their lips, and their notes were repeated by the musicians with every squadron.

Settling into the familiar motion of an easy rising trot, Ballista found himself wishing Maximus had not mentioned Rikiar. The doctor had not had to amputate, and the leg was not infected. Yet the Vandal had been far too weak to be moved. Ballista had left two of the four slaves of the *familia* travelling with the army to care for the invalid. Rikiar was accommodated in one of the inns at Summus Poeninus that had escaped the fire. He had money, and strict instructions not to attempt to travel until he was stronger. When the time came, he was to hire a wagon or litter to take him down to Italy, then buy passage on a ship to Sicily.

Although there was no certainty, the worst was past, and Ballista thought it unlikely that his bodyguard would die from the injury. Far more worrying was that Rikiar was bedridden, and unable to fend for himself. The slaves were recent acquisitions in Mediolanum, and could not be relied upon for protection. Ballista had not believed his words to Maximus. Years before, Ballista had served with Volusianus. The Praetorian prefect had always been thorough. The deaths of the son and secretary of the treacherous senator had shown that Volusianus had not lost that quality. If Ballista was right that the prefect had been party to the abortive attempt on the life of the emperor, Rikiar was very much in danger.

Violent death had been Ballista's constant companion since he had come into the empire as a hostage for his father, the ruler of the Angles on the distant Suebian Sea. Innumerable men had died in those twenty-seven years. Many had been killed on Ballista's orders, or by his own hands. Others, colleagues and friends, he had been unable to save. Two years before, old Calgacus had joined the number of the dead. The Caledonian had been with Ballista since childhood in the north, had travelled with him to Rome. For the next quarter of a century, first as a slave, then as a freedman, Calgacus had accompanied Ballista. In Africa and Hibernia, on the Danube and in the east, wherever Ballista was posted, Calgacus had been by his side. Hiding his affection behind a litany of querulous complaints, the Caledonian had always been a reassuring fixed point in a world of uncertainty. Then, one night, out on the steppe, a Greek called Hippothous had murdered the old man. It had been Ballista's fault. He had hired Hippothous as secretary, welcomed him into the *familia*, failed to see the terrible madness in the Greek. The death of Calgacus had yet to be avenged. It weighed on Ballista's conscience. He did not want it joined by that of Rikiar.

'To a walk!'

Again the command was relayed down the column. They were less than half a mile from the ridge.

As the gentler motion of the horse lulled him, Ballista's mind wandered to his wife and sons. Julia and Dernhelm, the younger boy, were at the villa in Sicily. Isangrim, the elder, had been summoned to attend the imperial school on the Palatine in Rome. Thirteen now, next year Isangrim would take the toga of manhood in the Roman custom. Yet he remained a prince of the blood of the royal house of the Angles. He was as much a hostage as Ballista himself had been all those years before in the same dusty schoolrooms.

Like some ominous creature rising from the depths, a ghastly thought swam up. Was Isangrim safe? Were any of them? Ballista had not remembered the voice of the conspirator until leaving Rome, after he had parted from his family. Yet Volusianus could not know that. Might the prefect think Ballista had shared his suspicions with his wife and sons? Desperately, Ballista tried to force his fear back down into the darkness.

'Halt!'

They were at the foot of the high ground. Ahead, the vanguard pulled up, still just in sight.

'Dismount. Check the tack. Tighten the girths.'

The road forked. The main route skirted around out of sight to the north of the hill, while a narrower branch ran straight up the slope.

'Chief scout, to me.'

The gelding stood quietly as Ballista rebuckled the straps that held the saddle in place. Pale Horse might well have tried to bite.

'Sir.'

The *speculator* who emerged from the ranks was older than most of the troopers. Ballista hoped his appointment was due to merit, not some favouritism or whim on the part of the unit commander.

'Take one reliable man up the hill. Keep off the skyline. You should be able to see down into the town. Anything suspicious, let me know.'

'Sir.' The scout sketched a salute, and walked away.

Ballista turned to the trumpeters. 'From now on all orders are to be passed down the column by word of mouth. No trumpet calls unless I give a direct order.' He pointed at one of them. 'Go down the line, make sure the trumpeter with each squadron knows.'

'Surely you are not expecting trouble?' It was Solinus. Ballista outranked him, and so had put the incompetent commander of the Third Thracians out of his mind.

'Best to be prepared.'

Ballista looked at the equestrian. He was older than Ballista, his face pale and drawn under the dirt. Evidently he had been no better prepared for the exertions of the march than his men.

Ballista looked away, to where the chief scout and his companion were starting their ascent.

'But if the enemy were already here, we would have seen a lookout up on the ridge.' There was an edge of apprehension in Solinus's voice. It seemed that he was not only inept, but a coward.

'We have not seen them, but they may have seen us.' Ballista raised his voice to address the men. 'Unsling the shields. Prepare to mount.'

Solinus looked as if he was waiting for some reassurance.

'Most likely, precautions are unnecessary,' Ballista said quietly.

The equestrian did not appear mollified.

'Mount!'

Ballista grunted with effort as he hauled himself back in to the saddle. Perhaps he had been too hard on Solinus. The march had worn all of them down.

Circling the gelding, Ballista called back down the line. 'Dress your ranks. Keep the gaps between the squadrons. Ride in silence. Listen for the words of command.'

The troopers jostled their mounts into position. It was an unpractised, inelegant display. Some of the horses flattened their ears; one or two still had the energy to kick.

'At a walk, advance!'

Soon they reached the river, and the road turned to the left. The arches of an aqueduct marched parallel with the road. A towpath was laid out along the near riverbank. There was no traffic on the road or the path, and there were no boats on the river.

The plod of hooves, the creak of leather and the jingle of harness echoed back from the slope. They drowned the sounds of the water. The steep ridge to the left, the broad river to the right: the road was an ideal place for an ambush.

Maximus touched Ballista's arm, then gestured up the hill.

One of the scouts was descending. The man had both hands on the reins, and was picking his way down with care. He was not in a hurry. Ballista kept the column moving, as the *speculator* angled down to meet them.

'Sir.' The scout rode up alongside Ballista.

'Report.'

'The town is quiet. No sign of the enemy.' The soldier looked as if he was wondering whether to say more.

'And . . .?'

'The town is too quiet. The streets are deserted. There is no one to be seen anywhere.'

'Fall in.'

The scout saluted, and reined around.

Ballista half turned in the saddle, and spoke loudly enough to be heard by the leading ranks.

'Husbands, and the fathers of unmarried daughters, tend not to come out to greet an *ala* of cavalry. Who knows what delights you will find in your billets tonight?'

Solinus looked as if Ballista had said something boorish. Yet, despite the disapproval of their unit commander, the troopers laughed. The witticism of this new officer was passed with approval from squadron to squadron, back down the column. Barbarian though the bugger was, they muttered, he knew about soldiering.

It was one of the penalties of command that you could never admit to doubt or apprehension, could seldom speak your mind. Of course civilians feared the arrival of soldiers. The threat of robbery and assault was combined with the danger of rape. Armed and belted men were unwelcome in any peaceful community. Yet if Ballista had been setting a trap, he would have cleared the townspeople from the streets.

They came around the shoulder of the high ground, and the town was spread out before them. Vesontio was built in a wide loop of the river Dubis. The ridge closed the neck of land. It was a fine defensive site. The road entered through an imposing gate. But the structure was ornamental. Long centuries of peace had negated the need for defences. The local elite had spent their money on other things. Instead of being linked to bastion walls, the gate stood next to a large nymphaeum, where the waters of the aqueduct were collected. Doubtless Vesontio would be embellished with many other examples of civic munificence – temples and theatres, statues and fountains – but the nearest houses prevented a view into the town.

'Sir!'

Ballista looked up the ridge to where the soldier pointed. The chief scout was coming straight down. He was riding fast, leaning back in the saddle to counteract the incline. Despite the difficulty of the descent, he held a corner of his cloak in one hand above his head. Every soldier knew the signal: *Enemy in sight!*

Ballista gestured for the column to stop.

A trumpeter raised his instrument.

Ballista leaned over, forced it down.

'Remember your orders!'

Rising on the horns of his saddle, Ballista waved the six outriders ahead to return. They had almost reached the gate before he recalled them.

The head of the *speculatores* had reached the bottom of the ridge without mishap. He reined up next to Ballista in a small avalanche of dust and stones. Ballista's bay sidled unhappily. He calmed the nervous beast.

'Cavalry, entering the town over the bridge at the far end of the main street.'

'How many?'

The veteran shook his head. 'Impossible to be sure. More than one standard, so more than a squadron. I would say at least an *ala*, maybe more.'

'How far across town?'

'The main street must be about a mile long.'

Solinus nudged his horse up next to Ballista. 'We are too late.'

'Silence!' Thinking hard, Ballista did not look at him.

The six men of the vanguard clattered up.

'How wide is the gate?'

The outriders looked at each other, disconcerted by the peremptory interrogation.

'How many horsemen can get through abreast?'

'Maybe three or four?' It was as much a question as an answer.

Ballista turned to the body of men strung out along the road.

'Form column of threes. Quickly, and do it in silence.'

'You cannot consider fighting,' Solinus said. The equestrian officer spread his arms, as if they could not contain the measure of the hopelessness. 'The men and horses are spent.'

'I am in command here.'

'Vesontio has fallen. It is our clear duty to retire and take the news to Gallienus.'

'I will determine our duty.'

'But—'

Tarchon moved his mount across towards Solinus. 'Best you keep your words locked behind the barrier of your teeth.'

The frightened equestrian officer said no more, but gazed off into the distance, somehow disassociating himself from this folly.

Only the whicker of a horse broke the silence.

Ballista studied the ridge and the town, trying to imagine how the topography would appear from above, in the view of a bird or a god. It might be too late, but the risk was worth taking. If it went wrong, the ridge could yet hold the key to the safety of the *ala*. But it would come at a price.

'What is your name?' Ballista asked the chief *speculator*.

'Fabius, sir.'

'Fabius, assume command of the rear squadron. Lead them back up the ridge. If we are chased out of the town, take the pursuers in the flank. Delay them as long as you can, buy the rest of us some time.'

'We will do what is ordered, and at every command we will be ready.'

'You understand what I mean?'

'Perfectly, sir. I never thought I was immortal.'

'Fabius, whatever the outcome, what you do here today will be remembered.'

'Thank you, sir.'

The old soldier rode away.

The *ala* was ready, three abreast. Ballista took his place at its head. There was no time for one of the long and elaborate speeches found in history books. Something short instead.

'Third Thracians, prepare to advance at a canter. Discard your javelins. The enemy are not expecting to have to fight. One charge with the sword, and the town will be ours. They will run.'

Wooden shafts rattled on the road, like hail on a tile roof, as the troopers threw their javelins aside. It was followed by the rasp of steel sliding from scabbards.

Ballista held his reins in his left hand along with his shield, and used his thighs to push his mount straight into a canter.

'Follow me!'

He did not look back.

Ballista drew Battle-Sun, looped the thong from the pommel around his wrist. There was comfort in the leather of the hilt. It was familiar, worn away to the shape of his grip. With Maximus on his left, and Tarchon on his right, there was no time to feel fear.

They thundered under the aqueduct, past the outer wall of the nymphaeum. The road dog-legged in front of the gate. Now the gateway loomed above them: lofty columns, gods and warriors picked out in bright paint against the white marble. Into the shadow under its vault, and out again into the noonday sunshine.

The main street ran straight as an arrow. About halfway along, by the far corner of a portico of gleaming pale stone, were the enemy. A clutch of standards flew over plumed officers in glittering armour. Behind them ambled the men. They were auxiliary troopers at the end of their march, taking possession of an undefended town, weary, saddle-sore, and unsuspecting.

The truth of the apparition dawned on the enemy. The standards swayed and dipped. The officers shouted, and trumpets rang out. Horses milled in confusion.

Ballista fought down the urge to charge hell for leather, to try to plough into them while they were still surprised, hit them before they had regained their cohesion. Three hundred paces – it was too far. Never break into a gallop until the last fifty.

A side street, overhung with awnings, deep in shade on the left. No sooner glimpsed than gone. Another to the right. Too late to think about outflanking. Two hundred paces. One charge, head-on. There was no room for subtlety. This would be terrible work, close to the steel. It would be over soon.

One hundred.

The monumental entrance to a grandiose forum flashed by, revealing an untenanted expanse of paving.

Fifty.

'Charge!'

Ballista kicked on into the gallop. The bay did not like it. The beast was running with its head on one side, fighting the bit. It was no warhorse.

The enemy were in order now, four abreast. But they were stationary.

In the front rank, a handsome young officer was haranguing them. Ballista could see his mouth opening and shutting, his curly fair beard wagging. The words were lost in the clamour of shouts, the jangle of harness, and hundreds of hoofbeats ringing like anvils.

No time for a countercharge. The enemy would have to receive them at a standstill.

An instant before the impact, it happened. It is hard to get an untrained horse to charge home. The bay dug in its feet, refused. Ballista was halfway up its neck. Another horse slammed into his from behind. The bay had lost its footing, was toppling sideways. Dropping his shield, Ballista struggled to get his right leg out of the grip of the horns of the saddle. The bay crashed to the ground. Ballista was thrown clear, his boot inches from the crushing weight. Nothing was worse than being trapped beneath a fallen horse.

Ballista landed hard, in a heap, the breath knocked out of his chest. Stamping hooves all around his head. Down here the tumult of battle was stunning, like a physical assault. Dragging himself to his feet, Ballista fought air into his lungs. Thank the gods, the loop of leather around his wrist had prevented him losing Battle-Sun.

Other horses were down, lashing out, trying to get up. Those on their feet bored and barged, wild-eyed and maddened. Their riders hacked at each other, hampered by the uncontrolled movements of their mounts. The momentum of the Thracians was gone. The melee was not moving. In the confines of the street, only the front ranks could get at each other. Those behind were mere spectators.

Maximus and the elegant young officer were trading blows. Tarchon was in trouble against two cavalrymen. The Suanian's movements were clumsy. He was fighting left-handed. Ballista had forgotten that Tarchon recently had lost the first two fingers of his right hand.

As a horse swung around, its quarters caught Ballista in the back. He was knocked to his knees. Again, only the thong on his wrist stopped him losing his sword. He twisted. The rider was cutting down at his head. Somehow he got Battle-Sun up to block. Before his assailant could recover his weapon, Ballista grabbed his sword-arm. Throwing himself backwards, his weight hauled the man from the saddle. The cavalryman landed on top of him. Ballista rolled, smashed the metal pommel of his sword down into the man's face. Three blows, four. No time to finish him; Ballista staggered to his feet.

Tarchon had lost his sword. Twisting and turning, like a cornered animal, he was fending off the attacks with his shield. The wooden boards were splintered and splitting. The Suanian could not hold out long.

The two riders were intent on their deadly work. Neither saw Ballista coming. He got a hold of the boot of the nearer, pushed him up, and over the far side of his mount. The other wheeled, but too slow. Ballista chopped Battle-Sun back-handed into his thigh. Screaming, the man sawed on his reins. All thought of fighting vanished, the rider forced his horse into the troopers waiting behind him.

Watching and waiting drains the resolve of any troops. It frays the nerves quicker than combat. In the thick of the fight, there is no opportunity to dwell on the risks run, or consider the seductive allure of flight. The supporting ranks of the enemy had seen enough. Sometimes it takes only one man to run, and panic spreads like wildfire on a parched hillside.

The street was transformed into a scene of rout.

Ballista grabbed the reins of a loose horse, vaulted up into the saddle.

The smart young officer had not given up. A couple of troopers still supported him.

'Cut him off!' Maximus shouted.

'No!' Ballista bellowed back. 'It is over. Let them go.'

Always leave the enemy a line of retreat, or they may fight to the finish.

Maximus backed his mount beyond sword reach.

The two troopers saw their chance and bolted after their comrades.

Abandoned, the officer gazed about, as if unable to comprehend the defeat. Then he, too, yanked the head of his horse around, dug in his spurs, and fled.

'Now after them!' Ballista yelled. 'Don't let them re-form!'

He booted the strange horse into motion.

The fleeing troopers had a start. Ballista's men would not catch them. But at the far end of the street, by the bridge, the enemy had placed a dismounted guard. If they stood, all this would have been for nothing.

Leaning forward, Ballista drove his horse faster. The high buildings that flanked the street passed in a blur of pale walls and dark, shuttered doors.

Faced with dozens of their own stampeding horsemen, the guards at the bridge looked to their own preservation. Cutting the tethers of their horses, they clambered aboard, and led the rout back over the river.

Almost at the bridge, Ballista had drawn a few lengths ahead. Often it was harder to stop a cavalry charge than it had been to start.

Ballista leaned back, pulling hard on the reins. Set back on its heels, the horse slid to a standstill.

'Halt! Form on me!'

Ballista turned his mount sideways across the street.

The pack was bearing down on him like a wave. If they did not stop, he would be dashed to the ground, ridden over, broken like a discarded plaything.

He flung out his arms, as if about to physically hold back the pursuit.

Hooves skidded, scrabbling for purchase, as the troopers dragged on the reins.

One horse, bolting out of control, swerved around him. It carried its helpless rider off over the bridge. But the rest bumped to a halt.

The Thracians were grinning, slapping one another on the back. They shouted insults at the retreating backs of their foes, jeered at their own man in his involuntary pursuit.

'The forty of you nearest the bridge, dismount.'

Elated by their triumph, by having faced danger and survived, the troopers continued their celebrations.

'Dismount now!'

In ones and twos, then all in a rush, the Thracians got down.

'One in four of the dismounted, lead the horses away. The rest, block the bridge. Shoulder to shoulder, form a shieldwall.'

As the orders were implemented, Ballista looked back to where the rest of the *ala* remained on horseback. He saw the crest of an officer in command of a squadron.

'Decurion, take your men south along the riverbank. Secure any other bridge you find.'

In the confusion of the departure, the only officer Ballista could spot was Solinus. It was the first time he had been seen since the charge.

'Solinus, take a squadron and hold any bridges to the north.'

The equestrian looked outraged. 'I must stay with the main body of my men.'

'You will obey orders, or suffer the consequences.'

Solinus hesitated, then, with a bad grace, shouted for men to accompany him.

Ballista unlaced his helmet, hung it on a horn of his saddle. He took a deep breath, ran his hand through his hair. It was slick with sweat, and felt odd being so short.

Allfather, he could not relax yet.

'*Stator*, to me!'

Where in Hades is the despatch rider? Has he fallen in the combat?

'Sir.' Another old soldier, by the look of him a veteran who had found a well-paid position, rather than a fast horseman.

'Requisition a fresh horse from the town. Ride back to the main army. Tell Gallienus that Vesontio is ours.'

'We will do what is ordered, and at every command we will be ready.' The ritual words were said with no enthusiasm.

Ballista looked at the others, gestured to a couple of the more promising-looking troopers.

'You two, do the same. A gold piece to the man that gets there first.'

Maximus sidled his mount up and handed over a flask.

Ballista drank. The wine was unwatered, strong. He felt it burn in his throat.

'Just in time.' Maximus pointed across the river.

A long line of rebel cavalry, several units strong, was on the road leading along the bank up to the far end of the bridge.

'And best of all, we are still alive, even old Tarchon.' Retrieving his flask, Maximus whispered, 'Your man Volusianus will be most disappointed.'

CHAPTER FIVE

The Town of Vesontio

Thirteen Days before the Kalends of July

VOLUSIANUS GESTURED FOR THE slave to add more water to his wine. He did not want a hangover the next morning. The same concern did not appear to be troubling the emperor. Gallienus was drinking out of a golden cup. Nothing was more common than glass, so the emperor claimed. Whatever the vessel, its contents were constantly refilled. Falernian and Chian, Lesbian and Caecuban, an inventory of the finest wines from across the empire. Gallienus never drank two cups of the same wine.

Isolated by his sobriety, amid the loud chatter of the intoxicated diners, Volusianus looked out at the campfires of the two armies. Two lines of twinkling lights spread across the darkling plain. Close to the river and the town were the tents of the imperial forces. A mile or so to the west were those of the rebels. Volusianus wondered if Postumus and his senior officers were drinking heavily the night before battle.

It was typical of Gallienus that he had commanded the upper floor of the amphitheatre of Vesontio be transformed into a luxurious dining hall. During the games, women and slaves occupied this level. With Gallienus, everything was out of season. New wines were served throughout the year, melons in the depths of winter. Expense and propriety were of no account.

Liveried servants came out to remove the plates, and the other flute player in the competition began to play. If anything, he was even worse than his predecessor. For all his huffing and puffing, his bulging eyes and distended cheeks, he seldom hit two correct notes in a row. He had a huge bald head, far too big for his stunted body. A few coarse hairs stood straight up on his shining dome. With his stamping and capering, he reminded Volusianus of a hairless ape, or perhaps a monkey that had been tamed, shaved and taught some tricks.

Conversation had dropped to isolated murmurs on the more distant couches. Gallienus was laughing. The majority of the diners joined in the emperor's mirth, although with what sincerity it was impossible to judge.

A servant cleared the table in front of the couch on which Volusianus reclined. Quite an amount of food returned to the kitchens untasted. The first course had consisted of a profusion of delicacies, including oysters, snails, and a salad of rocket and wild chervil. Although he enjoyed fine food, Volusianus had eaten sparingly, mainly confining himself to a little chicken, and some dry bread and lettuce. If you consumed a range of aphrodisiacs the evening before a battle, one way or another, sleep would be hard to find.

Bravo!

Mocking cheers greeted the end of the performance. Had there still been food to hand, things might have been thrown. No one was yet drunk enough to hurl the cups.

Gallienus raised his hand for silence.

The first flautist shuffled to join the one that had just finished. The former was taller, but had a hunchback, and was as hairy as the latter was bald. Standing together at the end of the imperial couch, the misshapen couple looked apprehensive, as well they might.

'Rhadamanthys himself, the judge of the Underworld, would find it difficult to decide such a contest,' Gallienus said.

All the reclining men, the good and the great of the empire, applauded the wit and elegance of their ruler's allusion to myth. Politely clapping, for once the irony was not lost on Volusianus. As Rhadamanthys was to the departed, so Gallienus was to those present: both dispensed decisions from which there was no appeal.

'There is next to nothing to choose between them,' Gallienus said. 'Both lack any talent, both should be flayed like Marsyas.'

This time, Volusianus did not join in the laughter. The reference meant nothing to him. Anyway, the Praetorian prefect had a reputation for austere independence to maintain. No one had ever accused him of being a sycophant.

'The winner!'

Gallienus tossed a bag of coins and a leather strap to the shorter flautist.

The loser went to break his flute over his knee. It took him three attempts. Then he held out his open hands. His dwarfish victor lifted the strap high, before cracking it hard down across the hunchback's palms. The latter howled.

Now the diners laughed without reservation. There was little the Roman elite enjoyed more than the humiliation and suffering of their inferiors. If the victims were deformed, it was funnier still. Although Volusianus did not share the origins of the well-born, he understood their mirth. Grotesques provoked laughter, especially when squealing in pain, and laughter drove away *daemons*. Any peasant knew that. And that was the problem. This was entertainment suitable for the barnyard or the backstreets of slums like the *Subura*, not for the imperial court.

Gallienus was not the emperor his father, Valerian, had been. The old emperor would never have brought buffoons and mime artists on campaign. Valerian had hardly tolerated them in the palace. The Praetorian prefect looked balefully at the table reserved for the jesters. It was next to that of Gallienus, in a place of honour.

Gallienus lacked the dignity necessary for his exalted office. Rather than senators or senior military men, he preferred the company of prostitutes and pimps, scum from the stage. He wasted his time writing poetry, or in endless inconsequential debates with philosophers. The money he squandered was the talk of Rome. A colossal statue of him on the Esquiline Hill; a grandiose portico in the Campus Martius: there seemed no end to the huge and incomplete building projects which drained the treasury. Most pointless of all was Platonopolis. What possible benefit could the *Res Publica* derive from a remote city in the Apennines, governed by the incomprehensible tenets of a long-dead Greek philosopher?

The servants brought in the main course with a flourish. A whole wild boar was the central piece, but there was a bewildering array of other dishes, whole flocks of pheasant and peacock among their number.

Before anyone could eat, the emperor stood to propose a toast. Gallienus wore a tunic of purple and gold. His sword-belt was jewelled. There were jewels on the laces of his boots. The gold in his blond hair shone in the lamplight.

Everyone got to their feet.

The emperor was looking straight at Volusianus.

'To absent friends.'

Gods below, surely not!

Gallienus giggled.

The stratagem would only work with surprise. Had all Volusianus' words of caution meant nothing?

Dear gods, do not let him name Aureolus, the general missing from the banquet. Any army was full of spies.

'To wives and lovers . . . may they never meet!'

Gallienus winked at Volusianus, and drained his cup.

Everyone downed their drink, the Praetorian prefect included.

The emperor remained standing. He held out his cup to be refilled. There was going to be another toast. Slaves busied themselves pouring more drink for all the diners. Volusianus sniffed the wine. Mamertine from Sicily, easy to quaff, deceptively strong.

Gallienus touched the hilt of his sword, his flushed face now sad.

'We are wearing them for Saloninus.'

All the *protectores* put their hands on their weapons, and repeated the toast.

As if overwhelmed by emotion, Gallienus slumped onto his couch.

Volusianus had been at the feast the ritual commemorated. They had been dining in the palace in Rome. All the officers had left their swords in an anteroom. Saloninus had been young. As a boyish prank, Gallienus' son had hidden the weapons. Amused, Gallienus had bidden that henceforth the *protectores*, the favoured inner circle of officers, would wear their sword-belts when summoned to banquet with the emperor.

'How long has it taken him to seek revenge?' Cecropius whispered in Volusianus' ear, so low that the third man on the couch, reclining beyond the prefect in the middle, could not hear.

It was five years since the rebellion in Gaul. Five years since Postumus had ordered the execution of Saloninus. The boy had been beheaded, his corpse left unburied. The shade of Saloninus was condemned to walk the earth for eternity.

Immediately after the killing, Gallienus had crossed the Alps. The campaign had yielded no result, and been soon abandoned. It had taken five years for the emperor to make another attempt.

'The wheels of divine justice turn slowly, but they grind very small.' Volusianus spoke at a conversational volume. 'Like Mark Antony, our noble emperor always rouses himself from his well-earned pleasures to do his duty. His vengeance is inexorable.'

The man who shared their couch muttered a prayer – 'May the gods guide his hand.' – but Cecropius merely smiled.

Volusianus was not sure how apposite was the comparison with Mark Antony. Unschooled, the only education he had acquired had been self-taught in rare moments of leisure after he had won high office.

At least Gallienus finally had taken the field. Volusianus did not doubt the emperor's courage, nor, on occasion, his ability to command in battle. Once he had crushed Postumus here in Gaul, Gallienus must march east. Combining his forces with those of Odaenathus of Palmyra, the imperial vicegerent of the Orient, it was the emperor's pressing duty to take the war to the Persians, and liberate Valerian from captivity. Once his father was free, they could dispose of Odaenathus, and true Roman rule would be re-established across the *imperium*. If Gallienus heeded his duty, all would be well.

Volusianus helped himself to some pheasant. The flesh of the Phasian bird was easy to digest. He still had much to do tonight, and he did not want to feel bloated on the morrow.

Three dancers from Gades had taken the floor. Clad in diaphanous robes, their thighs shimmered lubriciously. That would excite those who had gorged on oysters and the like.

Volusianus looked up at the night sky. The moon had advanced. It was near the second watch. Almost time he was going.

High-pitched screams.

Volusianus was off the couch, sword half-drawn before he registered the cause of the commotion. Cecropius was standing next to him, also hand on hilt. Most of the other *protectores* were on their feet.

The couch of the buffoons had collapsed. It had knocked over the nearby tables. Serving platters and cups were clattering along the flagstones. The jesters themselves were rolling and scrabbling on the floor. Their clothes and faces were covered in spilled wine and sauces, bits of food in their hair.

Gallienus was slapping his palm on his couch in amusement.

The merriment spread through the dining hall.

Sheathing his weapon, and getting back on his couch, Volusianus arranged his face into the smile of an indulgent uncle. The collapsing couch was an old joke, going back to the Emperor Heliogabalus.

As decorum returned, Volusianus wondered what should be done if Gallienus did not do his duty. Certainly the emperor could fight, when he was minded, and the rank and file of the soldiery would follow him anywhere. Yet Gallienus was inconstant; his attention flitted from one thing to another like a gadfly. The character of the emperor was undermined by a fatal levity. The prefect had always prided himself on staring difficulties in the face, not shying away from difficult choices. You had to be honest with yourself.

The first conspiracy had been too hasty, and it had been badly planned. Volusianus accepted that it was his own fault. He looked around, took in the whole banquet. Cecropius was next to him. On the other side of the dinner was the *protector* Heraclian. Also over there were the two senators, Acilius Glabrio and Nummius Faustinianus. The prefect was careful not to let his gaze linger on the conspirators. But when he regarded the man who had foiled the plot, Ballista suddenly looked up, and caught his eye.

Volusianus raised his cup, and smiled.

Ballista did the same. The barbarian's dark blue eyes were black in the lamplight.

He knows, Volusianus thought. The gods alone knew how – Volusianus had been assiduous in covering his tracks – but somehow Ballista suspected the involvement of the Praetorian prefect in the failed assassination of the man he was sworn to protect. A combination of small things, since they had left Rome. On the march or in the imperial council, Volusianus had found Ballista watching him. Now and then

Volusianus thought that he had seen a considering, or even a saddened expression on the face of the northerner.

Ballista would not understand. There had been no treachery. When an emperor appointed a Praetorian prefect, he handed the officer a sword.

If I reign well, use this sword on my behalf. If I reign badly, turn it against me.

Gallienus had not been ruling well.

Gallienus had not been the first emperor to hand Volusianus the sword. Valerian had plucked Volusianus from obscurity, had appointed him commander of his horse guards, then elevated him to Praetorian prefect. Valerian was a good emperor. Now Valerian was a prisoner of the Persians. The captivity brought shame on the empire, threatened the very safety of Rome. If his unworthy son would not campaign to free Valerian, he must be replaced with an emperor who would. Volusianus remained loyal to Valerian.

It was time to go. Volusianus dabbed his chin with a napkin, and got up from the couch. He walked across to the emperor. Gallienus watched him coming.

Volusianus saluted. Even under Gallienus, a banquet was no place to grovel on the floor in full adoration.

'My lord, with your permission, I will inspect the encampment.'

'So soon?' Gallienus took a swig of wine. 'There is more to come from the buffoons and mimes.'

'My lord, if I want to laugh at a clown, I don't have far to look – I laugh at myself.'

The emperor raised his cup at the quip.

'The watchword for tomorrow, my lord?'

'Let it be "Saloninus".'

'"Saloninus", my lord.'

As he walked out, the chant *Saloninus! Saloninus!* followed Volusianus down the stairs.

* * *

The pavilion of the Praetorian prefect gleamed with opulence. It smelled of cinnamon and cedar wood.

Volusianus dismissed his valet. Alone, he unbuckled his sword-belt, and hung it by the pillow of his camp bed. Heavily, he sat down. It was late – no more than four hours until daybreak.

Aureolus had his final instructions. Volusianus had watched the general ride off with his men down the dark street. With luck, no one in the enemy camp would have seen them leave. The night was dark, their route obscure. The flamboyant party of Gallienus high on the amphitheatre should have drawn all waking eyes.

After the departure of Aureolus, the prefect had walked the lines. The sentries had been awake, most of the men asleep. Volusianus had given the watchword to the officers. Everything was done. His duties concluded. Tomorrow was in the lap of the gods.

Volusianus knew he should sleep. Grunting, he pulled off his boots and tunic, and placed them near to hand, in case he should be woken unexpectedly. Naked, he got into bed.

It was a warm night, and he lay under a single sheet. He looked at the one lamp left burning. It was small, its bronze workmanship exquisite. By its gentle light, he looked around at the interior of the tent: the gilded and chased armour on its stand; the tables and chairs of expensive wood; the exotic rugs on the floor. Such things had been unknown in his childhood in the backwoods of Etruria. The furniture of the hut had been of local timber, home-made. The family had slept in one room, the animals the other. There had been five children: four brothers and a sister. Only Volusianus had survived infancy. His father's smallholding had got into debt. The land had been sold. The army had offered Volusianus a means of escape. The Praetorian prefect had come a long way.

Volusianus thought of his own son, born into such very different circumstances. Young Publius had served as quaestor. That magistracy had brought admission to the Senate. Publius had the outlook of a member of the Roman elite – attitudes and values that Volusianus could imitate, but never truly possess. The youth lived a carefree life of privilege, passed his time in hunting and parties. Publius knew nothing of the machinations of his father, nothing of the failed conspiracy. His innocence would not save him should Volusianus be exposed. That could not be allowed to happen.

Three of those in the plot were dead. Apart from Volusianus himself, four remained alive. Cercropius and Heraclian, the military men, could be trusted; the latter perhaps with less certainty. The senators, Acilius Glabrio and Nummius Faustininus, were another matter. Yet surely they must realise that if they turned informer, they would be denouncing themselves. Even if they did speak, Gallienus got on badly with the Senate. The emperor might prefer to trust the word of his Praetorian prefect. Volusianus was in two minds. Should Gallienus deviate from the path of duty, should he relapse into frippery and indolence, another attempt on his life must be made. Next time, it must succeed. In that desperate venture, the senators could be useful. But in the meantime, or if such action never became necessary, they remained a terrible danger. Many men died in a civil war. In the chaos, the causes of their demise often remained obscure. It might be best if the two senators were among the fallen.

Finally, there was Ballista. Even though the northerner was a barbarian, Volusianus liked the man. Ballista was an old comrade in arms. They had fought together at the battle of Spoletium that had brought Valerian to the throne. An overzealous underling with a personal animosity had tried to use the conspiracy to bring about the death of Ballista. A bad mistake. It had cost the underling his life. Ballista had not only survived – he had stopped the assassin driving the knife into Gallienus. Although he had no proof, Volusianus was ever more convinced that Ballista believed that the Praetorian prefect himself was implicated.

Volusianus had hoped that the problem might solve itself. Twice already on this campaign, he had sent Ballista on missions where death was the likely outcome. Both times, the northerner had returned. Volusianus prided himself on a cold-eyed pragmatism. Always stare a problem in the face. Except on the battlefield, make no hasty decisions. But, once your mind was made up, see that course through to the end. The principle established, consideration of the means could be left until after tomorrow. The gods willing, Ballista's place in the line of battle might resolve the issue anyway.

His mind at ease, Volusianus rolled over, and settled to sleep. It was a shame, but Ballista had to die.

CHAPTER SIX

The Plain of Vesontio

Twelve Days before the Kalends of July

SOMETIMES THE GODS NEED help in making their meaning clear. The livers of the first two victims had not been propitious. Postumus did not intend that of the third to be the same. As the priests went about slitting the stomach of the sheep, drawing out its viscera, Postumus surreptitiously slipped the small V-shaped piece of iron into the palm of his hand.

The army was drawn up waiting. It was early. The sun had not yet burned off the mist, but the sky held the promise of a fine day.

The chief priest placed the steaming entrails on the altar.

With due reverence, Postumus took the liver in both hands. Holding it up for close scrutiny, he squeezed the piece of offal. Blood ran up his forearms.

Everyone waited for his judgement.

'Victory!' the emperor shouted.

Postumus held the liver high in his right hand. Those nearby could see the V-shaped impression, the Greek character *nu*, the first letter of *Nike*.

The officers and soldiers cheered. It was the same sign seen years earlier when Postumus took the auspices before he defeated the Franks at Deuso.

Hercules Deusoniensis, the soldiers muttered.

The chamberlain of Postumus' household handed him towels to remove the blood. The emperor wrapped the piece of metal in one, and gave it back to his trusted servant.

At Deuso the sign had been real. Postumus had known it was sent by Hercules. In those days Postumus had felt the presence of the god, had known his divine patron was at his side. Everything to which he had turned his hand had been crowned with success. Recently he had felt bereft. The previous year his forces had tasted their first defeat, and Gallienus had retaken the province of Raetia north of the Alps. With his favour waning, would the god now take offence at this trickery?

There was no time to dwell on the attitude of the deity. All the time-honoured rituals before battle must be observed.

Postumus mounted the tribunal. It was neither high nor elaborate, being made from piled sods of turf, but it elevated the emperor a little way towards the heavens. From the top, Postumus looked down on the serried ranks of his army.

'Soldiers of Rome, today we are not fighting for the cause of one man. We are fighting for freedom and justice. You all know that I had no ambition to become emperor. You and the people of Gaul called me to the throne. Abandoned by the tyrant Gallienus, the provinces of the west were overrun by the barbarians. Lit by the fires of burning towns, the Franks and Alamanni and Thuringians raped and murdered and pillaged across Gaul and Spain; the Caledonians and Hibernians ransacked the length of Britain. If you had not elected your own champion, there would be no one left to mourn the dead.'

Postumus paused for effect. He was pleased with the image of mourning.

'Neither you nor I had a choice. But that effeminate who dares to pretend to be emperor had a choice. You all know that I wrote pledging that I would not cross the Alps. We offered him peace. In his deluded pride, he has crossed the mountains, and chosen war.'

A breeze was beginning to get up. It caressed the crests of the soldiers' helmets, shivered the standards above their heads. Few of the multitude could hear, but Postumus had ordered that an officer from every unit stand at the foot of the tribunal, and repeat the gist of his speech to their men.

'In war three things matter – courage, discipline, and the favour of the gods. Of the latter, we have just seen the evidence – the will of the gods made manifest. How could it not be so? The gods favour those whose cause is just. We did not seek this war. Fighting in self-defence is always just. The gods will punish the impious wretch who forces thousands of his miserable subjects to their deaths for no better reason than his own vainglory.'

A low murmur of agreement ran through the troops.

'There is no need to remind you of your courage. How many times have we defeated the savage Franks and Thuringians? If you need to be reminded, look at where those very barbarians now stand in our battle line. Once savage foes, our valour has made those warriors our loyal followers.'

The presence of the allies could not be ignored. Yet Postumus' words had been carefully chosen. They omitted that only some of the barbarians had been defeated. There were still Franks fighting against him in the Pyrenees. The chiefs who had brought their war bands to Vesontio had been well rewarded. The empire of Postumus would be in a parlous state without the silver mines of Spain.

In any event, the mention of the barbarian warriors was greeted by silence. Most of the soldiers regarded the Germanic allies as akin to ferocious, semi-trained animals. Better to have them on your side, but not to be trusted.

'As for discipline . . . Last night, officers and men, we ate our frugal rations under the standards. At sunset, the sentries did their rounds, while the rest quietly went to their tents. All that disturbed our sleep were the sounds of drunken debauchery from the ranks of our enemies. This morning we are rested and confident. Those who will soon run before our swords peer bleary-eyed at the rising sun. Their heads pounding, sick in their stomachs, their hands trembling, they curse their own improvidence.'

Just a few final words were needed.

'When Gallienus drags himself from the palace and the brothels and bathhouses, when he is forced by his evil daemon to take the field, he brings their contents to his camp. His senior officers follow his example. The wealth of Italy and Africa, of the whole empire, is heaped up in their quarters. When you have chased them back through Vesontio, sent those that survive scuttling towards the mountains, all that treasure shall be yours!'

At this, the armed men roared their approval.

'Let our watchwords be *Liberty and Abundance*!'

As the trumpets rang out, the officers saluted, and rode to their posts.

Postumus remained alone, looking out from the tribunal. The mist had gone, and the sun cast long shadows across the gently rolling plain. The morning smelled of woodsmoke and horses.

Everything was laid out before him as if in a painting: the plain and the armies, the wooded hills to the north, and, beyond the enemy, the river and the town to the east. Postumus studied the disposition of his own forces. It was utterly conventional. The heavy infantry held the centre. They were backed by the archers. The cavalry were divided between each wing, and the reserve was composed of Postumus' Praetorians and horse guards.

The breeze cool on his face, Postumus shifted his attention to the enemy. Gallienus' army mirrored his own. The heavy infantry looked closely matched in numbers, probably approaching twenty-five thousand men on either side. Although it was hard to be sure, Gallienus seemed to possess more bowmen. Certainly there were more infantry where the enemy reserve was drawn up on a small rise some way to the rear. Judging by the number of standards, Gallienus had some three thousand Praetorians to the thousand of Postumus. The solid block of men at a little distance from the Praetorians could only be the five hundred warriors in Gallienus' German guard.

Although the numbers of infantry were somewhat against him, Postumus saw that other things stood in his favour. Despite the reports of spies, Gallienus had few horsemen in the field. On Postumus' right the issue was balanced, with around two thousand troopers facing one another. But on his left, Postumus' three thousand cavalry appeared to have no more than a couple of thousand adversaries. That was where the battle would be won. Drive off the enemy riders, prevent all his own from galloping after them, then – with all speed, before the reserve could intervene – turn in and hit Gallienus' foot soldiers in the flank while they were fighting Postumus' infantry. Committed to their front, all troops run if attacked from the side or rear. It was an eternal truth of war. Once panic starts, it spreads through an army quicker than the plague through a slum.

Of course, the stratagem would take timing and personal intervention. Neither courage nor a clear head had yet deserted Postumus in battle. In his mind, as if choreographing a gladiatorial fight in the amphitheatre, he played out the stages of the conflict. Once Gallienus' infantry broke, there would be chaos. There were three barriers to their escape. Their camp and the suburbs of Vesontio were at their back. Beyond those crowded tents and narrow lanes, there was just one bridge over the river to the main town. Crammed together, those caught up in the rout would be helpless, their backs open to the sword. In the council the night before, the more bloodthirsty of Postumus' entourage – Marius well to the fore – had eagerly anticipated a massacre. Postumus had issued orders against unnecessary killing. All that was needed was to make the other army run. If Gallienus did not fall in the fighting, he was unlikely to long survive a defeat. His own men would see to that. The enemy soldiers were Roman citizens. The empire would not be served by the wholesale butchery of myriads of her trained fighting men.

The blare of distant trumpets, and faint cheering, broke into the thoughts of Postumus.

A glittering cavalcade was making its way along the front of the enemy army. Over the heads of the senior officers, standards shone in the morning sun. One of the riders, a large man, was mounted on a white horse.

Out in front of the pack cantered a lone horseman, a purple cloak streaming out from his shoulders. So Gallienus had risen from his debauch, and come to the fight.

Postumus glanced over his shoulder to the west. He had not intended to look back. Unlike that of Gallienus, his own army had an unobstructed line of retreat. An excellent road ran across the plain for a couple of miles, before it crossed a low, wooded ridge. The latter was an ideal site for a delaying action. If the day went badly, most of the army should get away.

A general should always plan for the worst, but these were ill-omened thoughts.

Seize the day. Do not give Gallienus time to let the wine fumes clear, and make a speech. Take the advantage of sobriety and early rising.

'Sound the advance!'

The trumpeters around the tribunal made the signal. It was picked up and relayed along the line.

Seize the day! Postumus settled his helmet on his head, tied its laces. *Carpe diem!* He descended the steps. An equerry led up his horse; another gave him a leg-up into the saddle. Radiating calm purposefulness, Postumus took station at the front of his horse guards.

Time never passes so slowly as in the advance to battle. The infantry plodded away, their backs seeming to get no more distant. The cavalry kept to a walk, matched their pace. The ground was dry, and the first fine haze of dust was being raised by thousands of boots and hooves. Soon it would thicken and obscure the entire field.

Trumpets ringing out further off. The enemy were beginning their advance. Now the thing was in motion, nothing but divine intervention – a thunderbolt from the clear sky, an earthquake, or the actual epiphany of a deity – could prevent the slaughter.

Postumus looked away at the wooded hills to the north. Only a tiny flight of birds rising from the trees disturbed the peace. Suddenly the diamond-sharp image of the valley of his childhood by the Rhine was in his mind: the dark thatch and bright red tiles of the roofs of the farms; the shaded green of the meadows; the silver of the broad waters of the river. He could smell the mud of the riverbanks, the ripening grain, hear the chatter of the swooping swallows. The army had been his life, but war was an abomination.

'Now the games begin!'

The reverie of Postumus was broken.

Maecianus, the commander of the horse guards, sounded excited, as if what was to come was no more than some eagerly anticipated spectacle in the circus.

Flights of arrows, like squalls of dark rain in a crosswind, fell this way and that on the infantry of both sides. Small figures jerked and dropped. The advancing phalanx of Postumus' men left the fallen on the grass, like a travesty of a meadow dotted with flowers.

There was something godlike, or perhaps merely inhuman, about watching from a safe distance as men died.

More trumpets called. The cavalry on both wings moved into a trot, then kicked on to a canter. Disciplined units, they would not hit full speed until almost upon their foes.

Now the dust was billowing up thick and fast.

'We should go,' Maecianus said.

'Not yet.'

Postumus may have fallen out of love with war, but he knew its moods, as a man knew those of an estranged and resented spouse. Few mounted fights were decided by the initial charge. Squadron by squadron, the troopers would charge, fight briefly, then wheel about, retreat and charge again. Fatigue and fear drained the resolve, like oil leaking from a cracked amphora. Unless some external force intervened, it all depended which vessel first ran empty.

A great roar rolled across the plain. The infantry were coming to grips. The dust now hung everywhere. The breeze made it churn and roil, but lacked the strength to disperse the choking clouds. Little could be seen of the battle, just the occasional flash of metal, and a glimpse now and then of a bright standard.

'Horse guards, prepare to advance.' Postumus turned to Victorinus. 'The imperial standard will remain with you and the Praetorians. If Gallienus gets to see through the murk, we don't want to tell him what we are about.'

'Sir.'

'At a walk, forward!'

As if a single beast, some many-headed creature of myth, the horsemen – knee to knee two hundred and fifty across and four deep – followed Postumus towards the left wing.

The first casualties were limping back out of the curtain of dust. A few were on foot, many still on horseback. Not all would be genuinely wounded. Some would be malingerers, others all too ready to help an injured comrade to safety.

The wind had shifted and was picking up. Postumus took a last look at the tranquil hills to the north from where it now came.

'To the trot!'

Riding into the dust cloud was as disorientating as entering thick fog: visibility of just a few paces, the noises of combat strangely muted, then suddenly loud, seeming to come from random directions.

A tattered squadron rattled out of the gloom.

'*Liberty and Abundance!*'

They were his own men. Sawing on their reins, they swerved aside.

'Close up! Form a wedge on me!'

For centuries, Roman emperors had not fought hand to hand. In the last generation, repeated foreign invasions and endless civil wars had ended that privilege. Desperate times called for desperate measures. Postumus drew his sword and hefted his shield.

Dim shapes in the murk.

'*Saloninus!*'

They were the enemy, several squadrons strong, but in no great order.

'Charge!'

Postumus dug in his spurs. The warhorse leaped forward without hesitation.

Not realising the numbers now against them, Gallienus' men countercharged.

For a horrible moment, Postumus thought he was deserted.

An officer slashed wildly at his head. Postumus took the blow on the boss of his shield, felt the impact run up his left arm.

Before Postumus could riposte, one of his guards cut the man down.

Another enemy thrust from the right.

Postumus deflected the blow with his sword, shaped to counter, but the trooper was gone.

The horse guards had thundered past their stationary emperor.

Inexplicably, Postumus was alone. Ahead, the unmistakable sounds of rout and pursuit: the rattle of horses pushed hard, screams of mortal agony, and whoops of exultation.

Everything hung on the next few moments. Any delay and Postumus' cavalry would be scattered, the victory thrown away in their wild chase.

Maecianus and a trumpeter emerged from the dust, more men at their back.

Postumus tried to give the necessary order. His throat was dry. The words would not come.

He grabbed the trumpeter by the shoulder, croaked in his ear, 'The recall. Sound the recall!'

The trumpeter tried to spit. Put the instrument to his lips. A thin, quavering note. He unstoppered a flask from the horn of his saddle, rinsed his mouth, spat, and drank. The second time, the recall rang out clear and true.

Postumus peered about. There was grit in his eyes, but he could see a little further. The wind was strengthening, dragging the dust away to the south. Two hundred, perhaps three hundred men with him, more walking their sweat-soaked horses back.

Taking the wine from the trumpeter, Postumus drank.

'Reform the line on me. In a wedge.' He gestured. 'This way, facing south.'

Any moment and the dust would clear, and they would see what awaited.

CHAPTER SEVEN

The Plain of Vesontio

Twelve Days before the Kalends of July

Ballista could hear the cavalry moving in the swirling clouds of dust: the thunder of hooves; the jingle and rattle of harness; shrill shouts of man and horse. Occasionally a rider or a small group of horsemen swept into sight. Sometimes they rode one way, sometimes another. They were no sooner glimpsed than they vanished again into the clinging murk. The troopers of both armies were armed alike; their allegiance could not be ascertained. No pattern could be discerned in their movements. It was impossible to tell who was winning.

It had been dry for days, the plain baking under the hot sun. Ballista had fought in the east, out on the great deserts by the Euphrates, yet he had never known a battle like this for dust. The stuff was everywhere, gritty in eyes and nose, catching in your throat, cutting visibility to a few paces.

Ballista strained his senses to penetrate the curtain. The whole battle hinged on the unseen cavalry combat. The survival of Ballista and the men of the Thirtieth Legion here on the extreme right of the infantry line depended on the outcome.

'Do you think they will come again?'

Maximus' question brought Ballista back. The enemy cavalry were not the only threat.

The Frankish warriors stood, panting, some five or six paces from the front rank of the legionaries. The barbarians had charged bravely enough. The legionaries had held them. Then – as almost always happened if one side did not break at the first onset – after a vicious melee, lasting perhaps at most a quarter of an hour, the combatants had drawn apart. Any man can only fight for so long, before limbs grow heavy, and spirits drop. Ballista had seen it happen on many battlefields. Yet the collusion remained a mystery to him. Why did both sides step back at the same moment, as if in response to some unheard mutual signal?

'Yes, when they get their nerve,' Ballista said.

It was always hard for men to get their courage up to cross those few paces back into danger, to close with the steel again – so much harder than the first rush. Ballista's orders were to hold the line. The battle was intended to be won elsewhere, by Aureolus and his men. The longer this lull in the fighting lasted, the better.

Ballista walked along the rear of the formation, patting legionaries on the back, calling encouragement to those whose names he knew in the front. *Well done, Titus; Keep it up, Marcus.* Trite sentiments, but the soldiers seemed to like them.

'Sir.' Ferox saluted. A great, half-healed cut ran across the centurion's face. The end of his nose had gone. When it healed, his looks would not be improved. It might make him resemble Maximus, who had lost the tip of that appendage years before. It was best not to raise the subject. No one wanted to have a nose that looked a bit like a cat's arse.

'Casualties?'

'Nine out of the fight, three of them dead.'

'Not too bad, Centurion.' Ballista pitched his voice to carry. 'I always said, no one fucks with the Thirtieth, especially not a bunch of sheep-shagging Franks.'

The legionaries grinned. 'Not with old Blondie on our side!' one of them shouted.

Ball-is-ta! Ball-is-ta!

The chant sounded brave enough. The men beat time with their swords on their shields. They were not yet too tired. There was still plenty of fight in them.

'Carry on, Centurion.'

Ferox was more than capable of leading this detachment in battle. The role of Ballista as acting commanding officer was largely symbolic. The army of Gallienus contained many more senior officers than was necessary. Incessant wars had led to a flood of promotions, and, with the western provinces lost, there were not suitable positions for all of the beneficiaries. Almost every unit in the line had one of the *protectores* at its head. The patrician Acilius Glabrio had the detachment of the Tenth Legion next in line to the left.

The ground trembled beneath Ballista's boots. The legionaries and the Franks fell silent. Everyone gazed to the north. Somewhere in that gloom, a large formation of heavy cavalry was charging. Ballista walked out beyond the extremity of the line.

Damn this dust. What was happening just out of sight?

A lone horseman spurred out of the murk. He rode as if the Furies of the Underworld were at his heels. Catching sight of the infantry, he hauled his horse's head, and galloped away towards Vesontio. Unless completely lost, he must be a trooper of Gallienus.

The sounds from behind the veil had changed: lots of horses, running as one; cries of exultation; yelps of fear or pain. The noises seemed to be heading past, moving east.

'Bring up the horses,' Ballista said to Tarchon. 'Maximus, stay with me.'

Ballista walked back to Ferox.

'Centurion, you have the Thirtieth. I will bring reinforcements to shield your flank. Until I return, Acilius Glabrio is your superior officer.'

Tarchon trotted up on a bay, leading Pale Horse and Maximus' black. The other two swung into the saddle.

'Follow me.'

Acilius Glabrio sat astride a showy chestnut behind the Tenth. Like Ferox's legionaries, their opponents had given ground, and were taking their time working themselves up for another charge.

'Too hot for you?' Everything the patrician said was a sneer.

'I am going to the emperor to request more men. Our flank is exposed.'

'Our orders are to remain. Leaving your post is against the military oath. But it will not be the first time you have deserted your betters.'

Ballista bit back a sharp response. 'Take over the Thirtieth.'

'The penalty for desertion is death.'

'Just do your duty.'

Ballista had no time for this.

'Did you lecture my brother on his duty?'

'Another time, Glabrio.'

'With pleasure.'

Ballista turned Pale Horse, and rode away.

Gallienus was with the reserve on a hillock to the rear. They were not moving, and there was no dust here. If conditions had been clear, they would have commanded a fine view of the field. As it was, they could see next to nothing of the fighting.

'What news?' The emperor's tone was relaxed, but his face was drawn and very white. Gallienus had won many battles. Ballista had been in action with him before. The pallor was more likely to be a hangover than apprehension.

'Our horse on the right are in retreat.'

Gallienus waved, as if brushing away an insect. 'Those were their orders – to draw the enemy.'

'My lord, this is no feigned flight. They are running.'

'No sign of Aureolus?'

Ballista spread his hands in a helpless gesture. 'Not before the dust . . . Now there could be anything out there.'

Volusianus spoke. 'Then how can you be sure our troopers are running?'

'I know the sound of defeat.'

A senator in the entourage sniggered.

'And Ballista knows the sound of victory.' As he delivered the reproof, Gallienus did not look at the senator. 'How many of my generals have defeated the Persian King of Kings?'

The officers behind the emperor were very silent. The animosity of some to Ballista was palpable.

'Take the Praetorians and the German guard, and protect that flank.'

For all he was suffering from last night's drinking, Gallienus could still act decisively.

'Not all the Praetorians, my lord,' Volusianus said. 'It is not fitting that the emperor should be unguarded by the Praetorians.'

Gallienus looked away, as if focusing on something only he could see.

Ballista suspected the emperor was conjuring up a panorama of the battle.

'Very well.' Gallienus snapped out of his reflections. 'Ballista, you will go with the Germans and two thousand of the Praetorians. We will be safe enough with the remaining thousand and the horse guards. If necessary, it leaves me enough to throw into the main line as a reserve. Volusianus, issue the required orders.'

Time dragged, and Ballista tried not to fidget with impatience as the Praetorian prefect laboriously wrote. For all his years in office, Volusianus wielded the stylus as if the device were new, seldom employed before.

At last the message was impressed in the wax, and the wooden tablet snapped shut.

Bowing in the saddle, even as he wheeled his mount, Ballista blew a kiss from his fingertips to the emperor, and cantered away.

The tribune looked dubiously at the writing. 'The script is not easy to read.'

'The sense is clear enough. Volusianus is a soldier, not a scribe. You are to follow my orders.'

'We will do what is ordered, and at every command we will be ready.' The words could never have been said with less enthusiasm.

'Two columns, one either side of the Germans. Prepare to march.'

Ballista went over and took station by Freki, the Alamann chief who led the German Guard.

'Like setting out over ice with a two-year-old colt, unshod, restive and unbroken,' Freki said.

'Things not to trust,' Ballista agreed. 'A yawning wolf, a tide on the ebb, a bride's pillow talk.'

'Expect little help from the Praetorians.' They spoke in the language of Germania. 'Good at beating unarmed civilians, not so happy against fighting men.'

'And you, Freki, what does your heart say today?'

The Alamann shrugged. 'It is true my people have no love for you Angles. Few people have. But you and I have given our sword-oath to Gallienus. We are like snow blowing from one tree to another.'

'One tree to another,' Ballista said.

Maximus made a sign to avert evil.

'Ready!' Ballista reverted to Latin. 'At the double, move out!'

Running in chain mail was hot, tiring and uncomfortable. Today the grit which had worked itself under Ballista's armour and clothes was rubbing his shoulders raw. Part of him wished that he had not sent Tarchon to take Pale Horse back to the camp. But only part of him. There had been dark words from the Suanian. An insult to his honour. He was as good a killer as ever. The loss of a couple of fingers signified nothing. The latter was not quite true. Yet it was not concern for the man but the gelding that had influenced Ballista's decision. This would be an affair for infantry. Having summoned Pale Horse from retirement, Ballista was not going to risk him unnecessarily. It would be unforgivable if, while he was preoccupied, the animal came to harm or were lost. He had a great fondness for Pale Horse.

'Here is good,' Maximus said.

Head down, concentrating on keeping going, putting one foot in front of the other, Ballista had not been aware of how far they had come. The wind had picked up, and backed into the north. Now it was in their eyes, but it was beginning to tear away the shroud of dust. To their left, Ferox's detachment of the Thirtieth Legion was in plain sight. Ahead the clouds were dispersing, and vague shapes, glints of metal, and patches of colour could just be made out.

'Halt! Form a line, at a right angle to the legionaries. Three deep, shields overlapping, ready to receive cavalry. Praetorians, take position on either side!' Ballista had to bellow the last instruction.

The Germans shuffled into formation, huffing and puffing after the run. Yet they completed the manoeuvre with alacrity, while the Praetorians jostled and barged in no order at all.

Let us perform brave deeds.

Freki recited the line of poetry quietly.

Silently, Ballista ran through his pre-battle ritual: first loosening the dagger on his right hip, then the sword on his left, finally touching the healing stone tied to his scabbard.

Out of the north wind, haloed by the dust, the enemy appeared.

Five, six hundred horsemen, helmeted, armoured, shields and swords in hand.

Here before sunset we will

Make noisy clamour of our spears.

The Praetorians did not react well to the sudden appearance of the enemy. From both bodies of guards came nervous shouts. The fancy white plumes of their helmets bobbed, as some tried to get into line, while others hung back. Centurions were shouting, belabouring the vine staffs on the backs of the recalcitrant.

'*Nithings*,' Freki said. 'This is how they repay their war-leader's gold. Men fit to be slaves.'

An officer in chased and gilded armour was haranguing the horsemen.

'Are you ready for war?' A purple cloak hung from his shoulders.

'Ready!' the troopers roared back.

Ballista settled himself in the front rank, Freki to his right, Maximus to his left. If this was where the Fates cut the thread of his life, he would die in good company.

'Ready!'

At the third response, the cavalry moved forward at a walk.

There was something inexorable about that slow, measured advance.

The Praetorians were still milling in confusion.

'At the trot!'

The enemy were some hundred paces away.

The Germans waited in silence.

Anxious commands and individual, unconvincing war cries issued from the Praetorians on either side.

'Stand firm!' Ballista bellowed in Latin, to make himself heard by the Roman guardsmen. 'No horse will run into a solid line. Stand firm, and they will not charge home! Hold the line and you are safe!'

'Liberty and abundance!'

The officer levelled his sword, and kicked his mount into a gallop.

'Postumus!' The troopers surged forward. 'Postumus!'

Fifty paces; the pounding hooves ate up the ground.

The very air seemed to shake with their coming. Ballista dug in his right boot, leaned his shoulder into his shield. His chest was reverberating with the noise; his vision filled with the wild eyes and gaping mouths of the horses, the wicked glint of steel above. Any second now.

Then, as if by the hand of a god, the onset was broken. Instead of a terrifying charge, there was chaos: horses swerving, colliding, planting their feet, skidding to a halt just ten paces out. Riders half out of the saddle, clinging to the necks of their mounts.

One horse, maddened beyond caution, crashed into the line to the right of Ballista. As it fell, skewered on the out-thrust spears, it smashed warriors to the ground. Caught by its massive shoulder, Freki was hurled backwards.

'There!' The officer with the bright cloak was shouting. 'Into the gap!'

Its momentum had taken the dying animal through the Germans. Without thought, Ballista stepped into the opening. The rider of the fallen horse was groggily getting to his feet. Ballista killed him with a backhanded cut to the head.

Recovering his blade, Ballista turned to face the enemy. Maximus was at his shoulder. For a moment they stood alone. The nearest troopers were urging their mounts into motion. Then the northern warriors closed up around them. The line was restored.

Ballista did not have to look to know the Praetorians on both flanks had broken. Screams of terror and agony told their story.

'Sound the recall!'

The cavalry commander knew his business. If he did not regain control of his men quickly, most would be out of the fight. Their bloodlust up, they would scatter, chasing the fleeing Praetorians back to their camp, and beyond into the streets of Vesontio.

As the trumpets sounded, Ballista called out his own order.

'Form circle, shieldwall!'

With discipline from experience, not the parade ground, the Germanic warriors obeyed.

The cavalry were re-forming a hundred paces away. The officer still had about three hundred men under the standards. The outcome hung in the balance. Many more would die before this was decided.

Freki came and stood by Ballista. They did not speak. There was nothing to say. They had to endure.

A despatch rider spurred up to the horsemen. He spoke to the officer. The latter pushed himself up on the horns of his saddle, peering over the heads of his men away to the north.

Another officer – his armour slightly less elaborate – was talking excitedly. The senior officer answered curtly. He was still staring north.

Ballista could see the crests of the wooded hills. A low cloud hung over them.

All the troopers were craning around. Consternation shivered through their ranks, like wind through a field of corn. From the rear of the formation, a rider wheeled his horse, kicked his boots into its flanks, and fled off to the west. In a heartbeat, a dozen others followed.

Was that a cloud or a pall of dust?

The troop disintegrating, the commander roared at them to stand. He was shouting that it was nothing to fear. It was all part of his plan. His words went unheeded. More of his men set off after the fleeing comrades.

Definitely a column of dust. Tall and narrow, before being tugged away by the wind.

The junior officer seized the bridle of his commander's horse, went to turn its head to the west. At a fierce order, he let go.

Ballista battened down a stab of hope. If he was wrong, the disappointment would be overwhelming.

The man in the purple cloak settled himself back in the saddle. He looked at the Germans barring his way. His eyes locked with those of Ballista. Then he nudged his mount forward.

Waving away the remaining soldiers who rushed to accompany him, the officer walked his horse within hailing distance.

'Gallienus is not worthy of your courage.' His accent was from the lands by the mouth of the Rhine.

'We have given him our sword-oath,' Ballista said.

'And you will not transfer your allegiance? Give your oath to another?'

'We will not, *Imperator*.'

Postumus raised his hand in farewell, or even in blessing, and rode away, after his routing men.

The tension broken, like men reprieved from the amphitheatre, the Germans dropped their shields, pounded each other on the back. Laughing, they said that bastard Postumus had balls. Not a bad man – not for a Batavian.

Ballista walked out from the line. His eyes followed the retreat of the rebel emperor. No more than twenty loyal men still rode at his back. Then Ballista looked to the north. Four columns of cavalry were cantering down from the hills. The general Aureolus had come. The long flank march – up along the river Dubis, around and through the hills – had succeeded.

As Ballista watched, trumpets rang out. The advancing cavalry halted and deployed into a long line. Horses pawed the ground, tossed their heads, full of running. There was no way Postumus could escape them.

Ballista waited to hear the trumpets sound the charge.

CHAPTER EIGHT

The City of Augustodunum

Six Days before the Kalends of July

FOR ALL THE MALICE of fortune, and the severity of the disappointment, life had to continue. The endless mundane demands on a Roman emperor did not cease, not even in the midst of civil strife, not even after a defeat in that war. The city had been in uproar when Postumus had ridden into Augustodunum. With much rioting, and wanton destruction of property, the locals had been set on lynching every Christian in the place. It was a sign of the disturbed times. Disasters, natural or man-made, including defeat in battle, were always blamed on the atheists who denied the traditional gods. It had not helped that in Augustodunum all the followers of Chrestus, the crucified Jew, appeared to be immigrants from the Greek east. Despite the troops at his disposal, Trebellius, the acting governor, had been out of his depth. Postumus had been forced to intervene, ordering widespread arrests.

Now, as the due processes of Roman law demanded, the leading Christians must be allowed to speak in their own defence.

'The prosecutor has said that all the events which shake and oppress our world are brought about by us, and ought to be imputed to us, because we do not worship your gods. As to that, since you are ignorant of the knowledge of God, and a foreigner to truth, you should know that the world is growing old. The winter rains no longer nourish the crops in the fields, in summer the sun no longer ripens the grain.'

Postumus let his gaze shift to the map of the empire which was painted on the rear wall of the school of rhetoric which he had commandeered as a courthouse. The Christian was an educated man. The amplitude of his oration was suitable for the surroundings. Trees withered, springs ran dry and the moon shrank, while harmony between neighbours – and integrity in court – evaporated. An educated man, but a fool. It was typical of the intransigence of these atheists that, even pleading their defence, he dared to insult an emperor to his face, had the audacity to call him a foreigner to truth, who presided over a court without integrity.

On the other hand, perhaps the Christian was no fool at all, but a realist. This trial could only have one outcome. The prosecutor, a young local orator called Eumenius, had been zealous in making his case. Perhaps his own Greek antecedents had inspired a measure of his zeal. Whatever his motives, Eumenius had proved conclusively that when Trebellius had ordered all those in the city to sacrifice for the success of Postumus at Vesontio, the Christians had not participated. They had poured no libations, tasted no morsel of the sacrificial meat. All that was at issue was the nature of their punishment.

'God does not hold back with the whip. There remains the eternal prison, the unquenched fire, and the perpetual suffering.'

The Christian was well into his stride. The sins of mankind were enumerated – malediction and lies and slaughter and theft and adultery – and the apocalypse approached. The beasts of the field, the serpents of the earth, the birds of the sky . . . all would mourn. No one could refute the will of God.

Postumus picked out Vesontio on the map. He had been so close, victory within his grasp. All that had stood in his way had been those Germans. Even then the day would have been his, if his men had not panicked at the arrival of Aureolus and his cavalry. Of course, Postumus had not made public that Aureolus would not intervene. There were informers in every army. A horse laden with Spanish gold, and promises of advancement, even the hint of elevation to the rank of Caesar, had bought the temporary neutrality of Aureolus.

At least Aureolus had kept his word. His troopers had sat motionless, no doubt chaffing and baffled, as Postumus had escaped from the stricken field. Yet the treachery of Aureolus troubled Postumus. A subsequent clandestine approach from another of the *protectores* of Gallienus had deepened his unease. Even in the aftermath of victory, those close to Gallienus were not to be trusted. Postumus did not need to look at the men who sat with him in this court. They were every bit as venal and ambitious as those around Gallienus. Somewhere in the back of his mind was an old story about a king who had lived with a sword suspended above his head by a thread.

'I willingly confess myself to be a Christian. I confound you and your gods. Why attack the weakness of my earthly flesh? Break the strength of my mind, destroy my faith, defeat me – if you can – with arguments. Defeat me with reason!'

The water clock had run empty. Postumus had no intention of quibbling like a Sophist with this fanatic. He turned to his advisors. Victorinus requested permission to speak.

'It is well known that Gallienus has passed an edict of toleration. In the middle of his folly, it is a rare moment of sanity.'

The Christian in the dock beamed at the Praetorian prefect, as if suspecting his God was moving in mysterious ways.

'Not because the worshippers of the Jewish criminal deserve anything other than death.'

If anything, the accused looked even more pleased at this seeming change of tack. Doubtless it was added proof of the unredeemed wickedness of those in power, and the world in general.

'But because the first quality of an emperor is mercy, even to those who are guilty. If a tyrant such as Gallienus occasionally shows mercy on a whim, how much more fitting that a good ruler, such as Postumus, exhibits that virtue as a matter of course. I recommend confiscation of their worldly goods, and perpetual exile. Let no citizen offer them fire or water on pain of death.'

Marius raised his hand to speak. Doubtless he would disagree. Was there no end to the squabbling of Postumus' courtiers?

'Often the uneducated see things more clearly than those unmanned by years on school benches. The windy theories of philosophers encourage pointless and harmful speculations. Out of his own mouth, this Greek has admitted that he does not worship the gods on whom depend the safety of the *imperium* of the Romans. The plebs of Augustodunum are right to demand vengeance.'

Marius glared around the fine marble portico, as if the famous Maenian school of oratory, and its product, the

Praetorian prefect Victorinus, in some way, were implicated in undermining the traditional ways of Rome.

'Gallienus is not to be taken as an example. His father, Valerian, was a good emperor. He did right by the gods, and feared nothing. Valerian ordered the Christians persecuted across the whole empire. Gallienus is a coward. He trembles before the words of these atheist scum, and their dead god. For five long years, Gallienus has been too afraid to even attempt to rescue his own father from the Persians. Emulate Valerian, not Gallienus. Throw these Christians to the beasts!'

Although, to a man, educated in the schools of higher learning, the councillors nodded their assent.

Transcended by his approaching martyrdom, the Christian began to shout joyful denunciations of lust, fraud, cruelty, impiety and wrath.

A centurion ended his rantings with a sharp blow across the back of the head with a cudgel.

The Christian lay, moaning on the floor. His spiritual brothers and sisters joined hands, and waited quietly.

Postumus composed his face into the sort of expression with which the divine Marcus Aurelius was depicted on statues: composed and thoughtful, in communion with the gods.

'War is coming. We should not deceive ourselves. In time of war, unity is essential. The Christians cause strife.'

Postumus paused weightily, aiming to give dignity to his words.

'Many things decide the outcome of a war. Among them, the will of the gods is by far the most important. The Christians deny the existence of the gods. If Gallienus tolerates the atheists, the gods will turn against him. If we do not suffer the impious to walk among us, there can be no doubt that the gods will support us, keep us safe in their hands, and bring ultimate victory.'

The emperor hunted for suitably elevated phrases with which to conclude.

'Piety and necessity combine. We must do the right thing by the gods and by man. With the authority invested in me by the Senate and People of Rome, and by the eternal gods themselves, I order that the Christians be taken to the cells under the amphitheatre, and, at a date to be determined, they be brought out into the arena to be executed under the gaze of the public in ways fitting their disgusting crimes.'

The councillors applauded decorously.

The guards led out the condemned. The speaker was dragged by his legs, his head bumping along the flagstones. Postumus took a sip of well-watered wine. It was not yet noon. There was much business to come.

The next case concerned the failure to return a deposit. It would take some moments for those concerned to be ushered into court.

War was indeed coming. Postumus looked again at the map on the wall. Postumus traced its route. The road from Vesontio to Augustodunum. The road down which Postumus had retreated, and along which Gallienus now was advancing. This morning the scouts had reported that the enemy cavalry had reached Pons Dubris. Once over the river, Gallienus would reach Augustodunum in a couple of days. Postumus decided to defer the execution of the Christians until the city was besieged. It would act as a tonic to the morale of the defenders.

Augustodunum was ready for a siege. Trebellius had not dealt well with the religious unrest, but he had gathered an abundance of provisions. Gallienus would cut the aqueducts, but there were wells in the town, and, if they failed, water could be drawn from the streams at the foot of the defences. The walls had needed only superficial repairs. Although built long ago, inspired by civic pride, rather than necessity, they were of massive construction – tall and broad, a solid core of rubble in concrete, faced with smooth blocks of sandstone. No fewer than fifty-four towers allowed torsion artillery and archers to enfilade all approaches. The Arroux and Accoron rivers acted as a moat to the north and east respectively.

The only weaknesses were the four gates. Yet they were protected by flanking towers, and, as soon as he arrived, Postumus had ordered battlements added to their ornamental superstructure. On reflection, he had not had the four portals in each gate bricked up. The defence of a town should never be passive. The threat of a sally would prevent the besiegers from ever relaxing or feeling safe.

The walls stretched for miles, enclosing a huge area. But there were more than enough soldiers to man them. The eight thousand troops who had been watching the southern passes through the Alps had gathered in the city under Trebellius. Thanks to the suborned inactivity of Aureolus, almost all the cavalry and over half the infantry had been able to escape the battle of Vesontio with Postumus. In all, there were about thirty thousand men under arms to defend Augustodunum.

Gallienus could sit outside Augustodunum until hunger, plague, or treachery forced him to break camp, and withdraw.

The prosecutor was ready to begin his speech.

'There ought to be a penalty for avarice, and greed should be chastised. Good faith among men cannot be maintained unless they are held in check by fear.'

Even in the midst of war, men did not cease from litigation and the pursuit of gain. Postumus saw his son scribbling notes. He had never understood the boy's fascination with the law. The thoughts of the emperor resumed their previous course.

Hunger might strike the besiegers sooner than Gallienus would expect. The forces Postumus had summoned from Britain and the Rhine were now bidden to assemble at Mogontiacum in Germania Superior. There would be fourteen thousand of them. From there, under the governor, Laelianus, they could move south, and prevent supplies reaching Gallienus from Italy via Summus Poeninus.

Similarly, the day before, Postumus had sent instructions for troops from Spain to cross the Pyrenees. A thousand legionaries, a matching number of auxiliary infantry, the five hundred allied Angles, and five thousand cavalry, the majority of them Moorish tribesmen, were to march to the valley of the lower Rhône. Once they were in place, it would become very difficult for Gallienus to get any aid through the southern passes of the Alps.

The latter had been a hard decision. It stripped the garrison of Spain bare. Postumus knew that as soon as they were withdrawn, the Franks, whom they had cornered in the Pyrenees, would issue forth. The barbarians had previously sacked Tarraco. Now many more communities across the peninsula would share the fate of that city. But it was a question of priorities. Once Gallienus was back in Italy – or, better, once he was dead – Postumus would be free to lead an army to pacify Spain. As with some diseases, a certain level of suffering was necessary to ensure long-term health.

'Whosoever denies a deposit, let him pay fourfold. So says the law. Without the rule of law, what hope is there for humanity?'

How these Gauls love the sound of their own voices.

Postumus' son was still writing furiously. Let them prattle and scribble, and leave the conduct of the defence to those who understood war. Augustodunum was a secure stronghold. No sooner was the thought formed than another insidiously appeared. Silvanus and Saloninus would have considered themselves safe behind the walls of Colonia Agrippinensis.

No, Postumus said to himself, *it's not the same at all.*

They were caught unprepared – few troops and scant provisions.

Not the same at all.

Postumus looked again at his son. The first duty of a father was to protect his children. No harm would come to his son. Not while Postumus was alive.

CHAPTER NINE

The City of Augustodunum

Four Days before the Kalends of July

FILTHY VERBAL ABUSE COULD only do so much. The man on the wall certainly thought more was necessary. He climbed on to the battlements, dropped his britches, and exposed his arse to the emperor.

'Impudent bastard,' Volusianus said. 'When we take the town, I will have him crucified.'

'You could crucify him upside down.' Gallienus was laughing. 'Or have him impaled – something fitting, like a stake up his arse. Still, rather than admire the view, we should keep moving.'

Indeed we should, Ballista thought.

The imperial entourage was out of effective bowshot. The defenders already had released a volley, the majority of which had fallen short. But, at a couple of hundred paces, they were well within range of the torsion artillery, which deserters had said were sited on every tower. In a few moments they would ride within range of three of the towers. Most likely, Postumus' men were waiting to try to catch the emperor and his generals in a crossfire.

Ballista had no idea where the ritual had arisen that the commander of a besieging force must put himself in danger by riding around close to the walls. Of course it was useful to see the defences for himself. But it could be done discreetly. Perhaps flamboyantly putting himself in danger was intended to raise the spirits of his own men, or lower those of the enemy, by demonstrating his contempt for the weapons of those inside the town. Maybe it was meant to prove his courage, and win the favour of the gods. The custom seemed universal. It was followed in the distant north of Ballista's boyhood. In the east, the Persian King of Kings was expected to get close enough to shoot an arrow over the walls. Whatever its origin or meaning, the practice was very dangerous.

Ballista could not take his eyes off the towers. Sweat was running down under his armour. The mail coat offered no protection against artillery. The bolt would punch clean through metal and leather, through flesh and bone. This ritual was not just dangerous – it was insane.

'Gallop!'

No one hesitated when Gallienus shouted. As one, the dozen riders kicked their mounts forward, bending low over their necks to make themselves smaller targets. The emperor must have seen the shutters over the artillery positions lifting a moment before anyone else.

The first bolt whistled over their heads. The second ploughed a furrow just short of their path. The final missile missed the last horseman by a couple of feet.

Gallienus reined in. He was bareheaded, his hair golden in the sun. Raising himself in the saddle, with a mocking flourish he saluted the defenders.

'I think we have seen enough – best we retire.'

Ballista admired his calm. The artillery would be reloaded in moments.

Gallienus spun his horse, and again went straight into a gallop.

Ballista pushed Pale Horse to follow.

Two hundred long paces to safety. Ballista's back felt horribly exposed. An artillery bolt would tear through his coat of mail like a knife through butter. One hundred paces. Hooves thundering; this seemed to be taking forever.

The emperor jinked left. A bolt shot wide and high to the right. Another raced past them on the left. Ballista heard the unmistakable twang of other torsion springs.

Gods below, where was it aimed?

By all that was holy, not at his back. Something warned him, and he pushed himself nose down into Pale Horse's mane. The wicked shaft hissed a hand's breadth over his head, missed his mount's head by no more than a finger or two.

Just over four hundred paces from the walls, the imperial horse guards opened their ranks to admit their emperor. Out of range, safe at last, Ballista drew a ragged breath. The men around him were laughing, light-headed with relief.

Well north of the town, over the Arroux river, was a theatre. Grooms were waiting to take their horses. Ballista handed Pale Horse to Maximus. Unsurprisingly, given the nature of the emperor, at the top of the building there were rugs and cushions, wine cooling in snow, liveried servants with trays of delicacies. There was a good view of the town.

Gallienus shrugged off and dropped his sword-belt.

'Well, my friends, what have we learned, apart from the enemy are very poor shots?'

The emperor reclined on a cushion. He gestured for Ballista to sit next to him. The others arranged themselves without ceremony. Volusianus remained on his feet.

'The walls are formidable, and in good repair.' As ever, the Praetorian prefect spoke slowly, as if choosing his words with much care. 'The river on this side cannot be forded, and the stream along the eastern wall is a serious obstacle. There is not an approach to the walls that is not enfiladed by towers. The gates are all flanked by projecting towers, and, although the circuit is long, Postumus has more than enough troops to man its entire length. There are no obvious weak points. As any attempt to storm the town would end in bloody failure, we must rely on treachery, starvation or regular siege works.'

'Starvation will not work,' Aureolus said. 'We could cut the aqueducts, but there are wells in the town, and, with some casualties, they could draw water from the streams at the foot of the walls. The deserters have told us that they have provisions for several months. In a long siege, there are open spaces within the defences that could be turned to growing crops. Only betrayal or making a breach will get us inside.'

The prefect of cavalry is a fine one to talk of treachery, Ballista thought.

Gallienus seemed to have accepted the excuse of Aureolus that he had been unable to intervene at Vesontio because his horses had been spent after their night march. Ballista was unconvinced. If the northerner had been emperor, at the very least the prefect of cavalry would have been relieved of his command; more likely, Ballista would have had him executed. Mind you, the head of Volusianus would have been exhibited on the next pike. There was nothing to connect Aureolus and Volusianus, but circumstantial evidence suggested both were disloyal. It would be much safer if both were dead. Living among the Romans, Ballista reflected, had not made him a better person.

'Philip, the father of Alexander the Great, said that no stronghold was impregnable if he could get a mule laden with gold inside.' Gallienus took a drink. 'We will have men approach the walls at night, and offer vast rewards to any who will open a gate or postern. Messages to the same effect can be tied to arrows and shot over the defences. Yet, by its nature, treachery is an uncertain business.'

Gallienus got to his feet, and walked to the parapet overlooking the town. The high command of his army went with him.

'We will divide the army into two main camps.' The emperor pointed out his dispositions. 'One to the south, the other off to the west. No major watercourses will lie between them and the defences. Smaller forts will block the roads on the north and east. When all four positions are fortified, we will connect them with a ditch and rampart, cutting the town off completely.'

'It will involve much labour,' Volusianus said. 'The men will be unhappy.'

'But discipline will go by the board if they sit around doing nothing.' Gallienus turned to Bonitus and Celer, the two siege engineers. 'What machines and devices would best serve to bring down sections of the wall in front of our camps?'

The talk turned to rams and penthouses, towers and ramps. The water level was too high for undermining. Ballista leaned his forearms on the warm, gritty stone of the parapet. Although he had successfully defended Miletus and Didyma from the Goths, he was best known for the siege of the town of Arete on the Euphrates. The Persians had taken Arete. The brother of Acilius Glabrio had died in the sack. Ballista had escaped. If Ballista ventured an opinion, the patrician would not fail to make some accusation.

Ballista looked out over the countryside, its peace vitiated by the movements of troops. Every siege reminded Ballista of that of Aquileia, the first he had witnessed within the empire. He had been young, just sixteen winters, when the centurion had arrived at the hall on the island of Hedinsey, and demanded Ballista's father give up one of his sons as a hostage to the emperor Maximinus Thrax. It had taken years for Ballista to forgive his father for his choice. Ballista had been happy in the north. An atheling, a prince of the Himling dynasty of Angles, his life had been a round of hunting and feasting, and sometimes fighting. There had been expensive books his father had imported for him from the empire. Only with hindsight was it obvious that the latter had been some form of training. If he had been allowed to remain on Hedinsey, Ballista would have wed Kadlin, the love of his youth. After he had left, she was hurriedly married off to a client chief.

The siege of Aquileia had not ended well. The army of Maximinus starving before the walls, some senior officers had formed a plot. Ballista had been forced to join. The conspirators had insisted that Ballista strike the first blow. It was an early lesson in Roman duplicity. Maximinus had been beheaded, his corpse exposed. Ever since, the shade of that terrible emperor had haunted Ballista.

Ballista had finally returned to Hedinsey the previous year. It had not gone as he had hoped. Kadlin had behaved strangely. Something unspoken on her part had hung between them. They had not parted on good terms. Ballista had fulfilled his mission, had returned his father from allegiance to Postumus to that of Gallienus. But in bringing that about, he had killed one of his half-brothers. There could be no further return to his homeland. The death of that sibling did not weigh upon him. It had been a fair fight, a duel to the death, and the man had been a traitor. His treachery had left another of their brothers, Arkil, and five hundred Angles in the power of Postumus. Kadlin's son, Starkad, was among their number. Ballista knew that he could not bring himself to fight Arkil, let alone a child of Kadlin. He would die before harming them.

His eyes followed the flight of a bird, soaring on the warm winds high in the sky.

The last he had heard, Arkil was serving Postumus in Spain, chasing marauding bands of Frankish raiders. This war would be decided here in Gaul. The possibility of encountering his brother or Starkad was very remote.

A thin mewing, like that of a kitten, came to his ears. It was a strange cry for a big bird of prey like a buzzard.

CHAPTER TEN

The City of Augustodunum

Two Days before the Kalends of July

'THE VALOUR OF TRAJAN, the righteousness of Antoninus, the self-restraint of Augustus.'

The Panegyric of Nummius Faustinianus flowed like honey, unctuous and mellifluous. A poet recited for his dinner, an acrobat tumbled, but a senator invited to the table of the emperor delivered a formal speech of praise.

Gallienus was not listening. Stretched out on the imperial couch, cup in one hand, the emperor petted one of the dancing girls. Her robe of sheer Coan silk was more revealing than if she had been naked. Volusianus could not help noticing her rouged nipples.

'Even if these good emperors had never lived, he himself is an example to all who come after.'

Gallienus' father would not have exhibited such casual disregard for the Senate. Among the vulgar and irreverent, Valerian had acquired a new nickname: *Colobius*. It was a slang term for an undershirt. Every day when the Persian king wished to go riding, the captive emperor had to get down on hands and knees in the dust. Shapur would place his boot on Valerian's shoulders, use the venerable man who had once ruled the better part of the world as a living mounting block. This is true, the Persian would say, not the lies told by the Romans. Now, with a new refinement of cruelty, Valerian was allowed to wear nothing but an undershirt. The thought was sickening.

'What is there in him that is not admirable? What that is not pre-eminent?'

Volusianus dragged his eyes away from the near-naked whore. There were slaves in his own quarters to fulfil the demands of nature in decent privacy. He had always prided himself on self-control, in pleasures of the flesh, as in all else. With advancing years, the goads of lust had become less frequent. In his measured way, he surveyed the pavilion. It was not a large party: ten couches, three men to a couch. Yet, two days into the siege, the entrenchment of the camp incomplete, it might be considered premature.

'The wicked he condemns openly and in public, but to the ignorant he extends a magnanimous indulgence.'

Nummius Faustinianus was earning his food and drink. The platitudinous flatteries sounded sincere. His smooth, groomed face betrayed no irritation at the lack of imperial attention.

Volusianus sought out the others who knew of the failed assassination. Elegantly propped on one elbow, Acilius Glabrio was listening with the restrained courtesy expected of a man of good breeding. Heraclian and Cecropius were talking quietly together. The flowery encomium might lack interest for such military men, but their closeness caused Volusianus a tremor of disquiet. That was nothing compared with the unease when he saw Ballista. The barbarian was staring at the purple hangings at the entrance, as if considering some weighty matter known only to himself.

The bastard knew, and he was biding his time. Volusianus furtively put his thumb between his fingers to avert evil. The gesture had been involuntary. You could take the peasant out of his hut, but something of the sty remained. Annoyed with himself, Volusianus reached for his cup. Ballista had waited too long. Soon he would be in no position to harm the Praetorian prefect.

Volusianus took a drink. His hand was perfectly steady.

Sound strategy demanded a cavalry raid deep into hostile territory. A flying column could win over the countryside and prevent aid reaching Postumus from the south. Ballista was well qualified to lead such an expedition. A timely and discreet message to the enemy could ensure that neither the column nor its commander returned.

The only question that remained was who should accompany the barbarian on such a doomed mission.

'What virtues stand higher than the love of family and the love of mankind? Here in the west, our noble emperor campaigns to avenge his cruelly murdered son. When the rebel is crushed, he will march east to free his father. Familial duty combines with piety to the gods and concern for humanity. Everywhere, Gallienus will cast down tyrants and restore liberty.'

Volusianus risked another glance at Ballista. The northerner remained lost in some private calculation. Not an easy man to kill. Many had tried. Few of them had survived. If the column was betrayed, Ballista might still fight his way clear. Perhaps something else was needed. A malign hand, close to Ballista, riding with the column. Most elegant would be to use one of the conspirators. But perhaps another might be best – someone untainted by suspicion.

The assassination of an individual, or the betrayal of an entire column? There was no need to decide precipitously.

Place the traitor in the heart of the camp, and Ballista would not return.

The oration of Nummius Faustinianus had come to an end. As was to be expected when the *protectores* were emulating the hard drinking of the emperor, it was superseded by earthier entertainment. Someone had wagered that Aureolus could not lift a large gilded statue of Hercules that stood in the centre of the imperial chambers.

The prefect of the cavalry swaggered out from his couch.

All around the pavilion, men noisily made bets. The *protector* Claudius offered odds of four to one against. Aureolus backed himself for a large sum. There was no love lost between the two officers.

Volusianus watched Aureolus roll his neck, stretch his muscles. In a civil war of a previous generation, a general called Laetus had held his men back until he was sure which side would win. The victor had executed Laetus. A night march was tiring, but the excuse that the horses of Aureolus' men at Vesontio had been all spent did not convince. Laetus had paid the price, but here was Aureolus, still at court, still wearing a sword in the presence of the emperor. Gallienus was too trusting. Volusianus suspected that he was not the only man in this tent with a clandestine line of communication to Postumus.

Aureolus braced his feet, encircled the god with his arms. He strained, but the statue did not move. Men yelled encouragement or deprecation. Aureolus heaved again, red in the face, veins standing out. Hercules swayed, then, inch by uncertain inch, tottered aloft.

With a roar, Aureolus let the statue crash back to the ground.

'Gold to gold,' Aureolus said, exulting. 'Does my name not mean "gold"?'

'It is a name given to gladiators!' Claudius shouted.

'Pay what you owe!'

Claudius threw the entire contents of his wallet at the feet of Aureolus.

'The son of a goatherd is used to manual labour.'

'At least I knew my father.'

'How dare you!' Claudius got unsteadily to his feet.

Aureolus sneered. 'No one has accused me of being the bastard of some degenerate.'

Claudius was red faced with anger. 'My ancestors were Dardanian kings – my line goes back to Ilus of Troy.'

'Dardanian kings, my arse.'

Both men had their hands on the hilts of their swords.

Gallienus was laughing, as if at the theatre.

Volusianus watched Ballista and another officer step between the drunken men.

'Your mother was a whore fucked by the drunken pretender Gordian.' Aureolus was spoiling for a fight.

The hangings were flung back, and a tribune of the Praetorians burst into the tent.

'The enemy are in the camp!'

As if a deity had passed through the room, there was silence.

'Here . . . now . . . in the camp . . . a sally.' Coherent words failed the tribune.

Gallienus leaped off his couch, snatched up his sword-belt. 'With me!'

All levity and inebriation vanished, he ran to the door.

As the emperor disappeared through the curtains, pandemonium erupted. The *protectores* grabbed their swords. Senators scrabbled for a knife, or some other makeshift weapon. Men got in one another's way trying to get out.

No longer young, Volusianus was left with the senators towards the rear of the stampede.

Outside, the night sky was a lurid red. The stench of burning in the air. The tent lines were on fire. All was confusion. A jabber of alarmed voices. No one was sure where the emperor had gone. The Praetorians on duty outside the pavilion must have left with Gallienus. There were no troops to be seen. The sound of fighting was to the north, towards the town. The senators scattered in different directions. Volusianus drew his blade, and followed some of the braver towards the enemy.

Apart from a few of the erstwhile revellers, the alleys between the tents were eerily deserted. Already blowing hard, Volusianus pounded along, eyes down, watching for guy ropes and other hazards. Sounds travel strangely at night. The noises of combat now seemed to be coming from the north-east. Volusianus followed a senator armed with a carving knife into an alley to the right.

At the next junction, the senator pulled up, hands on knees.

'Which way?' It was Nummius Faustinianus.

Volusianus did not answer. He looked up and down each alley. No one in sight.

Bent over, Nummius never saw the blow. He grunted as the steel bit into the back of his neck, then collapsed.

'Straight to Hades.'

Always strike first, then speak.

Volusianus went to be sure that Nummius was dead.

'Sir?'

A Praetorian was in the alley, his eyes full of confusion.

'An assassin sent by Postumus.' Volusianus straightened up. 'Search him.'

Accustomed to obeying his commander, the Praetorian sheathed his sword, put down his shield.

There were two ways out of this. One was more certain.

The guardsman crouched down, hands roaming over the corpse.

Again Volusianus glanced around. Some figures in the distance. Too far to see much.

A Praetorian was not a senator. Something made the guardsman look up. The sword caught him across the face. The impact knocked him sideways, on to his knees. Sword still in hand, he dragged it up into a guard. Volusianus chopped down into his wrist. The sword dropped to the ground. The clatter of soldiers running, at no great distance. No time to delay.

Volusianus set himself for the killing blow.

Through the dark blood, the guardsman's teeth gleamed white where his jaw had been sliced open. There was a look on his face like that of a dog unjustly beaten.

Volusianus finished him with a powerful thrust to the face.

The gods were kind. Still no one near. Volusianus put his boot on the Praetorian's chest to retrieve his sword.

Time to go. That was one less conspirator. Nummius would not have to accompany Ballista.

Bloodied sword in hand, Volusianus set off towards the flicker of the fires.

CHAPTER ELEVEN

The Pass of Aspalluga in the Pyrenees

The Kalends of July

THIS COULD BE THE last time.

The Frankish warriors were assembling at the top of the pass.

It would not be the last time that Starkad would fight, but perhaps the final battle under the standards of Postumus. He remembered the Latin oath taken by the Atheling Arkil as if it were yesterday:

By Jupiter Optimus Maximus and all the gods, I swear to carry out the emperor's commands, never desert the standards or shirk death, to value the safety of the emperor above everything.

Arkil had said three years. Postumus had insisted on five. But the emperor had replied graciously to the atheling's recent petition to revert to his reckoning. Three winters had passed since the oath.

Postumus had treated the Angles well. Keeping his word, he had not led them against their own people. The Gallic emperor had been open-handed, given them the pay of Praetorians, more than twice that of a legionary. The wallets of Arkil's men bulged with coins. There had been little to spend them on this last year, blockading the Frankish raiders in the mountains. Their baggage was laden with precious things: gold and silver plate, filigreed weapons and slaves.

In return, the Angles had fought well for Postumus, on the Rhine, in the Alps, and here in Spain. They had not shirked death. Less than half of their original number were left. The five hundred surviving warriors had earned their passage on the promised ships out of Burdigala back to the shores of the Suebian Sea.

Despite the pleasures of the towns of Gaul and Spain, Starkad very much wanted to go home. Of his twenty-eight winters on Middle Earth, three had been passed away from Hedinsey and the north. He missed his family, his friends, their way of doing things.

Starkad could see individual Franks stepping out from the ranks. Their helmeted heads could be made out distinctly. It meant they were within seven hundred paces.

'They mean to dance,' an elderly warrior said.

'They do,' said Starkad.

'The wolf-warriors are Woden-inspired. Baying, howling, they call down the power of the Allfather's slavering beast. Blind to pain, hard to stop, they are the ones to fear. Kill them, and the rest will lose heart.'

Who did Guthlaf think he was addressing – a child, a southerner? Starkad had stood in the shieldwall, faced the steel, been made an eorl, commanded a longboat before they came into the empire. When Arkil was wounded, it had been Starkad who had led the survivors across the Alps out of Raetia. Since then, it was accepted that he stood second to the atheling in the war band.

'The atheling has chosen a good position.' Guthlaf was not done. 'The pass is narrow. They cannot outflank us. Either side of the path, the ground is stony. It will break their formation. Except for here in the centre, they will reach us in ones and twos.'

Starkad did not reply. The old man's continuous litany of advice irritated him more than anything, except when Guthlaf made reference to Starkad's parentage.

A dozen Franks were leaping, tossing their spears in the air, working themselves into the ferocity of fanged and clawed animals.

Starkad looked along the line, where the Angles waited in silence. Bright painted shields, the burnished gleam of helmets, coats of mail and the points of spears. The white horse on a green field of Hedinsey flew above the reserve, where Arkil would take his station. Starkad's own white dragon standard twisted and hissed in the breeze.

The Franks were moving. They would walk until they were close.

This would be a desperate fight. Trapped in the high mountains, the Franks were starving. They had to break out or die.

Silently, Starkad checked his sword and dagger slid smoothly from their coverings, pushed them back, and touched the piece of amber tied to his scabbard as a healing stone. He would not disgrace his ancestors, whoever they were.

Arkil walked out on his own in front of the line. Like all the Himling dynasty, he was tall and broad, with long fair hair down to his shoulders. Woden-born, they were natural leaders of men.

'No need for many words. They are Franks, we are Angles. They have run from us before, they will do so again.'

Arkil drew his blade. The Himlings possessed many famous swords. This was *Gaios*, the growling one, half as old as Woden and responsible for nearly as many deaths.

'One last fight, and we can go home!'

The warriors beat the shafts of their spears against their shields.

The line parted to admit Arkil. As he passed Starkad, the atheling clapped him on the shoulder.

'Heart and courage, boy, heart and courage.'

The Franks were some two hundred paces away. A low *hooming* sound came from their ranks. It was the beginning of the *barritus*, the war-chant of the north.

Raising their shields, the Angles answered in kind. Deceptively gentle at first, the *barritus* rose to a roar. Reverberating from the wooden boards, it drowned out that of the Franks. A measure of manhood, the *barritus* foretold the outcome.

A hundred paces out, the Franks began to descend faster.

'*Shieldburg!*'

The front rank of the Angles kneeled, shields overlapping, spear butts planted. The second brought their shields over, locked their bases on the bosses of those below. Starkad hefted his spear out over Guthlaf. The war-hedge was formed.

Inspired by the Allfather, the bestial warriors leaped ahead of the Franks. Others, eager to get this ordeal over, followed. Guthlaf had been right. Their line was splitting apart.

The shaft of Starkad's spear was slick in his hand. His chest felt both hollow and tight.

A huge Frank was running straight at Starkad. In his frenzy, the warrior had cast off his armour. Spittle flecked his beard.

Fate will often spare a man, if his courage is good.

Uphill, the Franks hurled their spears first. Starkad thrust out his shield, away from his body, angled to deflect the missiles. The spear-points thumped down into wooden boards, clanged off metal armour. Screams and grunts of pain told that some had got through.

The rear ranks of the Angles threw. Peering around the rim of his shield, Starkad saw Franks fall. The near-naked warrior was not one of them.

Heart and courage . . .

The Frank launched himself. Somehow, twisting in the air, he avoided the out-thrust spears. He landed on Starkad's shield. Staggering back, driven almost to his knees, Starkad dropped his spear. Maddened, the warrior was tearing the shield away, jabbing around its edge with his sword. The tip scraped off the shoulder of Starkad's mail. The weight was crushing, the noise deafening. Starkad fumbled to get his dagger free. The next thrust slammed down onto the crown of Starkad's helmet. His vision blurred, the clangour of the blow stunning him. Starkad punched upwards. The razor-sharp steel slid into flesh. Starkad punched again, three, four times. Blood was stinging his eyes, running hot up his arm.

Starkad heaved the mortally injured man aside. Everywhere warriors were hacking, slashing, locked in the snarling embrace of violence. The slope against them, the shieldwall of the Angles was being ground backwards.

Guthlaf was left alone, still on his knees, almost surrounded.

Starkad stepped forward. Deflected a spear from his left with his shield, took a cut from the right on his blade. Reaching Guthlaf's back, he thrust out over the old man at his assailants.

An unseen blow smashed into the left side of Starkad's helm. He reeled sideways. From far away he heard a yell of triumph. Somehow, legs unsteady, he fended off another strike. This could not end well.

Suddenly, with a strength unexpected in one of his years, Guthlaf surged upwards. Shoulder to his shield, he hurled back the man in front. Almost too quick to follow, he struck out on either side. Two Franks went down in a spray of gore. Unrelenting, Guthlaf pressed the attack. Shields cracked, helmets buckled, mail coats snapped. The Franks pulled back.

There is a moment in battle when one side knows it has lost, when mind and body can take no more. Like a flash flood, in defiance of nature, the Franks ran up the pass.

Out! Out! Out!

The traditional war cry of the Angles echoed back from the hillsides.

Starkad stuck his sword point down into the earth, sank to his knees. Exhausted, he wiped at the blood on his face. Was it his own? His head hurt so much, it was hard to think.

Guthlaf pulled him to his feet, pounded him on the back.

'You fight well,' the old warrior said, 'like a true Himling.'

Starkad shoved him away, reached for his hilt.

The wild, uncaring joy of battle was in Guthlaf's eyes.

'Nearly as well as your *father*!'

That was too much. In a blind fury, Starkad brought up his blade.

'Starkad, enough!' Decades of command gave Arkil's voice authority.

Reluctantly, Starkad lowered the blade.

Arkil addressed the warriors. 'Finish off their wounded, tend to ours. The Franks will not return – strip the gold from their dead.' The atheling lowered his voice. 'Starkad, a word.'

Only the hearth-guard of Arkil, the dozen men who had sworn never to leave their lord, stood apart from the frenzy of pillage. The atheling gestured for them to remain, and led the young eorl away.

'Do not be hard on old Guthlaf.'

Starkad could not speak.

'He loves you like a son.'

'His words bring shame on my family, the House of the Wrosns.'

'It was meant as a compliment.'

Starkad looked away. Across the pass men stooped to their labour, an incarnadine parody of harvest.

'All my life I have heard men whisper, seen them smile. All my life I have overheard the things said about my mother.' Starkad was near to tears.

Arkil moved close, looked into Starkad's eyes. Those of the atheling were dark blue, sloping to the corners.

'Are you my man?'

'I gave you my sword-oath.'

'Then listen to what I say. Holen of the Wrosns was a good man. He raised you as his own. You should not blame your mother. Kadlin was young, so was Dernhelm. They were to be married. None of us knew Dernhelm would be taken as a hostage.'

Starkad stepped back, as if slapped.

'He abandoned my mother, left her pregnant, as if of no account. It was the act of a *nithing*.'

Arkil stiffened. 'Remember to whom you are talking. Remember, Dernhelm is my brother. In many ways he was the best of us.'

Head spinning with fury, Starkad did not consider his words. 'If he comes within range of my sword, he will die.'

Arkil shook his head, sadly. 'The hand's joy in the blow is brief. It is a terrible thing to be a patricide.'

The atheling held up a hand to silence any reply. 'An order has come from Postumus. We are to march to Gaul.'

'Then we are going home?'

'Before we embark at Burdigala, we are to prevent supplies reaching Gallienus from the south.'

'The three years are up.'

'It is still the third year. The emperor keeps his word. We will keep our oath to Postumus.'

PART THREE

THE CAVALRY

CHAPTER TWELVE

The Camp before Augustodunum

The Kalends of July

*T*HE FIRST DUTY IS *to sacrifice to the gods and pray them to grant you the thoughts, words and deeds likely to render your command most pleasing to the gods and to bring yourself, your friends and your city the fullest measure of affection and glory and advantage.*

Ballista had borrowed Xenophon's work on the duties of a cavalry commander from Gallienus' *A Studiis* when appointed to lead this raid into enemy territory. There were advantages in campaigning with an emperor devoted to culture, a ruler always accompanied by a secretary whose task was to oversee the travelling imperial library. No doubt there was wisdom in the opening precept of the ancient Greek text. Xenophon, however, had not neglected more mundane concerns, and nor had Ballista. Over the last two days he had been busy inspecting the mounted archers from Emesa. The Syrian light cavalry had a nearly full complement: four hundred and eighty-three men of the five hundred and twelve who should have been with the standards. Their personal equipment and tack had been well cared for and clean. No more than a dozen horses needed replacing. Their new commander, the *protector* Heraclian, already appeared to have them well in hand.

It was doubtful the same would apply to the Third *Ala* of Thracians. They had not impressed Ballista on the forced march down from the mountains to Vesontio. At Ballista's insistence, Solinus, the ineffective commander, had been replaced. This might cause resentment from those officers who owed their position to Solinus. Their new leader, a Gaul called Lucius Proculus, by all accounts had led a distinguished career in the army, but personally was unknown to Ballista. Whatever his capabilities, he had not had time yet to bring about significant improvements.

Ballista had ordered the heavy cavalry drawn up for inspection on the plain east of Augustodunum. He walked down with Lucius Proculus and Gratus, the prefect of the camp for the whole expedition. They were followed at a respectful distance by two more lowly officers, the chief armourer of the unit and its horse-master.

As instructed, the Thracians were formed in two dismounted lines. Each trooper was in full war gear and stood by his horse's head. The animals were bridled, but their saddles were placed on the ground, the leathers stripped off to reveal the wooden frames. From a distance – each squadron with horses of a distinct colour – the whole looked rather splendid.

'The Third *Ala* of Thracians, sir.' There was something rustic about the accent of Lucius Proculus. 'Three hundred and seventy-two men with the standards, eighty-four on detached duty, fifty posted missing, six dead.'

On any campaign there would be casualties and a high number of men absent from the standards for unknown reasons. Most of the latter would be stragglers, although some would have deserted.

'What duties call for eighty-four soldiers to be absent?'

'According to the rolls signed by Solinus, they are on various duties around the winter quarters in Mediolanum – collecting remounts, purchasing forage, guarding a crossroads, escorting a tax collector.'

Lucius Proculus answered correctly, with no hint of apology. The damage had been done long before he took command. To any experienced officer – to Lucius Proculus as much as to Ballista himself – it was evident that the Third *Ala* was thoroughly corrupt. Soldiers bribed their superiors – the centurions in the infantry, decurions here among the cavalry – to obtain leave under the guise of spurious detached duties. If the sum was large enough, they might never expect to reappear – in which case the junior officer might collect their pay as well as the initial bribe. It was a prevalent vice, which would spread through any formation, unless the commanding officer was both upright and active. Solinus had been neither.

'When we return, the circumstances attending all those away from the standards will be investigated.'

Ballista knew the implicit threat would not endear him to the squadron leaders of his new command, but it was important to make his mark from the start. Restoring discipline was always painful.

Ballista indicated to the armourer the inspection should begin.

'Soldier Malchus, eight years' service, pay-and-a-half, immune from fatigues.'

The soldier in question seemed older than eight years' service would imply. Either he had joined up much later than was normal, or he had re-enlisted.

'Have you served before?'

'No, sir.'

'How old are you?'

'Can't rightly tell, sir.'

Malchus had a sly and knowing look. Ballista suspected that he might have served with another unit under a different name before deserting and later re-enlisting with the Thracians. Whatever his past, his weapons and armour were spotless.

'His mount?' Ballista asked.

'Four-year-old horse, black, white face and off-fore, approved by the Prefect Solinus.' The horse-master read from a papyrus roll.

'Lead him round.'

Even at a walk, the horse pecked on the leg with the white marking. At a trot it was as lame as a cat.

Ballista picked up its foreleg. The hoof was cracked.

'Not fit for service. Make a note to indent for a remount.'

The horse-master juggled the papyrus roll, while opening a writing tablet.

'Indent one black remount for the first squadron, sir.'

'One sound remount, any colour,' Ballista said.

'Sir.' The riding master did not attempt to hide his disapproval.

'Next.'

'Soldier Titus, fourteen years' service, double pay, immune from fatigues.'

Again the man's equipment was polished and gleaming, and this time the horse was sound.

'Put the saddle frame on its back. No, not there, not halfway up its neck.'

'The further forward the saddle, the easier the ride,' the horse-master said.

'And the quicker it will break down with all the weight coming down through its front legs.' Ballista raised his voice. 'All saddles are to be fitted in the middle of the back, at the centre of the horse's motion.'

Even in the correct place, when the trooper mounted on the frame, it was obvious that the arch of the pommel constrained the withers, compressing them in their upper portion.

'The saddle is too small. Horse-master, it will need to be changed for another. If an alternative is not available in the unit, a new one must be made.'

And so it went on throughout the morning and into the afternoon. The arms and armour of the troopers shone from burnishing. Yet the mounts and their tack were a disgrace. Horses that were too old or too young, were spavined or gone in their wind, had sores or mange, or any number of equine ailments. Saddles where the cantle was not high enough, the fork insufficiently elevated, or the seat too low.

Mid-afternoon saw an unwelcome visitor. Clad in just a sweat-soaked tunic, Ballista was inspecting a horse's dock. The root of the tail was rubbed perfectly raw, the result of an ill-fitted crupper.

'Ah, Ballista, there you are.'

Acilius Glabrio looked down from a tall, showy chestnut. He spoke as if he had found a slave malingering on one of his estates.

'Glabrio.'

'I have been asked to summon you to the imperial war council.' The patrician's tone implied his task was extraordinary and distasteful. 'One hour. You might consider bathing, and a change of clothes.'

Without waiting for an answer, Acilius Glabrio wheeled his mount and cantered away.

Hiding his irritation, Ballista turned to Lucius Proculus and the other officers of the Thracians.

'Make a note of where we are in the inspection. Have the *ala* back on parade tomorrow, at the first hour of daylight.'

'Do the men already seen need to attend?' the horse-master said.

'The entire unit. Everyone is confined to barracks tonight. Have the men grease all the leather of their tack. We will take the road in two days' time. I intend the *ala* to be ready.'

Lucius Proculus snapped out orders.

Ballista walked back with the prefect of the camp.

'A poor showing,' Gratus said. 'Pretty on parade, not good in the field. Solinus ran them badly. Too many men immune from fatigues. They might be trouble, so might some of the decurions. That horse-master is no good. But the majority of the men will come round. They need a firm hand. Lucius Proculus can work them up on campaign.'

In the few days they had been together, Gratus had impressed Ballista. The former centurion radiated a calm competence. Ballista considered his other senior officers.

Lucius Proculus had served in many commands. The Gaul was said to be a notorious womaniser. His family estates were in the territory of the rebels, and it was well known that his cousin led the horse guards of Postumus. Some might think his loyalties could be compromised. Yet any number of men with Gallienus were addicted to the pleasures of the flesh, and many had family links to the other side. A cousin of Ballista's own wife was a senator on the council of the Gallic emperor.

Heraclian previously had charge of the *equites singulares* of Gallienus. The posting to the Emesene archers was a demotion that might rankle. But Heraclian had a distinguished war record. He had fought under Gallienus at Mediolanum and in Raetia. Presumably he would do his duty.

The fly in the ointment was Acilius Glabrio. There were more senior officers with Gallienus than the size of the army warranted. Yet why in Hades did this small cavalry expedition – less than a thousand riders – need a second in command? If Ballista was incapacitated or killed, either Heraclian or Lucius Proculus could have assumed command. Gratus equally was qualified. If there had to be a second in command, why did it have to be Acilius Glabrio?

The patrician hated Ballista. For almost ten years he had nurtured his loathing. His brother had died at the siege of Arete. Acilius Glabrio was convinced that Ballista had run, abandoned him to his fate. It was a travesty of the truth. Ballista thought back to the dusty city by the Euphrates. The brother had been drunk, had refused a direct command. Ballista had stripped him of command, confined him to house arrest, pending a court martial. That night the Persians had got inside the walls. Acilius Glabrio's brother had kneeled in the dust, requested to fight alongside Ballista as a private soldier. When it was obvious that the city could not be saved, they had sought to make their escape. The Persians were gaining on them. Acilius Glabrio's brother had volunteered to make a stand, let the others win free. Ballista remembered his final words: *You do not care for patricians, but I will show you how one of the Acilii Glabriones dies.*

There were many things that weighed on Ballista's conscience: things done, others left aside, oaths broken. The death of Acilius Glabrio's brother was not one of them.

They were nearing the tents. Gratus bade Ballista farewell.

The presence of Acilius Glabrio would be unpleasant, but it need be nothing more. Since Arete he had served under Ballista in the east. They had defeated the Persians at Circesium – even if the patrician's impetuous charge had cost them some of the fruits of the victory. This expedition was nothing like so desperate. A quiet ride through the Gallic countryside, intercepting unarmed wagon trains, cajoling or intimidating the locals back into allegiance to Gallienus. Perhaps there was nothing to worry about.

Unbidden, Ballista's thoughts latched on to something else troubling: the deaths of the senator Nummius Faustinianus and a praetorian in the raid on the camp. Everyone assumed they had been killed by Postumus' men. Except the raiders had only penetrated the north of the encampment, and the corpses had been found in the south. Had someone used the disturbance to settle an old score?

Ballista put the unwelcome thought out of his mind, and went to bathe.

CHAPTER THIRTEEN

The Road to Lugdunum

Twelve Days before the Ides of July

BALLISTA ORDERED THE COLUMN to pitch camp. A mile beyond the small town of Cabilonnum there was a broad meadow beside the road, and a wood beyond that – ideal terrain for cavalry to spend a night on campaign. Ballista dismounted, and watched them start to bivouac.

They had not set out early. The second hour of daylight had been half gone before they left Augustodunum. For the first two miles they had walked the horses at an easy pace. The Emesene mounted bowmen had plodded along quietly, but straight away there had been some confusion in the ranks of the Third Thracians. Ballista had spurred up and down the line, separating in season mares from stallions, sending animals which bit or kicked to the rear of the squadrons.

At the first halt the troopers had slipped the bits from their horses' mouths and let them drink, had tightened their girths. The Emesenes had checked the feet of their horses without being told. The men of both units had been reminded that they had only a quarter of an hour to see to their animals, and to relieve themselves. For some reason, soldiers seldom availed themselves of the opportunity. Men requesting permission to fall out to squat was the bane of cavalry on the march.

After that they had alternated between a walk and a trot, with a brief stop every hour, and a longer pause at midday.

On the two occasions that Ballista had ordered them to dismount and walk, there had been audible grumbling from Syrians and Thracians alike. They had done nothing wrong – leading horses on foot was a punishment for drunkenness or insubordination. Ballista pretended to have heard nothing. You would have thought horse soldiers would have realised the benefits. They got the feeling back into their legs, and their mounts got a little air on their backs and had a spell relieved of the weight. Contrary to the belief of townsfolk, the nomads of the steppe, if they had no remounts, often walked without complaint. But cavalry troopers were not renowned for either foresight or compassion, towards their animals or anything else.

Ballista stretched, rolled the stiffness out of his neck.

'You cannot be tired,' Maximus said. 'We have hardly covered twenty miles all day.'

'I am getting old.'

'Getting soft, like these excuses for soldiers.'

'They are not doing too badly so far.'

Not too badly, but there was a deal too much noise – swearing and cursing – from both units as the horse lines were arranged. As far as their numbers allowed, every squadron was to be set for the night sixteen horses wide and two deep, with good intervals between the ranks. Knowing their mounts must be seen to before themselves, two men in each *contubernium* of eight went off to collect forage. Their horses were to be unsaddled and groomed by their messmates.

'Leave the blankets on while they cool down.' Ballista's order cut through the general hubbub. 'Give them a little water while they are rubbed down, feed them afterwards.'

Acilius Glabrio cantered past on his big chestnut. The patrician ignored his commanding officer, and took no notice of the men. To be fair, there was nothing the second ranking officer in the expedition had to do, unless specifically instructed. Ballista had given him no orders.

A large tent was being erected in a shady corner of the meadow. It was a wonder how Acilius Glabrio had managed to have the elaborate thing transported, given that Ballista had limited every senior officer, including himself, to just three riding horses and four baggage mules. The restriction had been observed scrupulously. Ballista was not surprised. Years before, setting out on campaign in the east, he had banned officers from bringing personal effects in wagons. The order had been ignored. Ballista had burned the offending vehicles, along with their contents. Acilius Glabrio had been among those who had lost their possessions. It was the sort of story that was told and retold throughout the army.

The memory brought Ballista little pleasure. He had been drunk when he burned the wagons. He was not sure it had even been his idea. Acilius Glabrio's dislike of him was not based on nothing. The presence of the patrician was unlikely to add to the smooth running of the expedition.

'You there,' Ballista shouted, 'what are you doing with that straw?'

His hand holding the wisp in mid-air, the Thracian trooper said nothing, but looked thoroughly put upon.

'The horses are wet. They need drying.'

The horse-master of the Third appeared. His eyes were bloodshot. Perhaps it was the dust of the day's march, but there was a smell of stale wine about him.

'Not wet as if they had forded a river,' Ballista said. 'It is not raining. Nothing but a little sweat. The work is unnecessary. Rub them down with the brushes.'

'Their coats look better if the straw is used first.'

'Their appearance is of less concern than their welfare.'

'It is not how we do it in the Third.' The horse-master sounded truculent. 'The prefect Solinus always had us well turned out. Fit for inspection by the emperor, he liked to say.'

'Solinus has gone.' Lucius Proculus strode up. 'The Third is mine now. You will do as the general says.'

The horse-master grunted, and stomped off. Ballista was sure he heard something about *fucking Gauls* and *barbarians* muttered. There was a sway to his walk; the man might well be inebriated.

'No, not like that!' Ballista stepped forward, took the bristle-brush from the soldier. 'Stand well away from the horse, lean your weight on the brush, like this.'

The trooper stood back, his demeanour suggesting the whole world was unfair.

'Only brush against the coat if it is caked in dirt. Otherwise always follow the direction of the hair. Neck first, work downwards.'

The Emesenes were openly laughing at the discomfiture of the Thracian. One or two called out comments in their native language.

'Silence in the lines!' Heraclian roared.

It could be assumed that their prefect did not know Syriac. Heraclian would have been angrier still had he understood what was said.

Ballista looked over to where the pack train was laagered. It was a sad indictment that the muleteers under Gratus had things better in hand than either group of soldiers.

An expedition where the two senior officers could barely bring themselves to pass a civil word, the horse-master of the Third was an inefficient drunkard, the soldiers under him unready for campaigning, and the troopers of each unit cordially disliked the men in the other, was not propitious. It was fortunate that the column faced no serious prospect of fighting.

* * *

Camp Outside the City of Lugdunum

Eight Days before the Ides of July

From the first camp to Lugdunum, via the market towns of Tinurtium and Matisco, in three easy stages. The road had run through lush farmland, maintained in the neat rectangular fields that showed the hand of Roman surveyors. The river Arar on the left was bordered by willows. At dawn and in the evenings, duck and other wildfowl flighted over the water. The weather had been kind, the heat not excessive. The troops had begun to settle into a semblance of a routine. And then, on the very first night in the town, there had been trouble.

Ballista sat in the shade of an oak, flanked by his four senior officers. All were in the resplendent full dress parade armour demanded by a military trial. Sitting in judgement was always distasteful to him. The authority weighed on his spirits. So often he had seen holding the power of life and death bring out the worst in otherwise amiable and compassionate men.

In many ways, this trial was the fault of his own thoughtlessness and complacency. Soldiers in towns had too easy access to drink and women, coupled with the temptations of gambling and lording it over civilians. Discipline went to Hades. And Ballista had been well aware of the antagonism between the Emesenes and the Thracians. This morning, too late altogether, he had ordered the troops out of their billets, and had them make camp here on the plain to the west of the town. Stable doors and horses ran through his mind.

Until the incident, things had been going reasonably well in the town. While not exactly welcoming the column with open arms, the inhabitants had not been overtly hostile. Lugdunum had been bustling with activity, ships unloading and taking on cargo at the docks, the markets full, the smog from the fires of the potters and glass-blowers hanging over the approach along the lower reaches of the Arar. It was as if the town was wilfully ignoring the civil war raging just to the north.

The only thing that had betrayed the air of normality was the complete absence of any member of either the town council or the council of the three Gallic provinces. It transpired that they had all been made members of Postumus' so-called Senate, and as such had been ordered to accompany their emperor to Augustodunum. Lacking any recognised civic or provincial authorities, Ballista had summoned the heads of the various trade guilds. The motley collection of merchants, many of them freedmen, had taken the oath which returned Lugdunum to the allegiance to Gallienus. The leader of the shipping guild had been appointed acting chief magistrate of the city. It was the best that could be done under the circumstances, but Ballista had issued an instruction to arrest and bring before him any councillor who might yet be found.

'Bring in the accused, the plaintiffs, and the witnesses.'

On the face of it, the case was straightforward. Two of the Thracians, a recent recruit and a veteran on double pay, had been drinking in a bar. Three Emesene archers, one of them a decurion, had entered. Words had been exchanged, which had escalated. In the ensuing drunken brawl the older Thracian had wounded one of the bowmen, while the younger had manhandled the decurion.

What was unclear was who had struck the first blow. The Emesenes swore it was the Thracians. How could it be otherwise? Thracians lacked self-control, and were notoriously violent in their drink. The Thracians proclaimed that was just the sort of falsehood you would expect from shifty little easterners. They lied as easily as they drew breath. It was their nature. The Thracians vociferously maintained that they had acted in self-defence. The impartial witnesses were no help. The owner of the bar said he had not seen the fight start, and was more interested in who was going to pay for the damage to his establishment. His two serving girls and three other customers gave completely differing and irreconcilable accounts.

The afternoon dragged on in a welter of outrage, racial abuse and self-justification. At last everyone had had their say, and Ballista turned to his assessors.

'A military offence is committed whenever a soldier acts contrary to the general discipline of the army.' Ballista quoted the military statutes. 'There are a range of punishments including beating, fines, imposition of fatigues, demotion to another part of the army, loss of rank, or, for the more serious crimes, dishonourable discharge or death.'

'There is no doubt the Thracians attacked my soldiers,' Heraclian said.

'We cannot be sure who initiated the violence.' Lucius Proculus, as was proper, was going to stand by his men.

'The older wounded one soldier, the younger assaulted a decurion. The penalty for both offences is death.' Heraclian was adamant.

'It is a general principle that the rank, previous record, and age of an offender is taken into account,' Lucius Proculus said.

Acilius Glabrio condescended to speak. 'In peacetime – but in a time of war, no such leniency can be shown. The prefect Heraclian is correct, the penalty must be execution.'

'We are away from the fighting,' Gratus said. As ever, the words of the prefect of the camp were slow and measured. 'In all the proclamations of the emperor Gallienus, the rebel Postumus is called a brigand. A campaign against bandits is not a true war. Technically it is no more than crushing rebellious slaves.'

'Anyone would think your parents had paid a fortune for you to attend the schools of the Sophists,' Acilius Glabrio said.

The former centurion Gratus ignored the jibe at his presumably lowly and impecunious origins.

'I urge mercy be shown.'

So there it was. Two officers favoured severity, and two mildness. Opinion was divided. Of course, while obliged to consult his senior officers, Ballista was not bound to follow their advice, not even if it were unanimous. Like an emperor in his *consilium*, a general had to make the ultimate decision.

Undoubtedly a case could be made for either exemplary punishment or salutary clemency.

'If a soldier strikes an officer the punishment is death. The younger Thracian swears that he did no more than restrain the decurion. Some of the witnesses support his claim. In such a case, military law lays down that the offender should be demoted to a less prestigious branch of the service.'

As Ballista spoke, Acilius Glabrio gazed off into the distance, as if the details of the statutes were beneath his attention.

'It is a capital offence for a soldier to wound another with a sword. If the weapon was a stone, he should be discharged from the army. By all accounts, the older Thracian hit the Emesene with a wine jar.'

Ballista resisted the urge to swat a fly buzzing around his head. A certain ponderous dignity was apposite in a judge.

'On detached duty, neither demotion nor discharge are practicable.'

Seeing the way Ballista's mind was turning, Heraclian looked furious. Acilius Glabrio appeared bored.

'The youth of the recruit on the one hand, and the years of blameless service of the veteran on the other, argue for mitigation. Both soldiers will be docked two months' *stipendium*, the money to be given to the owner of the bar. After that time the veteran will lose the rank of double pay. Both men are to do extra fatigues for a month. The case is closed.'

The troopers were given a chance to stammer their thanks before being escorted away.

Thank the gods that was over.

Ballista had much to do. The next stages of the march needed planning, and he had yet to inspect the baggage train.

'Sir.'

The officer of the watch, a decurion of the Emesenes, ushered before the tribunal two civilians. One was the well-upholstered and groomed figure of the ex-slave who was head of the guild of shippers. The other had a self-assured bearing, but his clothes were ragged and muddied.

'As acting chief magistrate of the city of Lugdunum,' the freedman obviously relished saying the words, 'and following your orders, I have detained and brought before you Argicius, son of Arborius.'

'This is an outrage,' Argicius said.

'The prisoner was apprehended trying to enter the town.'

'I will have the skin off your back, give you a harsher whipping than you ever had as a slave, for daring to lay hands on a member of the council of the three Gallic provinces.' Despite his tatterdemalion appearance, Argicius was unabashed.

'For all his airs, this Argicius is a traitor, a member of the rebel Postumus' sham Senate.' The freedman was relishing the humiliation of the landowner. Most likely, his pleasure was fuelled by a lifetime of condescension from the latter and his class.

'He was caught attempting to slip through the gates in disguise. No doubt the pretender has sent him to stir up trouble, or as a spy – or worse, an assassin.'

'I was not in disguise, was not *slipping* into town, and have not been *sent* by anyone. I was returning openly to my house.' Argicius addressed himself to the bench of military officers, the ex-slave not being worthy of his notice. 'Whose authority has allowed this servile tradesman to usurp a magistracy, and persecute his betters?'

'On my authority. I am Marcus Clodius Ballista, *protector* of the emperor, commander of the mounted expeditionary force of the noble Gallienus Augustus.'

'Why have I been detained?'

'I think it is I who should be asking the questions.'

'I have nothing to hide.'

The self-righteous certainty of Argicius reminded Ballista of Christians brought before the authorities. At least this local dignitary was unlikely to announce that he wanted to die.

'As you have not followed the usurper to Augustodunum, have you come to pledge allegiance to your rightful ruler? And why are you dressed in rags unfitting to your rank?'

'Travelling from one of my estates in the west, I was abducted by a band of those brigands called *bacaudae*. Their treatment accounts for my apparel.'

'How much ransom did you pay?'

Argicius drew himself up proudly. 'I would rather die than give money to such scum. While they were insensible from drink, I made my escape.'

'Then I must congratulate you on your resource.'

Argicius smiled at the compliment.

'And now that you are providentially restored, you have the opportunity to swear your oath to Gallienus.'

Argicius said nothing.

'Your reluctance gives credence to the accusation that you are a partisan of Postumus.'

Although disconcerted, Argicius rallied. 'When Postumus seized power, there was no choice but to acknowledge him.'

'Then acknowledge Gallienus now.'

Argicius shook his head sadly. 'My son was being educated in Augustodunum. Now he is a hostage. Should Postumus hear that I have renounced his cause . . . Better I suffer than my actions cause the death of my son.'

Heraclian leaned over, and spoke quietly in Ballista's ear. 'Send him to Gallienus. With the right pressure, he might induce treachery among the besieged.'

'I have sharp hearing,' Argicius said. 'I will do nothing that will endanger my son.'

Ballista had been wrong. Argicius had all the intransigence of a Christian. In effect, he had announced that he wanted to die. Ballista thought of his own son in the imperial school on the Palatine.

'The prisoner will remain in military custody. He will be given time to reconsider.'

Ballista rather admired Argicius. This local landowner had courage.

CHAPTER FOURTEEN

Camp Outside the City of Lugdunum

Seven Days before the Ides of July

THE MAN SAT ALONE in the tent. An officer's rank brought a certain privacy. Yet the tent was small, even mean, and its furnishings sparse: a camp bed and a stand for his armour; two trunks – one for clothes, the other for documents – both serving as tables; a large bowl for washing; another cooling a jug of wine; a smaller bowl of indeterminate use; a couple of cups and plates; items of cutlery; writing materials; a lamp and a short brazier. The latter he had ordered lit, despite the warmth of the evening.

To Lucius Petronius Taurus Volusianus, Praetorian Prefect, Vir Ementissimus, from your friend with the cavalry.

If the seal of this tablet is broken, the letter has been intercepted and read.

That was redundant. Even if the seal appeared intact, its contents might well have been discovered. The messenger who would take the letter would be skilled with a hot wire and knife, with marble dust and glue. The ability to lift and replace a seal, leaving it looking pristine, was not that uncommon. Despite all the precautions, the risks were great.

The man picked up a stylus, and resumed writing in ink directly onto the wooden inside of the hinged tablet.

You order me to communicate with regularity. After the departure of the bearer of this despatch, the identity of only four other frumentarii with the column has been made known to me. Henceforth I will limit correspondence to the essential.

There would be other *frumentarii* in the camp. It was the way with the imperial spies. The watchers were always watched. The Praetorian prefect had taken direct command of the *frumentarii* a few months earlier. Volusianus was known to be extremely thorough.

Ballista has been diligent in his duties. He has been hard on the Thracians, but, as a result, in no great time will have them ready for combat. Depending on which of the two courses you will instruct me to take, his actions may not have made my mission easier. There was an outbreak of indiscipline in Lugdunum. The opinion of we officers on his council was divided on punishment. Ballista decreed clemency. This will have prevented animosity among the Thracians towards him. Again, subject to how you tell me to proceed, it may not have facilitated the task which you have entrusted to me.

The man paused. He twisted the ring on the middle finger of his left hand as he reread what he had written. It sounded verbose, the qualifying clauses like the whining of a bureaucrat, exculpating himself from a failure that had not yet happened. Volusianus had no time for excuses. Something more positive was needed.

Less explicable has been Ballista's behaviour concerning one Argicius, a member of the false Senate of Postumus, who was captured in Lugdunum. This Gaul talked a great deal; like all of them, he loves the sound of his own voice, but would not commit himself to Gallienus. Rather than force the man to take the oath to his rightful Emperor, or sending him to the imperial camp outside Augustodunum, Ballista has given the Gaul time to reflect. It seems Argicius will accompany the column. Although under military arrest, the adherent of the rebel is not confined in chains. Given that a relative of Ballista's wife is in the councils of Postumus, it appears to lend support to the doubts you expressed about Ballista's loyalty to Gallienus.

The man put down the stylus. Volusianus had to make a decision – give him a clear order, tell him which of the two plans he should implement. If the Praetorian prefect decreed it, the assassination of Ballista would be far from easy to accomplish, but it would not trouble the man's conscience. For all his high rank, and marriage into a senatorial family, the northerner was nothing but a barbarian. Although it had to be admitted that Ballista was a proficient leader of troops, good enough to earn a grudging respect, even from one who might be tasked with his destruction. No, it was the other option that Volusianus had said he might take that was troubling. The betrayal of the entire column to the enemy was unworthy of a Roman officer. The troopers may derive from Syria and the wilds of the Balkans, but they were Roman citizens from birth, and deserved better than such treachery.

Either way, the man had to know. Forcing the hand of Volusianus was not something to be undertaken lightly. The man steeled himself to finish the letter.

The column marches west tomorrow. Once deep in rebel territory, it may be difficult for your messengers to reach me. Tell me in your next communication which plan should be implemented, and it will be done.

There – it was written. Taking the smallest of the three metal bowls, the man dropped in some pieces of wax, and placed it to heat on the brazier.

There was no point agonising over the mission. The writer owed much to Volusianus. Anyway, once the matter had been broached, if he had refused, there was no way that he would have left the tent of the Praetorian prefect alive.

With the stylus, the man stirred the melted wax. Then he took the bowl with a pair of tongs, and poured the contents into the recesses of the tablet, covering the writing on the wood.

His family were in Italy. The commander of the *frumentarii* had a long reach, and was utterly ruthless. It was futile to rail at fortune.

When the wax had cooled, he smoothed it flat, and considered what innocuous message he might write on its surface.

Leading Roman soldiers into a trap would be distasteful. Better by far if Volusianus gave permission to act against Ballista alone: a fatal accident on the march, or in the confusion of battle; failing that, a dose of poison, or a malign hand in the night.

CHAPTER FIFTEEN

The High Country of the Arverni

Five Days before the Ides of July

'THERE IS GOOD GROUND for a camp, about two miles ahead, by a river.'

'Thank you. Pass the word to the officers, Fabius, then go and mark out the horse lines.'

The chief scout saluted, and rode away.

Ballista had toyed with the idea of appointing Fabius the decurion of a squadron of the Thracians. The man had shown his mettle in temporary command of one at Vesontio. No doubt a *turma* under his charge soon would have been knocked into shape. But such a promotion would have necessitated removing a serving leader. While at least five of the sixteen decurions of the Third might be judged barely fit for their duties, summarily getting rid of an officer might further antagonise their troopers. Even after his mild punishments in Lugdunum, the men showed little love for Ballista. The prefect of the heavy cavalry, Lucius Proculus, would have to do his best with the unpromising material available.

Instead of upsetting the structure of the Third, Ballista was pleased with his new arrangement. Fabius was raised to chief scout for the whole expedition. The veteran had been instructed to second a dozen proven men to serve under him, six each from the Thracians and Emesenes. Not only did the column now have keen eyes and ears as outriders, but, working together, the scouts might serve as an example of harmony to allay the antipathy between the soldiers of the two units.

All in all, Ballista's spirits had risen in the two days since they had left Lugdunum. The weather had been glorious. The sun shone from a ceramic blue sky. It was hot, yet a gentle breeze kept it from becoming oppressive. The road had been good. On either side, grain ripened in fields bounded by ditches. At intervals were cool stands of mature trees, ideal for the rootling and foraging of the pigs which made Gallic hams and bacon famous. The countryside seemed oddly deserted, but every passing mile showed that this was a wealthy agricultural province.

The previous night they had camped outside Forum Segusiavorum. Although well appointed, with baths, theatre and forum, the town was not large, and only one of its councillors had been elevated to Postumus' simulacrum of the Roman Senate. The dignitaries who remained had pledged their allegiance to Gallienus. The senator from Lugdunum, Argicius, had proved most useful. While technically still a prisoner, he had made introductions, and smoothed the transition. It transpired that the estate from which the *bacaudae* had kidnapped Argicius was nearby.

On the road, Ballista finally had found the time to inspect the baggage train marching at the rear of the column. The mules – two hundred pack animals, and sixty-two for riding – were in good condition. Perhaps they tended to be a little squat, but a small, blocky animal was to be preferred to a tall and rangy one. There were over fifty muleteers, all civilian volunteers. Taller than the Thracians, they towered over the slightly built Syrian bowmen. The heavy work of packing, and manhandling the beasts in muddy or difficult going, called for big, powerful men. Yet expertise was needed as well as brute strength. While you could train a cavalry trooper in five or six months, it was recognised that it took a year before a muleteer really mastered his skilled and multitudinous tasks.

On the debit side, the baggage train was bloated with well over a hundred horses on leading reins. The five senior officers were entitled to a pair of remounts each; the decurions, as well as troopers on either double *stipendium* or pay-and-a-half, a spare horse apiece. The problem lay with the number of men in the Third Thracians drawing additional pay. With the pack mules naturally in single file, the baggage stretched for over a mile. Still, with the ten slaves of the senior officers to aid the muleteers, there was a man for every four spare horses, and about one for every six mules bearing burdens. The prefect of the camp, Gratus, seemed to have everything in hand.

After the midday halt, they had ridden up into the high country, towards misted hills. Clouds piled up above the distant peaks. This was a harder landscape, the habitat of the shepherd, not the farmer. Cracked slabs of granite thrust up through the earth on the flanks of the valleys, and fast upland streams tumbled over green, mossed boulders. Yet the road remained easy. Contrary to popular supposition, not all Roman roads ran straight. This one graded across the slopes. Often it was shaded by overhanging trees.

Riding with the mule train, Ballista crested the final ridge, and saw the campsite. His admiration for Fabius increased further. The campsite the chief scout had chosen was ideal. A broad upland meadow sloped down to a stream. It was sheltered by the surrounding peaks. The grass was thick, just the right colour – not too brown, despite the recent sun.

Ballista's satisfaction vanished when he took in the activity of his command. The Emesenes, who had led the column, were busy grooming, having already watered their mounts. Now it was the turn of the Thracians, and all was confusion. The entire unit was attempting to use the stream at once. Worse, the majority of the troopers were off gathering forage or seeing to their own bivouac. It left individual troopers leading four or five horses. Some led the animals to the edge to drink standing on the low bank, others waded into the flow wherever seemed good to them. Unsurprisingly, the horses were playing up, slipping and getting in one another's way, showing their teeth and snapping. The men jerked at their heads, shouting angrily at their charges and fellow soldiers. None of the officers intervened. Lucius Proculus, still mounted, gazed at the muddle, as if unsure what measures to take.

A sudden alarm and the Thracians would be scattered to the four winds. Most of them would be separated from their mounts, and left stranded on foot. Thank the gods, the war was far behind. Suppressing his irritation, Ballista nudged Pale Horse down towards the little river.

'Lucius Proculus, a word.'

The prefect saluted.

'It might be better if the horses were watered one squadron at a time.' Ballista phrased his words as advice, rather than an order. Even so, he spoke quietly, not to be overheard. 'You could tell your decurions to supervise. Each trooper should have the reins of only two animals. They should all enter the water at the same place, lead the horses downstream, make sure all have enough to drink, then all use the same spot to get out.'

'Sir.'

The officer turned his horse, ready to implement the suggestions.

'And, Lucius, would you care to dine with me tonight?'

'It would be a pleasure, sir.'

The face of the Gallic prefect remained impassive.

* * *

'Since everything in nature moves according to the same laws of fate, all things may be signs for him who can read them.' Argicius was warming to his theme. 'Surely all those thousands of stars do not shine for nothing.'

It was the custom for a general frequently to dine with his officers. It could be a pleasure, could bind men together. That was not the case in Ballista's command. Acilius Glabrio gave every indication that only patrician manners kept him at the meal. Heraclian was taciturn and drinking heavily. Lucius Proculus and Gratus were polite but unforthcoming. At least the civilian Argicius, the sixth man reclining on the rugs, was urbane and loquacious.

The moon was big and bright in the clear night sky.

'No star was favourable or propitious at my birth. Venus did not shine, nor did Jupiter in that hour. Neither sun nor moon were in an auspicious place. The only star that weighed on my nativity was Mars, who presages savagery, nothing peaceable, the wielder of the scythe.'

Ballista took a sip of *dulce*. The raisin wine of the Vocontii region was sweet and thick. Too much was bound to produce a sore head in the morning.

'My fate is immutable – exile, confiscation of my estates, and poverty. But not execution.' Argicius smiled. 'So, you see, I am armoured against all dangers of the present. It makes no difference if Gallienus or Postumus drives me from my home, takes my worldly goods. And I draw comfort that the stars foretell that my family will rise again in the third generation. The consulship, honours and wealth are assured.'

'Surely the former is a self-fulfilling prophecy should word of your proclivities reach the emperor.' Acilius Glabrio raised an eyebrow. 'Astrology is illegal, the punishment banishment.'

'I would not dream of inquiring into the future of the throne.'

Acilius Glabrio grimaced slightly, as if the wine he had drunk – or perhaps the company – offended his palate.

'The gods, if they exist, are distant, and have no interest in humanity. The stars reveal nothing. It is a superstition best left to slaves, rustics and foreigners. The African Septimius Severus went to great pains to hide the hour of his birth, but everyone knew when that emperor was dying. What do you say, Gratus? Did the conjunction of the heavens predict your extraordinary rise to office?'

'I would not presume to meddle in higher affairs, the things of my betters.' Gratus spoke smoothly, but with a hint of mockery. There was a hidden steel in the prefect of the camp.

Acilius Glabrio rounded on Heraclian. 'How about you, Prefect? Did you have foreknowledge of advancement and its sudden *pitfalls*?'

Heraclian glared over the rim of his drink. 'Utter bollocks!' He drained his cup, held it out for a slave to refill.

'Me, I am a devout believer,' Lucius Proculus said. Everyone looked at him. He had volunteered no previous conversation. 'Venus was very much in the ascendant when I was born. Gave me an innate love of women. When I was serving on the Danube I captured a hundred Sarmatian virgins.' He took a swig of wine, eyes unfocused, as if looking back over the years.

Ballista wondered if the Gaul was drunk. He had not seemed to be drinking immoderately, like Heraclian.

'Had ten of them the first night, made all of them women, as far as was in my power, in the space of fifteen days. What it was to be young!'

'Perhaps we should drink a toast to lust and depravity?' Acilius Glabrio suggested.

'Perhaps we should not,' Ballista said.

This evening had gone on long enough.

'Gentlemen, we have an early start. Boots and saddles at dawn. I give you a final toast – the Emperor Gallienus and victory.'

Gallienus and victory!

They all finished their drinks, said polite words of thanks and farewell. Ballista noted that Argicius had been happy enough to make the toast.

Lucius Proculus lingered, as the others departed.

'Is something on your mind?'

The prefect checked that the rest of the party were out of earshot. He seemed perfectly sober now.

'I wanted to thank you.'

'You already have. That square of cheese from Tolosa was good, but the rest homely stuff.'

The Gaul laughed. 'Better than we might expect to eat on campaign. No, I wanted to thank you for earlier, down at the stream. It was thoughtful of you not to criticise me in front of the men.'

'I would not undermine the authority of any officer.'

'Not a view shared by Acilius Glabrio.'

Ballista said nothing.

'Your instructions were needed.' Lucius Proculus squared his shoulders, almost as if on parade. 'My life has been under the standards – auxiliaries, then the legions. The unsettled times have not favoured a normal career. This is the first time I have served with the cavalry. My home in the Alps was not suited to horses.'

'Felix!' Ballista summoned one of his slaves. 'Get the papyrus roll that is by my bed.'

Once the servant had gone into the tent, Ballista turned back to Lucius Proculus.

'The senior decurion of the Thracians was appointed before your predecessor undermined the unit. He seems sound. You might consider taking him into your confidence, let him run things day to day, learn from him.'

The slave returned.

'Ah, Felix.' Ballista took the book, and gave it to Lucius Proculus. '*On the Duties of a Cavalry Commander*, Xenophon – not sure how much use it will be.'

As soon as the prefect left, taking the rolled papyrus, Maximus sauntered out from the shadows.

'Seven women every night for half a month, not an evening off . . . Sure, he has almost my stamina, or is a terrible liar.'

'A last drink?' Ballista said.

Maximus picked up a cup. '"As far as was in my power . . ." Perhaps Lucius Proculus is not all the man he boasts?'

'What did you find out?'

'About two of your officers – bugger all. Me being a member of your *familia*, the two servants of Acilius Glabrio seemed disinclined to share any confidences about their master. Odd that, given the patrician hates you. As for your man Gratus, there seems nothing to discover. His slaves are newly purchased. They have no idea about his family or career, not even where he is from in Italy.'

Ballista sipped the *dulce*. He dismissed an urge to get very drunk with his friend.

'Now, the other two are more interesting. By the way, I had to drink an awful lot tonight, and spend a great deal of money, loosening their servants' tongues.'

'You are getting as tight-fisted as Calgacus in your old age. Anyway, you have never turned down a drink.'

Maximus ignored the comments. 'Now old Heraclian is not a happy man – bitter as a jilted woman. Claims he saved Gallienus' life back at the battle of Mediolanum.'

'So it is said.'

'Anyway, he hits the drink on his own in his tent at night. Been heard muttering about all he has done, and this being the thanks he gets, shepherding a bunch of effeminate little Syrians – he who led the emperor's horse guards. What he really hates is having to run about at the whim of some hulking great barbarian. That will be you.'

'I had gathered. Hardly an insight.'

'Maybe not, but it is always salutary to be aware of those with no love in their hearts.'

'Wherever you go, the malice of men is infinite.'

'Have you been reading poetry again?'

'No.'

'Like a bard, I have saved the best for last.'

'You missed your vocation.'

Maximus refilled his drink. 'Your priapic Gaul, Lucius Proculus, had a couple of clandestine visitors while we were in Lugdunum. Came after dark, left his quarters before dawn. They talked in Celtic. The servants don't have the language. The only words they got were *Gallienus* and *Postumus*.'

Ballista considered this. 'Could be nothing. Proculus has estates in the Alps. They are in the territory of the rebel.'

'In the dead of night, away from prying eyes? And his cousin commanding Postumus' mounted guards?'

'A proprietor like myself understands the endless responsibilities of a landed estate.'

'Really? I thought the lands in Sicily were owned by your wife.'

Ballista smiled. There were few secrets between them.

'It was good to hear that old Rikiar is on his way back there.'

A look of sadness passed across Maximus' scarred face.

'Would you not be there now?'

'I would, with all my heart, but you would be bored.'

'At least there would be a maid or two to get my leg over. Not be stuck in a field with hundreds of hairy-arsed men.'

'Your looks should spare you any unwanted attention. Where is Tarchon?'

'Bedded down Pale Horse, then went for a drink with some of the Thracians. Shall we have another?'

'No, I need to sleep.' Ballista tipped the rest of his wine on the ground. 'An offering to the gods.'

Maximus finished his cup. 'Silly Roman habit. The deities of my homeland are not given to waste.'

* * *

A very light touch behind his ear, and Ballista woke without a sound.

'Loose horses in the camp,' Maximus said.

Ballista had been sleeping in his clothes. He rolled out of his camp bed, pulled on his boots, buckled on his sword-belt.

Outside the tent, horses stamped and snorted and called; men shouted. Some way off, heavy things crashed to the ground. He must have had more wine than he thought to sleep through. Maximus was right – he was getting old.

The night was dark. Clouds had covered the stars while he slept. Ballista's tent was in the centre of the camp, by the baggage train. The mules shifted, smelling the air, listening. The disturbance was to the north, in the horse lines of the Thracians.

They walked. The chain tethering the mules clinked, as they watched the men pass.

Three loose horses thundered out of the gloom. Eyes very white, mouths open, their hooves pounding. They careered straight towards the two men. Without a word, Ballista and Maximus separated a little, held their arms out wide, stood very still.

Unless maddened, or evil-natured, a horse will seldom run a man down. Even so, at the last moment, Ballista closed his eyes. A clatter and scrape of hooves sliding and skidding. A violent buffet of air. The pungent smell of hot horse. Ballista opened his eyes. The animals were a step or two away, halted, but plunging, pawing the earth.

Ballista reached out, in a smooth motion took hold of a halter. The horse sidled, considering flight. Ballista swung up bareback. The horse backed, uncertain.

'Whoa.' Ballista spoke soothingly. 'Gently, gently, old man.'

He turned the beast back the way it had come, all the time talking softly.

The new-found calm of Ballista's horse spread to the others. They stood as patient as plough oxen, as Maximus mounted one, got a hand on the halter of the other.

Together they went on at a walk, Ballista still talking gentle nonsense to his horse.

The moon came out from behind the clouds. Its light revealed the chaos in the Thracian lines. Men chased horses here and there. Their hallooing and cursing was not helping. Nor were the orders bellowed by Lucius Proculus or the decurions. A tent was on fire, where a torch or brazier must have been overturned. The horse-master of the unit staggered about, as if befuddled by drink, and unable to comprehend the unexpected turn of events.

Ballista halted, looked away to where the shadows of clouds moved up the hillside.

'Bugger!' Maximus said.

Ballista peered where he had pointed. The Hibernian had always had sharp sight.

Not a shadow. A dozen or more horses, close together, the indistinct shape of men on their backs.

'Horse thieves,' Maximus said. 'Must be those *bacaudae* that got Argicius.'

The brigands were too far, the Thracians in no condition to give chase.

Tarchon, unkempt and ugly, like something from a bad dream, appeared.

'Pale Horse,' the Suanian said. 'The bastards have got him.'

CHAPTER SIXTEEN

The High Country of the Arverni

Three Days before the Ides of July

All morning they had lain up in a copse at the foot of the ridge. Now, in the afternoon, they were climbing. The ascent was difficult. They went on foot, slowly and carefully. Unlike some of the soldiers, Ballista had faith in the landowner Argicius.

Two nights before, after the raid of the *bacaudae*, order had been restored. The loose horses had been caught and tethered, the fire extinguished, more vedettes posted. While the troopers tended the horses, treated those that had been hurt in the tumult, Ballista had convened a council of his officers. Sensibly, although technically a prisoner, Argicius had been summoned. Only the Gaul knew the country. He could lead a party straight to the lair of the *bacaudae*. Argicius, however, knew the ways of the brigands. They would have left a man hidden somewhere on the surrounding heights to observe the column. If the troops marched directly, the bandits would scatter, vanish into the hills and forests, and there would be no chance of recovering the horses. The approach must be subtle.

Twenty horses had been lost. In the morning, Ballista had ordered the majority of the decurions and men on additional pay among the Thracians to hand over their spare mounts to those of their comrades who found themselves unhorsed. The exchange made, with much reluctance bordering on insubordination, the expedition resumed its journey to the west. On the march, Ballista had selected volunteers to the number of a squadron – sixteen from the Thracians, and sixteen from the Emesenes. The merging was more for their different fighting styles than to ameliorate the ill feeling between the units. Fabius, the chief scout, was seconded to command the *turma*.

That night, some twenty miles from the site of the raid, Ballista and the chosen men had slipped quietly from the camp. Argicius had led them back by an unfrequented and roundabout route skirting to the north. Nothing disturbed their progress, except the creatures of the night: owls glided overhead on silent wings; a vixen, intent on slaughter, stopped and regarded them with suspicion. By dawn they were ensconced in the wood at the base of the high ground. There they had passed most of the day, safe, as far as they could tell, from prying eyes. Once, a shepherd had driven his flock along a nearby path. Ballista was glad none of the sheep had strayed, the man not turned aside. Outside pastoral poetry, all shepherds were little better than brigands. This one, given his proximity to their base, must be in league with the *bacaudae*. Even so, it might have felt wrong to kill him out of hand. And there would have been the problem of what to do with his bleating flock.

At the ninth hour, about three hours before sunset, they had moved out. One in four of the troopers remained as horse holders among the trees. In single file, the rest followed Argicius along a goat track up the mountain.

Ballista slapped at a mosquito on his arm. The sun was low now, casting long shadows through the pines. The shield slung across his back was chafing his neck, the weight of his sword digging into his shoulder. Before leaving the camp, he had inspected the men, ordered them to leave behind all the ornaments from their belts and equipment – everything that could rattle. Despite the precaution, the sounds coming up the track were alarmingly loud: heavy footfalls; laboured breathing; chinks of metal on metal or stone. Dismounted cavalrymen seemed to make even more noise than foot soldiers. If the gods were willing, the racket would be absorbed by the close-set trunks of the trees, or carried away by the westerly breeze soughing through the foliage.

'The lair is over the next rise,' Argicius said quietly. 'Tell the men to spread out.'

Ballista slid back down the path, whispering instructions. Six archers on each flank, the armoured men in the centre. Keep this side of the skyline. Don't make a sound. Listen for my command.

A fallen bough provided good cover at the top. Having removed his helmet, Ballista peered through the pine needles. Only Maximus and Argicius had crawled up alongside him.

Down in a hollow, the camp of the *bacaudae* was already in shadow. A wattle and daub building like a tower stood in front of a cave. On either side were stock pens. They were full of animals. Among the horses, the coat of Pale Horse gleamed in the half-light. Away to the left were two guards. They had their weapons with them, but were sitting, drinking from a flask. As far as their attention was on their duty, it was directed towards the main path coming up from the south. They never glanced up the slope to the east, where Ballista and his men were concealed.

A pig was turning on a spit over a fire-trench by the cave. Women were basting the meat. The smoke billowed up the slope, bringing the delicious aroma of woodsmoke and crackling. An enormous wooden table was set outside by the building, the plunder of some ransacked villa. It was already piled with bread. Pitchers of wine and bowls of sauces and vegetables stood ready. All Ballista and his men had eaten today was cold bacon and hard biscuit, washed down with *posca*, the sour wine of their rations.

The *bacaudae* were preparing for their feast. In the open space before the table, they were naked, washing themselves at huge vessels of warmed water, rubbing each other down with stolen unguents and oil. Their swords and knives were stacked by their places at the table. Only a few had shields. Yet Ballista counted no fewer than fifty men. Surprise and training and superior equipment would have to overcome their numbers.

'Let's be dealing with them quick,' Maximus whispered, 'then be eating their meal, before it spoils.'

'No, let them get drunk first,' Ballista said.

Argicius had said that the bands of the brigands which infested Gaul contained many deserters from the army. They would be trained swordsmen. Not all the *bacaudae* were runaway slaves, peasants, or criminals freed from gaol. It was best not to underestimate them.

The plague of bandits had intensified in the last couple of years. Preparing for the civil war, Postumus had withdrawn to his field army all the soldiers previously stationed guarding crossroads and bridges in the countryside. Things had got much worse since the rebel emperor had ordered all members of his so-called Senate to go to Augustodunum. With the owners of the biggest estates gone, the desperate and the hungry had sought food and security elsewhere. Lesser landowners prepared to act outside the law, and bandit chiefs had filled the void. Among the leaders of the *bacaudae*, Argicius claimed, were Druids – hedge-priests, inspiring their followers with messianic visions of a new order, even the fall of Rome itself.

Their ablutions finished, the bandits pulled on their baggy trousers and short tunics, and went to recline on the bales of straw which served as couches.

'The one at the head, the place of honour, is Helianus, their leader,' Argicious said. 'Always was a violent man. Preferred taking things by force to honest work on the small farm he once had outside Forum Segusiavorum.'

Helianus was a well-set man of middle age. A bright torque of gold encircled his throat.

A crowd of servants, ragged and cowed in appearance, issued from the cave to minister to the needs of the outlaws.

'Dear gods, no,' Argicius muttered. 'You see the woman serving Helianus?'

She was tall, stood very rigid as the brigand dried his hands on her tunic, and, to the laughter of the diners, squeezed her breasts.

'The wife of my neighbour. They killed her husband, six months ago, when they burned their villa. We thought she was dead, with the children, in the ashes.'

'You did not see her when they held you captive?'

Argicius smiled without mirth. 'They kept me outdoors, tethered with the animals. None of the servants was allowed near me. No one spoke to me, or brought me food, except

Helianus. Occasionally he would toss me a scrap or a bone. He thought the isolation, together with his beatings, would encourage me to pay the ransom.'

'You will not be wanting him to see tomorrow,' Maximus said.

'May the earth lie lightly on him, make it easier for the dogs to dig him up.'

The pork was carved and platters brought to the table. It smelled and looked wonderful. No wonder recruits were not hard to find. Neither a peasant nor one of the urban poor would eat meat except at the occasional festival. A full belly and stolen wine; companionship and women for the taking: there was much in life with the *bacaudae* to appeal to the desperate and downtrodden.

Ballista tallied the numbers. There were about fifty brigands, and some twenty slaves, both men and women. The latter were of no account. They had no reason to fight for those they served. Ballista had a dozen Thracians. With Maximus, Tarchon and Fabius, as well as himself, there were in all sixteen men in mail, equipped for close combat. Seventeen, if Argicius were counted. The landowner was unarmoured, but had requested a sword. With the odds as they were, much would depend on the skill of the eastern archers.

The *bacaudae* had settled to a roisterous enjoyment of their feast, throwing down wine, tearing into the food, laughing, joking and boasting. It was all to the good. Ballista wanted them befuddled with drink. But the sun was setting, and the bowmen needed to see to find their targets. It was time to ready his men.

Ballista and Maximus slid back from the crest, then moved along the reverse slope. A quiet word, a pat on the shoulder; everyone was in place, knew what they had to do.

Back behind the fallen bough, Ballista was surprised how much darker it was down in the hollow. He hoped the archers still had enough light, hoped that they had the sense not to look directly at the fire, and ruin their night vision. There was no time to waste.

Ballista stood, and stepped over the branch. He cupped his hands around his mouth, and made the call of an owl. Like wraiths, figures emerged from the undergrowth along the crest. Intent on their revelry, the *bacaudae* noticed nothing.

Placing his boots with care, Ballista set off downhill. Maximus and Tarchon were on either shoulder, Argicius just behind. Half a dozen armed men moved down at either side, Fabius leading those on the right.

Bowstrings twanged, loud even over the sounds of drunken debauch.

Arrows thrummed out of the gloom. Some thudded into the boards of the big table, or buried themselves into the straw bales, but several brigands were plucked from the bales on which they sat. A babble of noise. The diners leaped to their feet, scrambling for their weapons. Three or four more went down, astonished, clutching at the shafts that suddenly protruded from chest or stomach. Now the living saw the line of grim men descending on them, sword in hand. For many, it was too much. They broke and ran, towards the safety of the tower, or pell-mell off to the left, and down the track.

Ballista glanced over. The two guards were already dead, the white fletchings of the arrows that had killed them bright in the gathering darkness. The Emesenes had done well. As he watched, another fleeing brigand was dashed to the ground.

Ballista's foot snagged on a root. He stumbled a few steps down the slope. When he regained his balance, he was out of the trees, in the level of the clearing. A bandit was charging at him, sword held overhead, screaming with fury or fear. Like a rustic chopping logs, the brigand brought his blade down. Sidestepping, with a neat backhand, Ballista cut the back of his opponent's thigh. The bandit collapsed forward on to hands and knees. A quick check that there was no other imminent threat, and Ballista finished him with a blow to the back of the skull.

Not all the *bacaudae* had given up the fight. Twenty or so had gathered into a rough phalanx around Helianus. The chief and those other outlaws with shields formed the front rank. They had brought the Thracians to a halt. From a couple of paces, the two sides jabbed ineffectually at each other.

'Behind you!'

At Maximus' shout, Ballista dropped to one knee, swinging his blade around. He felt its motion through the air as the sword swished above his head. Battle-Sun bit deep into the brigand's knee. Momentum blundered the man into Ballista, bowling him over. Releasing his grip on his shield, Ballista rolled; with his left hand, he yanked out his dagger. Without pause, he swarmed to his feet. No need. Maximus and Tarchon were cleaving the assailant apart, skilled butchers dismembering a carcass.

Helianus and his followers had backed to the door of the tower. Two by two, with a discipline that betrayed their military origins, they vanished inside. Last through was the brigand chief. The door slammed shut, and there was the sound of heavy bars being dropped into place.

Lit by the wavering flames of the fire pit, the victors stood, breathing hard, but otherwise motionless amid the carnage.

An arrow whickered out from a high window of the tower. Its point sparked off the mail of a soldier. The man swore, jerked up his shield.

'Back to the cover of the trees!' Ballista shouted. 'Rally to me!'

Time seemed to have stopped. Night had fallen. Somewhere at the rear of the cave, women keened. Out in the clearing, the wounded moaned.

'Fabius, roll call,' Ballista said.

'Two wounded, neither serious.'

'Parley!' The voice came from the tower.

'Speak!' Ballista shouted.

Helianus appeared at the upper window, his torque catching the light of the fire.

'Grant us our lives, and our weapons, and we will leave this district.'

'You can't let him live.' Argicius' voice was urgent.

'Keep him talking,' Ballista said softly.

'What hostages will you give?' Argicius called.

Ballista moved across through the trees.

'Argicius, my cousin, you have returned.' The bandit chief sounded genuinely amused. 'Your stars must have brought you back.'

'Shoot him,' Ballista said to the nearest archer.

'You are no kin of mine!' Argicius shouted.

'Have the heavens not told you how this will end?'

The arrow missed Helianus by a hand's breadth. He ducked back out of sight.

'Faithless bastards, you wonder why we become *bacaudae*!' Helianus yelled.

'That door will be hard to force,' Fabius said. 'We will take casualties.'

'No need,' Ballista said. 'Fabius, have the bowmen keep their heads down. Shoot at the windows. Maximus, Tarchon, with me.'

A few hurried words, and they set off. They raced across the clearing to the ruined feast. The straw bales that had served as couches were not large. Each man grabbed one. As they hauled them to the corner of the tower an arrow whisked past, unpleasantly close. Ballista heard Fabius shouting at the archers to shoot faster.

The straw piled up, they braved the clearing again.

Damnation, there were no half-burned logs projecting conveniently from the fire.

Ballista ran back to the table, gathered an armful of abandoned cloths or napkins. He felt, rather than saw, another shaft from the building whip through the air.

At the fire pit, he threw the others some of the cloths, wrapped the remainder around his hands. The heat was intense. It singed Ballista's face and hair. Ignoring the discomfort, he grabbed a burning brand.

In moments they were back by the bales, sheltered from above. It was the work of moments to set the straw ablaze. The wattle and daub of the structure would burn well. Ballista spat on his painful, blistered palms.

When they had gathered their breath, they split up, each running a different zigzag line to the cover of the line of trees.

Flames were licking up the side of the tower. The laths crackled as the heat increased.

'There are women and children in here.' The voice of Helianus came from inside.

'If so, send them out!' Ballista shouted. Then, much lower, he spoke to Fabius. 'Have the bowmen ready. It may be a lie.'

Almost at once the door opened. Everyone waited, all attention on the empty black rectangle of the opening. Half a dozen figures emerged hesitantly – by their stature, two evidently children, the others probably female. They clustered together, uncertain.

'Over here!' Fabius called.

Like a herd of nervous animals, the refugees stampeded into the trees.

'Check them for weapons,' Ballista said. 'Make sure they are really women.'

'Hardly the time for that?' Maximus said.

Ballista ignored the joke.

'We surrender!' Helianus now had to shout to make himself heard above the crackling roar of the gathering fire. 'Have mercy!'

Ballista turned to the Emesenes.

'Shoot them all down as the flames drive them out. Show them no quarter.'

CHAPTER SEVENTEEN

The High Country of the Arverni

The Day before the Ides of July

THE SLAVE STROPPED THE razor, removed the hot towels, and started to shave Ballista. The skill was a reason for his purchase, along with his training as a cook. The other slave that Ballista had bought in Mediolanum was experienced with horses. Felix the barber-cook and Astutus the groom could provide all the services that Ballista and his two bodyguards needed. Ballista's *familia* in Gaul was small.

Some owners renamed new slaves. Ballista did not. It seemed somehow unfair. Most likely they had become accustomed to their slave-names; some would have carried them since birth. Ballista wondered if the cook considered himself *Fortunate* and the stable boy *Cunning*. Ballista had once owned a horse called Astutus.

Ballista could have brought a couple of his household slaves into Gaul. But his wife's house-bred servants were unaccustomed to the rough life of an army camp, and there were always dangers, even on the quietest of campaigns. Julia would have been upset if one of them had died.

'All done, master.'

Felix handed Ballista the mirror. It was polished bronze, the handle inlaid with hunting dogs; a gift from Julia. Ballista studied his face in its slightly distorted reflection. Felix had done well – not one cut to staunch with cobweb and vinegar. Contrary to Maximus' dire prediction, the fall down the mountain in the Alps had added only one new scar on Ballista's nose. It matched the one already on his chin.

Ballista altered the angle of the mirror. Some months earlier, in a vain attempt at disguise, he had had his head shaved. It had been hard to bring himself to do so. Ballista's family, the rulers of the Suebian Sea, were known as the long-haired Himlings. Now the hair, growing back, lay just over his ears. It was longer than the neat short cut of a Roman military man, not elaborately curled and shaped in the style fashionable among the elite of the empire. Fitting neither Rome nor the north, it could serve as a metaphor. Doubtless, Ballista thought, a Sophist could write an entire oration on the subject; something like the *Encomium on Hair* of Dio Chrysostom.

'Thank you, Felix. Would you bring our breakfast?'

Summoned by the mention of food, Maximus and Tarchon wandered to the opening of the tent.

Ballista sat back on the folding camp stool, the sun warm on his face, and looked out over the camp. They were back in the meadow chosen by Fabius the scout before the *bacaudae* struck.

The two slaves brought out warm bread, freshly cooked bacon and hard-boiled eggs, and local beer. Gratus had been put in charge of foraging. The prefect of the camp conducted this additional duty with the same efficiency as he oversaw the baggage train. Ballista and his two bodyguards ate in companionable silence. Felix and Astutus waited discreetly, but with a certain trepidation. They would get the leftovers, and the slaves knew the appetite of these barbarian warriors.

Ballista did not want to think of the meal after the burning of the tower of the *bacaudae*, and the extermination of its inhabitants – some pierced by arrowheads in futile flight, others perishing in the flames. The squadron with Ballista had spent the night among the dead in the lair of the brigands. The smell of burned flesh, mingled with that of the pig roasted on the spit, had robbed Ballista of both appetite and sleep. Others – Maximus and Tarchon included – had not been so squeamish.

Not all the *bacaudae* had perished. Many had fled down the track. But they had lost their leader and their base, and were scattered. It would take time for them to regroup, for a new leader to emerge, or for them to gravitate to another band expanding into the vacated territory.

In the morning, the captives of the bandits had been rounded up. The troops had led the thirty men and women, and two children, down to the copse where the horse-holders waited. The soldiers, merciless killers the night before, had been transformed by the sentimentality of their kind into rough but avuncular figures. They had fussed over their charges, let them ride their mounts, as the tattered band slowly walked to the prearranged rendezvous with the column.

'The sick horses are ready for inspection.' Heraclian and Lucius Proculus were well turned out. Their polished armour gleamed in the morning sunshine.

'Have you eaten?' Ballista asked.

The prefects of both units thanked him, and said they had. The slaves looked relieved.

Ballista washed his hands, dried them on a towel held by Felix, and got to his feet.

Eighteen sorry-looking beasts were assembled. The horse-master of the Thracians was the officer on duty. This morning he did not smell of drink.

'Five-year-old bay gelding, branded with the letter epsilon, mount of Abbas of the Emesenes, persistent cough,' the horse-master said.

'Treatment?'

'A drink of ground lentils every night. No improvement.' The horse-master was not without all knowledge. Practical remedies were handed down in a cavalry unit.

'Try a daily drench – ammoniacum gum, turpentine, acacia, juice of poppy, in water, well shaken. Any others coughing?'

'No, sir.'

'Still, it might be contagious,' Ballista said. 'Enter him on the draft to be sent back.'

'Fourteen-year-old, chestnut mare, no distinguishing markings . . .'

And so it continued. Seven of the next eight horses were lame. Two merely had worn hooves, and could be led with the column. The rest were added to the draft of those returning to the main army.

The final nine horses all belonged to troopers of the Third Thracians. The unpleasant odour told Ballista what was wrong with them before he looked at the injuries to their backs.

'A hot onion poultice will deal with the abscesses, and bring down the swellings overnight. The open sores have been dressed with honey and linen cloths.'

Well might the horse-master sound defensive. His remedies were sound, but the wounds were the result of the troopers insufficiently cleaning either the horses' backs or their saddle cloths, or not properly securing the saddles. His failure had allowed the negligence.

Ballista made his decision.

'These horses can remain with the column, travelling with the baggage. If they are properly looked after, not ridden and the dressings renewed every day, it should not be long before they are fit.'

How often had the importance of caring for their mounts been dinned into the horse-master and his Thracians?

Ballista kept his voice businesslike.

'Their troopers will accompany you and the decurion selected to take the broken-down mounts back to the main army. They will ride spare mounts taken from those on additional pay among the Third *Ala*. They are to be docked a month's pay.'

'We will do what is ordered, and at every command we will be ready.' The horse-master pronounced the ritual words with a mixture of relief and resentment.

'Be prepared to leave tomorrow. Dismiss.'

Argicius was waiting outside Ballista's tent.

'You have come to say farewell?'

Ballista had ordered a decurion and a *contubernium* of eight troopers of the Thracians to escort the prisoners released from the brigands to Forum Segusiavorum, then Argicius to his estate. Those tasks accomplished, the detachment was to patrol the roads to hinder the return of the *bacaudae*.

The senator smiled. 'And to thank you.'

'No thanks are owed. I did my duty. Without your help, Helianus and his bandits would still be at large. And Pale Horse would be lost.'

'You are fond of your charger.'

'Very much so.'

Argicius looked around, meaningfully.

Ballista waved Felix away. The old adage that slaves are not to be trusted had been proven by the information Maximus had gathered from the officers' servants the other night.

'You are releasing me with no oath taken to Gallienus?'

'Your son with Postumus is motive enough for your reluctance. I hope he remains safe.'

'As I hope does your son in Rome.'

'Travel safely.'

'And you.'

They shook hands, and Argicius left.

It was almost time for the midday meal. Ballista whistled for Felix to bring him a drink. He sat in the shade. They would not break camp until tomorrow. There was no great urgency. Last he had heard, the siege of Augustodunum dragged on. The column could take its time marching west, then south, administering the oath of allegiance to the locals. There was no sign of any reinforcements or supplies being brought up to Postumus.

Felix brought a mug of beer. Campaigning in Gaul meant he could enjoy the drink of his youth. Ballista wondered if the stars spoke the truth that Argicius' grandson – or was it great-grandson? – would rise to fame and the consulship? Safer if he did not.

All in all, it had been a good day. Both the unfit horses and the brigands' captives had been turned to some advantage. Admittedly, Ballista was sending away a blameless *contubernium* of the Third Thracians with Argicius, but he had also got rid of a useless decurion. The drunken horse-master, another hopeless decurion, and nine inefficient troopers from the same unit were going with broken-down mounts. Lucius Proculus, guided by his second in command, could promote worthier men in the place of the missing three officers. The Thracians at the storming of the lair of the *bacaudae* had performed creditably. There was nothing like action to promote morale and a bond between officers and those they led. The Third *Ala* of Thracians might soon become a fine unit of cavalry.

And, best of all, Ballista was reunited with Pale Horse.

CHAPTER EIGHTEEN

The Road South of Augustoritum, Aquitania
Ten days before the Kalends of August

'No one else has refused.' Ballista raised his voice to carry, not just to the woman, but to those ranged along the perimeter wall of the villa.

'The city of Lugdunum, the towns of Forum Segusiavorum, Limane, Acitodunum and Augustoritum, as well as every estate along the road, all have returned their allegiance to Gallienus.' The litany of names might convince her.

'I am not the keeper of their conscience.' The woman, who had said she was Vitruvia, the mistress of the property, was not swayed by the repetition.

'This is not something to be taken lightly,' Ballista said. 'One of your menfolk should decide. Your father or husband?'

The woman looked down at him. 'My son is away. My husband was killed by the troops of Gallienus the last time the tyrant crossed the Alps.'

That explained the intransigence. Gallienus' first campaign, five years before, at the outset of the rebellion of Postumus, had been bloody, but indecisive. Somehow Ballista had to make clear the hopelessness of her position.

'We have almost a thousand men under arms. A couple of hundred men with makeshift weapons, your tenants and slaves, have no chance against them. Resistance is futile.'

'We will trust to our courage.'

Was there no getting through to her?

'Take the oath with your lips only. Think what you like in your heart. Do not bring destruction to your home and your *familia*.'

'The gods always favour the just cause.'

She was impressive, this Vitruvia. A tall and commanding woman of middle years, about Ballista's own age, blonde ringlets framing her face. From what Ballista could see at this distance, she was beautiful. He very much wanted to spare her, and her household, the horrors that were about to be unleashed.

'I will give you an hour to reconsider.'

* * *

An hour later the answer of Vitruvia was the same.

No one could ignore the preparations for the assault. It drew all eyes. From a nearby hill, Ballista sat astride Pale Horse and watched. Off to the north, the Thracians had felled a decently sized tree, and lopped off its branches. Now half of them – about a hundred and fifty men, in relays – were manhandling the improvised ram laboriously down the track towards the main gate. The Emesenes, also on foot, accompanied them. The archers' bows were strung, ready to sweep the defenders from the wall. They were still well out of range. There was some time to go.

The slow approach had a terrible fascination. Ballista dragged his gaze away, took in the whole scene. Like many rich estates in the Gallic countryside, the villa was fortified, almost like a military camp. It was strange. Few towns in Gaul had any defences. Perhaps the depredations of the *bacaudae* made such things necessary for rural settlements, and as yet the brigands lacked the numbers to assault a town.

A stone wall, roughly ten feet high, with a raised walkway inside, enclosed the large rectangular area of the farm. A cross-wall divided the space. The northern half, against which the ram was inching, contained barns and stables, slave quarters and outbuildings. The main dwelling and an elaborate bath-house occupied the southern portion. There were fruit trees and rose gardens, neatly bordered with ornamental hedges, around the owner's house.

Civil war was hell. It was appalling enough when soldier fought soldier, sometimes brother against brother. But it was infinitely worse when civilians were caught up in the madness. Everything broke down. Decency was abandoned. Life became cheap. It revolted Ballista. In the east, the Persians had called him Nasu, the daemon of death. It was not a title he relished.

The other eight squadrons of the Thracians formed mounted pickets around the estate. They were drawn up beyond bow-shot, but the threat they posed to all quarters was evident. Their presence ensured that not all the defenders could concentrate at the north gate to resist the battering ram.

Some military thinkers considered that odds of three to one were necessary to carry a fortified position. Despite Ballista's earlier rhetoric, his men probably amounted to little more than twice the number of those trying to keep them out. It would not affect the outcome. The wall was low. It had no ditch or towers. The soldiers under Ballista – although far from an elite, especially the Third *Ala* of Thracians – were trained in the use of their weapons. Those who stood against them were more accustomed to a plough or spade. This could only end in one-sided bloodshed. Ballista had issued orders that there was to be no wanton killing. The troops would not be restrained from looting the villa, but there was to be no unnecessary violence, no rape; the unresisting were to be spared. Easy commands to say, harder to enforce.

'Some women are born stubborn,' Maximus said. 'Just like some are born lascivious. It's all in the stars. If only old Argicius were here, he would explain it all.'

'You have become taken with astrology?'

'Sure, it is the most wonderful thing. There was this astrologer who predicted he was going to be torn apart by dogs. To prove him wrong, the emperor condemned him to be burned alive. A sudden downpour put out the fire, and do you know what?'

'He was devoured by a pack of dogs?'

'You have a natural talent for this.'

'All bollocks,' Tarchon said.

Maximus laughed. 'Irony has never played a large role in your life.'

'Talk, talk, all you ever do, talk bollocks.' The Suanian looked put out.

'So you are saying that this is not my fault?' Ballista said to Maximus.

'Even a man such as yourself cannot be defying what the heavens ordain. Besides which, what else could we be doing? Return and tell Gallienus that all these towns and places have come over to him. All except one farm, where a pretty woman told us to fuck off, and stick our emperor up our arses. So we did.'

'Necessity is a hard master.'

'As are the stars. Now, when I told Argicius the day and the hour of my birth, he was dumbfounded.'

'Really?'

'Yes, really. The conjunction of the heavens was most extraordinary at my birth – Mars was mounting Venus, with Jupiter gazing on in admiration. Argicius said I was destined to travel the world.'

'That was an insight. You being from Hibernia, and him talking to you here in Gaul.'

'Scoff all you like, but I am bound for great things.'

'Great talking of bollocks,' Tarchon said. 'The ram is in range.'

The first arrows were being released from the walls around the gate. The estate must have possessed some bows for hunting. The few accurate shots embedded themselves in the shields the Thracians held over those hauling the tree trunk.

The Emesenes did not reply until within about a hundred paces. Then, as one, they let fly an awful volley, which arced down onto the defenders. Even from where Ballista waited, the screams were audible. He saw a couple of men fall.

'We wait until the ram reaches the gate,' Ballista said.

Time dragged as the battering ram seemed to inch forward. Only a few of the bravest of Vitruvia's followers continued to shoot back. One or two of them paid the price. Ballista watched a man hit by two shafts topple off the walkway.

The ram was no distance from the gate. The defenders were hurling javelins, rocks . . . anything that came to hand. The missiles were bouncing and clattering off the big oval shields of the Thracians.

Ballista told the trumpeter of the squadron with him to sound the advance. The notes were repeated by the other seven *turmae* ringing the farm.

They cantered down the low hill towards the south-east corner of the wall, where it protected the main house. With no possibility of a counter-attack, there was no great need to maintain formation.

As they crossed the grass, they heard a muffled thud. Now out of sight, the ram had made first contact with the wooden boards of the gate. By the normal laws of war, the lives of everyone in the besieged place were now forfeit. Ballista wondered if his orders for clemency would be obeyed.

They reined in at the base of the wall. A few things were thrown as they dismounted. A trooper grunted with pain. The designated horse-holders took hold of four sets of reins.

A pair of troopers held a shield horizontal between them. Ballista put a boot on it, and they boosted him up the wall. Along the wall, others did the same.

His own shield ready, Ballista scrambled over the wall. No attack came. He drew his sword. All along the defences, peasants were dropping the farm implements intended for weapons. As the Thracians clambered up, the peasants leaped down from the walkway. Like rabbits, they ran into the illusory safety of the maze-like hedges around the gardens.

Ballista jumped down. As he landed, his right ankle turned. The pain was intense. He went to one knee. Looking about, there was no threat. He let go of the shield, sat down, clutched the ankle.

'Are you all right?' Maximus said.

'In a moment.'

How could a twisted ankle hurt so much?

He had injured the joint before. Now it seemed to carry a weakness.

Allfather, the pain was as bad as if it were broken.

The Thracians dropped from the wall, ungainly in their helmets and armour. They lumbered into the gardens after the fleeing rustics.

'No killing!' Ballista shouted.

The troops gave no indication of having heard.

Already there were screams and yells, and the sounds of things breaking.

An Emesene archer appeared. Panting, he said the troops were through the gate. Resistance was at an end.

Ballista looked around for the trumpeter to sound the recall. The man was gone. The decurion had vanished as well. Not much of a surprise with the latter – the officer was one of the three unreliable ones still left with the Third.

'Help me up. We need to restore discipline, get to the house, before they wreck the place.'

There was always the danger that some fool would overturn a lamp, burn the place through clumsiness or malice. Once soldiers got their blood up, no stupidity or brutality was beyond them.

With an arm around Maximus' shoulder, and Tarchon acting as shield-bearer, Ballista hopped along a gravel path.

The villa had wings, which projected to make the plan of the enormous building resemble a squared-off letter U. Hobbling through the courtyard, figures could be glimpsed rushing through the corridors. Suddenly a portrait bust was thrown through a window. The marble shattered as it hit the ground. Shards of glass tinkled around it.

Up the steps, and into the main entrance hall. Rough armoured men were milling, wine jugs in hand. They were tearing down wall-hangings, smashing objects of art for the mere pleasure of their destruction.

'Get that trumpeter.'

It was a musician from another squadron, but it made no difference.

Tarchon seized the man. When he protested, the Suanian cuffed him around the ear, as one would a child. The trumpeter's companions shaped to intervene. Tarchon said a few words – a foul melange of Latin, Greek, and his native tongue – and they thought better of it.

'Sound the recall.'

The habit of discipline slipping back, the musician did as he was told. The sound was loud in the confined space, but would not carry far outside.

'Follow me.'

Ballista limped back out to the top of the steps, told the man to make the call again. Now the brassy notes floated off across the settlement. Ballista instructed him to keep sounding the recall until told to stop.

Gradually the courtyard began to fill with soldiery. Some had managed to get drunk already, and reeled somewhat. Quite a few were concealing items of plunder about their persons.

Heraclian appeared. Red-faced and flushed, he looked like he had been on the drink himself.

'Prefect, get your men to round up the prisoners. Secure them in the farmyard.'

Whatever angry *daemons* drove Heraclian were released on his troopers. He shouted and cursed them. After he had kicked one, they got moving.

'A glorious victory,' Acilius Glabrio said.

Ballista ignored the sarcasm. 'Any casualties?'

'No dead. Three wounded, one seriously.'

Further exchange was cut off by the crowd of soldiers parting. Two Thracians dragged Vitruvia from one of the secluded gardens. The matron's clothes were torn, one of her eyes bruised. There were weals on her arms.

'I said no violence was to be offered to non-combatants.'

'The bitch has killed our decurion.'

'What?'

'Told him there was treasure hidden down a well, pushed him in. When we came around the corner, she was throwing rocks down on him. Poor bastard is dead.'

There was an angry murmur from the crowd.

Ballista addressed Vitruvia. 'Why?'

She looked him in the eye. 'He offered me an insult.'

'An insult?'

Despite her distress, despite having taken a life, she managed to choose her words with care.

'The sort that the son of Tarquin the Proud offered Lucretia.'

Ballista turned to the soldiers holding her.

'Is that true?'

Both started talking at once: *No, nothing of the sort! It was a lie!*

Their mendacity was obvious.

'My orders were explicit.' Ballista's voice was very cold. 'I will ask you one more time. Is it true?'

One of the soldiers shrugged. 'Don't know. He told us to give him some privacy.'

The other grinned placatingly. 'There was some screaming, maybe a bit of a struggle.'

'Nothing to do with us.' The first trooper let go of Vitruvia's arm, as if the contact might implicate him. 'We were obeying orders.'

'Which decurion?'

They named the one who had been with Ballista.

'It seems the lady has saved me the trouble of punishing the offence. Get the corpse, before it pollutes the well. His effects are to be auctioned. The proceeds go to the squadron. Throw the body out on the dungheap. It is denied burial. Leave it for the birds and beasts.'

The soldiers looked stunned at the posthumous savagery.

'The penalty for disobeying an order is death. And let go of that woman.'

Ballista searched the sea of unfriendly faces. Gratus – solid and dependable Gratus – looked less hostile.

'Prefect of the Camp, take this woman under your protection.'

Nothing shook the equanimity of Gratus.

'We will do what is ordered, and at every command we will be ready.'

The soldiers were still antagonistic, but they parted as Gratus led her away.

'What did I tell you?' Maximus said. 'All in the stars. Was I not saying that someone would be devoured by dogs.'

CHAPTER NINETEEN

The Villa of Vitruvia, Aquitania

Nine Days before the Kalends of August

THE OFFICER DISMISSED HIS servant, and went into his tent. It was late, his duties done. All the men and animals under his command were fed and watered, the guards posted, all settled for the night. Everything was normal, except for the corpse of the murdered decurion that still lay exposed on the dungheap.

It was impossible not to respect the action of Ballista. It was the deed, not of a barbarian, but a Roman of old. In the past the axes of Roman generals often were seen dripping with Roman blood. Military discipline required harsh punishment. If armed force were allowed to deviate from the right path, it would destroy the army. When Aulus Postumius was dictator, his son rushed forward from his position in the battle line. The youth defeated the enemy, but his father ordered him beheaded for disobeying orders. Torquatus had done the same. His son had vanquished the enemy general in single combat, stripped him of his armour, but Torquatus ordered him slaughtered in the manner of a sacrificial animal. Those stern aristocrats in the long past days of the Republic had known it was better for a father to do without a brave son than the fatherland do without military discipline. Nowadays they looked to nothing but their own pleasures.

The officer unbuckled his sword-belt, hung it on the stand with his armour. He moved across the narrow space to the trunk on which the wine jug was cooling in a bowl, poured himself a last cup. On the other trunk, amid the papyri and styluses of his records and correspondence, was a writing block that had not been there when he left. It was late, and he was tired, and he almost called for his slave before realisation struck.

He picked the thing up, as if it was fragile or dangerous. How in Hades had it got here?

Be a man.

It was expected. No need to be alarmed now it had arrived. How it had appeared was unknowable and unimportant. He looked at the nondescript impression on the seal. A cockerel, it meant nothing to him. He broke the wax, opened the two hinged pieces of wood.

The letter was written in a feminine hand. You had to admire the depth of the craft.

To my dearest nephew from your loving aunt Terentia.

I had so much hoped that you would come and see me at the house in Brixia while you were wintering in Mediolanum. But duty must come first. Since your uncle died, it has been hard. But the neighbours are kind, and your cousin Decimus has taken over the running of the farm.

Your parents sent a little money from Rome, may the gods watch over them.

Should you get the opportunity, we would welcome a gift of some of the square cheese of Tolosa, perhaps a jar or two of dulce.

The family details were correct. He had an Aunt Terentia – an aunt of whom he was very fond. She did live in Brixia, but this was not written by her. Terentia was illiterate. He felt a chill of apprehension. It was a perfect camouflage, but also a covert threat.

Neat, even fussy, in his movements, he held the block over an empty bowl and, using a knife, scraped away the wax. The hidden message was in ink on the inside of one side of the diptych. It was brief.

To my friend with the cavalry from your friend with the army.

Let it be the one, not the many. Should that fail, necessity demands the many.

The man felt a surge of relief. Volusianus had made a decision – issued a clear instruction. Thank the gods, he was not ordered to betray the entire column. Now to conceal the evidence. He put the bowl on the brazier.

Stirring the melting wax with a stylus, an unease crept over him. Commanded to kill an individual, was it right to feel something akin to joy? Of course it was better to murder Ballista than to send a thousand or so Roman soldiers to a treacherous death. Yet it was the lesser of two evils. He was not the man he had wanted to be, all those years before, when he had enlisted as a soldier. He had seen himself promoted through the ranks by open courage and honest adherence to discipline, not as a sly hired killer. But he had no choice. The letter made that clear. His aunt and cousin were in Brixia, his parents in Rome. Should he fail, let alone refuse, they would

suffer for his dereliction. The retribution of Volusianus would be both thorough and horrible.

Holding the hot bowl with a pair of tongs, the man poured the molten wax back into the leaves of the writing block. His mind turned to ways and means. There was poison. He had the knowledge and the ingredients. In his baggage was a vial of colchicine from the Caucasus – the poison of Medea. It was fast-acting. One draught was inevitably fatal. Only the ignorant sought additional recourse to magic. A doctor could mix citron with myrtle juice, frogs boiled in wine, administer it in the urine of a child . . . Whatever he did, it would make no difference – the victim would die.

Instinctively the officer's right hand went to the ring on the middle finger of his left. The ring contained another draught of the colchicine. Sometimes suicide was better than capture.

Yet to administer poison to Ballista would be difficult, and far from subtle. If the slave Felix could be corrupted, he prepared all Ballista's food. Yet the northerner ate every meal with his two barbarian bodyguards. All three would die. There could be no question of natural causes. Poison would be obvious. Somehow the slave would have to be killed before he could be put to the torture. Unless done by a wife, any poisoning had ramifications.

It would have to be a blade. Ballista slept in his tent without company. At other times he was often alone. Perhaps Ballista's attentions to the Gallic woman Vitruvia might provide an opportunity. Best the knife was not wielded by the man himself. There were four *frumentarii* with the column whose identity was known to him. They would follow his orders. Much more than messengers and spies, they were trained assassins.

CHAPTER TWENTY

The Road South of Vesunna, Aquitania

Seven Days before the Kalends of August

BALLISTA WALKED ON HIS own up from the horse lines. The horses had been watered and fed at first light. Ballista had tested several double handfuls of the oats. They were clean and free of dust, had the right sweet, fresh smell. Those grains he dented with a thumbnail were not brittle. When bitten, the kernels had chipped as they should, rather than torn. As a precaution, chaff had been mixed with the hay to stop the horses bolting the feed unchewed.

Animals always lost weight and condition on campaign. Their saddles ceased to fit. If not constantly adjusted, serious injuries would result. Apart from the right tack and furniture, thorough grooming and good feeding were vital for the health of the horses. Last night they had been given a bran mash with linseed – good for their droppings – and horses needed some variety in their diet. Overall, Ballista was satisfied with the way they were standing up to the rigours of the journey. Inevitably, some had gone slightly lame or completely broken down. The former were now being led with the baggage train. The latter had been left at the town of Vesunna, where replacements had been requisitioned. Even the mounts of the Thracians were not doing badly, now that the drunken horse-master had been replaced by a trooper promoted from the ranks, a man who understood the necessary care.

'Fine morning, sir.' The soldier's accent was from the Rhodope Mountains south of the Danube.

'It is indeed.'

The men were at their own breakfast: the bacon, biscuit and sour wine of their rations, supplemented by fresh food purchased along the way. Ballista was surprised at the change in the Thracians, like the one who had just addressed him. Their anger at his treatment of their dead decurion had soon dissipated. It turned out that the officer had been far from popular – a martinet, all too ready to lash out. Ballista himself had regretted exposing the corpse, without so much as a coin for the ferryman. Denied passage over the Styx, a soul wandered the earth for eternity. Yet sometimes discipline depended on exemplary cruelty.

The Third *Ala* seemed both more contented and a handier body of men. Certainly, there had been no more open insubordination, not even any dumb insolence, since they had left the villa. The troopers had begun to go about their tasks with a certain pride. Either from the writings of Xenophon, or, more likely, from the advice of his senior decurion, Lucius Proculus was learning to lead a wing of cavalry. Only two junior officers remained who gave cause for concern. Another month or two in the field, and the Thracians would be a proper fighting formation.

Of course, men had gone missing from the column. At roll call the previous evening, three Emesenes and two Thracians were absent from the standards without explanation. On the march there were always stragglers, and, at any time, some soldiers decided a military life was not for them any more and deserted. More surprising was that a couple from Gratus'

baggage train were gone. As the muleteers had all volunteered for the campaign, most likely some illness or accident had detained them.

It was not as if the journey had been hard since they left the villa of Vitruvia. Twenty-five miles a day: walk, trot, walk, halt on the hour, a rest at midday, pitch camp early – the set routine for a mounted detachment. The road had continued to be good. Once they had come down from the high country, were clear of its dense wooded slopes, the landscape broadened into great sweeping fields, bordered with thick hedges. This was ideal country for hunting on horseback: hounds chasing by sight, a fast horse, a breathless gallop, and the thrill of the jump. No wonder the Gauls were addicted to the pastime. Gallic hounds and hunters were renowned across the empire, and cost the earth.

They had ridden past orchards and vineyards, dovecots and fish ponds. Tracks shaded by poplars left the road to run to neat, white-painted farms. Harvesters in the fields did not flee, but waved, called out greetings. Rural shrines stood at crossroads, offerings on their altars. Everything was ordered and peaceful. The open countryside here offered no inaccessible fastnesses in which the *bacaudae* could build their lairs. All the communities along the route had given their allegiance to Gallienus.

The town council of Vesunna had insisted on certain conditions. They had requested that Ballista surround the town, draw up his men as if for an assault, and then formally summon the unwalled, and utterly indefensible, city to surrender. Ballista had gone along with the theatrical performance. He did not blame the councillors for taking every precaution. If

Gallienus lost the civil war, there might be repercussions from Postumus for those who had gone over without so much as a token resistance.

'You been eating the horses' rations again?' Maximus said.

'No, that will be the mules.' Ballista gave the expected reply. The joke was time-honoured among the cavalry.

Maximus was waiting with Tarchon under the white dragon standard. The *draco* was attended by the new standard-bearer. Lucius Proculus had recommended the young soldier for the post. So far Eprius seemed keen, well aware of the honour of serving close to the commander of the expedition.

'We saved you some food,' Maximus said.

'That is kind.'

'You get very bad-tempered when you are hungry.'

Maximus handed Ballista a plate. Fried steak and newly baked bread; the slave Felix continued to please.

Ballista sat on a folding stool, and ate.

Before he had finished, a trumpet sounded the order to break camp. The call was repeated throughout the lines. At once, the encampment was full of ordered activity. Fires were kicked out, bedding rolled, and the tents began to come down. It reminded Ballista of one of those elaborate mechanical devices for plotting the course of the stars – multiple cogs and dials, all moving individually, but meshing together towards one end.

The men designated flankers for the morning cantered out, chewing their rations as they went.

Also still eating, Ballista got to his feet. Felix removed the stool, and put it with the tent and other paraphernalia to be packed.

Those who had stood picket in the last watch of the night rode back, yawning and stretching. Ballista was pleased to note that their tent-mates had saved them some food. The expedition was shaking down into something approaching efficiency and discipline.

Away beyond the southern perimeter, the scouts under Fabius were already fanning out in pairs on either side of the road. Although there were no reports of any troops loyal to Postumus in the area – in fact, there were thought to be none this side of the Pyrenees – it was best to proceed under a war footing.

Ballista finished his meal, and gave the plate to Felix. Along with Maximus and Tarchon, he strolled after his standard-bearer and slaves towards the baggage train.

Cinch – Take – Break. A muleteer stood on each side of the beasts, securing their loads with a diamond hitch. *Take – Good – Tie.* The traditional cries echoed across the meadow. The mules were blindfolded, reins thrown over their heads to trail on the ground. They stood quietly, five paces apart, in a long line stretching back from the bell mare. It was strange how, when the blindfolds were removed, and the reins back on their necks, they would plod after the horse's tinkling bell, seldom needing any prompting or guidance. Herodotus had been right. Even in the animal world, custom was king.

Eprius led up the horses. Ballista had ridden Pale Horse for the last couple of days. To give the gelding a rest, today he would be mounted on the black. It did not have the stamina of either Pale Horse or the bay, but it had an easy action, and was comfortable.

Column of fours! At a walk! March!

The orders passed from squadron to squadron, yodelled to make them carry. If the listeners had not already known the words, they would have been meaningless.

The Emesenes had the lead for the first section of the journey. They jingled off to the south. After the midday halt, the Thracians would move up from the rear. Ballista, and his entourage, swung into the saddle. He intended to ride with the baggage in the centre of the column.

Gratus was accompanied both by Acilius Glabrio and Vitruvia. The latter was riding astride a fine horse lent by the young patrician. Seeing her as he approached gave Ballista pause for thought. It had not been difficult to find out who she was, or why she had defended her villa. The councillors at Vesunna had revealed her identity. She was also known as Victoria, and she was the mother of Victorinus, the Praetorian prefect of Postumus. It had surprised Ballista. Yet daughters of upper-class Roman families were married off at fourteen. If her son had been born a year or so later, Victorinus could be about thirty, and Vitruvia little older than Ballista himself – somewhere in her mid-forties.

Given her relationship to one of the chief supporters of the rebel, she should have been sent to Gallienus. It was not because of her ordeal at the hands of the decurion of the Thracians – a thing no longer mentioned, as if the rape had not happened – and not because she was personable and attractive, that Ballista had decided she should remain with the column. Given that the high country behind was infested with *bacaudae*, an escort would have been necessary, and Ballista was unwilling to divide his command. As she refused to take the oath of allegiance to Gallienus, she could not just be released. No, it was nothing to do with her agreeable personality or appearance. Really there had been no other choice. Besides, her presence had a good – even civilising – effect on the senior officers.

'Beautiful countryside,' Acilius Glabrio said, with something like affability.

'Beautiful,' Ballista agreed.

'I was just saying to Vitruvia that, given the evident wealth of the landed estates, it is a wonder that we do not see more Gauls in the Senate at Rome, or serving abroad in the empire.' Acilius Glabrio addressed himself to Vitruvia. 'Perhaps your fellow countrymen only thrive in their native climate?'

Vitruvia smiled. 'Next you will be saying that we lack all restraint in bathing, drinking and eating.'

'Gauls are fair-skinned – they suffer from the heat.'

'And we are impulsive and improvident, credulous and braggarts.'

'I would not dream of repeating such outdated slurs.'

'Although it is true that my countrymen are all too fond of the sound of their own voices, almost as addicted to high-flown oratory as, say, a patrician of Rome.'

Ballista rode in silence, as Acilius Glabrio and Vitruvia teased each other with mild flirtation. Even after all these years in the empire, Ballista would have felt uncomfortable joining their urbane Roman conversation. But it was good to ride in the sunshine with this remarkable woman.

Fabius and one of his scouts came back down the road. They rode without undue haste. There was no cause for alarm.

'Village up ahead, beyond the woods, about a mile.'

'Thank you.' Ballista turned to Vitruvia. 'With your leave, madam, Acilius Glabrio and I should attend to our duties.'

'But of course. Roman officers are not to be detained by the idle chatter of women. Duty always comes first.' Behind her formality was a hint of gentle mockery. 'But when duty is done, Marcus Clodius Ballista, it would be my pleasure if you would dine with me tonight.'

'The pleasure would be all mine, madam.'

The settlement lay in a dale. It was not large – just one street. Ballista had halted the head of the column at the edge of the woods, about five hundred paces from the village. He had a good view. All looked normal. There were a few people on the street, others working in the surrounding fields. Either the inhabitants did not know the cavalry were coming, or they were unperturbed. Even so, it was best to be careful. All the officers knew what to do.

'Carry on, Prefect.'

Despite his new-found almost affability, Acilius Glabrio did not salute.

Ballista watched the patrician moving to the front, having a last few words with the men. It was irritating that the troopers seemed to like the man.

Without trumpet calls, half the Emesene light horse followed Acilius Glabrio out of the trees, straight down the road. As they hit a gallop, the rest of the horse archers issued out in two groups. Heraclian led one party over the fields to the west, the senior decurion the other to the east. It was the sort of cross-country riding the troopers enjoyed, flat out, flying over ditches, leaping hedges. The Syrians were natural horsemen.

No need to keep dressed lines – the aim was speed, every man urging his mount, competing to be first.

The villagers did not scatter and run. Those in the fields stood still, gawping. The ones in the village shuffled to the edges of the street. No one rushed to hide, or bolt their houses. By the time Acilius Glabrio reined in at the far end of the settlement, the place was surrounded. The manoeuvre had been pointless. There was no lurking ambush. But the Emesenes had performed well. It was good practice, and might stand them in good stead later.

'A little early, but we will take the midday rest here.' Ballista gave Gratus the now usual orders. 'See there is no looting, and no molesting the villagers. Bring the village headman to me to administer the oath. Demand the keys to barns and smokehouses. Requisition food for men and horses. Check if there are any horses suitable for remounts.'

'We will do what is ordered, and at every command we will be ready.'

'And beat the woods. They might not be hostile, but they may have hidden their animals.'

Ever dependable, Gratus set off to do his bidding.

The baggage and Thracians following, Ballista let his black horse amble down to yet another placid Gallic village. After the early vexations, this expedition was an undemanding and agreeable excursion.

CHAPTER TWENTY-ONE

The Road South Towards Aginnum, Aquitania

Seven Days before the Kalends of August

THE LUXURIOUS LARGE TENT had been lent to Vitruvia by Acilius Glabrio. The patrician must have been fuming. The only guest being entertained under its elaborate hangings was Ballista. The northerner was relishing almost every aspect of this evening.

Vitruvia had been allowed to bring four servants: two maids, a steward, and a cook. The latter far outclassed Ballista's boy. They had eaten oysters from the Atlantic coast, fish from the Garonne, and suckling pig, all washed down with astringent white Massilian wine. Now they were nibbling the famous square cheeses of Tolosa, and drinking sweet raisin *dulce*. The heavens knew how she had obtained the delicacies on the march, let alone persuaded Gratus to transport them with the baggage train. But beautiful, rich women had their ways.

'Acilius Glabrio, you know is wrong,' Vitruvia said. 'Once, we Gauls entered the Roman Senate in numbers, commanded troops along all the frontiers. The families that were granted citizenship by Julius Caesar faithfully served the early emperors. But Roman mistrust persisted. After the rebellion of Civilis, most Gallic families renounced the wider world, turned inwards to our estates and local towns.'

They were reclining side by side on a couch made of straw covered with an ornamental rug. Ballista was unarmed. He had given his sword to her steward when he arrived. A *protector* could dine at the table of the emperor wearing his sword-belt, but not at that of a lady.

'Of course, things must be different for your people. A love of adventure, and a sense of duty has led your countrymen to serve across the empire. There are Angles over the Pyrenees in Spain. And you – although they say it is treason even to whisper it – you once wore the purple. Few women have had the honour of dining alone with a man who has sat on the throne of the Caesars.'

Her blue eyes shone in the lamplight; her blonde hair tumbled to her shoulders. In the face of such beauty, Ballista was somewhat tongue-tied.

'No, not at all, nothing like that. My father . . .' Ballista had no wish to talk about his family. 'I came into the empire as a hostage. None of it was my choice. Some things just happen.'

She looked into his eyes, very serious.

'For all his lowly origins, the elite of Gaul see Postumus as one of their own. Gallienus was far away, and Postumus vowed to protect them. Whatever oaths you exact – at Lugdunum or Vesunna, wherever you march – their loyalty remains with Postumus. Privately they pray he will triumph at Augustodunum. They will not desert Postumus, unless he dies, or tries to lead his armies over the Alps.'

This was uncomfortable talk, much nearer treason than mention of Ballista's brief elevation.

'You know I cannot take an oath to Gallienus. My son . . .' She let her words trail off.

'My family are in the domain of Gallienus,' Ballista said.

'There is nothing to stop your wife and younger son taking a ship from Sicily. They could be in Spain or Gaul in days.'

'My elder son is closely watched in Rome.'

'Then we are both trapped, bound like Ixion to the wheel.'

Vitruvia took a sip of wine, then leaned over him to take some grapes.

She was very close.

'Who is to say we should not take what pleasure we can find in our entrapment?'

Ballista could smell her perfume, her skin, feel the warmth of her body.

'My servants are very discreet.'

Ballista felt her breath on his face.

'I have been widowed for five years. Do you know one of the things I miss?'

Her mouth was inches from his.

'I am sure you can guess.'

Ballista felt a hollowness in his chest.

She smiled, her eyes dancing and playful. 'All the doctors say it is very bad for the health of a woman to live alone.'

It would be so easy. Just incline his head a fraction, reach for her. Something held him back.

'I should be going,' he said.

'You sure?' She pouted, knowing and mischievous. 'Other men would be happy to serve. You should not be bound by your stern northern morality.'

'Thank you, it has been an enjoyable evening.'

Vitruvia laughed. 'It could have been more enjoyable.'

She got up from the couch. She did not seem annoyed. 'You are a strange man, Marcus Clodius Ballista.'

* * *

Ballista lay in the camp bed in his small leather tent. He felt frustrated and foolish.

By the light of a tiny metal lamp, he looked around. His armour and helmet on a stand by the laced-up entrance; a travelling chest; a folding stool; his sword-belt and a pot to piss in by the side of the bed: nothing to distract his thoughts.

Her candid advance might have followed from her attempt to talk him into treason – an inducement, or a taste of pleasures he could enjoy were he to come over to Postumus. Denied public office, those women who wished to influence politics had to use other means. Vitruvia was a redoubtable woman. She had killed the officer who had tried, quite probably succeeded, in raping her. Outwardly at least, she appeared quite recovered from the assault. Her son was Praetorian prefect, and her family at the heart of the rebel regime. Yet, Ballista knew, such thinking had not shaped his refusal.

Why had he turned down something he had wanted, a decision he now regretted? Vitruvia was right – northern morality was a harder master than Roman. As the historian Tacitus had written, adultery was not a frivolous pastime; no one called it fashionable. But that was not the heart of the matter.

Years before, Ballista had developed a ridiculous superstition. If he were unfaithful to Julia, the next time he went into battle he would be killed. The superstition had been exposed as worthless. He had had an affair. In numberless fights since, he had not died. Yet somehow, like a sly rodent, the superstition had crept back. The brief reunion with Julia in Rome had been blissful. Their old intimacy had been restored. It had been enough for the superstition. Infidelity comes more easily to the unhappy.

Soothed by the platitudinous thought, he composed himself for sleep.

* * *

Ballista woke quietly. He kept his breathing deep and regular, gave no sign he was awake. Not moving, through slightly opened eyes, he checked his quarters. The lamp had almost burned out, barely illuminated the interior of the tent.

There was little surprise in seeing the figure by the entrance. As a youth, Ballista had killed the tyrannical emperor Maximinius Thrax. The conspirators who had forced him to the act had desecrated the corpse, denied it burial. Ever since, the *daemon* of that awful ruler had haunted Ballista. It was always the same. The smell of the emperor's waxed cloak. The same words: *I will see you again in Aquileia.* Julia had argued it was nothing but a dream. Ballista had not been convinced. Now he prepared himself for the familiar, but horrible, nocturnal ordeal.

There was no smell of waxed cloth.

Ballista threw off the blanket, rolled off the bed.

A glint of steel, as the figure rushed across the tent.

Landing on the ground, Ballista grabbed for his weapon.

His assailant stumbled over the stool.

Ballista got to his knees, fingers tugging at the hilt of his blade.

Regaining its balance, the apparition slashed at Ballista's head.

No time to draw Battle-Sun; Ballista blocked with the scabbard. Steel bit through the wooden sheath, rang against the sword within. The force knocked Ballista down, sideways.

Quick as a snake, his attacker recovered.

Ballista struggled up again. The attacker loomed over him. Battle-Sun remained wedged in the damaged scabbard. The assassin chopped down, overhead, grunting with the effort. Holding it two-handed, Ballista again got the scabbard in the way. The edge of the steel missed the fingers of his left hand by a hair's breadth. He had to get to his feet, or he was dead.

The man who had come to kill him drew back, readying himself, seeking an opening to thrust.

In the near darkness, something shining on the floor. Ballista grabbed the piss-pot, flung it unhandily through the air. The metal bowl missed the man, but the contents splashed into his eyes. Automatically, a hand went to wipe them. It bought the moment Ballista needed. Wrenching Battle-Sun free, he surged upwards. One-handed, the assassin could not turn the blow. With all his weight, and the fury of fear, Ballista drove the tempered steel into his face, turned the blade, withdrew it, and struck again.

CHAPTER TWENTY-TWO

South-west of Aginnum, Aquitania

Four Days before the Kalends of August

'Sure, after what you did to his face, his own mother would not have recognised him.'

Maximus was right.

'A nice, clean thrust to the stomach now, and everything would have been fine.'

'Foresight has never been one of my virtues,' Ballista said.

They had exposed the corpse the next morning for everyone in the camp to inspect. Average height and build, skin neither particularly dark or fair, brown hair, no distinguishing features, tunic, trousers and boots, a sword-belt with no wallet or ornaments; given the ruined face, it was unsurprising that no one had claimed to recognise the assassin.

'I am still thinking he was a civilian,' Maximus said.

'Not all units have their recruits tattooed.' Ballista had explained this before.

'At the roll call there were men missing from the baggage train.'

'And there were absent Thracians and Emesenes.'

'Outsider sneak into camp.' There was a certain admiration in Tarchon's tone. 'Furtive-sly-fuck.'

'It might not be Volusianus that sent him,' Maximus said. 'Postumus would like you dead, too.'

'My tent is no different from that of any other officer.'

'The white *draco* outside?'

'In the darkness a stranger would still have needed a guide.'

They rode on in silence, the unsettling speculation accompanying them like a fourth horseman.

The column had struck off the road before it reached Aginnum. Out gathering forage, Gratus had been told by a peasant stories of armed men crossing the Pyrenees from Spain – strange tales of outlandish pale giants and small men with faces dark as ghosts, outlandish warriors come to fight for Postumus. There were two passes in the south-west: one emerged at Imus Pyreneus, the other at Iluro. The small settlements were said to be no more than thirty miles apart. They took the direct route, cross country. The rumour might well prove unfounded. The scouts of Fabius had yet to find any trace. Yet, no matter how unlikely, the prospect of action was good training for the men.

They journeyed across vast plains, forests of cork-trees and pine on the eastern horizon. The sandy soil absorbed the tread of their horses, the only sounds of their passing the creak of leather and the jingle of harness. The only witnesses shepherds clad in the black skins of their sheep.

As so often, the chief scout cantered back.

'River ahead, steep banks, fast flowing, no bridge, no sign of a ford.'

'Thank you, Fabius. We will ride ahead, and take a look. Would you ask the senior officers to join me?'

The river was exactly as the scout had said. There must have been heavy rain upstream. The green waters slid past, powerful and inexorable. It was not wide, but presented a difficult barrier to cross.

'A pity your peasant did not mention the river,' Acilius Glabrio said to Gratus.

'I doubt he has travelled more than ten miles in his life,' the prefect of the camp replied.

'That may be why some would not take such people's advice on strategy.'

'You did not object at the time,' Heraclian said.

They sat astride their horses on the lip of the bank. Ballista looked at his bickering commanders, as if seeing them for the first time. The three Italians had nothing in common beyond their country of origin. Acilius Glabrio was tall and thin, both fine-featured and elegant. Away from the woman Vitruvia, the patrician made no effort to restrain his sarcasm, or hide his disdain of his colleagues. Heraclian was squat and bull-necked, face ruddy from the wind. He would have looked out of place anywhere except an army camp. An air of resentment, of barely suppressed anger, hung about him. Gratus, on the other hand, could have passed unnoticed in any surroundings. His features were regular, but nondescript. They slipped easily from mind. Beyond his duties, he seldom expressed an opinion. On the few occasions he did, they were uncontroversial, soon lost from memory. Yet there was something calculating in his eyes, a hint of steel behind the bland exterior. Finally, there was the Gaul, Lucius Proculus. Plump, smooth and urbane, even oleaginous, ready to defer to advice, admit his failings. It was hard to reconcile his appearance and behaviour with his descent from fierce Alpine brigands, let alone credit the claims he had made once at dinner to be a prodigious and tireless womaniser.

Ballista was convinced that if the assassin had been an outsider, he would have needed a guide through the dark maze of the camp. Even if he were a soldier or muleteer, a solitary walk in the dead of night might have provoked comment. But no picket would challenge, no unsleeping decurion question – they would not as much as notice – a man accompanying a senior officer.

'Well, you led us here!' The simmering antagonism of Heraclian was turned on Gratus. 'How in Hades do you suggest we proceed!'

'We will move west along the bank,' Ballista said. 'There is likely to be a bridge or a ford at no great distance.'

There was not a bridge or ford for miles. They rode for almost an hour along the bank under the shade of willows. Eventually they came to a place where flood-wood had caught in a fallen tree.

Ballista called the column to a halt.

'We can swim the horses across,' Heraclian said.

'Everything will get wet.'

Heraclian rounded on Gratus.

'Dear gods, we are soldiers, not Vestal Virgins.'

'The food and forage will be ruined.' The prefect of the camp was polite, but firm. His self-control was out of the ordinary.

Ballista ordered the men to water the horses, take their midday rest. He summoned two squads of muleteers to bring up ropes from the baggage train, then chop down two of the willows, and sent others to cut saplings from a nearby stand of elms.

The men ate as the horses cropped the grass, and axes thwacked into the trees.

When the trees were down, and their branches lopped, the muleteers ran them out, and tied them to the fallen willow to fashion a rudimentary footbridge. It was narrow, and springy underfoot, but, tightly lashed, was secure enough for one man at a time. In case any fell, Ballista had a rope strung across the river just downstream. Although reassuring to view, its utility was dubious, the men being in armour, and heavily burdened.

The horses were unsaddled, the mules unloaded, and the men prepared to carry the equipment and baggage over on their backs. Ballista sent Fabius and his scouts across first. Once the scouts were on the other side, it was time for their horses.

The bank where the horses must enter was about six feet above the stream, and nearly perpendicular. The one opposite was as high, but shelved gently.

The first horse was led up. It placed its feet with care, sniffed the air uncertainly. Two troopers held its head. When it had been brought to the edge, another pair of troopers approached from behind. They put a rope under its rump, leaned in with their shoulders. At a word of command, the four threw the horse forward. It fell, legs thrashing, hit the water with a tremendous splash. All horses can swim. The troopers prodded and clouted it with the poles cut from the saplings until it turned and made its way across. On the far side the scouts, standing hip-deep, grabbed its halter and hauled it up the bank.

When all thirteen mounts were over, the scouts dried them, tacked them up, and set off to spy out the land. Ballista ordered the Emesenes to begin crossing. With more than four hundred men and horses, one at a time, the process would take hours. After a time, his presence no longer necessary, Ballista wandered off to where the elms stood. Taking no chances, Maximus and Tarchon followed.

Ballista sat in the shade, and dozed. The sounds from the river seemed distant, somehow soothing. Unbidden thoughts of his home came to mind: the tall elms by the hall of Hlymdale on the island of Hedinsey; sitting with his mother, looking out at the trees from his father's chamber up under the eaves. It had been the previous year. It was unlikely he would return, see his mother again. He had never wanted to leave. He loved Julia, loved his sons, but part of his heart remained in the north, with his family, with Kadlin, the first woman he had loved. Now Kadlin was married to Oslac, his half-brother. Some lovers in this world live dear to each other, lie warm together. At the day's beginning, Ballista went by himself.

It was late in the afternoon by the time the Emesenes were across, the shadows lengthening. Ballista decided the baggage and mules of the horse archers would cross before the light failed. The rest would camp tonight where they were with the Thracians. Ballista was unhappy at having his force divided. From his reading, he remembered a Roman army caught on either side of a river by a rebel army in the Social War. It had been cut to pieces. Oddly, no other examples came to mind. Perhaps the danger was so obvious that prudent commanders avoided splitting their forces in the proximity of the enemy. Yet sometimes risks have to be run, and Fabius and his men had found nothing untoward. Even so, Ballista ordered the outposts doubled.

It was a black night. Clouds had rolled in with the north wind. They built huge fires to banish the darkness. By their light the men were almost festive. They sang old marching songs, happily roared obscene drinking choruses. Some danced, clumsy like performing bears in the shifting firelight. Then, amid the jollity, a man would sing something from his distant homeland. The camp fell silent as they listened to a tune of loss and longing, something that captured the essential melancholy of the military condition, of rough men a long way from home.

Felix had obtained some fish. He cooked them on skewers in the fire. There was no fresh bread, but biscuit and sour wine. Ballista ate with Maximus and Tarchon.

When they had finished, Ballista announced that he would walk the lines. The bodyguards said they would go with him. Ballista hesitated, having a half-formed notion in mind, but acquiesced. They were right. Someone had tried to kill him, and it was unlikely the assassin had acted alone.

They crossed the bridge, the water black and shining beneath in the reflected light. Heraclian, the prefect of the Emesenes, was sitting outside his tent, working on the reports of the day by lamplight. After a few words, Ballista moved on through the lines. The archers gathered around their fires, greeted him amiably. Shadowed by his bodyguards, Ballista walked out beyond the camp, where the darkness was near impenetrable, until he was challenged. Ballista gave the counter-sign. The picket assured him all was quiet, all well. Recrossing the bridge, the three men went through the lines of the Thracians. Lucius Proculus had retired to bed. Again, those troopers who had also not turned in were affable. This was the life, sir – proper campaigning, an easy ride, hot food, a drink, and companionship.

Ballista had left the baggage train until last. Gratus appeared, assured him the mules and spare horses were fed and watered, the men likewise; everything was bedded down. Ballista wished him a good night.

The big tent of Vitruvia was by the bank. Light and soft music came from within. One of her maids must be playing the flute.

'I will be all right on my own,' Ballista said.

Maximus and Tarchon grinned at each other.

'We will stay nearby,' Maximus said. 'Well out of earshot. I have no ambition to listen.'

Vitruvia's steward went in to announce Ballista. He came out, and said that his mistress would be delighted to welcome the *protector*.

As Ballista went through the hanging, he saw Acilius Glabrio. The man was on the couch, reclining where Ballista had laid a few nights before. Vitruvia was next to him. She got up. Acilius Glabrio did not.

Vitruvia crossed to where Ballista stood. Although tall, she had to rise on to her tiptoes to brush her cheek against his. Her perfume was different.

'An unexpected pleasure,' she said.

Ballista glanced at Acilius Glabrio. He wished that he had not. The young patrician was smiling, and raised his glass in mock salute.

'I came to check you were safely quartered.' The words sounded clumsy and unconvincing to Ballista himself.

Vitruvia smiled. 'I would have been safer the other night, if you had accepted my offer.'

She said no more, did not offer him a drink.

'I had best be going.'

Ballista turned, and left.

Outside, Maximus and Tarchon materialised out of the night. Neither spoke. They walked back in silence.

No one prohibits anyone going along a public road, Ballista thought savagely. *You could not blame Acilius Glabrio. No one stops a man buying what is openly for sale. She was little better than a whore.*

Ballista had been unsure of his own intentions. Now he felt foolish, angry with himself. It was not as if she had not given him warning. Yet, irrationally, he felt betrayed. How could she . . . and with Acilius Glabrio? That sneering, preening young aristocrat – *him*, of all men?

CHAPTER TWENTY-THREE

South-west of Aginnum, Aquitania

Four Days before the Kalends of August

LET IT BE THE *one, not the many. Should that fail, necessity demands the many.*

The words ran through the man's thoughts. *Should that fail.* Indeed it had. The much vaunted training of the *frumentarius* had been no match for the skill at arms of Ballista. Volusianus had been right – the northerner was a hard man to kill. The barbarian had butchered the *frumentarius.* Caution had counselled that the assassin not wear the MILES ARCANUS amulet that showed his calling, but it had been a stroke of luck that the corpse had been mutilated beyond recognition. Had even his assumed identity been revealed, it would have been difficult.

The assassination had failed. There was no question of another attempt. Now the two barbarian bodyguards never left the side of Ballista. At night one was always on guard, clad in mail, armed and vigilant. Every morsel they ate was first tasted by one of their slaves.

Somewhere outside the tent a horse whickered. An army camp was never silent. The man sat back, listened to the familiar nocturnal sounds: the tread of a guard; the stamp of a mule; the jingle of the chain of its tether; a cough, and a low murmur of voices; in the background, the noise of the river.

It was odd to regret the survival of a man to whom he had talked affably earlier in the evening. Odder still that the survival of Ballista must entail the death of so many others.

The man regarded the innocuous-looking writing block. Volusianus would not be pleased when he read the message it concealed. The Praetorian prefect seldom condoned failure. The man could not afford the next venture to fail.

Necessity demands the many.

Necessity was a stern master. The killing of the assassin had left three *frumentarii*, apart from himself, in the camp. One would soon slip away, taking this unwelcome communication. Another had already made his clandestine departure. They would both be missing from the morning roll call. It mattered not at all. Every day a few men were recorded as absent without leave, swelling the numbers of the deserters and stragglers. By then the chosen *frumentarii* would be far away. One would be riding north-east to Volusianus in the siege lines before Augustodunum. The other would be bound south, to make contact with the troops of Postumus which the peasant had said had crossed the Pyrenees.

Only one *frumentarius* would remain with the column, available to do his bidding. There would be no room for error engineering the ambush.

This treachery went against the grain, went against everything in which he believed. All those years before, he had not hesitated when offered a transfer into the *frumentarii*. There was a dark glamour about those secret soldiers with their base on the Caelian Hill. They were better paid, and they were a route to promotion. Of course, he had known from the start that it would come at a cost: eavesdropping and dissimulation;

the betrayal of those into whose trust he had inveigled himself; the efficient liquidation of an individual or two. But the latter were guilty of treason. It was just inexpedient, or perhaps embarrassing, to bring them to open trial. Better they leave this world quietly. Everything the *frumentarii* did was for the safety of the emperor, for the safety of Rome.

This was different. The thousand or so men in this column were guilty of nothing. The Emesenes, Thracians, and muleteers were doing nothing but their duty. They were serving Rome, loyal to the emperor. Now many of them would die to ensure the destruction of one man, an officer of barbarian origins called Ballista.

When given this mission, back at Augustodunum, the man had spoken up boldly. If the assassination failed, Ballista might also survive an enemy ambush. Volusianus had appeared untroubled. It did not matter if Ballista was alive, as long as he was captured by the rebels. Once he was in the camp of Postumus, no one at the court of Gallienus would believe any accusation the barbarian might make.

You did not serve in the *frumentarii* without questioning motives. What information did Ballista have that made it imperative he did not remain at liberty? If it was against the emperor, why was he not inconspicuously put out of the way, or discreetly arrested, smuggled into the cells under the palace, or some other gloomy place, and then questioned at length? Such things happened all the time. Yes, this was indeed different. What were the accusations that Volusianus feared Ballista might voice?

A faint scratching at the entrance of the tent. The messenger would not be early. It must be later than the man had thought.

He got up, and unlaced the hangings. The hooded figure took the writing block, and departed without a word.

The man sat down again, tapping a stylus against his knuckles. He was trained to investigate, not to disobey orders. Volusianus was Praetorian prefect, commander of the *frumentarii*, his superior officer. Volusianus had promoted him to centurion, then appointed him orefect. Without Volusianus he would never have risen so unimaginably high. He owed everything to the Praetorian prefect. The diligent execution of this task, and he might rise higher still.

In any case, he had no choice. As if he had not already been painfully aware, the letter he had received at the Villa of Vitruvia had reminded him that his family would suffer if he was fool enough to disobey the Praetorian prefect. If he tried and failed, there was the poison in the ring. Better he should die by his own hand than his family suffer the retribution of Volusianus. Unlike those degraded Christians, the Praetorian prefect was not known for turning the other cheek.

CHAPTER TWENTY-FOUR

The Foothills of the Pyrenees, Aquitania

The Kalends of August

THEY CUT THE TRACKS of the enemy early in the morning. Horsemen, many of them, heading east. Some of the hoofprints showed that the horses wore hipposandals. Only cavalry mounts were likely to be shod. Close inspection found hobnails that had been lost from military boots. So there were infantry with the horsemen.

The enemy were in no hurry. Ballista found a hoofprint with a distinctive notch, followed it on foot for a distance. Its spacing showed the horse had gone at an easy walk. The piles of droppings indicated the same. Sometimes the riders had reined in to let their horses relieve themselves. Wheel ruts overlaid the tracks. Wagons delayed a column.

'They must have come down from the mountains at Iluro,' Fabius said. 'Now they are heading for the city of Tolosa, and on into the province of Narbonensis.'

Ballista agreed with the scout. The enemy were aiming for the lower reaches of the Rhône. From there they could stop supplies from the south reaching Gallienus at Augustodunum, perhaps even threaten northern Italy via the southern passes over the Alps. Either might force Gallienus to raise the siege.

'If Postumus has emptied Spain of its garrison, the Moors will cross the Straits, the peninsula will be overrun,' Acilius Glabrio said. 'And it is said there are still bands of Franks roaming the high country.'

'The rebel is putting his own safety above that of his subjects,' Heraclian said. 'As you would expect from a tyrant.'

There were Angles serving with Arkil, Ballista's half-brother, in Spain. Kadlin's son, Starkad, was among them. Ballista pushed the thought from his mind.

'On this hard, impacted going, it is impossible to judge their numbers,' Gratus said. 'There may not be that many of them. Surely even the rebel would not abandon Spain to such a fate.'

'The droppings are fresh, no more than a day old, two at most,' Fabius said. 'There can be no certainty, except there are more of them than us.'

'What do we do?' Lucius Proculus said.

'Follow them,' Gratus replied instantly. 'Our mission is to prevent aid reaching Postumus.'

The prefect of the camp was right. They were soldiers. It was their duty. Ballista gave the orders. They would proceed with caution, in full armour, covers off the shields, the scouts ranging two miles in advance.

The road ran along beside a meandering river. There were swans on the water, gliding between low, muddy islets and pale, twisted drift wrack. Off to the right, beyond the river, green forested foothills rose from the plain. Beyond them again were the great misted mountains, snow on their peaks.

They rode through the morning, until Fabius returned to report that there was a settlement around a bend ahead, and the tracks ran towards it.

Ballista led the column off the road, and through the trees that fringed the river. Although there was little undergrowth, progress was slow. But time was not an issue, and they were effectively screened from the road.

They halted level with the village. It was set back from the road, on the slope of a hillock away from the river, about half a mile from where they stood. One main street, two alleys opening off it, a straggle of outbuildings, stock-pens, and some farms at a distance. There were a few animals in the fields, but no one to be seen.

Orders were passed from man to man – no trumpets, no shouts. Acilius Glabrio would go in with one squadron of the Third. They would have the task of springing any trap that might have been set. The rest of the Thracians, under Lucius Proculus, were drawn up in line under the trees. The Emesene horse archers were divided between the flanks, ready to fan out and surround the village. The mule train was left a few hundred paces back the way they had come.

The sun was directly overhead. They waited in the dappled shade. Nothing moved in the settlement, and no one came down the road. Although it was midday, it was unnaturally quiet.

The river at their backs was broad. Yellow irises waved in the slow current. On the opposite bank, six cormorants perched in a dead tree, very black against the bare white branches.

Ballista thought about the composition of the enemy force. They might not all be Roman troops. Arkil had already been in Gaul when Ballista had returned to the north. They had not seen each other for more than half a lifetime. They had got on well when young. Arkil was quiet and amiable. Yet, like all the Himlings, he was a natural warrior with the gift of leading men. Ballista would not want to face him in battle. Kadlin's son had been born after Ballista had left. Ballista would not recognise him. Still, there was no reason to think they were with this expedition from Spain.

'Time to go,' Ballista said.

Acilius Glabrio swung up into the saddle. A quick check that the squadron was ready, and he nudged his mount forward.

Once they were clear of the cover, Acilius Glabrio pushed them into a gallop. They flew across the water meadow, crossed the road, and headed up to the village.

Still nothing stirred among the buildings. Ballista scanned the road in both directions. No movement disturbed the drowsing landscape.

A cow lowed, and shambled away from the approaching riders.

The troopers bunched a little as they neared the outskirts. Ballista disapproved. It made them a better target for any hidden archers. They might have drawn together for some illusory safety, but they did not slacken their speed.

Ballista watched them funnel into the street, Acilius Glabrio at their head. If there was an ambush, it would be now. At any moment wicked arrowheads would slice through the air, tearing into man and beast; shouting men, steel in hand, would surge out and block the street. In the blink of an eye, the bucolic scene would resemble a slaughterhouse.

Nothing happened.

Ballista saw Acilius Glabrio emerge from the far side of the village, circle his horse, and begin to ride back. For all his faults, you could not doubt the courage of the young patrician.

'Mount up!' Ballista called.

Acilius Glabrio had set pickets. The rest of his squadron were searching the place by the time Ballista arrived. All the houses were closed, their windows shuttered. The troopers kicked in the locked doors. They went from one eerily empty house to another.

'It is as if they knew we were coming,' Maximus said.

'Rumour moves faster than a cavalry column,' Ballista said.

Ballista looked around. The hamlet was in a good site, raised from the flood plain, excellent visibility in all directions. He made a decision.

'We will halt here for the day. Heraclian, have the Emesenes set outposts half a mile out in all directions, and vedettes a mile beyond that. Fabius, press on further down the road to the east with your scouts. We don't want any surprises. Lucius Proculus, get the Thracians to round up the cattle from the fields. It is the Kalends of August. Piety and the tradition of the army demand a sacrifice, and a feast tonight.'

The soldiers in earshot grinned. An afternoon out of the saddle, and a roast meal to follow.

'Eprius, go and tell Gratus to bring up the mule train.'

The young standard-bearer saluted.

'And, Eprius, ask the Lady Vitruvia if she would care to join the officers for dinner.'

Eprius grinned, and turned to go.

* * *

The first of August was the birthday of the Emperor Claudius. He may have been poisoned by his wife, but dynastic politics had led to him being declared a god. The army sacrificed an ox on the birthdays of the deified emperors. Curiously, although Claudius had died more than two centuries before, the tradition continued. The conquest of Britain under Claudius might explain the tenacity of the custom.

The emperor Pertinax also had been born on the Kalends of August. He, too, had been murdered. Septimius Severus had posed as his avenger, and decreed Pertinax a god. Yet the sacrifices for Pertinax had lapsed with the end of the Severan dynasty. No provinces had been added to the empire under the auspices of Pertinax, and, of course, he had been killed by the army.

The arrival of the food broke Ballista's musings on public memory and forgetfulness.

There were six at dinner: the Lady Vitruvia and the five senior officers. They had requisitioned the largest house in the village. Three couches had been found. As the host, Ballista had made the arrangements. Acilius Glabrio reclined with Lucius Proculus, Heraclian with Gratus, and Vitruvia with Ballista. It had given Ballista a petty pleasure to separate the woman from Acilius Glabrio.

Ballista leaned back to let Felix taste a piece of beef from his plate.

'Mistletoe,' Vitruvia said.

Ballista looked puzzled.

'We Gauls believe it an antidote to all poisons,' she explained.

Acilius Glabrio smiled fondly at her. 'If you kept to all the old ways, Lucius Proculus here would be punished for his ample girth.'

The Gallic officer seemed in no way offended.

'The prohibition was against pot-bellied young men. You read it in Ephorus or Strabo – the idle chatter of Greeks about our wode-smeared ancestors. If it was ever true, we have long left such barbarism behind. We are as Roman as those born on the seven hills. For generations, the schools at Augustodunum have produced the finest Latin oratory in the entire empire.'

'Yet most defendants talk Celtic in court,' Acilius Glabrio said.

'Peasants tend not to attend expensive schools.' Lucius Proculus helped himself to some of the game pie that accompanied the beef.

'To listen to a Roman patrician talk,' Vitruvia said, 'you would think everyone in Gaul was still a head-hunter or a Druid.'

'The Emperor Maximinus Thrax talked to a Druidess,' Ballista said. 'A tall woman called Ababa – she predicted his death.'

Lucius Proculus took a drink. 'Druids still move among the ignorant, but they are no more than charlatans and hedge-magicians. The educated worship our traditional gods – Epona, the goddess of horses, the Matres, the goddesses of plenty. Yet none of us would heed the nonsense peddled by Druids.'

'So you say,' Acilius Glabrio laughed, 'but I think Strabo was right. An essential levity of character makes all you Gauls insufferable when victorious, and scared out of your wits when worsted.'

'Alexander the Great did not share your view,' Vitruvia said. 'When he asked some Gauls were they not scared of him, they replied that they feared nothing except the sky might fall on their heads.'

'And is the sky not falling with the civil war?' Acilius Glabrio asked.

'A minor irritation,' Lucius Proculus said. 'Our courage is fortified by the knowledge that the soul is indestructible. Like the universe, it will last until the final cataclysm, when fire and flood will cleanse the sins of mankind.'

'With such views, you would be at home in Platonopolis, the city our emperor has founded in the Apennines,' Acilius Glabrio said.

'I am not sure that I am suited for an ascetic life.' Lucius Proculus looked thoughtful. 'Although they say the philosophers have many widows living with them.'

Maximus came into the room. The conversation died.

'A messenger has come from Augustodunum.'

It was the first communication since Lugdunum.

'Have him enter.'

The officer was travel-stained, evidently exhausted.

'Report.'

'The emperor has been wounded.'

'Will he live?'

'It is not known.'

There was a deathly hush.

'The army of Gallienus has abandoned the siege of Augustodunum. By now, it will be retreating across the Alps.'

CHAPTER TWENTY-FIVE

The Foothills of the Pyrenees, Aquitania

The Kalends of August

'WE ARE TRAPPED,' Heraclian said. 'How far is it to the Alps?'

'Three, maybe four hundred miles, as the crow flies,' Lucius Proculus said.

'Much further by road, and the enemy forces from Spain are between us and the mountains.' Heraclian sounded despondent.

'Get the messenger a chair,' Ballista said to Maximus. 'He will be tired and hungry.'

'What do we do?'

The unexpected news had undermined Heraclian's resolve.

'You have done your duty. Given your situation, it is honourable to surrender.' Vitruvia could not keep the triumph out of her voice. 'The Emperor Postumus will welcome your allegiance, and that of your men.'

'My estates are in Italy,' Acilius Glabrio said. 'My family are in Rome. Gallienus will confiscate our lands, condemn my relatives.'

'As we speak, Gallienus may be dead,' Vitruvia said. 'You have no choice.'

'The lady is right.' Heraclian was desperate. 'We are cut off. Hundreds of miles of enemy territory between us and safety.'

'There is no question of surrender,' Ballista said. 'We have each taken the *sacramentum* to Gallienus. We are bound by the military oath.'

The family of Acilius Glabrio were not the only hostages in Rome. Ballista's eldest son, Isangrim, was on the Palatine. Julia and Dernhelm were not out of danger in Sicily. Now, more than ever, he wished he was with them.

Ballista turned to the messenger. 'What happened?'

The officer had been sitting, too exhausted to eat.

'The emperor was riding around the walls, challenging Postumus to come out and fight. He had been urged not to by Volusianus, by all the *protectores*. Gallienus was hit by an arrow.'

'Where?'

'In the back.'

'Was he conscious when you left?'

'Yes, but very weak. Volusianus had ordered the siege to be lifted. The army was breaking camp when the emperor summoned me. He was in a litter, his voice little more than a whisper, but he gave me the orders himself – "Find Ballista, tell him to save himself."'

'*Save himself*,' Heraclian said. 'He has released us from our oath!'

'No, that is not what he meant. We are bound to Gallienus.' Ballista recited the words of the *sacramentum*: '*By Jupiter Optimus Maximus and all the gods, I swear to carry out the commands of the Emperor, never desert the standards or shirk death, and to value the safety of the Emperor above everything.*'

'We need to plan our route,' Lucius Proculus said.

'The direct road is to the east, through Narbonensis,' Gratus said.

'But the troops from Spain block the way.' Heraclian had rallied a little. 'If we are going to run, we should skirt around to the north.'

'The Cebenna mountains lie that way,' Lucius Proculus said. 'It is a hard place, bad country for horsemen.'

'No forage for the animals, no food for the men – we would starve,' Gratus said.

'We can go hungry, live off the land,' Heraclian said.

'Not if the land has nothing to take,' Acilius Glabrio said. 'We go east, fight our way out.'

'We go east,' Ballista said. 'With luck, it might not come to fighting. We have the advantage of surprise. Postumus' reinforcements from Spain do not know we are here. Even if we do not manage to slip past them, they are encumbered with infantry and wagons. We are all mounted. We can outmarch them.'

'Mules cannot keep up with horses for any distance on a forced march,' Gratus said.

'If it becomes necessary, we will abandon the baggage train.'

'And what about the Lady Vitruvia?' Acilius Glabrio asked.

Ballista had not thought about her. The mother of Postumus' Praetorian prefect was a valuable bargaining counter. But was it right to expose a woman to the rigours and dangers of a forced march? For all his previous words, he thought there would be fighting.

'The lady will be released at the next town through which we march.'

Gratifyingly, Acilius Glabrio looked put out.

'In the morning we will review the troops and the spare animals. Now we should finish our meal. It would be a shame to let such good food go to waste.'

* * *

The next morning, the troops had been drawn up in the water meadows to the south of the village. Almost four hundred Emesene horse archers, three hundred Thracians with javelins and swords, fifty muleteers and servants. The inspection was thorough: saddles and tack, the loads on the mules. One mile of travel with a loose pack or ill-fitting saddle would do more to ruin an animal than ten miles added to the journey. Horses were taken from the led animals to ensure everyone was well mounted. The unfit animals were left turned out in the fields around the settlement. Rations for five days were issued to the men. At a stretch, they could be made to last ten. The grain handed out was oats. If the mule train had to be abandoned, horses as well as men could eat them.

They had started late in the day, and ridden through the afternoon. To their right was the river, sluggish and broad, both banks fringed with trees. Further off, more trees on the foothills of the Pyrenees. On the left were vineyards and fields, separated by ditches and hedges, all well maintained, but empty of workers. Beyond the cultivated land, other hills rose. Perhaps they were outliers of the Cebenna mountains which dominated the centre of southern Gaul. Ballista's knowledge of the geography of this part of Gaul was vague. The itinerary he possessed showed the roads in a schematic plan, but was near useless for the topography.

After a couple of hours they had come to the site of an enemy encampment. The ashes of the cook fires were cold. The camp was two nights old. Normally each *contubernium* of eight men would have its own fire. The number of fires and the amount of horse droppings suggested a force of both infantry and cavalry, at least seven or eight thousand strong. Some of the latrines were carefully dug, indicating regular troops. In other places, around the horse lines, human faeces fouled the ground. Substantial numbers of irregular horsemen had come up out of Spain.

They had made their own camp further down the road, when the sun began to dip to the horizon behind them. Roman infantry often entrenched their camp. Numbers and time prevented cavalrymen on their own constructing even rudimentary defences. Rather than dig ditches, troopers had to see to their mounts.

Infantry marched at between ten and fifteen miles a day. Ballista's column had covered about ten miles after passing the enemy encampment. The troops they were following should be at least ten miles ahead. Ballista had allowed fires to be lit, but doubled the outposts and vedettes.

They had ridden on this morning. The countryside was unchanged. Again, they saw no one labouring in the fields, met no travellers on the road. The scouts of Fabius, sweeping south to the river and north across the farmland, reported no encounters. The force they were shadowing could account for this emptiness. If they had sense, civilians avoided soldiers – took to the woods and hills until they had gone. Irregular cavalry seldom were amenable to strict discipline. Only a fool would remain to be robbed and beaten, perhaps worse. It might work to Ballista's advantage. Fewer eyes to see his men, fewer tongues to spread the news.

Lulled by the steady clop of hooves, the gentle motion of Pale Horse, Ballista wondered about the assassin who had entered his tent. Postumus had been shut up in Augustodunum. Until the siege was lifted, the lines of contravallation constructed by Gallienus should have precluded news of the progress of the cavalry column reaching the rebel. Certainly they would have made it difficult to despatch the killer. Of course, some unknown adherent of Postumus might have taken the initiative. The governor of Aquitania was thought to be on the Atlantic coast at Burdigala. He remained loyal to the Gallic emperor. The governor had no regular troops, just a local militia. Unable to take the field against Ballista, he might have decided to employ underhand means. It was possible, but somehow seemed unlikely. Where would the civilian governor have found an assassin in the peaceful and mercantile city of Burdigala?

Ballista's thoughts turned to Volusianus. He was convinced that the Praetorian prefect had been implicated in the failed plot to kill Gallienus earlier in the year. And he was sure that Volusianus was aware of his suspicions. The Praetorian prefect wanted him dead, and Volusianus commanded the *frumentarii*. That was what the secret soldiers did – the discreet elimination of individuals judged a danger. Did that account for the killing of the senator Nummius Faustinianus in the camp outside Augustodunum?

If Ballista had accepted Vitruvia's offer, he would not have been in his tent. He was honest enough to acknowledge that he was jealous of Acilius Glabrio enjoying her favours. It might be mean-spirited, but he was glad that affair was about to come to an end. According to the itinerary, tomorrow they would reach a town called Novum Oppidum. Obviously a small place – it merited no picture in the itinerary, nothing more than its bare name – but it would be safe enough to leave the woman there.

The harsh, clattering call of a disturbed bird. Ballista tracked the distinctive, looping flight of the jay as it came up from the woods by the river. It took a moment to realise its import.

'Column, halt!'

Ballista fought down his impatience as the signal was relayed down the line, and acted upon.

'Form line facing south!'

From a column of fours, it was simple to turn into a line of battle four deep. But again there was the agonising delay.

'Prepare for action!'

Those around him looked quizzical, but unalarmed. Was this yet another drill?

Ballista ignored them, surveyed the troops. The Emesene bowmen, who had been leading, now were on the left. The Thracians with Ballista formed the centre, and the mule train the right. All were in position, the troopers tugging the covers off their shields, the archers pulling their bows free of their cases, opening their quivers. The muleteers all had swords, or some form of blade.

The line of trees down by the stream was some three hundred paces distant. The foliage of the low-hanging willows and alders was bright green, thick and glossy in the sunshine. It shifted gently in the breeze. Nothing else moved. Like a pastoral poem, it was an unreal and treacherous image of bucolic peace.

Ballista looked around, surveyed the terrain. Behind the hills were quite steep here, about half a mile away. Running up to them were arable fields, quite large, not many hedges or stone walls – nothing that would too much impede manoeuvring cavalry. The road stretched off laterally west to east. In front, the open meadows dropped down to the trees.

'Lucius Proculus, take two squadrons back to the hills. Plant your standard on the top, form a line to which we can fall back.'

Ballista gestured a trooper forward.

'You, ride to Gratus. Tell him to withdraw the mule train to the hills, behind Lucius Proculus. As fast as it can go, no time to lose.' He summoned another rider. 'Find Heraclian. His light horse are to be ready to skirmish with whatever comes out of the woods.'

Now for the key element of the defence. Ballista raised his voice.

'Senior Decurion, to me!'

The officer rode up.

'I will assume direct command of the seven even-numbered *turmae*. You have the other seven. We will form two lines. Prepare to conduct a fighting withdrawal.'

The officer went off to instruct his men.

Ballista walked Pale Horse forward. Still nothing untoward down by the river.

'Even-numbered *turmae* two through to fourteen twenty paces forward, form on me, keep the gaps between the squadrons.'

The designated *turmae* moved up. The Thracians now were arranged like the squares in the board of a game of *latrunculi*.

They waited. Horses dropped their heads, snatched mouthfuls of grass, swished their tails, although there were no flies. Nothing would be lost if he was wrong. Unexpected deployments kept the men on their toes.

The baggage train beginning to pull back may have precipitated the action. Glints of steel among the trees. Half-seen movements in the shade.

A murmur like a collective sigh from the troopers around Ballista.

File after file of horsemen emerged from the line of trees. If only Ballista had more men, more shock cavalry. Now would be the moment to charge, downhill, over good going, hit them as they came out of the cover, before they could dress their lines.

No point in crying for the moon. Deal with what fate decreed.

Ballista studied the enemy, counted their standards. Opposite Ballista was an *ala* of regular auxiliary cavalry, armed and equipped exactly like the Thracians, not outnumbering them by much.

The flanks were not so good. Irregular light horse to the right – Moors, by their loose robes and long, dark braided hair. Unarmoured, javelins in hand, they did not pause to get into any formation, but straight away set their unbridled little ponies to chase the baggage train. Clouds of them, racing up the slope. Lacking formal standards, their numbers were unknowable. Not all that many – perhaps about five hundred.

Things were much worse on the left. Many, many more Moorish horse. Two, three thousand, impossible to say. The Emesenes had spread out into a long skirmish line. Although well out of range, even from uphill, the horse archers released one volley. The arrows fell short, but it let the tribesmen know what they faced. Unlike their compatriots on the other wing, these Moors, for all their numbers, did not charge. They milled, perhaps getting their courage up to set off into the killing zone.

Ballista looked east, the way his men had been headed. Sure enough, some distance off rose a tall thin pall of dust: close order cavalry, moving in column, most likely another unit of regular heavy cavalry. He had not marched all the way into the ambush. Perhaps the Allfather had sent the bird that had warned him. The trap had been sprung too early.

On the right, the Moors had caught up with the tail of the baggage. Mules can never outrun horses or ponies. The Moors rushed in, but, when the last muleteers turned to fight, they wheeled away, despite their overwhelming numbers. These North African horsemen were true light cavalry. They would only charge home if their foes were already defeated, running for their lives. Now they began to circle, like venomous insects. The bolder at the front hurled their light javelins. The first muleteers fell. They had swords, mismatched bits of old equipment, but no missiles, nothing with which to fight from a distance. Some of the Africans' javelins struck the animals. The wounded mules staggered or ran, adding to the confusion. At least the majority of the baggage train so far was out of range. Through the dust raised by stamping hooves, Ballista saw them driving as fast as they could go up towards the hills.

High, wild yells from the left signalled the onset of the rest of the Moorish horse. Most peeled away to outflank Heraclian's Emesenes. Yet some set their ponies straight up the slope. When they had ascended to within a couple of hundred paces, they were met by a volley of four hundred arrows. Tribesmen were plucked from their seats; ponies stumbled and crashed to the ground. Those unhurt lashed their mounts. They knew they had to get much closer before their javelins could hit back at their tormentors. Almost at once another squall of arrows hissed among them. More white-robed figures writhed on the ground. It was too much. The Moors yanked around the heads of their beasts, and fled pell-mell back down the slope.

Heraclian's men had done well. But it had only bought a little time. Hundreds of tribesmen were working around their left. Soon Heraclian would have to retreat, and both flanks of the Thracians in the centre would be exposed.

A peal of trumpets from below. The regular cavalry of the enemy were formed up, and beginning their advance. They came up through the meadow at a walk. Yet Ballista knew he had only moments.

'Senior Decurion! The *turmae* at the ends of each line are to face outward, protect our wings.'

The order was no sooner given than enacted. The Third *Ala* of Thracians had improved out of all recognition since Lugdunum. As the unit was under-strength, there were no more than about twenty men in each *turma*. But now at least there were forty or so men guarding each flank of the main body.

The enemy horse were about a third of the way up the incline.

'Front line, prepare to charge! Drop your javelins, we will do this with the sword.'

Troopers fidgeted, eager to get this over. The tension spread to the horses, who tossed their heads, tried to sidle. One or two lashed out with their feet.

'Wait for my command!'

Ballista knew the waiting was the hardest part. But a cavalry charge was a fragile weapon. Released too soon, the men scattered, horses got blown, all impetus was lost.

'Steady! Wait for the word!'

A hundred and fifty paces. The din of fighting from both flanks. Ballista forced himself not to look.

Concentrate on the task in hand. Just a little closer, a little longer.

A hundred paces. Maximus and Tarchon on either shoulder, young Eprius with the standard tucked in behind.

'Charge!'

Ballista brought his heels into Pale Horse's side. Schooled to war, the gelding leaped forward. Fifty paces to cover. They went straight to a gallop.

The enemy hurled javelins. They had thrown too soon. Uphill, they lost momentum, fell short. None came near Ballista, and he did not see anyone fall.

The thunder of hooves echoed down to the woods, seemed to shake the ground.

Cavalry never crash into each other. Unless one side runs, or both pull up, at the last moment their mounts bunch and swerve, opening the ranks, and they ride through each other, hacking and slashing. Horses often have more self-preservation than their riders.

Ballista set Pale Horse between two of the enemy. He took a blow from the left on his shield, struck backhanded at the throat of the man to the right. Instinctively the enemy ducked. A fatal mistake. The edge of the blade caught him in the face. At the moment of impact, Ballista hauled back his hand in a sawing motion. Reeling in the saddle, the mortally injured rider was left behind.

There were four ranks of the enemy. Ballista struck right and left, urging Pale Horse on with his thighs. Momentum was everything. Another blow to his shield, then something got past, clanged off the mail on his left shoulder. He thrust at the last man, sword sideways. The tip punched through armour. Ballista thrust home, between the ribs, and instantly drew back his elbow. Even so, the impact almost wrenched Battle-Sun from his hand, near sprained his wrist.

They were through. Open grass ahead.

'Form on me!'

Ballista brought Pale Horse to a stop, turned him on his back legs.

Maximus and Tarchon crowded close. The white *draco* was still flying above their heads. Young Eprius had come through unscathed. The troopers jostled back into place. All five *turmae* still under Ballista had lost troopers, but they had got through. Now they were steeling themselves to fight their way back up the slope.

Although numbers were on their side, the enemy were at a disadvantage between the two bodies of the Thracians. They were at a standstill, evidently unsure which threat to face.

'Each squadron, form a wedge on the senior officer. Prepare to charge.'

Best strike before the enemy regained their composure.

'Charge!'

Now the incline was against them. They were at no more than a canter when they reached their foes. This time many of those ranked against them pulled aside. Ballista rode through without giving or receiving a blow.

Ballista maintained the pace. They rode through the gaps between the *turmae* in the second line. Ballista kept them going. They jumped a low hedge bordering a field. About two hundred paces beyond their compatriots, Ballista called them to a halt. With almost parade ground precision, they swung around.

With a roar, the Thracians under the senior decurion charged. The plan was simple. Each line would charge down, wheel, charge back up, then retire through the supporting troops, turn, and wait for their comrades to do the same. The process repeated, gradually they would fall back on the hills.

Ballista surveyed the field. To the east the baggage train had all but vanished, men and beasts dead or fled into the hills behind. Only a knot of about a dozen muleteers were left. They were cut off. The Moors swirled around them. The muleteers were using their animals as cover. They were throwing stones, tent pegs, anything that they could find. The last stand could not last long.

To the west, Heraclian had been forced to withdraw the Emesenes. They were still shooting, but were well to the rear of Ballista's men. On both sides only a thin screen of forty or so troopers shielded the Thracians. Everything depended on the enemy commander. If he could seize the moment, control his troops in the frenzy of battle, victory was within his grasp. Send the Moors to overwhelm the screens on each wing, then throw in the regular cavalry as well, attack the Thracians from three sides. The disciplined retreat would disintegrate into a rout.

The Thracians under the senior decurion were returning. They cantered through Ballista's line. They were appreciably fewer in number. There were empty saddles among them. Often riderless horses would continue to run with the rest. Ballista turned and watched the squadrons take station to his rear. One squadron did not halt. It rode straight on towards the hills. They moved in order. The men were not panicked, each seeking his own salvation. They were following their decurion out of the battle. It might be best for that officer if Ballista did not survive.

Downslope, the enemy cavalry had cleared the hedge. They were taking their time getting ready to renew the attack. Was it a sign that their morale was weakening? Had four brief melees been enough? Noises from the flanks drew the eye, and dispelled the illusion. Ballista had not yet spotted the enemy general, but now he knew he was a man to respect. Somehow, through all the confusion, he had got his orders to the Moors, and the tribesmen had been induced to obey. From east and west hundreds of dark figures were bearing down on the pitifully few riders that guarded the flanks of the Thracians. At those odds, even the Moors might close, fight hand to hand, and, like a pack of jackals, tear down the troopers. Once the screens were gone, it would soon be over.

Ballista looked over his shoulder. The crest of the hills were empty, only a few hundred paces away. Yet, when the Thracians broke, assailed on all sides, it would be too far.

'Maximus, Tarchon, stay very close to me.' He spoke quietly. 'You too, Eprius.'

When the battle was lost, there was just a faint chance that Ballista and his bodyguards could cut their way clear of the disaster. Through the regular cavalry, down to the woods, across the river and away. Victorious troops always prefer to kill the unresisting, often shy away from those who still fight.

The flank guards to the west had disappeared. Dragged down, hordes of Moors were hacking at their broken bodies. Only a dozen still remained to the east. They were selling their lives dearly. But they were surrounded. There was no hope. When they were gone, only the massacre remained.

Trumpets rang out from somewhere, high over the stricken field.

Miraculously, the Moors were pulling back.

The trumpets sounded again.

They came from behind.

Ballista gazed at the hills. Over the skyline rode the head of a column of cavalry – ten abreast, standards flying. More men than had been with Lucius Proculus.

Dear gods, surely not more of the enemy?

The arrivals were deploying into line. They manoeuvred slowly, with complete assurance. They halted, about a hundred men wide, the depth impossible to judge from below.

The Moors were shouting, pointing at the newcomers. Then, as if they had reached some collective decision, they were spinning their ponies around, and urging them away down the slope.

Ballista squinted up at the scarlet standard. It was fluttering in the breeze, not easy to make out what was on its face.

A different note. One never more welcome to Ballista. It was the trumpets of the regular cavalry of the enemy down the slope sounding the retreat.

A gust of wind flattened out the standard on the hill. Picked out in gold was the numeral III. The Third Thracians, and there, at their head, was Lucius Proculus.

Where in Hades did he find all those men?

CHAPTER TWENTY-SIX

The Foothills of the Pyrenees, Aquitania

Eleven Days before the Ides of August

'THEY WON'T CHARGE UP the hill, not today,' Ballista said. 'The ground is against them. Their horses are as spent as ours. It is always hard to get men to go back into combat for a second time in one day.'

'What if their infantry come up?' Heraclian said.

'There is no sign of them,' Ballista said. 'They may have continued their march to the east. With luck, by now they may be somewhere towards Tolosa.'

'Tomorrow?'

'We will not be here tomorrow.'

The officers stood, looking down at where the enemy had regrouped in the valley. Two *alae* of regular auxiliary cavalry, the second having ridden up from the east. Combined, they were around a thousand strong. They were supported by perhaps three thousand Moorish irregular light horse.

'Lucius Proculus, it was a brilliant stratagem of yours to mount the surviving muleteers on the spare horses,' Ballista said. 'Get them in line with the troopers who were on the hill. We are all in your debt. Without you, every one of us would be dead or prisoners.'

The Gaul made a self-deprecating gesture. 'It is the oldest trick.'

'You convinced me that it was the head of a newly arrived column.'

'Up on the skyline, I hoped no one below would be able to see that we were only one rank deep,' Lucius Proculus said.

Ballista turned to Acilius Glabrio. 'What are our casualties?'

'Forty-four Thracians missing, ten Emesenes, and twenty-two muleteers. There are others wounded.'

Ballista calculated the losses. About eight hundred remained, including the wounded, and the muleteers and servants. Odds of worse than four to one.

'There is something else,' Acilius Glabrio said. 'Gratus has gone.'

'Dead?'

'Perhaps captured. His deputy in the baggage train said Gratus spurred his horse into the Moors.' Acilius Glabrio looked puzzled. 'Apparently he was shouting his own name. The Moors let him pass. It was as if they were expecting him.'

That might explain the ambush. Since the assassin had struck, it had been likely there had been a traitor in the camp. Ballista had no time to dwell on it now. He called for the chief scout.

'It is my fault, sir,' Fabius said. 'The tracks run on to the east. But some of their cavalry must have crossed the river. At several places there were signs that they had gone down to water their horses. I should have checked the far bank. Once across, they doubled back through the woods to the south.'

'The fault is mine,' Ballista said. 'I only ordered you to scout down to the river, not across. Seventy-six men have paid for my error with their lives.'

'Soldiers know the risks, sir. Men die in war.'

'And the civilians with the baggage?'

'Them, too. They are volunteers, like us.'

'Thank you, Fabius.' Ballista was grateful to the chief scout. The guilt remained, but he would deal with it later. 'Fabius, I need you to find us a path through these hills. North, then north-east. We will run to the Cebenna mountains, try and lose them in the wastes of the high country.'

'A bad place for cavalry,' Lucius Proculus said.

'Needs must. Our only other choice is surrender.'

'To the Moors?' Heraclian laughed. 'Not likely to go well, after the numbers my men slaughtered.'

'Then it is the mountains.' Ballista addressed Fabius again. 'Set off as soon as your men are ready. Take fresh horses, and second more men into the scouts, if you need them. Where the path branches, or its route is not obvious, leave a man to direct us. We will follow tonight. The watchword is *Salus*.'

'*Safety* it is, sir.'

'And, Fabius, if you can find some shepherd or other local, we need a guide. Promise him a large reward, but make clear to him the consequences of betraying us, or getting us lost. Do not let him escape. Keep him tied up.'

The chief scout left.

There was much to do before evening.

'Lucius Proculus, bring me the decurion who led his men out of the fighting.'

Ballista recognised the officer. He was one of the last pair of the favourites appointed by Solinus, the former prefect of the Thracians.

'I am not to blame.' Like many guilty men, rather than contrite, the decurion seemed angry. 'The orders were not clear. After we had charged the enemy, I thought that we were to retire to the hill.'

Ballista eyed him coldly. 'The other officers understood the orders well enough.'

'It was my men – there was no stopping them.'

'So your men misunderstood my orders, not you?'

The decurion looked around the senior officers, as if hoping to find support there. None was forthcoming. The fierceness had drained out of the man. Now he looked scared. The exposure of the corpse at the villa of Vitruvia had earned Ballista a reputation as a savage disciplinarian, a commander who did not spare those of rank who transgressed.

Cowardice in the face of the enemy; deserting the ranks; disobeying an order: all merited death. At the very least, the decurion should be cashiered or dismissed from the service. Yet the time might not be right for draconian punishment.

'In future, make sure you are certain about all orders. If in doubt, ask. Get your squadron ready to march.'

The decurion saluted, and walked away.

The decision might have been a mistake. Ballista knew that his clemency had been influenced by his own error with the scouts. A man pardoned when at fault often felt not gratitude, but resentment. After this, the decurion could prove to be yet more of a liability.

Ballista put it out of his mind. If they were to live through the next day, the retreat had to be organised. Someone had to command the party that had to be left behind. Not the decurion he had just sent away. The task called for a reliable officer – one with seniority. Neither Heraclian nor Lucius Proculus could be spared from their units. Acilius Glabrio was too hot-headed.

The task would call for exceptional patience. It would have to be Ballista himself.

'Heraclian, two squadrons of your Emesenes will stay here as a rearguard. I will remain with them. Acilius Glabrio, you will command the column until I rejoin. The mule train, as the slowest element, will lead. They will be followed by the Thracians. As skirmishers, the Emesenes will be best at the tail. Have the men remove the ornaments from their equipment, wrap the horses' hooves in rags, stuff straw in the bells on the mules. This must be done in silence. You will march after dark, at the start of the second hour of the night.'

'And if you do not rejoin?' Acilius Glabrio did not sound as eager for the possibility as he might once have done.

'You must try and lead the men back to the Alps to safety.'

'What about the wounded?' Acilius Glabrio asked. 'Those too injured to ride out of here?'

'How many are there?'

'Eleven, perhaps a dozen.'

Acilius Glabrio did not have to consult the list in his hand.

There was only one answer, and it was not good.

'They will have to stay here.'

'Leave them to the mercy of the Moors?' Heraclian was horrified.

'Whoever leads the enemy has the barbarians well in hand. They will not harm our men.'

'When the wounded realise that they are being abandoned, they might make an outcry,' Acilius Glabrio said.

'I will ensure they are quiet.'

'And the Lady Vitruvia?' Acilius Glabrio said.

'She will travel with the mule train.'

The officers avoided one another's eyes. They all understood the implications for the wounded if the woman could not be left.

* * *

The moon was waning, but with few clouds the night was not dark. It would help the column find the waiting scouts, and not stray from the track. The men were drawn up behind the skyline, out of sight of the enemy in the valley.

Acilius Glabrio loomed up on horseback.

'The men are ready.'

'No reason to delay,' Ballista said.

Acilius Glabrio did not move.

'I should be the one to stay behind,' he said.

'It is my decision.'

'My brother . . .'

'Was a brave man. He chose to stay in Arete. I choose to stay here.'

Acilius Glabrio smiled, his teeth very white in the dim light.

'I may have misjudged you. Should we survive, we might be friends.'

'Your family might not agree. The smoke-blackened busts of all your ancestors would glower with disapproval.'

Acilius Glabrio laughed. 'You do not understand. The portraits are not just to be emulated, they are to be rivalled. A patrician must follow his own mind, be true to his own *virtus*. We can discuss this tomorrow.'

'Or later, in Hades.'

'I was rather hoping for the Elysian Fields.'

'Travel safely.'

'And you.'

Acilius Glabrio turned his horse.

'Take care of Vitruvia.'

'I will,' Acilius Glabrio said, 'although I would have rather been her first choice.'

The patrician rode away.

Hissed orders were passed down the line – none of the usual trumpets and hallooing.

Despite all the precautions, the noise of the column moving out seemed loud in the quiet of the night: the creak of leather, the muffled clop of hooves, the occasional clink of badly wrapped metal.

Ballista wet a finger, held it up. What breeze there was came from the north. He hoped it was not enough to carry the sounds over the crest, and down towards the river.

Ballista walked back to the top of the hill, where his standard flew. The white dragon stirred sleepily in the light air.

The campfires of the enemy were strewn across the valley floor, like fallen stars. So many of them, all harbouring men with hostile intent.

Ballista went on a way down the slope towards where he had stationed the guards. Maximus fell in beside him. Tarchon and Eprius were with the wounded.

'Who goes there?'

'*Salus*.'

'Approach, friend.'

The exchange was loud. Everything had to appear normal.

After the challenge, the silence hissed in his ears. Nothing betrayed the stealthy departure of almost seven hundred men and more animals. The light of the enemy fires blinked as unseen men passed in front. It was only the second hour of darkness; not all would be asleep. And, like Ballista's rearguard, they would have pickets posted.

'For the love of the gods!' The shout rang out from the crest.

As one, without a word, Ballista and Maximus turned and sprinted back up the incline.

'You heartless cowards! We are your brothers! You can't just—' The words were cut off.

Tarchon was standing over the dead man, blade in hand.

'He just killed him!' Eprius said. 'Butchered him in cold blood!'

'They were my orders,' Ballista said.

Ten pairs of frightened eyes gazed up from the blankets around the fire.

'If you alert the enemy, we will all die.' Ballista hardened his heart, looked at each of the injured in turn. 'In the morning, they will accept your surrender.'

'The Moors? Like fuck the savages will,' one of the wounded said. Despite everything, the man spoke softly.

'The chances will be better then than if they storm the hill tonight. In the darkness and confusion, their officers will have no control.'

None of the wounded spoke, their silence an eloquent accusation.

'Heart and courage. Duty is hard.' The platitudes were hollow in Ballista's own ears.

'Knew he would get us killed.' An Emesene with a terrible wound to his chest spoke in his native tongue. 'Always said he was a murderous bastard. All the northern barbarians are the same.'

'And you were not wrong,' Ballista replied in the same language. 'You forget I served in the east for years.'

'Is it true you had the Persian king's favourite concubine after you beat him at Soli in Cilicia?'

'Strange things happen in war.'

'A man could die happy after a concubine of the King of Kings.' The Emesene coughed. It opened his wound. Ballista went to re-dress the bandage. The archer waved him away. 'No point, I will not last the night. Still, a drink would ease the waiting.'

Maximus unstoppered a flask, and gave it to him.

'A coin for a shave seems pointless. Perhaps one for the ferryman?'

Ballista took the wallet from his belt, solemnly gave each man a coin.

'Keep quiet, boys.' Ballista reverted to the Latin of the army, so they could all understand. 'The long watch is over. There is nothing else to be done.'

The brief outcry seemed not to have reached the enemy. Their camp was the same as before. Perhaps, as the night drew on, fewer figures moved about, momentarily blocking the light from the fires.

Ballista's men were too busy to dwell upon their situation. There were some fifty troopers comprising the two squadrons. Five pairs were out front, one of the two decurions with them, watching for movement from the hostile encampment. Ten more archers were up the trail, keeping the horses safe. The rest were tending three fires each. It was hard and repetitive work, cutting and hauling wood in the darkness. The other decurion chivvied them on. It was vital to keep the fires burning as big and bright as if eight men were around each – essential to have the right number. Assuming the enemy had belatedly seen through the ruse of Lucius Proculus, they had a good idea of the numbers with the column.

Another half an hour or so, about the beginning of the third hour, and they could let the fires begin to dim. Not until then could they attempt to slip away, and make their escape.

The waiting was hard. Ballista was tempted to help the troopers feeding the fires, but he could not stop staring at the flickering lights spread across the blanket of the dark at the foot of the hill.

The plight of the wounded brought old unhappy things to mind. Acilius Glabrio's brother was not the only man Ballista had been forced to abandon at Arete. It had been harder to leave Mamurra, and not just because he was a friend. Mamurra had been in a countermine dug out under the walls to intercept a Persian siege tunnel. If Ballista had not ordered the entrance to the mine collapsed, the Persians would have swarmed through and taken the town. Ballista had left Mamurra entombed. Most likely, Mamurra had still been alive. He had left his friend to die: killed by the Persians, or crushed by the falling roof, or – most ghastly of all – to starve alone in the blackness.

Some nights, when sleep deserted him, he imagined that Mamurra, against all the odds, had survived. It was not a comforting thought. If the roles had been reversed, Ballista would have wanted vengeance on the friend who had left him to his fate.

Vengeance was a duty. Ballista's mind pursued its own course unbidden. Calgacus was dead, and his murderer was alive. Ballista had not avenged Calgacus. Somehow, on this hillside in Gaul, it seemed impossible that Ballista would ever track down Hippothous. In the unlikely event that he reached the Alps, how on earth could he hope to find one man among the millions that inhabited the empire?

'The third hour,' Maximus said, 'and all is well.'

Ballista gazed at the moon. The Hibernian was right. It was time to go.

They told the men to leave the fires, make their way back, and wait with the horses. Then they went and summoned in the pickets.

Ballista took a last look at the enemy encampment. As he did so, he heard a snatch of music – voices and flutes. It was gone before he could catch the tune. Mark Antony had heard music when his god abandoned him. Ballista put the thought away. It was nothing but a trick of the acoustics, some late revelry echoing up the hillside.

They collected Tarchon and Eprius. Ballista bade farewell to the wounded, wished them luck. There was nothing else to say.

They trudged guiltily out of the circle of light.

'The *draco*,' Eprius said.

'Leave it,' Ballista said. 'It is white, in the light of the fires. They may notice it gone.'

'To lose the standard brings the worst luck.'

Ballista considered it in silence.

'As its bearer, should I give it up, my *daemon* would turn against me.'

'Fetch the dragon.'

Half a lifetime in army camps ensured you respected the superstitions of their inhabitants.

CHAPTER TWENTY-SEVEN

South-west of the City of Tolosa, Aquitania

Eleven Days before the Ides of August

THE TRACK FROM THE camp up into the hills was hard and stony. There was no sign of the passage of the main column. No droppings, and not so much as a hoofprint showed in the pale moonlight. Where the track first branched, one of Fabius' scouts was waiting to guide them.

Riding on, they began to come across the usual detritus left by a body of cavalry on the move: a discarded flask; a hipposandal that had been shed by the mount of a trooper; broken bits of tack; piles of horse dung; human faeces. Ballista got down and picked up a couple of bits of cast-off equipment.

They went on at a walk. Although they had heard no sounds of pursuit, it was hard not to put their spurs to their horses' flanks. The urge had to be resisted. If a mount stumbled in the gloom, if it went lame, there were no replacements.

The second time the track divided, Ballista called a brief halt. He dropped the hipposandal where the paths diverged, and threw the flask down the route they would not take. It was unlikely to delay the enemy for long, but every moment might count.

Around midnight, they came up with the main column. Ballista had been in the saddle for three hours. Under normal circumstances he would have expected to be some fifteen miles from the camp. But in the darkness of the hills, they were unlikely to have made anywhere near as many. Somewhere along the march, Fabius had discovered the hut of a shepherd. Its occupant, tied atop a mule, now served as a less than willing guide. They watered the horses from their canteens, and pressed on through the night, the stars the only witnesses to their flight.

Dawn found them wearily debouching from the hills on to a wide plain. They pitched camp by a stream. While all but the pickets slept, Ballista questioned the shepherd. There was a village to the north. It took two hours on foot to reach. From there an unmade road ran north-east to Tolosa. The rustic had never been that far. Although his experience was circumscribed by a day's walk, the shepherd knew that the Cebenna mountains were at a considerable distance, well beyond Tolosa.

Ballista's understanding of the geography had been wrong. The high country they had left was an outcrop of the Pyrenees, not the foothills of the Cebenna. That was the trouble with itineraries. They showed the cities and towns, the roads that linked them, accurately noted the miles to travel. Yet they were no more than abstract diagrams, and did not depict the reality of the topography. As soon as you left the marked roads, you were lost. Roman armies had been campaigning in the east for centuries, yet, when they did not follow the Euphrates or the Tigris, time after time they went astray. In Germania it was much worse. The great rivers lay across the line of advance, and Roman forces habitually stumbled through a fog of unknowing. Still, Ballista had not expected to be so wrong-footed in the middle of the empire.

It was extraordinary that Roman surveyors could draw exact plans of the land allotments around a town – the dimensions of every meadow and vineyard plotted, and in the right location – but they had never been called upon to produce a map that could be used by an army.

Ballista slept for four hours. Then Maximus woke him, and he had the trumpeters sound reveille. While the animals were fed, the officers made their morning reports. There was something comforting about the unchanging routine.

Not one man was missing, but during the night ten horses and four mules had broken down. Although nearly half the baggage train had been lost in the ambush, there were still over a hundred mules, and almost fifty spare horses. New mounts were allocated, loads redistributed, and the animals that could not go on were cut loose. Most would recover. Some local peasants would thank the gods for their unexpected generosity.

The men ate their rations. No fires had been lit. They gnawed hard tack and cold bacon, drank sour wine. An hour after the horses had been fed, boots and saddles was sounded.

Fabius had ranged in front. By the time the head of the column reached the village, the chief scout had released the shepherd, and taken an unfortunate pedlar. The new guide loudly claimed that he had never been to Tolosa. The villagers – glad it was him, not them – swore that he was a lying bastard that travelled the route regularly.

'Company,' Maximus said.

A mist hung over the distant hills behind them. Perhaps it was smoke. It was impossible to say.

'Are you sure?' Ballista asked.

'I have good eyes, but I am not a magician. The other hills are clear.'

'How far?'

'Might be ten miles.'

Ballista called Fabius over, explained what he wanted the scout to find, then sent him ahead.

'Tighten girths, and prepare to mount.'

Ballista swung up on Pale Horse. He spoke gently to the gelding, while the men got ready.

'Mount up. Column of fours. Prepare to march.'

The horses were warmed from their morning's work.

'Move out.'

They set off down the back road to Tolosa at a trot.

* * *

Ballista lay on the riverbank where the willows came down to touch the water. Through the foliage he could see where the road forded the river about half a mile away.

Maximus and Tarchon were next to him. The three were not wearing helmets, armour, or anything that might reflect the sunlight. The tall reeds along the edge of the stream provided additional cover, and their horses were concealed with Eprius in the depth of the copse.

Fabius had discovered the ideal place. It was the second small watercourse they had crossed. The first had been in open grassland, its sides too steep.

Maximus was chewing air-dried beef, Tarchon desultorily plaiting some reeds. Anything to help pass the time. Ballista just lay very still, waiting. If something went wrong, if they did not return, Acilius Glabrio would lead the column. Ballista could have left this to Fabius, but something made him need to see for himself.

The boughs of the willows moved gently in the stream. Peasants across the empire believed that trees had souls. The educated thought groves were inhabited by nymphs and other supernatural beings. In the heat of the afternoon you might disturb a dozing satyr. The soldiers of Sulla had captured one, and taken it to the general. There were sacred woods in the north, and Ballista found nothing strange about the idea. Silently, he mouthed a prayer to the unknown deity of this stand of willows.

Maximus touched Ballista's arm, then pointed. Small grey shapes were moving up across the land from the south-west. As they came nearer, they resolved themselves into individual riders. As was their custom, the Moors kept no discernible order. Each man urged his mount where he thought best. It made their numbers hard to judge. Yet these were outriders, and comprised no more than a few dozen.

Their ponies were small, stunted and ugly. Yet they covered the ground with great rapidity. Soon the leaders were at the river. They walked their ponies through the ford, letting them drink as they went. Trotting up the near bank, they fanned out, went on a couple of hundred paces, and halted. Some studied the track, others looking about more generally. They were alert, but not suspicious.

There were only a few isolated trees on the far, western bank. All three men saw the solitary Moor coming. They did not move or make a sound.

The Moor halted at the lip of the bank. His dark, fierce face studied the copse. As he turned his head, the long black braids jostled on his shoulders. Like many of his race, he rode without saddle, bridle or reins. Seated on a cinched blanket, he controlled his mount with just a switch. Now he tapped the pony's rump, and, sure-footed as a cat, it stepped down the bank.

In midstream a touch to the shoulder stopped the pony. Immediately its head went down, and it lapped the water which swirled around its legs. The Moor lifted himself with one hand; with the other he raised his dirty, off-white tunic. He urinated without dismounting. Unlike those of the steppe, evidently the nomads of North Africa had no prohibitions about fouling running water.

His clothing adjusted, the Moor resumed his seat. He clicked his tongue in his cheek. The pony's head came up, water dripping from its whiskers. The Moor made the noise again, and the pony moved forward. It was heading straight for the hidden watchers.

The pony stopped at the bank, regarding the mud and reeds dubiously. The Moor flicked the switch, and the pony scrambled up, chesting the reeds apart. They loomed over Ballista and his companions. Another few paces, and they must stumble across them. Ballista could smell the horse, the rank, unwashed rider. He gripped the hilt of his sword. Concealed by the glade, they might be able to take the Moor down unseen by his compatriots. But he would soon be missed.

With an explosion of clattering wings, a partridge got up right under the feet of the pony. The beast's head jerked up. Eyes wide, it sidestepped with fear. The Moor cursed, brought the crop hard down onto the neck of his mount. The pony started forward, its hooves stamping a few feet from Ballista's head. The Moor hit the animal again. Intent on regaining control, he passed without seeing the prone figures. They heard his noisy passage through and out of the trees.

'Very filthy fucker,' Tarchon said. 'Piss in river, but never wash.'

Ballista laughed, more with relief than anything else.

'Here they come,' Maximus said.

Two units of regular cavalry were approaching the ford. In column of march, four abreast, standards flying, they moved at a trot. A Roman officer under a red standard rode at their head. Ballista tallied the ranks. The *alae* were nearly at full strength, almost five hundred each. Behind them came a meteor trail of more Moors – at least two thousand barbarians, perhaps half as many again.

The regulars took the ford still at a trot. In the sunshine, the water that splashed up flashed like diamonds. Without breaking stride, the horsemen followed the tracks along the road to the north-east, drawing their savage allies in their wake.

Ballista exhaled noisily. Maximus patted him on the back.

'Sure, you are as cunning as a fox,' the Hibernian said.

'A fox knows many things.'

'Fox very fucked if Moor had stepped on him,' Tarchon said.

They were all grinning like idiots. The plan had worked.

When they had come to the river, Ballista had sent the baggage train on ahead. Accompanied by only the one squadron of Thracians commanded by Ovidius, the decurion who had fled the ambush, it would act as a decoy. The main body of troops, leading just twenty of the spare horses, had ridden up the riverbed, and got out of the stream where the trees camouflaged the ground churned up by their exit. By now they would be several miles away to the south-east.

'The Moors won't overhaul them until tomorrow,' Maximus said. 'As you did not tell Ovidius or any of the muleteers which way we are headed, the barbarians will have to waste another day riding back here to pick up our tracks.'

'Things not go well for Ovidius and mule-fellows when caught,' Tarchon said.

'Ovidius will surrender.'

'Should not be a problem,' Maximus said. 'Your man has the heart of a deer.'

'Still good you did not send woman with Ovidius,' Tarchon said.

'A courtesy to Acilius Glabrio,' Maximus said. 'Someone has to keep our young patrician warm at night.'

'We should be going,' Ballista said. 'There is hard riding between us and the column.'

Ballista stood and stretched. He was exultant. The stratagem had bought them a two-day head start. Yet there was another reason for his joy. Arkil had not come up out of Spain with the enemy. There was no danger of meeting the Angles led by his half-brother in battle.

CHAPTER TWENTY-EIGHT

South-east of the City of Tolosa, Aquitania

Seven Days before the Ides of August

THEY WENT EAST FOR three days, over rolling hills that were wood-crested and misted in the mornings as they rode into the rising sun. They crossed shallow rivers and paved roads which lay across their line of march. Avoiding the towns glimpsed in the distance, they moved along dusty tracks through a landscape of cornfields, small villages, isolated villas and rural shrines. When they rested at midday, the white wall of the Pyrenees seemed to hang suspended above the blue horizon to the south. There was a timelessness to their travel. Each ridge revealed another view, in all aspects reminiscent of that seen from the previous height.

They covered perhaps thirty miles a day. Ballista did not want to push the column too hard. There was a long way to go. Even so, a dozen troopers had to be remounted from the spare horses. There was little time to forage. The men ate their rations, the horses the oats from the saddlebags.

Fabius released the pedlar when a local merchant had the misfortune to be apprehended on one of the roads they crossed. The new guide was no more enthusiastic than the old. But their course lay due east, and there was little likelihood of getting lost.

On the third evening the sun was molten gold, the clouds red in the west. On a black hillside below fires burned, as if embers dropped from the sun. The enemy had recovered their trail, were less than a day behind.

The officers sprawled on the ground outside Ballista's tent. It was a weary and somewhat dispirited war council in the darkness.

'The guide says there is a small town to the north.' Fabius respectfully stood in front of his superiors. 'A place called Sostomagus on the road east out of Tolosa.'

'If we go there, everyone for miles will know our position,' Heraclian said.

'It makes no difference,' Acilius Glabrio said. 'The enemy will follow our tracks wherever.'

'After the ground they have made up, their animals must be foundering,' Heraclian said. 'Ours are tired, but not done in. We press on east, outrun them.'

Ballista shifted on the hard ground. 'We are almost out of supplies.'

'The philosopher Diogenes used to masturbate in the market place.' Acilius Glabrio grinned in the gloom. 'He said if only rubbing his stomach would similarly solve hunger.'

'Thank the gods, few soldiers follow the tenets of Cynicism,' Lucius Proculus said. 'Very bad for discipline in the camp.'

'There is no choice.' Ballista spoke to end the debate. 'We have to go to the town. Take what we need, then force march east. The itinerary shows a main road to Narbonensis. We should make good time.'

Even Heraclian accepted the inevitability of the decision.

'Boots and saddles at first light.'

* * *

The paved road from Tolosa to Narbo Martius ran like a white scar through the green countryside. Once in a while, despite all his years in the empire, Roman roads could unsettle Ballista. There was nothing like them in the north. They were about much more than the practicalities of marching legionaries or transporting goods. The huge labour and cost of their construction was a statement. Nothing could stand in the way of Rome. Nature itself was shackled and transformed, must yield to the power of the eternal city.

Ballista realised that nowadays only an outsider, a barbarian like himself, would think such things. The roads had been here for centuries. Whatever the intent of the builders, whatever the effect on the Gauls' savage antecedents, a contemporary born in the empire would just see a road. Every symbol was perfectly blank unless someone invested it with meaning.

The road ran clean through the little town of Sostomagus. Ballista studied the place from a vineyard about a mile away. Three cross-streets branching off the road. A forum in the centre, with temples and a basilica. White houses with red tiled roofs. Smoke rising from the furnaces of a bathhouse. No town walls. The usual tombs along the roads out of town. Everything was utterly unexceptional.

It was still the first hour of the day, but people were about on the roads. Peasants were driving in laden donkeys. No doubt they were thinking how they would spend the meagre coins they got for their produce: pick up some necessities they could not grow or make at home, then maybe treat themselves to a jar or two of wine, perhaps a girl in one of the taverns. Merchants were abroad with carts, their minds set on greater sums and grander schemes, and not troubled by the inherent mendacity of their calling. The philosophers were right. There was something underhand in buying an object cheap, then selling it somewhere else, completely unaltered, for more. When not demonstrating the ease of assuaging sexual desire, Diogenes had roundly denounced such practices. The elaborate carriage of some wealthy family was setting out for Tolosa. At this distance it was tiny and toy-like. They had picked a good day to leave, Ballista thought.

It was time to shatter the placid calm of Sostomagus.

'Everyone clear about their orders?'

The officers said they were.

'Then let us begin the games. And remember, no individual looting, no violence and no raping. Once the town is secured, the Thracians gather supplies, and the Emesenes round up any useful horses. Fabius, you will find a new guide, and Acilius Glabrio, bring the town councillors to me in the forum. This has to be done quickly. I want us to be back on the road after midday.'

Ballista checked the straps on his equipment, waiting until the officers were back with their men. Since Gratus had deserted, there had been no opportunity for the organised gathering of provisions. Ballista had assigned the task to Lucius Proculus and his Thracians. Most probably, the Gaul would do an adequate job. With the baggage train gone, they could carry less, so he did not need to requisition as much.

A single trumpet sounded. The Emesenes rode out from under the vines. They divided into two unequal groups. One went to cut the road to the east. The larger pounded off to the west. Some of the latter would continue north to encircle the entire town.

After the horse archers had gone, leaping fences and hedges, racing through the fields, the Thracians trotted out of the cover. In more sedate fashion they proceeded directly up the drovers' track to Sostomagus.

Ballista watched, his thoughts elsewhere. The unexplained departure of Gratus was deeply troubling. They had known little about the officer, but was he really a traitor? Had he guided the assassin to Ballista's tent? What possible motive could have impelled Gratus? As an Italian, it was difficult to see what inducement might have possessed him to go over to Postumus. When the assassin had struck, Gallienus still had Postumus cornered in Augustodunum, and had been likely to win the war. Even after the emperor was wounded, and withdrew over the Alps, there was no realistic prospect that Postumus would follow, and make a bid for Italy. Gratus was unlikely ever to be able to return home. Postumus was not the answer. Ballista suspected the solution lay at the imperial court, at the door of the Praetorian prefect Volusianus.

A trumpet call from the town announced that Sostomagus had been secured.

Ballista spoke to Pale Horse, and at the sound of his voice the gelding plodded forward. By the time he reached the town, the led horses at his back, the Thracians were about their work. Doors had been kicked in, and troopers were emerging carrying sacks of foodstuffs. The inhabitants, too shocked to protest, let alone resist, stood wondering what deity they had offended to bring this misfortune upon their heads.

In the small forum, the town councillors were corralled in front of the basilica. Acilius Glabrio rode over, accompanied by Fabius.

'Bad news,' the young patrician said. 'They say a column of troops went through, heading east, two days ago.'

Fabius opened his hand. In his palm were some hobnails lost from military boots. There was truth to the story.

'How many?' Ballista asked.

Acilius Glabrio shrugged. 'Thousands and thousands, according to the locals. Numberless infantry and cavalry – you know what rustics are like.'

'Civilians always overestimate.' Ballista looked at Fabius.

'The road is paved,' the scout said. 'No tracks, impossible to say.'

'It has to be the rest of Postumus' men from Spain,' Acilius Glabrio said. 'Once again we are between Scylla and Charybdis.'

Ballista scratched the stubble on his chin. It would have been good to have a bath and a shave.

'There is no time to delay. Pass the word – we will march out before midday.'

The two men saluted.

'And, Acilius Glabrio, would you ask the Lady Vitruvia to attend us?'

Ballista had dismounted to take the weight off Pale Horse's back. He was sitting on the steps of a temple when Acilius Glabrio returned with the woman. He got to his feet politely.

'I trust you are well, madam?'

'Tolerably well, thank you.' Somehow she made even the exchange of pleasantries sound teasing.

'You will be glad to hear that you will no longer have to accompany the column. I have arranged for one of the town councillors to offer you the use of his home. With your servants, you should be comfortable. When you are rested, and the troops gone, you can journey home.'

She seemed far from pleased.

'You drag me halfway across Gaul, and then think to abandon me in this backwater, knowing those dreadful Moorish barbarians will be here tomorrow! There is no telling what they will do.' Her eyes flicked to Acilius Glabrio. 'I understood that I was to be released in a proper town. I will be safe in Narbo.'

'You will be quite safe here,' Ballista said. 'The Moors are under Roman command. They will not be allowed to sack a friendly town. There is much hard riding between us and Narbo, and, should we encounter the enemy, I would be unable to guarantee your safety.'

She stepped closer to the two men, spoke softly. 'Your war is lost. Postumus would welcome both of you to his council.'

'We have family on the other side,' Ballista said, 'as you do here.'

'A shame.' She got on tiptoe to kiss Ballista on each cheek, then, a trifle more lingeringly, Acilius Glabrio. 'Then I will bid you both farewell.'

When she had departed, Ballista turned to Acilius Glabrio.

'I am sorry,' he said.

'Do not be – not on my account.' The patrician appeared to be about to say one thing, before changing it to another. 'Those around Gallienus will not be pleased. If the emperor lives, the war will continue. Holding his mother as a hostage might have undermined the loyalty of Victorinus. The rebel Praetorian prefect is a powerful figure.'

'If we escape, I will face that problem,' Ballista said. 'The mountains of Cebenna are no place for a woman.'

'Then we are not going to Narbo?'

'No, but once they have spoken to Vitruvia, those who are chasing us may think that is where we are bound.'

CHAPTER TWENTY-NINE

The Cebenna Mountains, Aquitania

The Day before the Ides of August

THE LOWER REACHES OF the Cebenna mountains were gentle enough, the air aromatic with thyme and lavender, the path white, its small stones shifting and noisy under the hooves of the horses. Higher, there were great slabs of wooded slopes and steep white valleys between ridges that swept in expansive curves.

They had left Sostomagus before midday, their mounts bulky and misshapen with sacks of provisions, the spare horses almost hidden under their loads of fodder. Eight days of supplies, more if they were rationed. Two squadrons of the Emesenes had remained for a couple of hours to prevent any news leaving the town until they were well on their way. Ballista had led the column several miles down the paved road towards Narbo Martius before turning off north towards the mountains. A pair of scouts had waited to guide the Emesenes.

Ballista looked up through the trees at the peaks; granite fangs tore through the thin soil, and were bared at the sky. It was no wonder that in myth virtue lived on the tops of mountains, inaccessible to man. Hercules had been offered a choice. The path to vice was broad and smooth, that to virtue steep and rocky. Unlike the hero, those destined to remain mortals tended to the easier way. In reality, most men avoided the high places. The foothills of the mountains formed an internal frontier. The empire was a lowland creature – its power ran from city to city along its roads. The roving population of shepherds and foresters in the mountain ranges were untouched by civilisation, as alien as any barbarians in the remote wastes beyond the borders.

On the second day they had come across a camp of charcoal burners. None of them knew Latin. Their dialect was such that Maximus and Ballista, who spoke the Celtic of the far west, struggled. Lucius Proculus from the Alps acted as translator. When they understood that one of them was to act as a guide, the charcoal burners had made no outcry, but their lack of enthusiasm transcended language. Ballista told the guide whom Fabius had taken from Sostomagus that he was free to go. The man had refused to leave the column, convinced he would not make it out of the mountains alive. Without doubt, as soon as he was alone, the wild denizens would rob and murder him.

The charcoal burner was a shaggy, taciturn creature. His attitude to being tied to the saddle-horn of his mount seemed to suggest that it was just the latest hardship in a life of relentless adversity. For three days he had led them through the high country – where he could, above the treeline, across bare plateaus of rock. When necessary they had descended, in single file, down vertiginous valleys, waded mountain streams, and then clambered back up to where the ceaseless wind rang in their ears. Through all the endless windings and detours, their course inclined to the north and the east. Another five days, the charcoal burner claimed, and they would strike the road which ran down to the valley of the Rhône.

Ballista rode next to the charcoal burner. The cold, fretting wind did nothing to dispel the stench of woodsmoke and ingrained filth. They had come out from the trees, and again were on an open tableland of rock. The charcoal burner spoke. Whatever the words meant, they expressed no surprise.

'He says we are being followed,' Lucius Proculus said.

Ballista halted the column, looked where the hairy guide pointed.

A thin, dark line was snaking down into the valley they had so laboriously just negotiated. Too far to discern individuals, there was no doubt that it was a large number of horsemen. Whoever led the pursuit did not lack persistence.

'They will catch us before we get out of the mountains,' Ballista said, 'unless we find a way to stop them.'

* * *

The new moon was a thin, perfect crescent high above the peaks. The heavens were full of stars. There was enough light, although under the trees it was banded and fractured. Shadows broke the outlines of the huddled men. Ballista avoided looking directly at where the campfires still glowed.

There were few places in the mountains where a mounted force could pitch camp. The broad and gently tilted tableland, sparsely dotted with pines, was an obvious choice. Ballista had been waiting since mid-afternoon. The column had ridden on, and he had settled down with Maximus, Tarchon and Eprius, and six of the scouts. Above the dense cover in which they lay was a steep slope, about thirty paces of bare scree, and above that the enemy encampment.

There was only one sentry in sight. Most of the time the Moor sat, sometimes he walked about. There was no timing or plan to his wandering. No one had come to relieve him. Africans were known for their poor discipline. Greeks and Romans would put it down to climate and geography. Hard places bred hard men, and the reverse. The African sun was hot; it thinned the blood, made it flow copiously if wounded. Fear of getting cut made the Africans cowards. The sun heated the blood, encouraged the wearing of loose clothing. Both led to a lecherous nature. Ballista was unsure how the heat could be responsible for the Africans eating dogs, or their reputations for being both savage and treacherous. As a young man serving in Africa, Ballista had never actually seen anyone consume a dog, and he had found the locals no more bloodthirsty or unreliable than other men.

Ballista gazed at the wheeling stars, judged the movement of the moon. Another hour, perhaps two until light. Men were at their lowest before dawn. Ballista got to his feet, crept to the three Emesenes. They saw or heard him coming. There was no need for words. Everything had been prearranged. The archers got up. Their bows were cased to keep the strings dry. They took them out, selected an arrow, slung the quivers on their backs. Quietly they moved to the treeline.

The Moor was sitting, skylined at the top of the scree. A difficult shot in the gloom, but there was only the softest breeze, and the bowmen were skilled. The faint creak of the drawn bows was almost lost in the low soughing of the wind through the foliage.

The Emesenes did not speak, made no discernible signal, but released as one.

The guard looked up, started to rise when he heard the thrumming of the flying shafts. One arrow missed. It vanished into the night. The other two both took him in the chest. The Moor collapsed backwards. If he was not dead by the time he hit the turf, his life ended before he could make a sound.

All around Ballista, figures arose from the forest floor. Dark-clad, faces blacked, they resembled creatures of the night, or shades released from Hades. Wordlessly, they set off.

Both hands were needed to scramble up the scree. The loose stones skittered out from under hands and boots. They clattered, horribly noisy, down the slope. The weight of Battle-Sun dragged at Ballista. At times he slid back in a miniature avalanche. The rocks were sharp under his fingers. He felt the sting of grazes.

At the top, the raiders paused, peering over the lip. The Moors had formed makeshift corrals by lashing ropes around the trees. There were a score or more mounts in each. The ponies looked up, their eyes very white in the dimness.

When they were satisfied no alarm had been raised, the men went forward. They spread out in pairs. Maximus came with Ballista. Together they ducked between the two ropes of a corral. The ponies shifted, their breath riffling. These newcomers smelled of horses, but not from their herd. Although African ponies were said to be ill-natured, these were more inquisitive than alarmed.

Ballista murmured soft words of reassurance as he moved through the ponies.

The Moors were sleeping some twenty paces from the corrals. No one moved in the ramshackle collection of tents and rough shelters. The more orderly lines of the Roman regulars were beyond the Moors.

There was no point in untying the ropes. Ballista drew his dagger. He had no intention of blunting the edge on Battle-Sun. A noble blade was not to be put to such a menial task. As he started to saw the top rope, Maximus set about the lower.

A pony stamped up from behind, nudged Ballista between the shoulders with its forehead. Pausing, Ballista half-turned, brought his face near its muzzle. He breathed into the beast's nostrils.

When the pony was quietened, Ballista went back to his task.

The ropes parted, the two men went back through the animals, and along to another corral. The procedure repeated with quiet efficiency, they moved on through the dark that smelled of warm horses. Each pair of men was to cut the ropes of three corrals.

'Who goes there?'

Ballista whirled at the challenge. A Roman, unhelmeted, but in mail – an officer. Some malign fate had sent him out walking the perimeters of the camp.

'Friend,' Ballista said.

Maximus had disappeared.

'Give the password.'

The knife behind his back, Ballista walked slowly towards the officer.

'It has slipped my mind.'

The officer drew his sword. 'Which troop are you with?'

'The troop of Maximus.'

Ballista stopped just out of reach of the sword.

'There is no . . .'

The officer jerked his blade up into guard. The wrong answer and the blackened face had alerted him.

Ballista brought the knife from behind his body, tossed it into his left hand, drew Battle-Sun.

Seeing the steel, the imminence of the threat, the officer made a fatal mistake. Rather than shout and raise the camp, rather than run, he lunged forward.

Ballista stepped back, turned the thrust with the edge of his sword. Steel rasped down steel. The officer regained his balance, cut backhanded. Again Ballista blocked, kept retreating.

The ponies were becoming alarmed. They were sidling away, hooves pocking the ground. Some threw up their heads, neighed shrilly. Any moment they, or the sounds of fighting, would wake the sleeping troops.

Intent on his swordplay, the officer pressed forward. Ballista continued to give ground.

A shout somewhere in the distance. A fleeting movement off to the left. This had to be ended soon.

'I want him alive,' Ballista said.

Sensing Maximus' approach, the officer whipped around. Ballista stepped in, brought the flat of his blade across the officer's head. The Roman staggered. Ballista kicked him in the back of the knee. The officer went down, dropped his weapon. Maximus landed on top of him, knocking the wind out of the prone man.

'Get him to his feet. Don't tie his arms, not until we have got him down that slope.'

Ballista looked around. The ponies in the next corral were bunching, thoroughly alarmed. Somewhere off were raised voices. The camp was waking.

Ballista ducked into the corral, advanced on the nervous herd. Close up, he waved his arms, shouted. The wild eyes looked at this apparition. They backed away.

From along the line, shouts answered that of Ballista.

Relentlessly hazing the ponies, Ballista whacked the nearest beast on the shoulder. It shaped to bite, then changed its mind. The pony turned, and kicked. Ballista jumped back. Now all the pony wanted was to get away. It charged forward, barging into those in the way. In a heartbeat the entire herd was running, out through where the severed ropes had contained them. Headlong, they crashed into the tents and shelters. Equipment went flying, tents collapsed, sleepy men were barrelled to the ground and stamped under sharp hooves.

The stampede hit the camp like a tidal wave. It is hard to comprehend the chaos some three hundred bolting ponies can inflict upon a slumbering and unsuspecting encampment.

In the corrals that were still intact, knots of ponies were running in tight circles, plunging and rearing, the madness of the wild in their blood. Ballista went to the nearest enclosure. Having severed the ropes with two swift strokes of Battle-Sun, he flattened himself against the trunk of a tree to stop himself being trampled.

Three, perhaps four more corrals had been opened before Maximus caught up with him.

'Enough,' the Hibernian said. 'We must be leaving.'

'The prisoner?'

'At the bottom of the slope with Tarchon and the others. We have to go.'

Ballista surveyed the destruction like a malevolent deity summoned from the night. Then he sheathed his sword and turned and followed his friend back into the darkness from which they had come.

* * *

'Health and great joy!'

All the guests at the dinner returned Ballista's toast.

'A successful foray!'

They drank to that, too, with the exception of the prisoner.

Of course, there had been no pursuit as Ballista's party had left the camp. All the next day, and probably the one after as well, the enemy would have been tending their wounded, mending equipment, and searching the surrounding mountain tracks for lost ponies. Many of the animals they found would have been injured; some they would never find. Those that had not fallen down ravines in their panic would have been spirited away by the shepherds and those other outcasts that haunted the mountains.

Fabius had been waiting with the horses a couple of miles from the devastated camp. There had not been a spare animal, and the prisoner – hands now safely tied – had been mounted behind Tarchon. It was not something that he had appeared to enjoy. They had caught up with the column by mid-morning. They had ridden through the rest of the day, camped, then continued through the next day.

When they had halted on the second evening, Ballista had invited the officers and the prisoner to dinner. There was little to eat or drink. They had been on half rations for days. The bacon and hard biscuit was served without fancy preparation. Felix and the other slave had gone with the baggage train. Ballista hoped Julia would not be annoyed – slaves were expensive, and the loss might seem profligate. Safely in her villa in Sicily, the exigencies of the situation might not be apparent.

Ballista sharply reined in his thoughts. He was getting complacent, letting himself assume that escape was certain. By now the enemy would have regrouped. The majority would still have mounts, and they would again be on the track – a day behind, two at most.

'I trust your head is much recovered?' Ballista asked the prisoner.

'It is greatly improved, thank you.'

The prisoner was a decurion of the Second *ala* of Gauls, bearing the title of *Postumus' Own*, serving in Spain. Quite rightly, he had volunteered no other information about the pursuing force. He had refused to give his word that he would not try to escape, and had spent last night bound and guarded.

'I am glad to hear it.'

'Thank you for the invitation to your table.' The prisoner was a professional officer among his own kind, and courtesy was to be expected. 'When my men overhaul you, I look forward to offering you dinner.'

Ballista smiled. 'If such an eventuality comes about, I will hold you to that. We all will.'

The officers raised their cups and laughed.

'Now, we have an early start and a long ride ahead tomorrow. All the men are already asleep. We should follow their example.' Ballista smiled at the prisoner. 'After all, tonight there is no danger of any alarm.'

The man smiled back.

'In the morning we head south-east. The guide tells me we will be in the valley of the Rhône, near the town of Avennio in three or four days.' Ballista produced a small container. 'But before we retire, I have one last flask of *dulce*. There is so little that it would be an embarrassment in our cups, but, if we drink from the flask, there should be just enough for a swallow each.'

'Long life and happiness.'

As they took their leave, Ballista spoke to Tarchon in an undertone. There was no need to bind the prisoner tonight; no guard should watch over him.

CHAPTER THIRTY

The Foothills above the Rhône Valley, Narbonensis

Thirteen Days before the Kalends of September

For three days the guide had led them north-east. As before, they had gone not along the valley bottoms where rivers ran, but along droves high on the ridges. Sometimes in the mornings, when the sun was still very low, the peaks shone deep red; at others they smoked with white mist.

Of course, the morning after the dinner, the prisoner had gone. The officer had taken a horse. No pickets had been set which might have prevented him. Since then there had been no sign of pursuit. Perhaps this latest stratagem had finally put the hunters off their scent.

On the fourth morning they had reached a huddle of huts and sheds and strange tall structures topped with wooden wheels. There was a stream that ran through the settlement. Its water was an unnatural yellow, its banks stained, as if corroded. The *contubernium* of eight soldiers from the Twenty-Second Legion that guarded the slaves condemned to work below ground were swiftly disarmed. The legionaries had been far from on the alert. As far as they had known the war was won, the forces of Gallienus withdrawn over the Alps. With luck, the column would descend into a peaceful and unsuspecting countryside.

The mining camp provided no remounts. The only beasts were some scrawny pit ponies and a string of donkeys used to take the ore down to the plain. Ballista ordered the requisitioning of all the food and fodder. It would leave every living thing at the mine – the overseers and slaves and beasts of burden – hungry, perhaps worse. Yet the first duty of an officer was the welfare of his command. If he led cavalry, the horses were as important as the troopers.

There was a good road down from the mine through the foothills. Not paved or straight, but at least it had been created by the design and tools of man, not by a combination of nature and the hooves of wild beasts, like the tracks they had been following. Lucius Proculus claimed to know the country where the path would emerge on to the plain. The utility of the charcoal burner exhausted, the monosyllabic and malodorous guide was released. As he had promised, Ballista rewarded him with several gold coins. He granted him a donkey from the mine to ride home as well. It was easy to be generous with other people's goods – although the recipient displayed no conspicuous gratitude.

By late afternoon, when they could see the plain from the last low hills, the sky to the north had turned black. The rising wind was cool on their faces. Ballista and his staff rode ahead, and halted in a group on a rise. The sunlight was retreating to the south. The land around them had turned grey. Veins of lightning pulsed in the towering thunderheads to their left.

'The *melamboreion*,' Lucius Proculus said.

Ballista looked at the Gaul.

'The black wind of the region. The storm will be bad.'

'We will shelter in the woods ahead.'

Ballista waved the column on.

There were spits of rain in the air as they cantered down the road. The first crack of thunder was no louder than a snapped twig. But the world around them now was drained of all colour.

There was no time to make an ordered camp. Fat pellets of rain were cratering the dust like hailstones. A terrible peal of thunder reverberated in their chests, shook the very ground.

They bundled under the trees anyhow. The rain was hissing down through the foliage.

'Every man stay with his mount!' Ballista yelled. 'Distribute the led horses. No man is to hold more than one of the spare animals.'

The orders were shouted down the line.

They dismounted, and hunkered down, holding the reins of their horses. Those who could sat with their back to a tree.

Ballista pulled the hood of his cloak up over his head, sat hunched forward. Water dripped off the end of his nose; somehow it still found its way down his neck.

It was very black under the trees. Night had come early. The rain fell in gusting torrents. Overhead the boughs writhed and groaned, tortured by the storm. Flashes of lightning suddenly illuminated the wood. Trees and horses and men leaped out of the darkness. For a moment they were there, frozen and two-dimensional, their outlines sharp, then they vanished again. The instantaneous crack of thunder accompanied them back into the darkness.

'Epona, the Mothers, hold us safe in your hands.'

In the intervals between the thunder, Ballista could just hear Lucius Proculus praying.

The horses threw their heads, tugged at the reins. They stepped sideways, panic in their minds, ready to tear off into the night.

Ballista spoke soothingly to Pale Horse. The gelding shone like some mythical creature in the gloom.

A terrible tearing crash. Horses screaming and men shouting. Somewhere in the wind-lashed wood a branch or tree had fallen. In a brief lull, horses could be heard running out on the plain.

Ballista pulled down the muzzle of his mount, talked endlessly, the words calm, although devoid of human meaning. The breath of Pale Horse was warm and sweet on his face. Each drew comfort from the other.

Away to the south, a yellow flame blossomed where lightning had struck a tree. Ballista and everyone else watched it burn through the ceaseless nocturnal vigil.

The rain lessened in the night, the wind weakened. Yet dawn was late coming.

Chilled, soaked to the skin, Ballista still talked to his horse.

Finally the storm passed. It was no more than drizzling when the light returned. Ragged dark clouds, still trailing tendrils of rain, fled south across a wan, washed-out sky.

They levered themselves to their feet, aching with cold and wetness, their limbs cramping. With the stiff gait of octogenarians, they led the horses out of the trees.

The sun came up, casting long and canted shadows, less bedraggled than their owners.

'Each *contubernium*, get a fire lit. Hobble the horses. Two men watch over them, the others cut firewood.'

The orders given, Ballista leaned wearily against Pale Horse's shoulder. The gelding turned its head, nuzzled his arm.

The drenched bracken steamed in the sun.

'Do you think there will ever be a day when the sun does not rise?' Lucius Proculus said.

'Ragnarok, the end of days.'

The Gaul regarded Ballista, uncomprehending.

'The stars will fall, and the wolf Fenris will devour the sun.'

Lucius Proculus nodded. 'Like the flood of Deucalion, when the gods washed the world clean. A cyclical destruction, so that mankind can start again free of sin.'

'No, Ragnarok is the death of gods and men.'

The Gallic officer looked appalled. 'Nothing survives?'

Ballista shrugged. 'In some tellings one couple survive, hidden in the tree of life.'

It was difficult to get the sodden wood to burn. Great, choking clouds of smoke billowed around.

When the fires had caught, they removed the hobbles and tethered the horses in ordered lines instead. They unsaddled them, removed their tack. Although carried on the spare horses in waxed cloth, much of the hay was ruined. Finding some from the middle of the bundles that was dry, they gave a little to their mounts.

Ballista dried Pale Horse himself, although both Maximus and Tarchon offered. Starting at the neck, as always, he rubbed hard and vigorously back and forward with one wisp of hay after another. A horse-brush should never be rubbed against the direction of the hair, but a wisp caused no discomfort or harm. The familiar repetitive motion eased his own muscles, warmed him as well. He was sweating under his damp clothes by the time he was finished.

They gave the horses a proper feed and watered them. Now, at long last, the men could tend to their own pitiful condition. They all stripped naked. Improvising lines with ropes, they hung their clothes to dry. The decurions made sure that the saddles and horse furniture were not too near the fires. They would harden and crack if the heat was too intense. The officers were less concerned about the men's own clothes scorching. Finally, they took a drink of sour wine, and chewed army biscuit, as they cooked their bacon. Decurions roared at the few stupid enough to use the tips of their swords to hold the meat in the fires. What sort of fucking soldiers were they? Did they not realise the blade would go brittle? What the fuck use was a trooper with a sword snapped in half?

Ballista sat on a milestone beside the road.

Heraclian marched over as if on parade. Unlike among some peoples, nakedness was not an issue for the Romans. They bathed communally. But here, in the middle of the country, without clothes Heraclian looked ridiculous. His face and neck and forearms were tanned mahogany, but the rest of him was as pale as a creature from under a stone.

It dawned on Ballista that he must look much the same, perhaps yet more absurd with his straggly, half grown back long hair.

Heraclian had a flask in his hand.

'I saved some decent stuff – smoked wine from Massilia. Should put some life in us.'

Ballista stood, thanked him, and took the flask.

Heraclian nodded at the milestone. 'Think he is worthy of being emperor?'

Postumus' name and titles were inscribed on the stone. Ballista took a drink. There were herbs in the wine.

'Are any of them? You could inscribe all the good emperors that have ever ruled on one signet ring. There was a tactlessness about Heraclian. For just a few days, Ballista had worn the purple. Heraclian probably had forgotten. On reflection, that was good.

'A strange sight.' Heraclian gestured at the men. Squatting, naked and muddy, amid their ramshackle possessions, wreathed in smoke, they resembled some troglodyte tribe not long emerged from their caves. 'Not where I expected to end up when I commanded the emperor's horse guards.'

Ballista passed back the drink.

'Thought it was all over when I was attached to this column. Thought some of those fuckers whispering at court had brought me down – me and my whole family. You cannot trust anyone around the emperor, not even old Volusianus. Fucking vipers, the lot of them. The court stinks of corruption. Nearer you are to the emperor, the fouler the stench.'

Heraclian paused his diatribe to take a drink.

'Thought I was being got out of the way, maybe a prelude to something worse. But then, before we left, my brother gets appointed governor of Thrace.'

'Then do you know why you were sent?' Ballista said.

Heraclian caught himself before he answered. He looked at Ballista, then at the milestone again.

'Do you think the empire is any more than skin-deep? One day *Romanitas* will fall away, be forgotten?'

'What?'

'This province has been Roman for centuries, and that milestone is in Gallic leagues.'

Heraclian drained the flask, shook himself like a dog. 'Best go and see my little Syrians are not buggering each other too much. Be back with the morning report.'

When they came, Ballista was fully clothed, as were the rest. The reports were not too bad. In the night a number of animals had got away, were now lost beyond recall. Four troopers, two from each unit, were added to the list of stragglers. Where in Hades did men go to absent themselves without leave in the middle of a tempest? There were four hundred and sixty-three Emesenes, officers and men, still with the standards, three hundred and one Thracians. Only thirty-six horses remained on leading reins. With what they had taken from the mining camp, the men had food for three days, the animals fodder for just two. Lucius Proculus assured them that they could get replenishments in the valley. There were no towns, but many villas, farms and villages.

The meeting was breaking up when Fabius arrived. One of the scouts had seen a rider watching them from one of the low hills to the south. The horseman had spurred off before he could be taken.

It might be nothing: a local landowner out riding the further reaches of his estates, hunting, or checking the damage caused by the wild night. Far from the towns, it might be a brigand. There was no telling. Still, they had best be moving. The order was given to mount.

When he had tightened Pale Horse's girths, Ballista took in the morning. A veil of thin dark clouds was moving south;

through them could be seen high, ribbed white clouds, and beyond them the perfect, pale blue of the sky. The storm had passed. The weather was unsettled, but today was going to be a fine day.

With the four senior officers, Ballista's bodyguards and standard-bearer, there were seven hundred and seventy-one effectives all counted. They were not out of supply. The column was not a force to be taken lightly, but they were still deep in enemy territory. The Rhône and the Alps had to be crossed. They were a long way from safety.

CHAPTER THIRTY-ONE

The Rhône Valley, Narbonensis

Twelve Days before the Kalends of September

THEY RODE DOWN FROM the foothills and out on to the rolling country before the plain. They went often at a canter. The halts were infrequent and brief. Before they entered the first of the two farms they came across, the column stopped, and Ballista had them furl the standards, binding them up with nondescript material, as if to protect them from the weather. In the farmyards they paid handsomely for the provisions they took, told the inhabitants they were a patrol of Postumus' men. They had been in the high country hunting *bacaudae*. Now they were bound south to apprehend a band of the brigands infesting the Louerion mountains. As a Gaul, Lucius Proculus did the talking, distributed the money.

Neither the generosity nor the subterfuge might prevent the inhabitants of the farms guessing their true nature, and spreading the news of their presence abroad. In any event, the rider from the morning might be spurring off to raise the alarm. This was a forced march. They had to be across the Rhône before the countryside was raised against them, before troops could come down from Postumus' army at Augustodunum, or the troops that had pursued them from the Pyrenees march up from Avennio.

In the late afternoon they pulled off the road, and into a sheltered valley that Fabius had found. Here, sheltered from prying eyes, they saw to the horses, and rested for three hours. As the light failed, they regained the road, and went on at a walk.

Men and horses were tired. It had been a gruelling campaign. They had a long day's ride behind them, and there had been little sleep in the storm the night before. They went slowly. Many of the riders slumped, asleep in their saddles, only waking if their horse stumbled. When the steady gait resumed, they fell asleep again. Each man was isolated by fatigue. The close order of the march relaxed. Riders began to fall behind. There was no point in setting a rearguard; no troopers or mounts were fresh enough for the task.

Ballista was more exhausted than most. The duties of a commander demanded that he rise before his men, turn in after them, and Ballista had not recovered the night's sleep that he had lost raiding the enemy horse lines. Twice he found himself thankful for the four high, projecting horns of a Roman saddle. Both times, only they prevented him toppling to the ground.

The night had clouded over. There was no danger of rain, but it was dark, the moon and stars obscured. The unmade road was a pale line in the blackness. Roads ran through Ballista's thoughts. Real roads that he had travelled: the desert track to Arete in the east, and the mountain path up into the Caucasus. Roads taken only in allegory or cautionary tales: the one to virtue, walked by Hercules, and the one to vice, that ultimately led to Tartarus and eternal punishment.

Ballista woke when Pale Horse put his head down to graze. They were in a stand of trees. Under the timber the night was darker still. They were alone. Nothing to be heard but the susurration of the breeze through the broad-leafed foliage.

Trying not to give way to a childish surge of panic, Ballista gently pulled up Pale Horse's head. No, there was no point in riding until he knew which direction to take. He let the gelding drop his head again, carry on cropping the grass. Ballista peered all around through the trunks in the stygian gloom. There! Where the trees ended was a wan path through the blackness.

It was one thing to find the road, quite another, disorientated in the dark, to tell from which direction it had been approached. Ballista looked both ways. He stilled his breathing, cocked his head, the better to hear. Nothing. Seven hundred and more riders swallowed up by the night. He stared at the sky, willing the clouds to part and give a glimpse of the stars. The heavens remained hidden.

This was ridiculous, being unable to tell east from west. Ballista dismounted, stiffly. Although Pale Horse was not given to bolting, he held the reins tight. Alone and lost was bad enough. On foot, things would be much worse.

Painfully – his back ached dreadfully – he got down on one knee. With the palm of his hand he felt for hoofprints. They were overlaid, stamped on top of one another, hard to distinguish.

Ballista led Pale Horse to the edge of the path where fewer riders may have gone, where this palimpsest of equine voyaging might be easier to read. His fingers traced an individual hoofprint. To be certain, he traced the outline of another – the toe and the heel. Now he had no doubt which way the column had gone.

Rejuvenated by relief – all aches and pains vanished, as if through the intervention of Asclepius or some other healing god – Ballista vaulted back into the saddle. With a slack bridle, he put Pale Horse to a smart canter, trusting the instincts of the gelding to keep them safe and on the path.

Should any doubt have persisted about the route, it was ended when Pale Horse came to a halt of his own accord. The gelding stood gazing into the dark, ears pricked. Another horse stood just off the track. At its feet was a huddled shape. Man and beast were fast asleep. In the fog of his weariness, Ballista would have ridden straight past them, unnoticing.

Ballista had to kick the Thracian to wake him. Having given him a leg-up, they rode on in silence. No fewer than a dozen times they stopped and roused others, both Thracians and Emesenes, slumbering where they had fallen. The mounts of three of the troopers had wandered away. The unhorsed were taken up behind their compatriots.

No one hailed or challenged them when they came to the tail of the column. Some of the troopers had tied themselves to their saddles. As defenceless as babies, their heads rested in their horses' manes.

A sullen, slate-grey band on the eastern horizon marked the coming day. Below it was luminescence of water. They had reached the Rhône.

* * *

They rested in a wood, set back from the river, throughout the next day. Lucius Proculus explained their position. They were between Colonia Valentia, about thirty miles to the north, and Arausio, rather further to the south. Both were on the far bank. There was too much traffic on the river, and the road connecting the towns was too busy, to cross unnoticed during daylight. There were no bridges, but some five miles towards Arausio was a ferry.

Having rubbed down and fed the horses, the men slumbered by their heads. They lit no fires. Those who woke did not stray beyond the confines of the wood. Ballista slept until midday, then sat under a tree with Maximus and Tarchon. They watched the broad waters roll past and the boats and ships plying up and down. The clouds had gone, and it was warm and peaceful. Someone had once told Ballista that there was a fish in the river called a clupaea. During the increase in the moon it was white, but when the moon was waning it turned altogether black. There was a stone in its head which cured quartan agues.

'It was strange what Heraclian was saying after the storm,' Maximus said. 'Sure, I was convinced that he was the traitor.'

'Angry man, bitter as a rejected woman, but too fuck-pig stupid,' Tarchon said. 'Treachery more oleaginous trade. My wager was Acilius Glabrio or the Gaul Lucius Proculus, both very slippery.'

'Hard to see why Gratus would have gone over to Postumus,' Maximus said.

'Money,' Tarchon said. 'Steals soul of man, makes him a stranger to honour. My cousin . . .'

Maximus ignored the reminiscence of old Caucasian betrayal, turned to Ballista.

'You will be thinking Volusianus was behind Gratus and the assassin.'

'It seems probable.'

'That will make for an odd homecoming. If we get home.'

In the mid-afternoon they roused the camp. The horses were fed early, and the men greased and checked their equipment. At dusk they moved out.

It was a fine late summer evening, the vault of the heavens studded with stars, the moon a luminous sickle. They drove up wildfowl from the banks, but there was no one but themselves to note their flight.

They turned a bend, and the river was in front of them – flat and sleek and blacker than the ragged rim of trees and the square, box-like house of the ferryman on the opposite bank. The flat-bottomed barge was moored at the landing by the dark and shuttered house.

Lucius Proculus cupped his hands around his mouth and hallooed across the stream.

There was no response.

The Gaul tried more times.

Still nothing.

Ballista told a trumpeter to sound reveille.

At last a yellow rectangle of light from a doorway.

'Who wants to cross?'

The figure holding the lantern sounded suspicious. An isolated ferry house might be a target for the *bacaudae*. Travellers paid for their crossing in silver.

'The *Second Ala Gallica Postumiana* and the *Third Ala Emesenorum Sagittariorum* out of Spain.'

If they did not speak, the Thracians might pass as the regular unit of Gauls that had chased the column, but the Emesene archers were easterners at a glance. A mixture of truth with fiction might allay suspicions. A ferryman on the Rhône would not know what units were stationed in Spain.

'Hold your horses!'

They could hear the ferryman laughing at his own joke clear across the river.

Other dark shapes moved down to the ferry. Soon, those waiting heard the splashing of the barge being punted across. Circles of phosphorescence showed where the poles broke the surface.

The ferry came up suddenly out of the dark. A rope trailing through the water ran through iron rings on stanchions on the side of the vessel. At the landing stage one of the three ferrymen jumped ashore, and secured the rope to a bollard.

'Where are you bound?' the chief ferryman asked.

'Down south – there are reports of bandits up in the Louerion mountains.' Lucius Proculus quickly changed the subject. 'Harder to wake you than the dead.'

'No one crosses at night. Not unless they are on official business. Only now and then we have to turn out for soldiers like you.'

The ferry was roomy and could hold thirty men and horses at a time. Even so, it would take at least twenty-four trips before both units were across. Ballista judged the course of the moon. Some ten hours of darkness remained.

'The men will haul on the rope. You ferrymen, give them their instructions. A gold coin each on top of the usual fee, if you get us over before dawn.'

'Best get started,' the leader of the ferrymen said. 'Have to punt across in daytime. The rope would foul the merchantmen going up to Lugdunum. The ones coming down as well.'

He wheezed with mirth. Ballista hoped his flow of humour would not continue through the long night ahead.

Ballista led Pale Horse down first. The gelding was untroubled when his hooves rattled on the boards. Some of the horses that followed tried to play up at the unusual sound. They stamped and snorted at the motion as the barge got underway. The troopers cursed. This was going to be a long and vexatious endeavour.

The red fingers of dawn were in the sky when the final horses clattered off onto the eastern bank. Ballista paid the ferrymen.

The jocular foreman looked at the highest denomination in his hand.

'It makes you laugh . . .' He paused for effect.

Tired and eager to be gone, Ballista very much doubted that whatever was coming would have that effect.

'Postumus hates the guts of Gallienus. He chopped off the head of his son. But he has never tried to stop his subjects accepting silver coins boasting the virtues of Gallienus.'

Ballista had not thought of the words and images on the coins.

'*Piety, Virtue, Liberality* . . . all the usual bollocks – see dozens of them, we do. Mind you, not so many of gold coins like these.'

Was the ferryman becoming suspicious?

'There again, don't see enough gold to know!'

No, it had just been the setting up of another laboured witticism.

'Enough to know – oh, that is a good one, if I say so myself! Oh, ha, ha!'

Smiling politely, Ballista wondered what to do. If the real Second Gallica and the Moors were not haring off to Avennio, but instead had resumed the pursuit, it would be best to destroy the ferry.

'Is it true those easterners there all fuck their mothers?'

The ferryman's attempts at humour obviously were not limited by discretion, perhaps not even by self-preservation.

But if the ferry was destroyed, what to do with its servants?

'Relentlessly,' Maximus said. 'A regular Oedipus, every one of them. Although the blind ones are of very little use.'

'You have got a funny accent.'

'Sure, I was on the stage before I joined the cavalry.'

'Really?'

'No.'

Irritating though the foreman was, Ballista could not bring himself to order the killing of the ferrymen. Besides which, once they had thrown the bodies in the river, their absence, and the wrecked barge, would draw attention.

Acilius Glabrio announced the column was ready. Ballista bade an amiable farewell to the ferrymen.

They rode south. Lucius Proculus knew of a track that left the road and went north-east into the mountains, where it joined the road up from Colonia Valentia. Two days from that junction, the road forked. There they could choose between the northern pass through the range of the Matrona, or the southern, which ran through the Alpes Maritimae – indeed, through the wild estates owned by Lucius Proculus himself.

It took two days, plodding upwards, to reach the road. On the third day they rode across a bridge over a chasm at the foot of Mount Gaura, and descended into the high valleys towards Mount Seleucus.

And there, in that remote place, their luck deserted them.

Drawn up across the road were the enemy. Three thousand and more, they filled the vale. In the centre of the array stood four hundred tall men clad in mail. All his life Ballista had known the standard that flew above their heads. A white horse on a green field – the banner of the Himlings of Hedinsey.

CHAPTER THIRTY-TWO

Mount Seleucus in the Alps

Seven Days before the Kalends of September

'I KNEW YOU WOULD COME.'

'What are you doing here?' Ballista said to his half-brother.

'A man has to be somewhere.'

When it was dark, Ballista with Maximus and Tarchon had gone to the enemy camp. They had walked openly, straight up the road to the Angles. A warrior on sentry duty had challenged them. Ballista had given his name: Dernhelm, the son of Isangrim. The sentry had brought them to Arkil.

'What happened to your hair?'

'A story for another time,' Ballista said. 'How did you find yourself here?'

'We were fighting the Franks in the Pyrenees when the command came. An officer called Julianus organised the expedition into Gaul – the four hundred of us, a thousand from the Seventh Legion, another thousand auxiliary infantry, the same number of regular cavalry, and about four thousand Moors.'

Arkil paused, considering.

'There was something strange from the start. Julianus knew about you before we had come down from the mountains. More than one messenger arrived in the night. You were keeping untrustworthy company.'

Again, Arkil stopped to consider his words. Ballista had forgotten the weightiness of his half-brother's conversation.

'Anyway,' Arkil resumed, 'Postumus had given his word that we would not be called on to fight our kinsmen. When most of the cavalry doubled back, looking to ambush your column, we continued east with the rest of the troops. Our orders were to help Vocontius Primus, the *Dux* of the Alps, secure the passes to Italy. That is why we are here with Julianus and the legionaries and some of the Moors. The auxiliaries and the rest of the African horsemen are holding the passes to the south.'

Arkil sighed deeply. 'Something in my bones told me that it was only delaying the inevitable.'

'Where is Vocontius?'

'Somewhere in the mountains. A nondescript Roman prefect was here looking for him yesterday.'

'What was the name of the prefect?'

'He spoke privately with Julianus.' Arkil shrugged, dismissing the matter. 'Things did not go well for our brother Morcar when you were in the north.'

'It was Morcar that betrayed your war band to Postumus.'

'Why?'

'I was away in the empire – he wanted you gone, too. Easier to supplant our father.'

'Morcar was always the worst of us.'

'What happens now?'

Before Arkil could answer, a tall young warrior stepped forward.

'We have given our sword-oath to Postumus.'

Ballista regarded him. The warrior was not yet thirty. There was something familiar about him. Pleasant-featured, but throughout the conversation he had been radiating hostility.

'When I was young, a puppy did not bark in front of grown dogs,' Ballista said.

Arkil looked embarrassed.

'Kadlin's boy, Starkad.'

That explained why he looked familiar. Ballista could see something of Kadlin in his face.

The young warrior glowered at Ballista.

'I was sorry to hear of the death of your father,' Ballista said. 'Holen of the Wrosns was a good man. We were friends.'

Starkad made a furious gesture, as if this was some sort of insult or untruth.

'You were not there to judge,' Ballista said.

Some strange *daemon* seemed to inhabit Kadlin's son.

'Starkad is right,' Arkil said. 'We gave our sword-oath to Postumus.'

'An oath under duress is no oath at all,' Ballista said.

'The words of a *nithing*,' Starkad snapped. 'You have broken your vows repeatedly.'

Ballista rounded on Starkad. 'For the memory of your father, I will overlook your words. And for your mother.'

'Don't mention my mother!'

Arkil stepped between them.

'Starkad, do the rounds of the sentries.'

The young warrior did not move. 'Julianus should be told that the *oathbreaker* is in our camp.'

'Do not insult . . .' Arkil checked himself. 'Do not insult the Atheling Dernhelm.'

Arkil drew himself up; his next words were forceful, but controlled.

'Julianus will not discover that Dernhelm is here. You will not tell him, nor will any Angle.'

Ballista remembered the natural authority of his half-brother. Arkil had possessed it when they were young. Some said it ran in the blood of the Woden-born Himlings.

Starkad turned on his heel, and stalked away.

Arkil put his hand on Ballista's shoulder, almost a gesture of consolation.

'All these years, and we meet under arms. Still, never let it be said that I would deny my brother a drink.'

* * *

The valley was broad and green and flat. It was bordered by steep slopes, bare at the bottom, timbered higher up. From the crests jutted strange isolated stacks of pale grey rock. The shallow and braided channels of a mountain stream ran under the incline to the right.

The enemy were drawn up in battle array. The Angles were in the centre, four deep. Each warrior occupied a frontage of a couple of paces to give him room to use his long sword. On either side stood some five hundred legionaries. They were closer packed, big shields almost touching. Even so, the more than two hundred African light horse on the flanks had a lot less space to manoeuvre than they would like.

Julianus, the Roman general, was taking the auspices on a low rise to the rear. Obviously the liver of the first sheep had been unsatisfactory, because another was being led up.

There was no priest with the *alae* of the Thracians and Emesenes. Ballista had told them the plan. They would have to take the favour of the gods on trust.

The valley faced south. As the sun appeared over the crest to their left, the Emesenes on either wing ceased stringing their bows and preparing their quivers. They blew kisses to the pale disc, prostrated themselves before their risen god. Emesa was the city of the solar deity Elagabal. The Thracians, with Ballista in the centre, stolidly continued checking their equipment and tightening the girths of their horses.

Ballista looked at the big standard flying above the Angles. The white horse of Hedinsey on a field of green. He remembered the first time that he had fought under that banner – the storm of a settlement of the tribe of the Rugii. Sixteen winters old, it had been hard for Ballista to hide his fear. He was scared now. He had never thought he would face that standard on the field of battle.

Silently, Ballista went through his pre-battle ritual: right hand to the dagger on his right hip, pull it an inch or so out of its sheath, then snap it back; left hand on the scabbard of his sword, right hand pull Battle-Sun a couple of inches free, then push the blade back; finally, right hand touch the amber healing stone tied to the scabbard. Courage was not the absence of fear, but its mastery.

In a sense the expedition would end here. Victory or defeat, by nightfall one of those actors would be posturing on the stage. Like an epic poem, the journey was circular in its composition: the Alps, Vesontio, Augustodunum, the Rhône valley, Aquitania, the Cebenna mountains, and back through the meadows of the Rhône to the Alps.

The intestines of the second sacrificial animal must have been propitious. Conspicuous in a scarlet cloak, Julianus was cantering along behind the line of his troops. A last few words of encouragement. Ballista had already said all he had to say.

Ballista regarded his own order of battle. The left flank of the Emesenes was commanded by Heraclian, the right by Acilius Glabrio. There was little cause for concern. The horse archers were hardly outnumbered by the enemy cavalry. They had room to wheel and feint. Their composite bows easily outranged the javelins of the Moors. If it came to close combat, the Emesenes were disciplined soldiers wearing light mail shirts. The Africans possessed neither of those advantages.

The centre under Ballista himself was altogether different. Little more than three hundred armoured horsemen were ranged against some fourteen hundred heavy infantry. Odds of worse than four to one against. One charge would have to decide the issue. No second chance. The outcome would depend on timing.

Trumpets rang out from the ranks of the enemy. They were answered from Ballista's lines. The Emesenes and Thracians mounted. There was always a strange complicity about battle. Unless an ambush, both sides had agreed to fight – although, like now, one force might do so with reluctance.

About three hundred paces separated the lines. It was as if each waited for the other to make the first move, to take the step from which there could be no return.

Ballista hefted the javelin in his fist, then nodded to the trumpeter behind him to sound the prearranged signal.

The Emesenes trotted forward in silence.

Whooping, the Moors set their ponies to answer the challenge.

The mail-clad phalanx of the enemy infantry did not move. Julianus was no fool. Momentum must be sacrificed for cohesion. Men on foot should stand to receive a cavalry charge. Let the Angles absorb the impact, then, when the horsemen were brought to a standstill, the legionaries could turn in, overwhelm them with numbers, haul them from the saddle, and butcher them on the ground.

The first volleys from the Emesenes were arcing through the air. Ballista saw a few Moors tumble from their mounts. The unscathed belaboured their ponies to close the gap. The Africans needed to get within range quickly. There was nothing worse than being shot down while unable to hit back. Ballista dismissed the flanks from his mind. The issue would not be decided by the skirmishing light horse.

'At the walk, advance!'

The heavy tread of horses on the powdery surface of the track, a deeper thud from those on the sward.

Ideally, cavalry did not break into a gallop until the final fifty paces.

'Steady! Hold the formation!'

Lucius Proculus was on Ballista's right at the apex of the wedge. The standard-bearer of the Third was behind the prefect, Eprius at Ballista's back. Maximus and Tarchon were close. The troopers rode knee to knee, javelins in their right hands, shields in their left. They had their orders, knew what was expected of them.

Two hundred paces.

Ballista saw the white horse on the green field billowing in the breeze. Other banners flew over the Angles. Among the many dragon standards of the leaders was the red of Arkil, and the white of Starkad that mirrored Ballista's own. It saddened Ballista that, whatever the Fates had spun, there would be fewer warriors under those brave banners tomorrow.

One hundred.

'To the trot!'

Now the earth trembled with their progress; the air rang with the rattle of their arms.

The gleam of helmets over the round, bright painted shields. The flash of swords. The fierce and bearded faces of warriors that had seldom, if ever, known defeat.

Fifty.

Still the Angles stood like statues.

'Charge!'

Pale Horse went straight to the gallop. The wind hissed through the metal jaws of the *draco* writhing above Ballista. The riders jostled and clattered, as they fought to maintain the formation.

Thirty paces out, a northern war horn high above the din.

The wall of shields parted. The standards inclined left and right. An opening appeared, like a sea parting at the word of some nameless god.

Ballista rode through, the horsemen thundering in his wake.

When they were clear, Ballista went to the left, Lucius Proculus to the right. Almost as if on a parade ground, the troopers divided.

Reining back to a canter, Ballista brought his followers around in a wide curve to the rear of the unit of legionaries that stood to the east of the Angles.

'Halt! Close up, dress the line!'

The Seventh Legion was not one of those hardened by endless campaigning on the Rhine or Danube. Called the *Twin*, *Loyal* and *Fortunate*, it had few battle honours on its standards. But in recent years its soldiers had fought the Frankish and Moorish raiders that had descended on Spain. They were no callow recruits unused to the emergencies of battle. Trumpets called, centurions bellowed, and the rear two ranks about-turned towards the unexpected threat.

Ballista let horses and men gather their breath.

A moment of stillness, the calm in the eye of the storm. Away on the wings, clouds of dust, distant shouts, where Syrian and African horsemen brought one another destruction.

'Prepare to charge!'

Ballista's words were swallowed in a terrible, booming, wordless roar. The ranks of the legionaries shifted like barley in the path of a storm. The long blades of the Angles caught the sun as they chopped into the flank of the Romans.

Fortune may have deserted the legionaries of the Seventh, yet they were still loyal. Discipline held. They wavered, but did not run. In their midst, the red-cloaked figure of Julianus urged them to stand firm.

'Charge!'

Ballista aimed Pale Horse at Julianus.

Two ranks of legionaries stood between Ballista and his quarry.

Ten paces out, Ballista hurled his javelin. The legionary at the front took it on his shield, but the force sent him staggering. He collided with the man behind. Ballista yanked back on the reins. Pale Horse skidded to a stop, lashed out with his front hooves. They dashed the entwined legionaries to the ground.

Ballista drew Battle-Sun as the warhorse hurdled the sprawling soldiers.

Julianus desperately unsheathed his sword. He slashed wildly. Ballista blocked with the edge of his blade. Rolling his wrist, he opened the guard of his foe. With calm precision, he thrust. The motion of Pale Horse behind his arm, the blow punched clean through the gilded armour guarding the chest of Julianus.

The horns of the saddle held Julianus upright for a moment. Then, the scent of blood in its nostrils, his horse reared, and the officer toppled down where hooves and hobnailed boots stamped.

It was too much. Assailed from two sides, their commander slain, the legionaries broke and ran.

'Let them go!'

Ballista felt weary, sickened with the slaughter.

Victory, wearing a mask from tragedy, capered across the field.

CHAPTER THIRTY-THREE

The Pass of the River Stura, Alpes Maritimae

The Kalends of September

'YOU DID NOT KNOW?'

'I had no idea.' Ballista did not look at Starkad, as if a glance might shatter the fragile truce between them.

They rode up the mountain track, side by side at the head of the column, only Fabius and the scouts in front.

'We were to be married. Then the centurion came and demanded a hostage. My father chose me. I never wanted to leave.'

Ballista kept his eyes on the way ahead. None of this was easy.

'I had been in Rome for a year when I heard that Kadlin was married to Holen, that there was a son. The news arrived together. There was no reason to suspect.'

'No one told you when you were in the north last year?'

'The night before I left, your mother came to see me. If Kadlin intended to tell me then, she did not.'

Now Ballista looked at Starkad. That first air of familiarity was explained. There was something of Kadlin about the tall young Angle with the shoulder-length hair, but in many ways it was like looking at a younger version of himself.

Starkad did not return the gaze.

Ballista looked back at the road. He felt a terrible sadness, for himself and Kadlin, for the son he had not known he had, and also for Holen, the friend of his youth who had raised another man's son as his own. He very much wanted to ask how Holen had treated Starkad; had he acted as a father? How had Oslac, Kadlin's second husband, behaved as a stepfather? The words would not come.

'There was much talk of your exploits – the Angle that had killed two emperors, defeated the Persian King of Kings.' Starkad ran his palm down his horse's neck. 'It pained me, because I knew.'

'Did Kadlin tell you?'

'No. There were whispers when I was a child. All my life you were a ghost in the hall. Arkil told me when I gave him my sword-oath.'

'Arkil is a good man.'

They rode in silence for a time. Ballista tried to frame the things that he had to say.

'You have hard decisions to make.'

'Exchange a stepfather for a stepmother?' Starkad grinned without mirth.

'You are welcome in my house.'

'Would all the household be welcoming?'

Ballista took a deep breath. 'I am still a hostage. My other sons are as much hostages. I would have you stay, but, should the emperor discover your parentage, you, too, would be held as a pledge for the behaviour of our people.'

Starkad looked sharply at Ballista. 'Even now you will not acknowledge me?'

'I would like to above all things, but, while you are in the empire, for your freedom, even your safety, I can not.'

'For three years I have dreamed of returning home.'

Ballista did not say that he had suffered the same dream for far longer.

'Then you will not stay?'

'My mind is set on leaving.'

Ballista had to master himself before he could speak.

'When you go back to the north with Arkil, there is another decision you must make. I would be proud for the Angles to know that you are my son. Yet, once it is declared that you are a Himling, you become a threat to others who would inherit the throne.'

'No one said that life was without danger.'

Ballista nodded. 'I will give you a letter to present to your grandfather. When you return to Hedinsey, you can trust Arkil – also Eadwulf.'

'"Evil-child"?'

'Eadwulf is no longer a child, and the epithet was unearned. Trust Arkil and Eadwulf, the other Himlings less so. The court of any ruler is a nest of vipers.'

'Your father?'

'A ruler has to look to the good of all his subjects, not an individual.'

The young man mulled this over.

'Will the emperor ever let you return?'

'It is unlikely.' The words caught in Ballista's throat. 'And I am not the man that I was. Half a lifetime among the Romans has changed me. Last year showed that there are those among the Angles that would not want me back.'

They relapsed into an awkward silence. It was five days since the battle, and this was the first time that they had spoken together without others present. There was still much that had not been said.

After the legionaries had broken, the column had remained at Mount Seleucus for another day. They had tended their wounded, buried their dead. A herald had come, and they had returned the enemy, both living and dead, that had been left on the field.

The night before the battle, Ballista had had to argue hard to win over Arkil. An oath given under duress was not binding. Postumus had sworn the Angles would not have to fight their kinsmen. The Angles of Hedinsey were allied to Gallienus. That emperor was more likely than Postumus to let the warriors return home. Arkil was an honourable man; the position had troubled him, but in the end his duty to the warriors that followed him had led him to agree.

The column was approaching a narrow defile. Fabius and the scouts rode into it, looking about. For four days since Mount Seleucus they had ridden east, the long and thin line of Angles, Thracians and Emesenes winding through the mountains. Where the path forked, they had taken the southerly route into the Alpes Maritimae. They had passed the small settlements of Rigomagus and Mustiae Calmes. The enemy had followed, but at a distance, made no move to interfere with their passage.

Lucius Proculus said that in another couple of days they would reach a place called Pedona. There they would turn north. Another day's ride would bring them down into the foothills. Two more and they would come out onto the plains of northern Italy.

They would go to Mediolanum. Gallienus would have gone there to recover from his wound. In that pleasant city,

Ballista hoped there would be time to get to know Starkad before the Angles began the long journey to the Suebian Sea. And where would Ballista himself be sent? Would Gallienus finally grant his wish to retire to Sicily? Or would he remain caught in the machinations of Volusianus? The Praetorian prefect had not wanted Ballista to return. Would Volusianus concoct another mission, or find some other way to be rid of Ballista?

The steady clop of hooves echoed back from the walls. The track had narrowed. The ravine was little more than thirty paces wide, and a small mountain stream ran under the incline to the right.

A handful of stones skittered down onto the path ahead.

Ballista looked up. The walls of the canyon were not tall, but they were sheer, banded rock. Only here and there a hardy pine clung to a tiny ledge. A movement at the very top. To the left he saw the silhouettes of figures against the sky.

'Back!'

Ballista turned Pale Horse.

'Get back out of the ravine!'

The column was going about, as the order was relayed. Young Eprius, however, sat motionless holding the standard. Mesmerised, he was staring up the cliff.

Ballista grabbed the bridle of Eprius's mount, hauled its head around.

A terrible clattering from above.

'Go!'

As if woken from a trance, Eprius booted his horse. It leaped forward, almost unseated the standard-bearer as it bolted after the others.

Ballista and Starkad were close behind, neck and neck. The roar of the coming avalanche loud in their ears, both bent forward, urging on their mounts.

The first large rock thundered down the cliff ahead. It clipped an outcrop, bounced out like a deadly toy. When it hit the track, it smashed into the ranks of the Thracians. Where there had been three horses and their riders was a shambles of blood and flesh and white exposed bones.

More boulders were falling. Clouds of dust rolled up from where they landed. The man-made landslide was between Ballista and safety.

'Eprius, halt!'

Ballista's shout was lost in the din. The white *draco* whipping above his head, the youth vanished into the roiling gloom.

Fabius and the scouts skidded up to Ballista and Starkad.

'Wait for the avalanche to settle,' Ballista said. 'We are not in its path here. They will only have loosened so many boulders.'

'Then they will start throwing things,' Fabius said.

'Smaller rocks,' Ballista said.

'Shields up,' Fabius ordered his men. 'The dust might obscure their aim.'

'We will go through the stream,' Ballista said. 'Keep as close to the other wall as possible.'

'Trouble just follows some men about,' Starkad said.

Ballista did not answer. He was looking up, and recognised the officer who had sprung the trap.

'That looks to be the end of it,' Fabius said.

They went into the stream, and into the choking murk. The water only seldom came above the horses' hocks. They moved at a walk. The stream bed was littered with broken stones. The horses stumbled. The riders yanked their heads up when they missed their footing.

As if from nowhere, stones and javelins flashed down through the dust cloud. Some thumped off the shields held above their heads. More splashed harmlessly into the stream, or pinged from the near wall of the ravine.

Eprius was pinned under his dead horse. The white *draco* lay in the stream.

Ballista gave his reins to Starkad, swung down. The water was icy in his boots.

Fabius and the scouts roofed them with their shields.

The standard-bearer was barely conscious. That was a blessing. His horse had rolled on him. It had broken his back.

'The dust is clearing,' Fabius said. 'You want me to do it?'

'Look away,' Ballista said.

'I am not a child,' Starkad snapped.

Ballista drew his dagger. With something akin to tenderness, he slit Eprius's throat.

* * *

'You sure it was Gratus?'

'Certain. He must have found the *dux* and his auxiliaries somewhere in the high mountains – most likely set an ambush in both passes.'

'There is nothing memorable about his looks.'

'I am certain it was him.'

At the repetition, Acilius Glabrio accepted the statement.

'You do really have to admire the dedication with which he pursues our destruction.'

The others – neither the Roman officers nor the Angle chieftains – seemed inclined to share the judgement.

Ballista's party had got out of the defile without further loss. They had caught up with the column where it had withdrawn to a broad, uncultivated meadow.

They were completely trapped. The avalanche had almost blocked the ravine. Fabius reported that a hundred or so of the ambushers had come down from the heights, and built a rough breastwork of rocks at the narrowest place. The chief scout estimated at least another hundred remained on the crest. The legionaries who had been shadowing the column had come up, and were across its line of retreat.

For three days they had sat in the trap. The fodder for the horses was almost gone. The animals had cropped the grass bare. Two days' half-rations remained for the men. The enemy had no need to attack.

'If you ask me,' Heraclian said, 'that Gaul has saved his own skin.'

Lucius Proculus had slipped away out of the beleaguered camp on the first night.

'His family have lived in these mountains for generations,' Ballista said.

'Generations of brigands,' Heraclian said. 'They are not renowned for loyalty.'

'He will keep his word.' Ballista was less sure than his words. 'We will be ready.'

Acilius Glabrio sketched a mock salute. 'We will do what is ordered, and at every command we will be ready.'

'First light,' Ballista said.

* * *

Before dawn, the campfires had burned down to ashes and glowing embers. The men got ready quietly in the half-light. But the enemy would know they were coming.

The avalanche in the ravine meant the attack could not be made on horseback. The Angles were accustomed to riding to battle, but preferred to fight on foot. They would attempt the storm of the pass. A hundred Emesene archers also would leave their mounts behind and accompany them. The bowmen were to try to force the men on top of the defile to keep their heads down, stop them from hurling missiles down as the Angles approached the wall. Heraclian and the rest of the Emesene horse archers would spread out across the meadow and guard the rear against the legionaries. Acilius Glabrio and the Thracians were to act as a reserve.

There was no subtlety to the plan. No book of stratagems would laud its cunning. It relied on brute force. Get to the wall, kill enough of the defenders to break their spirit and make them run. Much favoured the enemy: the narrow approach that prevented numbers telling; the rocks scattered across the track that made the going bad underfoot; the breastwork of stones itself; the men on the heights; above all, the knowledge that sooner or later the legionaries would break through and take the Angles in the rear. And the ravine faced east; when the sun came up, it would shine into the eyes of the attackers – yet another weight in the scales against them. Everything depended on Lucius Proculus.

Allfather, Ballista prayed, let the Gaul keep his word. These were his mountains, the inhabitants his people.

Ballista joined Arkil and Starkad at the head of the Angles. The warriors were checking their companions' equipment. Before Thermopylae the Spartans had combed one another's hair. In the gloom the scene was less heroic, resembling nothing so much as the grooming of a troop of primates.

'No time like the present,' Arkil said.

The Angles divided into two groups, each some twenty wide and ten deep. Arkil would lead the vanguard. When his men tired, they would retire, and those under Starkad would assault the wall. The eastern bowmen brought up the rear.

'Take care of yourself,' Ballista said.

Starkad bridled. 'This is not the first time I have stood in the shieldwall.' The youth seemed ready to take offence at anything his father said.

An old warrior called Guthlaf chuckled. 'I will look after your little boy.'

Starkad looked furious.

Flanked by Maximus and Tarchon, Ballista walked up to Arkil. As was right for one of the Woden-born Himlings, he took his place in the front rank. Careless of the honour of the other Angle warriors, his bodyguards remained with him on either shoulder.

'Let us be on our way,' Arkil said.

The light was strengthening.

At first the path was easy, yet it was hard not to feel a foreboding entering the shadowed ravine. Soon, all formation was lost as they clambered over the fallen boulders.

Arkil halted them some fifty paces from the wall, out of range of javelins and rocks from in front or above. They jostled back into some form of order. The white horse of Hedinsey flew over their heads.

Here the pass was only some thirty paces across. Two thirds was blocked by the hastily improvised breastwork; the stream ran through the remainder. The enemy waited, three or four deep, behind the wall and in the shallow water. Helmeted, clad in mail, protected by big oval shields, armed with javelins and swords, these were well-equipped regular auxiliaries. More of them, indistinct figures, were on top of the cliff to the left.

The Angles held their shields in front of their mouths. They began the low hooming of the *barritus*. It built slowly.

'Are you ready for war?' An officer among the enemy shouted the traditional question.

'Ready!' the auxiliaries bellowed back.

Three times came the Roman call and response.

The throaty roar of the *barritus* reached a crescendo, almost drowning the final yell of the Romans.

Something deep and atavistic stirred in Ballista's soul. The thunder of the *barritus*; the white horse on the green field; the close companionship of his own people: he was born for the fight. The spirits of his ancestors were with him, the war leaders of the north: Hjar, Himling, the long line of blood back to Woden the Allfather.

'Out! Out! Out!' Arkil shouted.

They set off.

The track was treacherous with loose stones. Warriors stumbled and collided. A rock plummeted and shattered in front of Ballista. Jagged splinters flicked through the air. Ballista glanced up. The Emesenes were shooting over their heads. Ballista saw one of the enemy on top of the cliff pivot and fall, the feathers of an arrow projecting from his chest. Yet the soldiers up there were not cowed. They braved the storm, continued to hurl missiles down at the advancing Angles.

A stone turned under Ballista's boot. He staggered for a few steps, regained his balance.

Not far now. Get to the wall and the men above will have to cease or hit their own.

A soldier behind the barricade hefted his javelin, aimed at Ballista. The northerner brought up his shield, well out and angled to deflect. The soldier threw. The missile whipped over Ballista's head.

Not all were so lucky. Metal points thumping into wooden boards, clattering into armour. Screams and the awful sound of tearing flesh where they got through.

The breastwork was four feet high. Too high to jump in full armour. A bearded face opposite, eyes wild above the rim of his shield.

Ballista thrust. The tip gouged into the desperately lifted boards. The soldier hacked, a mighty blow down to the head. Ballista took it on his own shield, the impact jarring his shoulder.

With his left hand, using the boss of his shield, Ballista punched at his opponent's face. The man jerked back. Ballista got his sword hand on the barricade, tensed to jump. Another enemy blade sliced at his wrist. Ballista let go, yanked back his hand. The steel knocked chips out of the stonework.

The rough wall made it difficult to land a killing blow. But it had served the defenders' purpose, halting the Angles. Ballista feinted and jabbed, seeking an opening. The auxiliary was a trained swordsman, getting his shield or the edge of his blade in the way of everything. He fought doggedly, always now on the defensive, never exposing his sword-arm or body to an attack. All he needed to do was hold his position, stay alive.

In a battle, time could cease to have any meaning. Ballista laboured on in a transcendent state, like some martial version of an eastern mystic. Thrust, feint, jab; endlessly repeated, and never succeeding.

A hand on Ballista's shoulder hauled him back.

'We need to go!' Maximus shouted. 'Your brother has ordered us to retire.'

Now they again ran the gauntlet of missiles from above. The Angles sheathed their swords, needing both hands to cover themselves with their shields and negotiate the boulders or drag along their wounded.

Arkil's men passed through those of Starkad. Ballista stopped with his son.

'Difficult work,' Starkad said.

Ballista, short of breath and tired beyond reason, grunted an affirmative. He saw an officer rallying the auxiliaries along the wall. He was unsurprised to see that it was Gratus. At the top of the defile, the enemy were gathering more stones ready for the next attack. The Emesenes were conserving the arrows in their quivers. The defenders moved about with impunity. They seemed unalarmed.

Lucius Proculus had said first light on the third morning after his departure. Perhaps Heraclian was right that the Gaul, like the brigands from which he was descended, had put his own safety first.

The ranks of the Angles parted, and Acilius Glabrio approached Ballista. The patrician spoke, low and urgent. In the meadow the Emesenes had been forced back. Now the Thracians were facing the legionaries. Outnumbered, they would not hold them long.

'Best we do not delay.' Starkad raised his voice to ready his men. 'You saw how tired were Arkil's warriors. Those Romans will be worse. Now we go and finish them.'

The Angles hoomed their approval.

Ballista touched the arm of his son.

'The best chance is the stream.'

Starkad said nothing, but shifted to the right of the line. Ballista went with him.

'Out! Out! Out!' Starkad screamed.

'Out! Out! Out!' the warriors chanted.

The water was no more than shin deep. It was icy, the bed of the stream slippery, stones shifting under boots sodden and heavy.

They splashed along with Starkad under his white *draco* standard: Ballista, Maximus, Tarchon, Acilius Glabrio, old Guthlaf and the others.

This time the rocks from the malevolent hands above glanced off the cliff face to the right, caused fountains of water in the stream. Again they thudded into upraised shields, an outsized and demonic hailstorm.

The warriors trudged forward with a curious high-stepping gait as they lifted their feet from the water.

The enemy waited stoically, crouched behind their shields.

Up on dry land, those Angles on the track charged the wall. The clangour boomed around the canyon.

Those in the river lagged behind. They closed at a walk.

Another bearded face behind another blue shield. Ballista sloshed at him, the water dragging at his boots, slowing his movements. Cut, parry, thrust; an endless cycle, never bearing a result. Ballista was bone-weary. A man can only fight so long.

Out of the corner of his eye, he saw an auxiliary fall. Before another could take his place, Acilius Glabrio stepped into their ranks. The young patrician was fighting like a madman, or some hero from early Latium. He launched a flurry of blows. Another auxiliary went down.

'With me!'

Acilius Glabrio pressed deeper into the body of the enemy.

Rousing himself for one last effort, Ballista hurled himself against his opponent.

Acilius Glabrio was cut off, surrounded. Another foe reeled back from his blade.

Ballista ducked his shoulder into the back of his shield. Legs churning the water, stones slipping out from under his boots, he drove into the auxiliary. Sheer strength and willpower drove the man backwards and down. Reversing his grip, Ballista stabbed vertically. His weight on the hilt, Battle-Sun snapped the links of mail the man wore. Two feet of steel penetrated ribs and vitals.

Another auxiliary swung at Ballista. The northerner swatted the blow aside with his shield. Maximus dropped the assailant with a shrewd chop to the back of the thigh. Tarchon finished him.

Acilius Glabrio was reeling. His helmet was buckled, blood coursing down his face.

Ballista put his boot on the dead man's chest, retrieved his blade. The water of the stream was running red. No poetic conceit, but a horrible reality.

Acilius Glabrio was gone.

The enemy were giving ground. Those in the rear were casting fearful looks upwards. There was the sound of rustic trumpets.

And then, some silent communication running through them as it would a herd of timid animals at the proximity of a predator, the enemy were running.

High on the cliff, where the stone-throwers had stood, was Lucius Proculus. With him was an array of hirsute mountaineers. The Gaul – brigand or not – had kept his promise.

Ballista looked around, fear in his heart. The white *draco*! And there under it, for all the world unmarked, was his son.

An enormous weariness threatened to unstring his knees. Ballista wanted nothing more than to stagger to the bank, and collapse. But there was still work to be done.

Ballista turned to Maximus. A lurching apprehension when the Hibernian was not to be seen.

Concentrate on the task in hand.

'Tarchon, get back down to Heraclian. Tell him to have the Emesenes come up along the stream. Bring the led horses. Once they are through the narrows, his Thracians are to withdraw. If the legionaries pursue, the Angles can hold them here.'

Without wasting words, Tarchon got out of the stream, and went off.

Ballista looked around. Starkad was striding out of the water, calling out commands. He had everything in hand.

Too tired to clean and sheath Battle-Sun, Ballista waded to where Acilius Glabrio lay.

The young patrician's helmet was gone. The current played with his blond hair. In a poem there were always last words. Not always in life. Acilius Glabrio was dead.

Leadenly, Ballista clambered out onto the track. Without conscious thought, he cleaned Battle-Sun on the tunic of a dead Roman, slid the blade back into its scabbard.

'Look what I have found,' Maximus said.

Relief that his friend was alive stopped Ballista instantly recognising the prisoner.

Gratus was bareheaded and unarmed. He stood wringing his hands.

'Why?' Ballista said.

Gratus was twisting a ring on his finger, as if screwing his courage up.

'Why did you betray us?'

Gratus smiled. 'Telling you would defeat the whole object.'

He raised the hand with the ring to his mouth, tipped back his head.

Ballista grabbed Gratus' wrist, dragged it away. Too late. A smell like almonds, only more pungent.

The first convulsion almost wrenched Gratus out of Ballista's grip.

Gently, Ballista lowered Gratus to the ground. He cradled his head. Maximus held Gratus down at the next paroxysm.

The poison was quick-acting. Before he died, Gratus said one thing.

'My family.'

EPILOGUE

The City of Mediolanum, Italy

The Ides of September

THE EMPEROR WAS NOT dead, but it would be a long time before he was recovered. Under the apse of the tall basilica, Gallienus sat rigid on the throne. When he moved, it was evident the wound still pained him.

Ballista finished telling the story of the expedition. After they had forced the pass of the river Stura, their journey down from the mountains had been hungry, but uneventful. The legionaries had not pursued them.

Under the eyes of Volusianus and the rest of the imperial courtiers, Ballista had been discreet in what he said. The treachery of Gratus was ascribed to the machinations of Postumus. No doubt was entertained that the assassin had not been sent by Gratus at the instigation of the Gallic rebel.

'You have done well,' Gallienus said. 'The gods hold you in their hands. You have always been a hard man to kill.'

'Emperor.' Ballista looked Gallienus in the face. 'I gave my word that the Angles would be allowed to return home.'

'And so they shall.' Gallienus grimaced slightly as he eased his back. 'Your father is a loyal ally.'

Ballista shifted his gaze to where the sacred fire burned on its portable altar. He framed the words in his mind, before looking back at Gallienus. So much depended on the emperor's response.

'The campaign was hard. I have served you faithfully, as I served your father. I am no longer young. With your permission, I would retire to my estates in Sicily.'

Gallienus did not reply at once. He regarded the vaults of the ceiling, as if some answer might be lurking there.

There was no sound in the basilica but the ticking of the fire.

'We have decided to accept the offer of a truce from Postumus.'

Gallienus did not look down as he spoke. There was something distant and hieratic about his pose.

None of the councillors moved; their faces betrayed nothing. They already knew of the accommodation, and how much it would have cost the emperor.

Ballista thought of the men who had died in the inconclusive war. Acilius Glabrio and young Eprius had been killed, and nothing had changed.

'Yet it is no more than that.' Gallienus looked down and studied each member of the council in turn. 'A truce, not a peace treaty. It is no secret that I will never forgive the man who murdered my son Saloninus. When I am recovered, we will cross the Alps again.'

The courtiers murmured approval. It was a quiet sound – nothing to disturb the *silentarii*, who maintained the decorum of the imperial court.

'The gods give with one hand, and take with the other. They did not shield me from an arrow in Gaul. But they have granted victory to our forces in the east. Our general Oedenathus has defeated the Persians.'

This was news to those assembled. Men exclaimed with pleasure, made comments to their neighbours, without addressing their remarks to the throne. This unseemly display provoked the chief *silentarius* to rap his staff on the floor.

The hubbub subsided.

'Oedenathus writes that next year he intends to march upon the Persian capital of Ctesiphon, and free our father Valerian from captivity. Should the gods not grant him success, when we have defeated the rebel Postumus, we will march east ourselves.'

This time the applause was loud and heartfelt. It ignored the rapping of the staffs of the palace officials. Volusianus led the ovation. The Praetorian prefect had shaken back the folds of his cloak, the more vigorously to clap his hands.

When quiet had returned, Gallienus spoke again to Ballista.

'So you see, we will not take the field until next spring.' The emperor smiled. He looked tired. 'As for returning to Sicily, that will depend on the Praetorian prefect. Volusianus wants to question you.'

* * *

'Come with me,' Volusianus said.

The imperial council was over. Volusianus led Ballista out of the basilica. Two Praetorians fell in behind.

The forum was full of petitioners, litigants, merchants and those perusing their wares. Volusianus paused at the top of the steps of the basilica. He still enjoyed the way people stopped and stared at the Praetorian prefect, the way they all stepped back out of his path. It gratified the soul. The peasant boy from Etruria had become one of the great – a man to treat with conspicuous respect, if not with fear.

Volusianus hitched the sword on his hip, and processed slowly down the steps.

Ballista walked at his shoulder.

Two guardsmen followed, just out of earshot.

Sometimes silence was a weapon. Volusianus said nothing as they paced the marble flagstones.

Ballista stopped.

The guardsmen halted.

Either Volusianus could walk on alone, or he had to stop as well. He turned to face Ballista. A minor victory to the northerner.

Volusianus waited.

Ballista spoke first. That skirmish had gone to the Praetorian prefect.

'You never intended the expedition to return.'

Volusianus looked past Ballista, up at the statues of the gods on the pediment of the basilica. He did not know their identity.

'Acilius Glabrio was a traitor, part of a conspiracy to assassinate the emperor.'

Volusianus always told as much of the truth as was possible. It gave verisimilitude to the rest.

Ballista stepped forward.

Volusianus did not flinch, did not so much as look at him.

'I do not know if that is true, but he was a brave man.' Ballista's voice was tight with fury. 'You were one of the conspirators. I recognised your voice in the mausoleum.'

Now Volusianus looked Ballista in the eye. 'It was necessary to gain their trust, to find out how far the plot had spread.'

If anything, Ballista seemed angrier still. 'Why not arrest Acilius Glabrio? You are not squeamish. It would not have troubled you to torture the truth out of him. Why not execute him when we were with the army?'

'Of all people, you should realise the power of his family,' Volusianus said. 'This way he is a dead hero, and the Acilii Glabriones remain, at least outwardly, loyal to Gallienus.'

'And the assassin? Why did he come to my tent?'

Volusianus made a gesture as if swatting away a fly, or something of no significance.

'A mistake on the part of Gratus.'

'Then Gratus was your man?'

'Gratus was my man.' Another fragment of the truth.

'And he went over to Postumus?'

'The *frumentarii* inhabit a dark world – often one betrayal leads to another.' Again, that was no lie.

Volusianus saw a fragment of uncertainty on Ballista's face. Now was the moment.

'The empire must be reunited, Postumus crushed, the Persians defeated, and the Emperor Valerian freed. Oedenathus must be brought to heel. "If I reign well, use this sword on my behalf. If I reign badly, turn it against me." Those were the words of Gallienus when he appointed me Praetorian prefect.'

Ballista said nothing.

'You wish to retire from public life, to live quietly with your family in Sicily. That is in my power to grant. Your elder son in Rome can go with you.'

'"If I reign badly"?' Ballista said.

'We all make choices,' Volusianus said. 'If you do your duty, then I will do mine.'

'Gratus' last words were "my family".'

'Then we understand each other?'

Ballista looked away. 'We understand each other.'

Volusianus put his hand on Ballista's shoulder. 'It is getting late in the year, but, if you make haste, you should be reunited with your family in Sicily before the end of the sailing season.'

Volusianus squeezed Ballista's shoulder. 'The winter is pleasant in Sicily. The locals call the island the House of the Sun.'

AFTERWORD

The Third Century AD

The best narrative reconstruction of the period is by John Drinkwater in *The Cambridge Ancient History: The Crisis of the Empire*, AD 193–337, volume XII, edited by A. K. Bowman, P. Garnsey and A. Cameron (Cambridge, 2005), 28–66. Another starting place is D. S. Potter, *The Roman Empire at Bay* AD 180–395 (London and New York, 2004), 217–262. Thematic surveys are offered by O. Hekster and N. Zair, *Rome and its Empire,* AD 193–284 (Edinburgh, 2008), and C. Ando, *Imperial Rome AD 193–284* (Edinburgh, 2012). The briefest of overviews, with the Baltic link explored in this novel, is H. Sidebottom, – 'Rome in Crisis', *BBC History Magazine* (September 2014), 24–28.

The Gallic Empire

The fundamental work on Postumus and his successors remains J. F. Drinkwater, *The Gallic Empire: Separatism and Continuity in the North-Western Provinces of the Roman Empire* AD 260–274 (Stuttgart, 1987). See also D. König, *Die gallischen Usperpatoren von Postumus bis Tetricius* (Munich, 1981), and R. J. Bourne, *Aspects of the Relationship between the Central and Gallic Empires in the Mid to Late Third Century AD with Special Reference to Coinage Studies* (Oxford, 2001).

The Campaign of AD 265

Even by the poor standards of the third century, the ancient literary sources for the second campaign of Gallienus against Postumus, probably in AD 265, are abysmal. See Zonaras XII.24; Augustan History, *The Two Gallieni* 4.4; 7.1–2; *Thirty Tyrants* 3.8–11; Peter the Patrician, Fr.182.

The siege of Postumus by Gallienus (in 'a certain city of Gaul' in Zonaras) has been placed at Augustodunum (modern Autun) because it was one of the very few cities in Gaul with defences at this period.

Roman Cavalry

K. R. Dixon, and P. Southern, *The Roman Cavalry From the First to the Third Century AD* (London, 1992) provides a splendid introduction to all aspects of the subject.

Grierson's Raid

The inspiration for *Falling Sky* goes back to watching John Ford's film *The Horse Soldiers* (1959) as a child. To find out about the events on which it was based, I read D. A. Brown, *Grierson's Raid* (Dayton, 1981), N. L. York, *Fiction as Fact: The Horse Soldiers and Popular Memory* (Kent, Ohio, and London, 2001), and M. Lardas, *Roughshod Through Dixie: Grierson's Raid 1863* (Oxford, 2010).

High levels of literacy and mass printing at the time of the American Civil War, coupled with modern print on demand publishing of out of copyright books, makes many contemporary memoirs readily available. Among these are S. A. Forbes, *Grierson's Cavalry Raid* (Springfield, Ill., 1907), R. W. Surby, *The Horse Soldiers' Raid: Grierson's Raid and Hatch's March during the American Civil War* (no place named, 2012), and

B. J. Dingles and S. A. Leckie (eds.), *A Just and Righteous Cause: Benjamin H. Grierson's Civil War Memoirs* (Carbondale, 2016).

Horses

Curious Roman practices of horse management are drawn from various ancient veterinarian writers and the *Cesti* of Julius Africanus. The former are introduced by Liliane Bodson in *The Oxford Classical Dictionary*, 4th ed., (Oxford, 2012), *s.v.* veterinary medicine, pp.1545–6. The latter is translated by William Adler (Berlin and Boston, 2012).

Ballista's practical horse management comes from 'Stonehenge' (J. H. Walsh), *The Horse in the Stable and the Field* (London, 1880), and Lieut.-General Sir F. Fitzwagram, Bart., *Horses and Stables* (London, New York, Bombay, and Calcutta, 1911).

Life in a cavalry column relies on D. Rickey, Jr., *Forty Miles a Day on Beans and Hay* (Norman, Oklahoma, 1963) and Lieut. J. Boniface, *The Cavalry Horse and his Pack: Being the World's Most Comprehensive Military Study of Equestrian Travel* (no place named, 2005, first published 1903).

Other Novels

As in all my novels, it has given me pleasure to include a couple of homages to other writers. In *Falling Sky* they are Cormac McCarthy, *All the Pretty Horses* (New York, 1993), and D. Alexander Brown, *Grierson's Raid* (Dayton, 1981). The latter is not a novel, but a history book that deploys techniques from fiction.

If you enjoyed *Falling Sky,* why not join the HARRY SIDEBOTTOM READERS' CLUB?

When you sign up you'll receive an exclusive short story, THE MARK OF DEATH, plus news about upcoming books and exclusive behind-the-scenes material. To join, simply visit **bit.ly/HarrySidebottom**

Keep reading for a letter from the author . . .

Hello!

Thank you very much for picking up *Falling Sky*.

This *Warrior of Rome* novel offers me a unique perspective. I wrote *Falling Sky* a few years ago, but it did not fit my publisher`s schedule. So when its time came I approached it with a measure of trepidation. Would I still like the novel? Only the most complacent and arrogant writers revisit their work with total confidence. Thankfully, I loved rereading the book. It has the historical authenticity and the strong sense of place that various newspaper reviewers have been kind enough to praise in my other work. Yet two other things really struck me. First, the sheer pace of the story. There is no down time as Ballista leads a cavalry column deep behind enemy lines over the Alps in Gaul, facing both the enemy in a vicious civil war and treachery in his own ranks. Second, the humour in the story. From the start Ballista is back with his *familia*. No matter how bad the threat, how desperate their position, Ballista, Maximus and Tarchon, as all soldiers do, express the deep bonds between them via teasing, mockery, and self-deprecating jokes. Frequently their banter made me laugh out loud.

Falling Sky is a *Warrior of Rome* novel. The events in Ballista`s life fall between *The Last Hour* and *The Burning Road*. It will have a deep resonance for those who have read the other novels, but those who have never read any of them can enjoy on its own this tale of action and adventure.

If you would like to hear more about my books, you can visit **bit.ly/HarrySidebottom** where you can become part of the Harry Sidebottom Readers` Club. It only takes a few moments to sign up, there are no catches or costs, and you will receive a free Ballista ebook short story.

Bonnier Zaffre will keep your data private and confidential, and it will never be passed to a third party. We won`t spam you with lots of emails, just get in touch now and again with news about my books, and you can unsubscribe any time you want.

And if you would like to get involved in the wider conversation about my books, please do review *Falling Sky* on Amazon, on Goodreads, on any other e-store, on your own blog and social media accounts, or talk about it with friends, family or reader groups! Sharing your thoughts helps other readers, and I always enjoy hearing what people experience from my writing.

If you have any questions, or would just like to get in touch, please do so via my website – www.harrysidebottom.co.uk – or my Facebook page – www.facebook.com/Harry-Sidebottom-608697059226497

Thank you again for reading this story, and I very much hope you share my excitement with *Falling Sky*.

All the best,

Harry Sidebottom

ACKNOWLEDGEMENTS

MANY PEOPLE SUPPORTED ME when writing this novel. Only a few are named here: Kate Parkin, who commissioned the book, Ben Willis, who edited it, and James Gill, who was there all the way through. At various points advice and encouragement was offered by my dear friend Donna Leon. As ever, it would never have been finished without the love and forbearance of my wife Lisa, my mother Frances, and my aunt Terry.

There are a lot of horses in the book. Although I was brought up in Newmarket stables, my lifelong friend Michael Dunne knew far more about them than me. With typical kindness Michael had agreed to read the first draft of *Falling Sky*. It is one small sadness, among many greater, that his life was cut short by a tragic accident. *Falling Sky* is dedicated to his memory.